BETWEEN HELL AND TEXAS

BETWEEN HELL AND TEXAS

Dusty Richards

PINNACLE BOOKS
Kensington Publishing Corp.
www.kensingtonbooks.com

PINNACLE BOOKS are published by

Kensington Publishing Corp.
119 West 40th Street
New York, NY 10018

All Kensington titles, imprints, and distributed lines are available at special quantity discounts for bulk purchases for sales promotions, premiums, fund-raising, educational, or institutional use. Special book excerpts or customized printings can also be created to fit specific needs. For details, write or phone the office of the Kensington sales manager: Kensington Publishing Corp., 119 West 40th Street, New York, NY 10018, attn: Sales Department; phone 1-800-221-2647.

PINNACLE BOOKS and the Pinnacle logo are Reg. U.S. Pat. & TM Off.

ISBN-13: 978-0-7860-4533-4
ISBN-10: 0-7860-4533-7

First printing: December 2011

12 11 10 9 8 7 6 5 4

Printed in the United States of America

Electronic edition:

ISBN-13: 978-0-7860-2919-8 (e-book)
ISBN-10: 0-7860-2919-6 (e-book)

Chapter 1

Texas hill country looked winter drab all around him when Chet Byrnes pushed the big bay gelding he called Julio off the ridge. The leafless mesquite branches stuck out and the brown grass waved in the relentless north wind under the cloudy sky. Kind of a day a man hunched under his denim jumper and rode along dreaming about a crackling fire to warm his hands. Fingers encased in the goatskin gloves, the heat would still feel good to his digits. Being home would, too, instead of out checking on scattered range stock this far away from the headquarters.

One good notion crossed his thoughts. The buttermilk ceiling rolling in from the Gulf might bring some rain. Wasn't a day in Texas a man couldn't use more water.

Then the sharp report of a rifle cracked the wind's heavy breath. Without even thinking about it, he ducked down in the saddle and set steel spurs to Julio. They bailed off the steep slope into the dry wash bottom and the thicket cover of cedars and live oak.

The powerful gelding slid to a stop amidst the tall, bushy evergreens. Chet jerked out the .44/40 rifle from the scabbard in a swift dismount. Rifle chamber quickly loaded with the lever action, his ears were tuned for another incoming round.

Where was the shooter? One round could draw a man's attention, but he needed the second one for a source and a direction where the shooter might be located. His heart pounded hard under his breastbone. Breathing came short at the realization of his tough situation. Alone and far from any aid or assistance from the ranch crew, he must wait out these back-shooters. For a short moment he'd forgotten all about the deadly feud that existed between his family and the Reynoldses—a sneaky bunch of cowards who with their relatives had killed his younger brother the previous spring. Dale Allen'd been up there in the Indian Territory on a cattle drive to the Abilene, Kansas stockyards.

Listening intently, all he could hear were some windswept crows calling. Three or four more hours of daylight until sundown. Another cold winter day. He could wait them out. No doubt they'd quickly get fidgety. Then they'd either charge down there to find him, or hang tail on their horses and ride like they were on fire for home.

After a breakneck run last spring up to the Indian Territory, he'd gathered most of the herd and later evened the score of his brother's murder with a gunfight in Abilene. But that never stopped a feud so deeply entrenched in revenge with ignorant people like the Reynoldses. If they came for him in this draw with its dense cover, he'd send some more of them to hell before they ever reached him.

Julio was busy snatching bunch grass through his small curb bit. He raised his head between bites as if testing the wind. Then, with a clang of the steel bit on his molars, he hurried to eat more, like he might not get another chance. Ground-tied by training with the dropped reins, the big horse would not leave him except to get more to eat—then the cow horse raised his head again and shifted around, looking south. Enough of a clue for Chet to belly down under the pungent-smelling boughs and try to spot the riders on the ridge above them, opposite of where he'd flown off the slope.

He caught sight of a red something, and next, through the limbs, he distinguished a rider huddled under a blanket jacket coming across the hillside. Armed with a rifle, the party stared hard down at the cedars for a sight of him. Satisfied this was one of the ambush crew, Chet took aim, the red cloth making a good target; drew a tight bead and fired. Then Chet rolled to the side and levered in a new cartridge. His shot had struck either the rider or the horse, for he left bucking and threw the man off on his back in a half-dozen short hops.

It was the others Chet worried about. If they'd seen his quickly dissipated gunsmoke in time, they might have him spotted. He needed to move aside from there and be certain they couldn't see him. There came another shot, but the round never came close to him. And he suspected the bullet originated from the same ridge, as he settled in a new spot a dozen feet away.

Muffled shouting. "Joe. You alright?"

"Hit hard—"

Good.

"Stay down. We'll get him."

Don't be so damn certain. Still flat on the ground, Chet removed a fresh brass cartridge from his jumper pocket and slipped it into the side breech. His rifle reloaded, he tried to peer through the boughs for another sight of one of them.

"Come on," he whispered to himself, anxious to get this settled. The word "We" must mean more than one was left up there. Had he been daydreaming, riding along, to draw that many assassins? Or had they simply gotten lucky running into him? He was near the south end of —*C* range. No matter, there were still at least two more gun-happy yahoos out there.

A hard-breathing horse was coming at breakneck speed off the hill, and he could hear the rider urging him. He rolled over and drew his .44. When the one on horseback busted into the space where Julio grazed and spooked him, the shooter never saw Chet on the ground half-under the cedar, and two shots from his Colt belched death into the rider's shocked face and chest. The horse lurched sideways into the cedars and his rider fell off, face-down.

Chet was on his feet and headed for his own wide-eyed horse. In his left hand, he caught the reins and "whoaed" to him. The other mount tore out of the grove and clattered down the dry wash, wasting no time to escape. In an attempt to scramble up the hillside, the frantic animal fell over, then rolled back on his side into the dry wash off a chest-high side wall.

Kicking and screaming, the horse finally righted himself and then bounded to his hooves. In lunges, he was going uphill with fear in his wide eyes, his tail tight to his ass.

"Damnit, did you get him?" someone shouted.

"No. He's gone to hell, too," Chet answered in a whisper, trying to locate the lastest one doing the shouting on the ridge. Then he saw the speaker and quickly drew a bead on him. Way too far away for a pistol shot.

There wasn't time to get his rifle off the ground, but he lunged for it anyway. At last, with the wooden gun-stock of the oily-smelling rifle in his hands, knowing the shooter must have seen him, he scurried to the right on the floor of sticky needles for another knot-hole in the green boughs to shoot at him from. When he reached the spot where he could see the black gun-smoke blasts of the shooter's rifle, he aimed into them. Two quick shots expressed toward him and Chet raised the smoking barrel to look for the results. There was silence, save for the wind.

Chet found his feet, then swept up the pistol he'd dropped and looked it over. Save for some resin-sticky needles, the revolver looked okay and he jammed it into his holster. With slow intent, he studied the ridge selectively from his cover and reloaded the Winches-ter. Were there only three of them? By his judgment, that was all, but he wasn't taking chances—that Reyn-olds bunch was never easy to kill.

The twice-shot man on the ground had never moved. He rolled him over with his right boot toe. This dead man had a name. Carley someone. Did day work for ranchers. He wouldn't no more. He located Julio and swung into the saddle.

Julio acted upset when Chet rode him out of the thicket to the north. Twisted in his seat, Chet could see three saddled horses together, grazing on the ridge opposite his position. Their horses. It took fifteen minutes or longer to work his way over there.

He found Adrian Claus sprawled out on his back, rifle nearby in the grass. A brother-in-law to the Reynolds clan, he'd been the talker on the ridge. If he was alive, he'd not last long. He was unconscious, the wound in his chest pumping blood though Claus's fingers. Chet booted his cow pony over and rode downhill where the one in the red jacket sprawled on the ground.

No more than a boy in his late teens, the stricken shooter blinked up at Chet and made a gasp. His open jacket showed he was losing lots of blood. He reached vainly for his handgun a few feet from his fingers.

"Better save those bullets for yourself," Chet said, resting his left hand on the saddlehorn. "They won't find you in time to save you from all the suffering. You a Clayton?"

"Joe Clayton. . . ."

He looked hard at the wounded one. "Are you boys that damn stupid?"

"Guess—" Joe's voice cut off and he closed his eyes against the obvious pain. "We figured we could take ya easy."

"You ain't the first or last to think that. Shame you won't be alive to tell 'em that."

"Yeah—"

Chet reined the bay around and struck out for the north. Half-sick to his stomach, he short-loped Julio for the house. Small patches of sunlight through the buttermilk sky swept the hill country, lighting the live oak and cedars on the slopes, and then the seams in the clouds closed in again. Another day and a chapter in his belly-souring life had come and gone. The taste of vomit was hard to swallow from behind his tongue. Three more of his enemies were dead, or would soon be when the last one slipped away back there.

He hunched his shoulders under the unlined jacket against the penetrating cold. Damn, was there no end to this killing and dying?

Chapter 2

Some lights were still on in the large sprawling ranch house and compound Chet called headquarters. Chet could smell the fireplace's oak smoke as he rode up the starlit valley. Julio acted as weary as he felt. Snorting in the road dust occasionally, the big horse at last awoke to the fact that he was close to the corrals, feed, and his associates. The two arrived at the hitch rail and Chet dropped heavily out of the saddle. He slung the wool army blanket over the seat of the saddle. He'd worn it for warmth most of the way home. His sea legs under him, he loosened the girths, picking with his fingers at the sweat-soaked leather.

Chet could hear his young buckskin stallion snorting at the buggers that shared his barn area. And then he smiled to himself. The quick-footed stud from the Barbarousa Hacienda breeding farm was one thing that always made him grin over his pride of ownership.

"That you, Chet?" his sister Susie shouted from the half-open lighted doorway.

"No, it's his ghost."

"The ghost looks lively to me." She laughed, then frowned at him. "You have trouble today?"

His 12-year-old nephew Heck must have heard him come in, too. "I'll put him up, Chet," he called out.

"You alright?" Chet asked the youth.

"Ah, sure. You must have rode him a long ways, he acts very tired."

"He earned his keep today. You better get some sleep. It's late."

"I will." With that, he led the horse off under the stars toward the corrals.

"Thanks," Chet said, and turned to his twenty-some-year-old sister. "Well, did it all go well around here today?"

"Good enough. I was about to think you'd found a bed for the night."

He slung his arm over her shoulder and kissed her forehead, going inside. "Naw, no one would have me."

"You aren't trying hard enough." She smiled up at him, then pushed the brown wavy hair back from her face. "Food's in the oven."

Susie was attractive enough to have any fellar she wanted in the countryside. But, like himself, she didn't have time for one—running the big house was no small chore. He removed his gloves, then hung his wide-brimmed hat on a peg and took off his jumper to hang it beside on the wall pegs. At the large open-hearth fireplace, he stopped and warmed his fingers.

"Cold out there, wasn't it?" She shifted the woolen shawl on her shoulders.

In a quick check of the large room, he made certain

they were alone. "Cold wasn't the problem. Three of them tried to ambush me today."

Her eyebrows hooded her blue eyes with concern. "What happened?"

He shrugged and looked hard at the overhead coal-oil lamp in the center of the living room. "They won't cause us no more trouble." Then, trying to revive her spirits, he smiled. "But that ain't no concern of yours."

"I knew something was wrong." She shook her head, leading him into the dining room. "Gut feeling. Worried me all day that something was wrong. This won't ever end. The killing, I mean?"

"Sis, we've talked about it enough. The only way to escape them is to clear out of Texas."

She used some hot-holders and took his heaping plate of food out of the oven and slid it before him. In a low voice she said, "I know, but our dad can't stand a long trip. I'd hate to bury a family member alone in some isolated graveyard and lose contact with them. Here we have our grandparents' graves, Mother's—"

"Sis, if we don't do something soon, there may not be enough of us left alive to even tend those graves."

"I know. I know."

Chet sat down and turned at the sound of someone coming into the dining hall. Dale Allen's widow, May, nodded and crossed to the table. May was on the chubby side, age twenty-three, and the past nine months had been hell for her. She'd lost Dale Allen's daughter Racheal as well, from what the doc called *some weakness*. Never a strong person, May did all she could to raise his other children and her own daughter—Chet's sister-in-law proved to be Susie's greatest helper. May's dark hair was thin, cut in a bob, and had no curl. She wore black, which did nothing for her appearance, but Chet felt certain she did all she could do.

"Did you have trouble today?" May asked, as he chewed on a piece cut from his slice of beef roast.

He nodded, not wanting to explain the day's entire incident. Susie filled his coffee cup from the pot she brought over from the stove. Then she took her place across the table and nodded to May. "He had more trouble with the Reynoldses."

Looking hard into her steaming cup, May nodded. "I thought so. Oh, I guess it won't ever stop."

Before taking another bite, Chet agreed with a head bob and went on eating. Finally he set his fork down and cradled the hot tin cup in his hands. "May, I'm planning on finding us a new place. We can't raise our families in this hill country. The place is full of mean people with no value in them for life."

"You still thinking about Arizona?" she asked, speaking subdued like usual.

"It could be the land where we could escape this madness. But—" He blew on the surface and the aromatic richness curled up his nose. "I don't know, Arizona may not be far enough."

May blinked her eyes. "When would we go?"

"I have no idea. Might take a year to sell this place and find another one out there."

She chewed on her thin lower lip, looking concerned before she spoke. "I need to go with you and the family. I don't have another. My people disowned me for marrying Dale Allen. I feel more a part of you all than I ever did growing up in that big house."

May's parents were the height of society in the area. They owned a large bank and several ranches. But May had never really fit in with them. Her younger sisters were charming young ladies in society, while Chet's brother's widow was always backward-acting and very tender. It didn't help that May, against their advice, ran off to get married. Dale Allen took her to a country preacher and they gave their vows with Chet as a witness. May was nothing like Dale's first wife, Nancy, a bright, laughing, attractive woman who died giving birth to their last child. At that moment in time, Chet figured that Dale simply needed a mother for his newborn daughter, Racheal, and the boys, Heck, twelve, Ty, ten, and Ray, seven. Racheal they later lost, and soon May brought in this world a baby girl of her own, Donna. She simply must have been a handy choice for Dale Allen.

However, Chet's brother had turned his back on May. He spent long evenings working on farm machinery in the shop, alone. While Dale Allen was a terrific mechanic, when Chet finally confronted him about his absent ways toward his family, both May and the boys, Dale Allen about cried. "The kids remind me too much of her."

Things were going better at last when his brother rode out ramrodding a fifteen-hundred-head herd for Kansas—then the last thing Chet ever thought about happened—the Reynolds clan attacked Dale Allen and the crew in the Indian Territory.

His father, Rocky, had been no help for years. He'd

lost his mind searching for the twins, and later did more damage to himself looking for the other son kidnapped by the Comanche. Their mother, Theresa, had passed away with little left of her mind over the losses of the three children to the red marauders.

His father's younger brother Mark's wife, Louise Byrnes, widowed by the Civil War, was headstrong, and she locked horns a lot with him. Her two sons, Reg, nineteen, and sixteen-year-old J.D., were Chet's right-hand helpers. A big family that shared the sprawling compound built originally to survive the Comanche. With two mildly creaking windmills, corrals, a large hay storage, granary, a dairy barn, bunkhouse and a rambling house all snuggled behind a twelve-foot-high wall. Behind the tall wooden gates that had not been shut in years lived his family.

Chet finished his meal and thanked them before heading to his small apartment in the bunkhouse. Scratching the thatch of brown hair on the top of his head, he put on his coat, ready to leave, and nodded to both of them. "Quit worrying, girls. We can figure this situation out. I thought they'd soon have enough of this dying business and quit. But I'm afraid they have their minds made up to die to the last man or woman."

"Good night," Susie said to Chet, and hugged May's shoulder. "We're both with you. You can count on us to do whatever we need to do."

"I'm counting on both of you." Hat on, he headed outside, dreading the cold night, leaving the warm fireplace. Heat in the bunkhouse was a wood-burning stove in the main part—little of its warmth reached his private bedroom.

At last, under the piled-on sogans in his bed, he quickly fell asleep, still wondering what those Reynoldses would try next. Before five AM, he was up, dressed, and back over in the kitchen filled with the aroma of food cooking. The two new Mexican girls, Juanita and Sonya, were setting plates and cups on the long table. A baby was crying somewhere, and Susie directed the breakfast operation in a starched white apron. Chet poured his own coffee and smiled at her.

Heck soon arrived with his two younger brothers, bringing in buckets of milk. Putting down the milk on a bench, all three boys smiled at the sight of Chet, then Susie sent them off to wash up. The youngest, Ray, ducked her herding and shouted, "Kill any Injuns while you were gone, Uncle Chet?"

"No, Ray. No Injuns this time."

"You remember you promised me a big headdress some day," he said over his shoulder, while Susie moved them out to the back porch to wash up.

Still grinning about Ray's remarks, he nodded at Louise's two older boys, who came in from the living room.

"We were about to go looking for you last night," Reg, the older and taller one said, shaking his hand. "Susie said you'd be coming along. Any trouble?"

"We can talk about it later."

Both boys agreed, knowing he didn't want a conversation about the feud during the meal. Chet felt family meals were no place to discuss such bloody incidents and most everyone respected that. When he looked up he saw, with her hair put up and usual demeanor, his aunt Louise, forty-two, sweep in to the room. Chet's father's brother Mark found her in Shreveport's society and brought her home before the war. Mark was supposed to have been killed in the final actions of the war. But they had only heard of his demise, with no news or record from the military. Chet never felt certain that his uncle had been killed, and he still looked for him to arrive any day, despite the intervening years.

Sipping on his coffee as the platters of food begun to be set out, Chet asked for silence to say his short prayer. He rose to straddle his seat and spoke softly. "Oh, Heavenly Father, guide and protect us through this day. May this wonderful food give us the strength to do the chores we are assigned. In Jesus' name, amen."

Everyone nodded and then took their places. Susie oversaw everything. She and the two helpers made certain everyone had what they needed. Sleepy-eyed, May soon joined them with her little one in her arms and nodded good morning to everyone. Apologizing for her tardiness, she set Donna in a high chair that Juanita brought to her, and then took her place.

"How tough are those new horses to break?" Chet asked the older boys.

Reg shook his head to dismiss any concern about the fresh horses he'd bought. Range-raised, they came from a breed Indian named Crooked Foot who brought the herd of forty head to the ranch last January, winter-thin enough to catch, herd, and handle. Systematically, the boys had been working on them in their daily routine to green-break them.

"That gray we're saving for you," J.D. said, with a wink at some of the others.

"I thought he'd be the gentlest one in the bunch." Chet laughed, recalling the hoof-pawing horse's first day on the —𝒞.

"Yeah, he'll make a real buggy horse," Reg said, before he took the dripping sorghum-clad piece of pancake from his fork into his mouth.

"We just don't have his attention yet." Chet picked up his refilled cup of steaming coffee. "But he'll learn. We need to put a running W on him, lay him down on a canvas for half a day and then see how wild he wants to be after that."

Reg quickly agreed. "That's about all that we've not tried on him so far."

"Good, let's do that first thing." The horse matter closed, Chet excused himself and went with a cup of steaming coffee into the living room to the large roll-back desk and swung the swivel chair in under his butt. His second-largest job, after being ranch ramrod, was keeping the books. A job that he hated worse than shoveling out a hog pen. He studied his list of items needing to be taken care of. He must make a payment to Grossman's Mercantile to settle the ranch's monthly account.

Among items on the bill was a glaring charge for three hundred dollars made by Louise for some special-order millinery items. A subject she'd never discussed with him before spending that large a sum. There would be hell over that between the two of them. No one else on the ranch abused his or her part in this outfit's finances except Louise. With her free spending to gouge him, he also knew she did less work than the rest, other than throwing her weight around on the other folks.

In a short while, with the house cleared out, he walked back in the kitchen for another cup of coffee before he went outside. Seated at the kitchen table, he found his father Rocky, head down, slurping up too-liquid oatmeal from a tablespoon. Disheveled, un-shaven, he looked up and then shook his head in disapproval at Chet.

"Now, by nab, I checked last night. Wasn't an armed guard on duty nowheres around this place. I tell you, boy, them sneaking red devils will be in here and murder us all in our sleep." He used the big spoon to make his point. "Them sonsabitches will swarm in here and murder us all. You can mark my words. You may be in charge, but you're doing a damn sorry job of keeping up the guard around here."

"I'll check on it," Chet said.

"Check on it, hell—why we'll all be dead. Bring me some more of that oatmeal." He handed the bowl to Susie, who shrugged on the other side of him, looking at Chet.

"Was it alright? The oatmeal I mean?" she asked him, loud enough to overcome his hearing loss.

"Just right, darling. Just right."

"I'm going to check on the boys," Chet said, setting down his empty cup.

Susie gave Rocky the cereal and patted his shoul-der. "Now you eat big, daddy."

Chet saw her actions were to distract his father, and nodded his approval, then left. A cold blast swept his face first, and the bright sun did not much warm the air. The confusion and dust down in the corral told him the taming of the gray was in process. He climbed the corral rails, and in time saw the struggling gelding being laid on the canvas sheet. The running W was a device of ropes on his legs that, with two men behind him pulling on the ropes, could trip him down. Then the crew tied his four feet together with soft cotton ropes. His older three boys, hands on their hips, studied the helpless pony on the ground.

"Looks good. What do you call him?" Chet asked.

"George, for George Washington, who once rode a gray horse."

Squinting against the sun, the three nodded in approval. J.D. said, "And it says in the Bible to beware of the rider on the gray horse."

"I heard that. How are the fattening pigs?" Chet asked them.

"They'll be fat enough to butcher pretty soon," Heck, the youngest of the three, said, about to bust his buttons with pride about the swine-fattening project.

"Reg, you better get the wood supply up for the scalding. Those Mexicans down there need the work and a share of the meat. We'll plan on it for next week."

"I'll get it done," Reg promised. "How long does George need to lay here?"

"You can let him up after lunch. If he don't tame down, do it every day for a week. He'll learn some time that we aren't to be messed with."

"You small boys better go gather eggs," Reg said to the two youngsters on the top rail, who moaned about it, but took his orders and, hang-dog acting, went toward the house for their baskets.

The four got down on their heels, and Reg asked Chet about the day before, while the younger ones went off to pick up eggs and were out of hearing.

"I was about as far south as our land goes. They tried to ambush me, but I made it to some cover and held them off."

"Who were they?"

"Joe Clayton."

"He's a brother-in-law," J.D. said.

Chet agreed. "Adrian Claus."

"He used to haul freight from San Antonio. They must have hired him." Reg made a frown. "Who else?"

"Someone named Carley."

"Frank Carley," Heck said in disgust. "He did some day work around. Must have needed money real bad to join them two."

"Three against one ain't bad odds." Chet said.

"No—are they all three dead?"

"They're in hell shoveling coal for the devil, you can bet on that."

"What will the law do about it?" Heck searched the others' faces.

"They may need to have a court hearing." Chet shook his head, with no idea about the outcome.

"I hope that's all," Reg said, looking sour about the whole thing.

"Here on, we just need to go in pairs. We need to add a few more tough hands to help us and maybe that'll stop their part of these ambushes."

"Maybe," J.D. added.

"If we can't stop them, we'll be forced to move out of Texas and find some new country."

"I'd hate like hell to ever figure them damn worthless Reynoldses ran us out," Reg said, and shook his head in disgust.

"It could be better than burying more of our own," Chet added, and the heads around the circle agreed.

The gray horse struggled on his side and everyone turned to watch him. This would be a long, exhaustive struggle to convince this horse that he belonged to —$\mathcal{C}$, and he might as well relax.

Chapter 3

Late that afternoon, Chet noticed two riders coming across the valley. He thought he recognized one of them—Sheriff Bob Trent. Susie came out on the porch, drying her hands on a towel.

"Who's coming?" she asked with a hard look at the far-off pair.

"Looks like one's the sheriff."

"Does my hair look alright?' she asked, feeling to see if it was out of place.

With a casual look at her, he nodded. "You look great."

"Damn you." She gave him a shove on the back. "Chet Byrnes, you wouldn't tell me a thing that was wrong."

"What am I supposed to do?"

She smoothed down her dress. "Nothing."

"He kinda stopped coming out here. You discourage him?"

"No."

"Sorry. Wasn't digging into your business."

"That's alright. I'll go be sure we have enough food for them for supper."

"I bet they'd eat fried grasshoppers and scorched armadillo if you served them."

"Yuck." She disappeared inside, and Chet smiled at his teasing her.

He stepped off the porch and went to the hitch rail to greet the lawman and his partner when they finally arrived.

"Howdy, Chet," Trent called out. "This is Billy Moore, a new deputy of mine."

He moved in and shook both their hands. "What brings you two out this late in the day?"

"Three dead men," Trent said.

"Unload, get down. We can go inside and talk. Susie's busy adding more water to the soup."

Both men laughed and swung down.

"He's teasing you, Billy," Trent said. "She's a damn good cook, and I'd bet good money she ain't watering down no soup."

"Good," the man in his mid-thirties said, sounding relieved.

They took seats in the leather-covered furniture around the living room. Hats and coats on the wall pegs, they held a council near the crackling large hearth.

"They brought three bodies into Mayfield last night and I happened to be there," the lawman began. "Tried to raise a lynch mob, buying whiskey for everyone, until I shut the damn saloons down and sent all of those drunks home."

Chet nodded, leaning on his knees. "Guess you want to know what happened?"

Trent nodded. "We came out to hear your side."

"I was checking stock in the south end. It was a cold and windy mid-afternoon. A rifle shot popped off and I headed like a flushed turkey into a dry wash for some cedar cover. They exchanged some gunshots with me. I saw one in an open spot and picked Joe off.

"Then the one named Claus come busting through the cedars shooting, and I got him. Number three was up on the ridge and swung around on horseback. He showed up in my gunsights and I used the Winchester on him. I think he was Carley. Happened so fast, I wasn't sure of much but the fact they wanted me dead."

"Well, Carley, Claus, and Clayton are all dead," Trent said.

"You see the corpses?" Chet asked.

Moore nodded. "We did before they buried them."

"Any of them shot in the back or at close range?"

"One of them shot himself, they figured, 'cause he was left to die."

"I was riding my own land, checking on my own stock, and they chose that site to die on."

Trent made a hard face of disapproval, leaning forward with his hands clasping his knees. "I sure wished you'd came to me last night before they got everything stirred up."

Chet nodded he'd heard him. "I damn sure didn't murder them, and anyone in this country except the Reynoldses will tell you that."

"Don't make my job any easier. State of Texas tells me I have to investigate all shootings, right or wrong. It ain't for me to decide."

"Who do you believe? Them or me?"

"Chet, we've talked about this feud between you and them for near onto two years. I have to try to stop it as the chief lawman in this county."

"Good. You go tell them Reynoldses to stop trying to kill me and my family and go mind their own business. We ain't looking for trouble, but they can't do like them boys did and expect us not to react. If you shoot at me or my kin, you better have a coffin ready."

Trent closed his eyes as if to escape the senseless business. "Chet, me and my few deputies can't be everywhere. For God's sake, let's try to avoid these damn shootouts."

"When a man or a gang shoots at me on my own land, I'm going to protect me and my family."

Trent made a deep exhale. "This has gone on too damn long. I'd like to court your sister Susie, but the situation of me being sheriff won't let me."

"You're welcome anytime you want to come. I won't ever impose on your or her privacy."

"Gentlemen," Susie announced from the doorway. "Everyone else came in the back door to avoid interrupting you three, but the food will soon be cold."

Trent shook his head, as if weary of the matter. "Ma'am, we ain't missing any of your sweet food. Susie, this is Billy Moore, one of my new deputies."

She made a short nod and smiled at him. "Nice to know you, sir."

"All my pleasure, Miss Byrnes."

"Come now, you all can talk later." She herded them inside the dining room with a nod at Chet.

Moore was introduced around the table with everyone standing; then they bowed their heads for the prayer. That amened away, chairs scraped to take seats and not much was said. Tension hung in the dining room that made everyone talk softly to the ones beside them or not speak at all.

Chet had no idea whether he would be required to testify to a justice of the peace or a grand jury, or the whole thing would be simply dismissed. One thing: the presence of the sheriff made things sobering, and even a cough drew sharp eyes from the others.

"Sheriff Trent is here because some men tried to shoot me yesterday. They failed and are on their way to their maker. He tells me that I may have to go in and testify in court. That is real serious business."

Everyone big and old nodded. But his words didn't relieve any of the uncertainty written on the family members' faces.

"This will work out," he added to his explanation.

"You have a herd to take to Kansas next spring?" the sheriff asked, to make conversation.

"No, after last year, I don't have much heart to do it," Chet said.

Trent's quick agreement spoke for him, saying he understood that the last year's losses of life were bad enough. Full conversation around the room never really opened up. Moore, the deputy, spoke some to May, and for the first time, Chet saw her open up a little. More than she had done in a long while.

Good for her; she needed to perk up when a man spoke to her.

The sheriff and his deputy left after supper, but not before the lawman warned Chet that there might be a hearing. When they rode off in the darkness, he and Susie stood on the porch in the growing cold.

"Still like him?" Chet asked.

Holding her arms tight, she neither nodded nor shook her head. "He's a good man, but we don't have much time for either of us to have a life of our own."

"Susie, I can hire more help. We might not have as good a place as we have now with you in charge, but we'd live."

She shook her head, and in the light coming from the window he saw her bite her lower lip. Then she turned without a word and went back in. He followed her through the doorway and closed it. Going over the repercussions of the day before, he stood inside the warm front hallway. No time, she said—that was a big part of his life. Without Dale Allen, the shortage of leadership was there; this was so even with his brother alive. Dale had avoided it most of the time— lucky that he had two great boys to help him. But nothing ever relieved his needed command—his allegiance to the —*C* and family kept him yoked as much as it did his sister.

He looked around the living room at the checker players and readers. "Guess we know we may have some court time now."

"How will you handle it?" Heck asked.

"When they decide to hold one, then I better go to San Antonio and see a good lawyer."

"Can I go with?"

He looked at the twelve-year-old. "We'll see, Heck. We'll just have to see."

Ready to turn in, he headed for the kitchen where the two Mexican girls, Juanita and Sonya, were finishing up the dishes. May busied herself sorting pinto beans at the table to be sure there was no trash or stones in them. She looked up at him.

"Susie's gone to bed," she offered.

Chet nodded. The evening must have knifed his sister deep with something she probably felt was over him. "Ring the breakfast bell. Good night, ladies."

The two teenagers giggled and he left them. Hat and jacket on, he told the crowd in the living room he was off to bed. The chorus told him good night and he headed for the bunkhouse. A sharp north wind cut his cheek under his right eye, walking in the starlight for the bunkhouse.

How long since he'd been to see her—Kathren? Too long. Maybe he'd simply drop by and offer to get something for her from San Antonio. He rubbed his beard-stubble-edged mouth. Somehow, he needed to try and rebuild their relationship if it wasn't too late.

Susie wasn't the only one having problems with old loves. He had his, right along with her. And there was that big charge Louise had made at Grossman's on the ranch account—he still needed an understanding with her on that matter.

Chapter 4

The village of Mayfield sat in the cool sunshine of that early February morning. A dozen houses, a small church, six businesses, and a blacksmith shop, smoke from the forge, and the sound of the new blacksmith, Harley Taylor, hammering on steel, rang out like a big bell. A brave rooster crowed while a red-tail hawk skimmed the ancient live oaks, looking for a meal. Chet arrived in town on Fudge, a sixteen-hand-high bay horse, and dismounted at Grossman's store. He hitched him at the rack and said hello to the middle-aged man in the fresh white apron sweeping off the board porch.

"In town early, aren't you?" The man, in his fifties with white sideburns, looked him up and down, leaning slightly on the broom.

"Early enough. I have a list of things Susie needs and I want to buy some candy."

"Oh, I wasn't complaining none about having your business."

"I know that. You're one of my steady people on this world."

Grossman dropped his chin. "I've heard they tried you again."

Chet paused and nodded. "They damn sure don't give up."

"I've been praying for the good Lord to intervene for you."

"I could use his help. I sure could."

"Oh, give me that list, I'll have it filled—"

"No rush, I'm going over to see Kathren. Any word on her dad's condition?"

"Doc says he's alive. Don't sound good. Guess he can walk some, but not far. How is your family?"

"Doing well as can be expected. Rocky is less in our world every day. If I didn't have Susie, May, and those two Mexican girls, I guess I'd go crazy. By the way, what in hell did Louise buy that cost three hundred dollars?"

They went inside. Grossman set the broom in the corner by the door. "Let me see. Two dresses and three hats plus some undergarments. You know what I mean by that?"

"I do. She say where she was going to wear all that?"

"No, she didn't."

Chet dropped his gaze to the floor. "That's a damn shame, 'cause I didn't want to miss the big affair."

"She show them to you?"

"Heavens, no. I saw them on this month's bill."

"She's always charged things." He looked hard at Chet over the matter.

"Hey, I'm not mad at you. I'm mad at myself for not facing her about this business."

The storekeeper nodded and opened the candy case. "What do you need?"

"Something for a twelve-year-old. Kathren's daughter, Cady."

"I'll mix the kinds of candy up, alright?"

"Fine. Is there much talk about that incident I had two days ago?"

The balding storekeeper looked up from his candy choosing. "I've heard some. Those Reynolds women always talk bad, like those three were just riding along minding their business—you know what I mean?"

Chet agreed, took the sack of candy, and thanked him. Exactly what he had expected. Always innocent, like that boy they'd lynched up in north Texas. Oh, sure, he was going to bring them back. Those others just tricked him into doing that. Yes, sure thing, ma'am. He closed his eyes to try and shut off all that talking in his head.

"Here's your check for last month." He fished the folded paper out of his shirt pocket. "I'll have to handle Louise. I'll get those things Susie needs on my way back."

"They'll be ready and waiting."

"And thanks, I hope they don't hurt you for being nice to me."

"No problem. Anyone mention having a hearing about it yet?"

"Trent did when he came by. I'll hire a good lawyer from San Antonio if they have one."

"Good, I was really concerned."

Chet nodded and left. The morning chill struck his face outside on the porch. He undid the reins and re-mounted the bay. Candy in his coat pocket, he short-loped Fudge east for Kathren's place.

Kathren Hines, a year ago, became a big feature in his life. There had been complications in both of their lives. Her husband had been another on the list of those three horse thieves they'd executed up in Parker County. She'd later told Chet he had long since left her for good, and she knew he wasn't ever coming back. His and Kathren's arrangement then turned serious. He was set to marry her in a week when he learned that Dale Allen had been killed by the Reynoldses up in the Indian Territory. The remuda had been stolen and the herd stampeded. Their marriage plans were set aside and none had been remade. Her father had had a serious stroke and she was overseeing two ranches herself with some hired help. Nothing turned out right— nothing. He booted Fudge into a faster lope.

Mid-morning sun time, he walked Fudge the last mile to her place under the live-oak cedar-clad hills. The temperature had risen some, and the gelding was cooling fine when he reached the yard gate and dis-mounted. Two stock dogs were barking a welcome, and he looked around for sight of anyone. She might already have ridden out to check on her stock for the day. His guts roiled. This business between them had not gone smoothly since he had returned from Kansas the past fall. They'd been on a heaven-sent ride up until his brother's death—Chet had even come by to see her before he went to settle the mess up there.

She came around the corner with a small shovel on her shoulder. Tall, with a willowy figure, dressed in men's pants and shirt, run-over boots, she still looked like a female. Her blond hair tucked under her felt hat, she appeared as fresh as usual to him. A smile on her face—not a wide one, but a grin, anyway.

Kathren set down the shovel. "I'm expecting rain and needed some work on a small ditch that diverts water into my garden."

He hugged her, then he kissed her forehead. "I could have done that."

"Chet Byrnes, you haven't time to think, let alone worry about my details."

"You never asked me."

"Word's out they tried to ambush you again." A serious look swept her smooth face.

"Two days ago. Three of them shot at me down on the south border of our ranch. I managed to make some cover and exchange some gunfire."

She nodded. "They're all dead?"

"Yes."

She hooked his arm in hers. Then she guided him toward the front door. "You know that you're using up your nine lives—fast?"

"I didn't ask them to come after me. I never had a cross word with any of them. They shot at me unannounced and I got under cover."

She opened the door and they became caught in each others arms, his mouth tight on hers in the open doorway. He forgot all about his problems, Louise's extravagant purchases, the Reynolds clan, all the rest, and savored her kisses. Damn. Why couldn't they be man and wife?

"We're chilling down the house," she whispered, and pulled him inside. With both of them indoors and her back pressed against the door, she returned more of his attention.

Finally out of breath, they snuggled with each other.

"Damnit, Chet. We're both trapped in this world." She closed her eyes, toying with his jacket front. "Why can't we both find some solace from all this bloodshed and my father's health?"

"I hear he's walking some."

She shook her head. "He'll never ride another horse."

"What can we do?"

"Sneak around—" She chewed on her lower lip and tears began to fill her blue eyes. "Damn, I wanted you and me—married. But the outside forces in our lives will never let us. I know. I know."

"Speaking of sneaking around, where is your daughter?" He held out the sack of candy from his coat pocket.

She peered into the bag. "You have bought her off again. You know, her father never brought her a piece of candy in her entire life. She's over at her girl-friend's place doing math today since the school up here has not been opened this winter."

"I guess you have more chores to do?"

"No, but I do have hot coffee on the stove. You sip on some and turn your back while I get into a dress."

He blew on the hot brew, seated at the table, facing the dry sink until she joined him, brushing on her blond hair that reached her shoulders and wearing his favorite blue dress.

"You still don't plan to ship any cattle this spring?" She poured herself a cup and joined him.

"I may ship some with someone else. But no—"

She squeezed his arm. "I know. Dale Allen's death and all. I can see what you're thinking and don't blame you, but who will we get to take our cattle to market?"

"I'll find you someone honest."

"Thanks." She smiled and leaned over for him to kiss her. "You've not been by much lately. Guess you have had lots to do, too."

They settled back on the wooden chairs, but were unable to take their eyes off each other. He finally cleared his throat. "I am going to have to find us a new place to ranch. These crazy people won't quit. I can't risk the others being killed or maimed. I need to—"

"Let's talk about it later." Her finger closed his mouth.

Slow like, he finally perceived her desires and reached over to take her onto his lap. But instead she took his hand and led him to the bedroom doorway and in sight of the bed. He closed his eyes. It all could wait.

Chapter 5

Clouds gathered off the Gulf when he set out for home in late afternoon. He needed to get Susie's supplies before Grossman closed the store. There were more barriers in his life. Kathren's father could never stand selling out his home and moving to God-knew-where—and there was no way she could ever leave her mother behind. Being frank, she'd spelled it all out to him, but that didn't dampen their lust for one another. The notion of not ever having her for his bride gnawed on his insides when he dismounted at the hitch rail in the twilight in front of the store.

Grossman brought out two bulging pokes of the things Susie'd ordered. "I have it all in these two bags."

Chet raised his hat and scratched the top of his head, looking at all the items she'd ordered. "I should have brought a pack horse."

"Aw, we can hang them on your saddlehorn."

"Poor Fudge may have a bucking fit and scatter it all over forty acres."

Grossman laughed, then shook his head. "We can take some of it out of them."

"Lord, no. It would be what she needed the most."

With one poke hung on the left side, Grossman said, "Mind yourself. Three strangers showed up about noon today. I never saw them before, but they didn't remind me of any workingmen." He searched around to be certain they were alone before he went any further. Satisfied, he shook his head. "I'd say they were hired guns. No reason why they'd even stop off in Mayfield. Someone hired them, or they were looking for work."

"Catch a name?" Chet asked.

"Cecil Crown was the name of the one who acted in charge."

"Crown? Never heard of him." The name by itself didn't even dent his recall, but in no way did he dismiss the five-letter name—his enemies were determined. "Any others?"

"One of them was a cocky kid and the third guy stood around looking over it all—never said a word while they were in the store. Kinda fish-eyed looking."

"No mention where they hailed from?"

"No." He exhaled hard. "I just hate to think—"

"So do I. Keep an eye out. Anything about the horses they rode?"

"Bays. Rode hard. Sure enough nondescript."

Chet knew the type. Dressed plain, rode plain horses, but they came all armed and ready to kill for what some would consider a small amount, then be gone like smoke on the wind. They no doubt spelled out more trouble for him if they stayed around.

"They didn't even get a drink at the saloon. Just bought a few staples and rode on. But I felt they knew where they were going."

The second poke hung on the right side, Chet thanked Grossman and then rode for home in a jog trot. The stars lit his way in a silver night. A coyote or two broke the silence except for the wind orchestra. Fudge took a few swallows of water at the creek crossing, and then jogged for home. The groceries hindered Chet's legs, so he rode standing up most of the way. Coming up the silver Yellowhammer Creek bottoms, he could see a lamp that Susie must have hung out for him. He felt relieved about being this close to home, and settled himself in the saddle seat.

"What's happening in Mayfield?" Susie asked, stepping off the porch to welcome him when he rode up.

"Same old sleepy place." He dropped heavily to the ground and unhooked his first bag. He carried it to the stoop. "Leave that one. That's too heavy for you."

"I'm not some little sissy."

"No one said you were." Then Chet shook his head as she heaved the bag off the saddlehorn.

"Go ahead, feels like lead." She laughed. "You go see Kathren too?"

"Yeah."

She carried her poke in both hands through the door ahead of him. "That doesn't sound good."

"Kathren's dad is still down from that stroke. She's running both places. No way she can move off, and I don't blame her."

"And you think we'll have to move?"

"If we want to live—Grossman saw three hard cases

arrive in Mayfield today. No talk, simply showed up. A hard case, a tough-acting looker, and a cocky kid, all riding nondescript horses and plain clothes showed up like they knew where they were at and never spoke to anyone."

"You think they're a threat to us?" She set her sack down on the kitchen floor and then frowned at him.

"They'll bear checking out." He put his sack on the table.

"I'm really sorry about Kathren Hines. You know how excited I was for you two—before it all fell apart."

He made a thin line of his lips and nodded. "There is lots there for both of us, but no way it can work out under the circumstances. They need her and I need you all."

"Good night," she said. "Morning will come early."

He paused in the doorway. "Louise ever tell you what she bought cost three hundred dollars?"

"No. Why?"

"I'm just wondering." He shook his head and went on out to put up his horse; obviously Heck was asleep this late.

In the starlight, he undid the wet latigoes and pulled them off, then packed the saddle and wet blankets inside the tack room. He put the saddle in the dark room on its horn and spread the blankets over the top to dry. With Fudge grunting and rolling in the dust under the half moon, he went to the bunkhouse. At the sink, he washed his hands and face, then dried them. The water pressure from the tank worked well.

The cold liquid made him wide awake for a moment, and he went on to his dark room.

A few minutes later under his covers, he was sound asleep. Nightmares plagued him and he woke up in a cold sweat some time before the five AM bell rang at the main house. Seated on the edge of the bed, he mopped his face in his calloused hands. Even in his sleep, the Reynolds clan ambushed him—this time shooting him in the back. There was no escaping them.

He dressed and went to the house. The Mexican girls were scurrying around, and Susie was turning several flapjacks to make a tall stack on a tray. At the sight of him, Juanita rushed over to fill and deliver him a mug of coffee.

"Gracias," he said.

The short, dark-eyed teen smiled big at him and, in her best English, said, "You're welcome."

"What's happening today?" Susie asked over her shoulder, and then she poured more puddles of batter on the hot grill.

"I'm going by the sheriff's office in Mason and talk to him about the inquest. If I need to, I'll go on to San Antonio and find a lawyer to be at the hearing."

"I'll pack you some clothes."

"I'll be gone several days if I need to go over there. I guess the crew can handle it?"

"We can handle it." Susie finished the tall stack and gave it to Juanita to put on the table. "Ring the bell, too, it's time they were up." She turned back to him. "I just hope you don't need to make that long trip."

Chet shrugged. "Whatever I need to do."

Before he left, he was going to talk to Louise, also

have the boys heat some water so he could bathe and shave. The crew came in, and May with her little one joined them. He watched the door to see if his aunt was coming—he was going to talk to her if he had to wake her up.

"Chet, you want J.D. and I to scout the west range?" Reg asked.

"No, you two need to stay close. I'm going in to Mason and check on what the law is going to do about those three. Trent said he had to hold an official inquest. I'm going to see if I need a lawyer, and if I do, I'll go onto San Antonio and hire one. Probably take the stage from Fredericksburg in there."

"We can handle it."

"Handle what?" Louise asked, sweeping into the room in her usually late manner.

"I may have to go to San Antonio and see a lawyer," Chet said.

"I thought you were hiring more men to work for you." She took her place at the far corner of the long table.

"Louise, there is no need for more hands to feed and pay in the winter time."

She shrugged his words away. "That is your opinion."

"You may not know, but we aren't taking a herd north this spring. We may ship some steers, but that's not like the income we'd make off a drive."

"If you were a real businessman, you'd consider how to do both."

"Louise, we can talk after this meal. No need in upsetting everyone over your opinions."

"I can tell you one thing, Chet Byrnes. This ranch could be run much better if you'd hire a competent manager."

He blew on his refill and shook his head in disapproval to cut off Reg before he could start to answer his mother. It would only make things worse. Besides, he could defend himself. Her sharp tongue wasn't hurting him, only balling up the flapjacks inside his stomach.

After the meal, she didn't even excuse herself and headed for the door. Chet excused himself and was right on her heels. Out in the cool predawn light, he called to her as she fought to put the shawl on her shoulders.

"What?"

"I don't know what you spent three hundred dollars on at the store, but there will be no more such purchases on the ranch account. There is no way to operate this ranch and pay such ridiculous expenditures."

"I own a portion of this ranch, and I am entitled to some normal expenses for myself."

"Louise, you don't lend a hand to any part of this operation. The rest of us work for free. I'll have no more frivolous spending like that."

"I may hire a lawyer and find out what my fair share is."

"When you sue us, you better have a roof to put over your head, because you won't live and eat here."

"Hmm." She sniffed up her nose. "You have not heard from me for the last time over this matter."

"I'll tell them at the store, no more large purchases

without my approval if you don't promise me you won't do it again."

She shook her finger in his face. "You aren't my boss. I'll do as I damn well choose."

"I haven't left that order yet, but I am going to town today and if you don't promise me you will check with me before you spend over thirty bucks on anything you order or buy, then it will have to be approved by me."

"Do as you damn well please. You will anyway." Then, as if realizing his threat was real, she turned on her heel and dropped her gaze. "I won't."

"You won't what?"

"I won't charge anything over thirty dollars without talking to you first."

"Thank you." He watched her stalk off to her living quarters. He'd struck her deep with that "notice" idea. No way she wanted a restriction placed on her buying that everyone could gossip over—he'd hit on Louise's remaining pride. That might work. He beat the side of his leg with his hat. Maybe?

Chapter 6

After his bath and shave, Chet had the boys saddle Scamp, a big bay, and then he went to the house to get some things to put in his war bag. Susie packed two more ironed shirts and his best pair of pants in it. He'd talked to Reg and J.D. about what they needed to do. For sure to keep the cattle out of the oats so they'd have hay next spring, and the Mexican work force could start plowing the corn ground, because before long they'd need to plant it. Susie and the house crew waved good-bye and he headed for Mason.

The winding road went through the live oak and cedar-clad hills, with cleared fields opening up wide farmland inside of stake and smooth-wire fencing. Most other oat fields looked green, the small blades tossed by the wind. Lots of threats recently, but not much serious rain, and they could sure use some.

With distractions talking to others on the road about finding drovers, he finally reached Mason in late afternoon and went by the jailhouse. The jailer told him that Trent was across the street at Han's

Diner. He thanked the man and crossed through the wagon and buggy traffic for the eatery.

"Well, Chet, what brings you to town?" Trent asked, seated in one of the first booths, eating a late lunch or early supper.

"I came by to test the water about the inquest." He hung his hat on the hook above his head, and then, at the sheriff's invite, joined him.

"Not much water to test. Judge Heingardner took our deposition and off the record asked for our opinion. The prosecuting attorney won't be here for another six weeks, so I think it is all quiet here. You said you weren't taking a herd north this year?"

Chet shook his head. "Not if I can help it."

"With an outfit like yours it is kinda hard not to go up there, isn't it?"

"It usually makes money, but it's twelve to sixteen weeks of hell to earn it. Then the long trip back."

"How's your sister?" Trent ducked back to spear a piece of the cut-up pork chop on his plate.

"She sent her best."

"I don't know why. I make a pretty poor suitor."

"Ah, you can't tell."

"I can." Trent used a piece of bread to sop up some gravy. Before he put it in his mouth, he added, "We've both got big jobs."

"Amen."

"I'm sorry," the skinny teenage waiter said to Chet. "I was busy and didn't hear the doorbell ring. Can I get you something?"

"Bring me the plate special and some coffee."

"I can do that, sir. Thank you." He left.

"What are you really doing over here?" Trent asked.

"Seeing if I needed to go find a lawyer for this business."

"No, not yet. I'm sure that the family will raise cain in San Antonio about the courts and the law doing nothing. But what can they do? Send a ranger down here. I'd welcome him."

"Grossman at the store told me there were three strangers in Mayfield the last few days. Closemouthed, but he felt they were gunhands looking for work or already hired."

Trent rubbed his finger over his mustache. "Damn, I'll need to get a deputy back down there. I thought things were getting down to a simmer on your deal— I mean after the shootout and all. But it's only got worse, huh?"

"There ain't any end to them. If every man in the clan was dead, the women would come after me."

Trent shook his head in disappointment. "I have another one north of here that's festering over a milk cow and a dispute over who owns her. It has only come to fistfighting so far. But killing is next."

"Thanks," Chet said as Trent got up to leave.

"I hear anything, I'll send word to you. No need to go to San Antonio, unless you just wanted to."

"No need in that—" Chet leaned back as his meal arrived. The young man apologized and told him he'd be back with his coffee.

"See ya. Oh—" Trent stopped and turned back. "Tell Susie I gave you my best for her."

Chet agreed. Damn shame he was a little older, but

he'd be a good man for his sister and she'd be good for him.

Meal over and paid for, he discovered the winter sun had already set when he led Scamp over to the livery and entered the lighted hallway. He planned to get a room at Maude's when all at once the hallway light went out. He only had a flash of it coming when someone struck him over the head from behind. He went to his knees and could hear several men cussing him, their boot toes trying to cave in his ribs. His world swirled. Later he awoke, hardly able to breathe from the pain in his chest. Mouth full of dried horse shit and dirt, he tried to spit it out from his smashed lips.

Someone far away was talking to him.

"Chet? Chet?"

"Yeah," he managed. "Who were they?"

Then three faces appeared in the coal-oil lamp held high enough that he could make out their faces: the old livery man, the town marshal Hinkle, and another man with a badge shining in the yellow light.

"I never *seed* them. They grabbed me and tied me up in the back room," the old man said.

"Whoever they were, they rode out before we could catch them," Hinkle said. "Lay still. We've sent for Doc."

"You recognize any of them?" the deputy asked, shifting his weight, and squatting on the ground beside him.

Chet tried to sit up, but instead, with the sharp pains his movements caused, he dropped back onto the ground. "I need some water to wash out my mouth. I must have ate a ton of this dry horse shit."

The old man said he'd get it.

"You know anyone who would do this to you?" the deputy asked.

"Not unless his name was Reynolds," Chet mumbled.

Chapter 7

Someone was calling to Chet. The painkiller really had him doped up. However, he could feel the stiff sheets he laid between and the thick wool blanket on top. Three images hovered above him—their faces began to come into focus. Susie was first, then J.D., and last Louise—what was she doing there, looking like she thought he was dying? Hell, oh, the pain struck him from head to toe like a lightning bolt.

"Lie still," Susie said. "Doc says you'll heal, but didn't say when."

"You get a look at any of them?" J. D. asked.

Chet barely shook his head.

"Damn, oh, Mom's going to stay and look after you," the concerned-looking J.D. said.

Only one they could spare out there at the ranch. *Thanks.*

"So," Louise said. "Is there anything you need besides a new body? Those two have to get back. Do you want anything from the ranch? The doctor said you'd have to be here for a week, so if you need anything, you better tell J.D. or Susie. They're going back this evening."

"Be careful." Shocked at his own weak voice, he closed his eyes. "Keep your finger on the trigger." Then he drifted off into never-never land. A million things he wanted to warn them about—but they were gone and so was he. . . .

Louise's voice came into his left ear—she was reading him a newspaper aloud. "The Simpson family who live on Thorny Creek reported a panther ate their litter of newborn piglets. Last Friday, a sow gave birth to seven shoats and made herself a nest for them on the side of a hill in some timber on their place. Some time after midnight Saturday, a fight broke out in that area of their farm and woke the entire family. It was the sow and the cat fighting, which seven-year-old Carl Simpson said sounded like the devil wailing up there. At dawn, when the family risked their lives to go see about the damage, they found the mother pig alive, however badly clawed up, but every baby pig had been eaten. The lion was not to be found."

"You're awake?" She put down the newspaper. "What can I do for you?"

How did Chet tell her he needed to stand up and vent his bladder? Why in God's name did they leave her to take care of him?

Louise looked critically at him. "You want to stand up. And for me to set that night jar between your feet and then get out of the room?"

"Yes."

"If I get you up, don't faint on me unless it is over the bed. I can't pick you up."

"I will try not to faint. But I can't raise my arms without screaming."

"I understand. Remember, I raised two boys and a husband. At various times they all had horse wrecks that broke ribs. I'll catch your elbows at your sides, you rock forward and maybe this will work to get you up."

He nodded, and on the second rock forward Louise got him up. She steadied him, then repositioned the jar and excused herself. It worked, and once completed, he dropped to his butt on the bed and winced at the shock of his pain, but the relief was worth it.

Her knock on the door he answered from back under the covers. "Come in."

Louise entered the room and replaced the pail. "It's near supper time and they are bringing you some oatmeal from the café."

"Fine, I'm not starving."

"But you have to eat."

"Yes, ma'am."

"I will have to feed you."

"Yes, ma'am."

Trent broke up his morning with Louise and she excused herself. When she was out of hearing, he asked, "That's your aunt, isn't it?"

Chet agreed. "You learn anything about who took me on last night?"

"Nope. No one saw them. No one knows anything, so they must have slipped into town. Not hard to do that late on a weeknight. Han's cook heard someone in the alley earlier, but didn't see anyone when he went outside and checked. They must have waited somewhere while you ate supper then followed you across the street. Their horses left piles of horse shit where they had them tied. I'd judge they waited in the alley for you to go across the street with your horse to the livery."

"Someone had to see three men." His jaw hurt to talk much.

"Not after five at night and it's already dark in this town. Everyone goes to bed. The sun sets at five. Why burn all that coal oil?"

"So parties unknown did this to me."

Trent sat back in the chair. "Chet Byrnes, they're out to get you. Three of them ended up dead. This time they came close to killing you."

"They won't get many more chances at me."

"No, you'll be dead next time."

"I ain't planning on it being me."

"I'll keep asking questions around town. I'm like you, I feel that someone saw them."

A knock on the door and Chet said, "Come in."

He wasn't ready for Kathren's wind-reddened cheeks and the shocked look on her face when she saw him.

"Good morning Sheriff Trent," she said, and rushed past him. "Are you alright?"

"I'm taking nourishment. What are you doing up here? You have two ranches to run."

"I'll see the both of you later," Trent excused himself and winked at Chet. "You have real company now."

She dropped to her knees beside the bed and kissed him. "Chet, Heck said they must have near killed you."

"They broke some ribs for the main part. You didn't need to come clear up here."

She narrowed her blue eyes. "I damn sure think I have the right."

"No. No. I mean I'm going to live and you have two ranches to run."

"Well, I also have a stake in you, too. Now who's looking after you up here?"

"Louise."

"Your Aunt Louise?" She looked near aghast.

He motioned for her to get closer and whispered, "I think she's all they could spare."

"I guess you're right. How long are you going to be here?"

"A couple of days, then I can go home, I hope."

"Why not come to my place? You won't ever rest back at the bar-C."

"We'll see."

"No, I'll ride by your place and make plans with your sister. The two of us can figure this out."

He shook his head, staring at the ceiling. "No, that might make you a target. That's happened before."

She put her forehead on his arm. "I can watch over you. To hell with those damn Reynoldses. I may start a war of my own."

"Kathren, you don't need them for enemies. One of us is enough."

"Kathren," Louise called from the doorway, holding a bowl and spoon. "Here, you can feed him this oatmeal while you're here."

Kathren rose and took it from her. "Thanks, Louise."

"I don't mind. You two have lots to talk about, I'm

sure. I guess every time a Scotsman gets sick they feed him oatmeal."

Kathren laughed. "Must be some magic medicine in it."

Louise shook her head. "Only makes their heads harder."

"Good. Get some rest, Louise, you look tired. I'll stay for a while."

"Thank you. He's tough. They didn't kill him. I will go sleep a few hours."

"Yes, you go get some rest."

Louise gone, Kathren brought his oatmeal over and took her time feeding him off a small spoon. He felt sure that with each bite in her company he was healing. Her soothing voice filled with concern was what he needed to recover, and, the feeding complete, he closed his eyes and went back to sleep.

On the third day, Kathren's arrangements were in place. J.D. brought the ranch buckboard to haul Chet to Kathren's place. A frosty Texas morn; they had a mattress and a pile of quilts to cover him with in the back. Louise sat with her son on the spring seat, and Kathren, who'd come back for him, rode her horse and led his.

The trip took five hours; Chet decided it was his ride to hell. The buckboard had no springs, and no one ever realized the bumps encountered save the patient who lay in the back. But a large dose of medication helped soothe some of the pain. Doc had shown Kathren how to rewrap his ribs. He stared at the sky most of the way—deep blue—and the day warmed the farther they went.

J.D. and Kathren helped Chet into the house. He was so tired he fell immediately asleep, and never got to talk to J.D. enough about the ranch operation. In his groggy return to life the next morning, he awoke long before sunup and managed to go outside by himself to relieve his bladder. He limped inside and Kathren ushered him back to the living-room bed set up for him.

"Why didn't you call me?"

"Lord, I'm not a baby."

"Almost one."

"Did J.D. mention anything wrong at the ranch yesterday?"

"No, things were going fine. The corn ground is being plowed and no incidents so far."

Weak as a pup, he laid back down and fell asleep.

Chet's efforts to recover were way too slow. Susie and Reg came to visit on Sunday. He'd lost all sense of time and days. His sister was her usual bright self and Reg, the nineteen-year-old, was all business, talking about horse breaking, plowing, and fence repairing. He'd been talking to Mark Ott about sending some steers north with their drive. But he thought Ott had all the stock he could drive up there.

"How many head do you figure we can send?" Reg asked, seated on a chair beside his bed.

"Oh, at least five hundred. We can use the income. You better hire some day help and begin gathering them."

Reg agreed. But he wasn't through. Chet could read it on his face. "I kinda waded in where I didn't belong."

"Yes?"

He looked around to be certain the women were out of the room before he started, "Heck and his stepmother May got into it. I'm still not certain what it all was about. I made him move to the bunkhouse. She's got enough problems with that baby."

"Did you ever think that is what he wanted you to do?"

Reg shook his head. "I damn sure ain't you at handling things."

"You did alright. Keep Heck busy. I'll be getting home in a little while."

"Don't rush it. We're getting all the things done that you wanted."

"I know, but I need to be back there." He still felt sharp pains every time he moved an inch.

After they left, Kathren came and sat on the edge of his bed. "Your sister is a great person."

He agreed. "She having problems?"

"No. She's holding up. Didn't her and the sheriff have something going?"

"I guess like we did."

"Shame, isn't it?" She reset the lock of brown hair on his forehead.

"Is your daughter ready to come home?"

"Don't worry about Cady, she's fine helping her grandmother."

Days passed slowly for Chet. He worked all he could to loosen up his muscles and get back his strength. He took less and less laudanum to wean himself from the painkiller. In a week, he was walking stiffly around, following Kathren to milk the cow and gather eggs.

They were coming from the barn when the sharp whang of a rifleshot cut the air.

"Git down." Chet motioned to the parked wagon and, holding his side in deep pain, scrambled on his hands and knees to join her under the wagon bed.

Two more shots slapped into the wooden box. They edged back and he made a face at her. "I warned you."

"Do you see the shooter?" Kathren asked.

"He's somewhere on that hill. Probably in those cedars."

"I can get out of here and crawl through the garden out of sight. Then slip in the house."

"Too dangerous." But his words were too late. She was already slipping like a serpent backwards and away from him.

"Damn it, Kathren." But his words were lost because she was already gone. Some small birds chirped and flittered around the homestead. He kept wanting to reach back for the Colt that wasn't on his hip.

Two more rounds sprayed dirt in his face. But he could see the gunsmoke from each shot coming from the center of the cedars where the shooter was stationed on the hill. Damn, and they'd found her place. He shook his head. How long would those no-accounts stay out there and shoot at this wagon? The fact that the two of them were unarmed was obvious, but they weren't real certain about it or they'd already have been down there.

He winced at the pain in his chest, trying to wiggle back farther underneath the wagon. The sharpness in his body distracted him. What was she doing?

The crack of her rifle broke the sound of flittering small birds. She emptied the long gun into the cedars and a horse screamed in pain. Men were cussing and he listened intently—one or more of them was hit. Good.

In a short period of time, she fired the rifle from another window in the house. She emptied it again. They must have pulled back some, for the results of her shots were not as rewarding. He couldn't see shit from under the wagon, but dreaded the pain of getting up. Then he thought he heard some horses galloping off.

This time she shot from the front door. No reply. Obvious she'd hurt them with the first rounds, and then, like most cowardly back-shooters, they'd retreated. But who in the hell were they?

No doubt Reynoldses or hired guns of the clan. He clenched his teeth and managed to gain his feet, standing behind the wooden box.

"I think you put them on the run," Chet said as she stepped outside the front door, reloading the Winchester in her hands.

"You alright?" Kathren asked, hurrying over.

"I'm not scratched."

"Should we go up and see what happened to them?"

"It will take me some time to climb that rise, but yes, let's go."

"I can get—a wheelbarrow, I guess."

They both laughed. Not a happy eruption, but it drained some of the held-back tension from both of them. She waited on the slope for him as he hobbled up the grade until they were at the small cluster of pungent cedar, the smell of gunsmoke still in the air. With her gun barrel she swept back a bough, and then her eyes narrowed at what she saw. He gave a hard effort to get beside her. On the ground was a dead man. His face a bloody mess where the bullet had struck him.

She turned away and for a moment he thought she would get sick.

"I'm sorry, Kathren." But his sore body couldn't hold her.

"I-I'll be fine in a minute."

A saddled horse lay on his side ten feet away, whimpering in pain. He'd need to destroy him. A plain bay horse—he knew without looking there was no brand on him. Which one of those three hired guns was he? Even with his face disfigured and shot up, he knew this man wasn't from the area. He'd bet a hundred this was one of those Grossman had told him about.

"Who is he?" she asked.

"A hired gun."

"You know him?"

He shook his head. "Never saw him before. I'm sorry I brought them down on you."

She chewed on her lip. Then she bent over and buried her face on his shoulder. "I'll survive. I simply wasn't ready for this."

He half-raised his right arm to hug her despite the pain that ran up his jaw and shot into his cheek. "Why in the name of hell won't they let go?"

"They're crazy. No other way to explain it." She stiffened her back and wet her lips. "They're so infected with getting revenge, they won't ever quit."

He agreed and closed his eyes. She stepped over with the rifle and destroyed the wounded horse with a loud report. With a nod of approval for her, he collapsed to his butt on the hard ground.

"You alright?"

Wearily he shook his head, considering what had happened. "I'll live. This should have been my job. Not yours."

"Listen, big boy, I'm not going to let them harm a hair on your head. You hear me?"

"Yes, ma'am."

Chapter 8

Kathren went back and covered the body with a blanket so the buzzards wouldn't pick out his eyes. Then she saddled a horse to ride into Mayfield to tell the authorities there had been another altercation. With his six-gun in his lap, Chet sat in a stuffed chair and waited on her return.

Sundown came early in late winter, and he had to light a lamp to set on the table before she rode in with four men. The justice of the peace, Gunner Barr, and three others he'd gathered up. They stopped in the dimming twilight on the hill to look at the dead man, and she rode on to see about Chet and fix some food for all of them.

She stoked the range with wood to start a fire, and he joined her on a ladder-back chair. Her first mission was to get the coffee water boiling and it soon nested on the range top.

"You made good time," he said, as she tied on an apron.

"I worried they might have came back for revenge."

A serious mask of concern covered her face as she looked hard at him.

He shook his head. "I regret the most that they came here to shoot at you."

"Guess I chose that when I brought you here. I'm not afraid for myself. Men like that are worthless and they have to be stopped." She set in to scrub off some potatoes in a pan of water and had the large cast-iron skillet heating on the range.

"Kathren, the worst thing that could happen for my part is that something happen to you or your family."

She looked up at him. "I think the same about you, Chet Byrnes."

The soreness in his mending ribs knifed him as deep as her words.

A short while later Judge Barr came into the house. His deep bass voice resonated in the room. "How are you, old boy?"

"Fine."

"Damned if you look fine. They must have mauled you over pretty bad."

"I'll heal. Who's up there on the hillside?" Chet tossed his head in that direction.

"They say his name's Peters. Jud Peters, him and two more rode in here from New Mexico."

Chet nodded. "I heard about them coming."

"Hired gun hands, I'd call 'em. Henton Green hired them, he says, as ranch hands."

"Green is an in-law to the Reynoldses."

"I know that. I'd wanted to schedule a hearing on

those other deaths, but I can see you ain't in any shape to ride into town." He made a dismissing head-shake. "It can wait."

The rest of the men came inside and spoke politely to Chet and Kathren. The three looked a little uncomfortable over the situation they found themselves in. They hung their hats on wall hooks and took up her invitation to wash up on the porch. When they filed out to clean up, each one going out made a small sign to Chet that he was glad to see him.

Judge Barr took the cups from her and set them on the table. She poured fresh coffee into them. Pointing out the sugar and canned cow, she took the granite pot back to the stovetop.

"Where were the other two while he was shooting at us?" Chet asked.

"I imagine they can draw up a dozen sworn witnesses that would say that they had been working on their ranch all day."

"That sure sounds like the past, alright."

The judge took a seat at the table and shook his head. "This is the toughest job I ever took on, and it don't get much easier. I hate to go over Trent's head, but I may wire Austin and ask for some Rangers. Four men dead, and you beat up within an inch of your life. Mrs. Hines shot at on her own ranch, all in one week. Obviously we can't handle it."

"Why not speak to him first?" Chet asked. "He's shorthanded and don't have the money to hire any more men."

"You're right."

The men came back in: Sam Fisher, a rancher from

south of Mayfield, Carney Briggs, who ran the TLN ranch, and Either Hanks. Hanks carried in an armload of split firewood for Kathren and then he stoked up the fireplace. His bald head shone in the flames' reflection when he rose.

"Sure wish you were going north this spring. I've got about three hundred head need selling." He took up a nail keg to set on. "Guess you're healing some?"

"Doing better, Either. I've got steers that need to be marketed."

The rancher drew the keg closer, and the others came with him. "What're we going to do?"

"There will be someone going north. It's the only source of money we have."

"And it takes a damn sight more money each year to just stay even," the oldest of them, Fisher, said.

Carney climbed into the conversation. "My boss said I needed to chose a sure-enough good outfit. He couldn't afford to lose them all like has happened with some drover outfits."

Their words in his ear made Chet more concerned than he had been before. Perhaps he should send word to Reg to come over and they could talk about finding a drover to handle it for them. He blew on his coffee. "Going to be a big concern for all of us until we see the final payoff."

"Dang sure won't be like having you in charge. I never missed a night's sleep. Even when word came back about the raid, I told Molly Ann, 'Chet will get her done right for us.'"

They raised their coffee cups and toasted him.

After her supper of fried ham, German potatoes,

canned corn, biscuits, and butter, she opened two jars
of sweet peaches for their dessert. They slept on the
living-room floor in bedrolls, and when Chet woke in
the middle of the night, the house sounded like a half-
dozen saws cutting oak timber. Kathren used the bed
in her daughter's room.

At dawn, she made them breakfast of scrambled
eggs, ham, and hot biscuits with more rich coffee.
They all left bragging on her and thanking her for her
hospitality. Barr told him they'd take the body back.

With pained steps—diving under the wagon the
day before had not helped him—he stood beside
Kathren in the sharp north wind on the porch and
waved good-bye to the crew. She soon hustled him
back inside.

"No coat, you'll freeze out there," she whispered,
closing the front door behind her.

He looked hard at her. "I need to get well quicker."

"I'm not surprised you'd say that, you impatient old
man. You wrecked yourself. Now it will take some
time."

"I don't have that time."

She shook her head to dismiss him. "Oh, yes, you
do. I've watched you put on that 'I'm alright' look.
You aren't, and you will simply have to heal."

That settled, he spent his awake time rebuilding a
saddle for her. Reg came on Sunday and she made a
fuss over him. Her daughter rode over, and she, too,
tried to spoil the six-foot-tall foreman. The laughter
and fun made the day pass faster.

Late afternoon, Chet went over ranch things with his man. The corn planting was all set. Heck had settled down a lot and Reg promised he had that in hand. When they got to the cattle herding, Reg managed to tell him the Johnson brothers had approached him about taking the —𝓒 cattle along with their herd. The deal about them was that they needed thirty of the new —𝓒 horses to have enough mounts for his crew to ride, and needed to pay for them out of their part of the drive's income.

"You think those boys can get there?" Chet asked, feeling Reg was serious about the two brothers handling their cattle.

"Oh, yes."

"You figure out the deal and we'll do it. We need Kathren's shipped, too."

"I'll include them. Those horses are worth what?" Reg asked.

"I'd think forty dollars a head. With all the work we have in them."

He agreed. "They're going to road-brand in two weeks. They want to leave mid-March."

"That's their call. I'd hold till later in March so I didn't overrun the new spring growth of grass. If it warms up some earlier, that might be fine."

Reg made a grim headshake. "I'll tell them what you said. They've been up there twice and had good results. Most of the steers they plan to drive have been handled enough, they shouldn't act like deer."

"I understand. You better head for home. Tell everyone I'm stronger and look to be back. Any trouble?"

Reg drew his even upper teeth over his lower lip

and then spoke. "We've had some altercations. But so far we've bluffed 'em."

"Serious?"

"We've got it under control. You keep healing."

Chet sat back in the chair. Cold sweat popped out on his face. He had intended to walk Reg out to his horse, but the sharpness of the pain in his body had immobilized him.

Kathren must have seen his discomfort and stepped in. "Well, let me show you to your horse." Her arm in Reg's elbow, Chet watched her show him outside and clap him on the leg when he mounted up.

Chet saw Reg salute her and gallop off. Damn, he hadn't wanted to show that to the boy. When she came back in, she closed the door. "It's got you again?"

He slumped in the chair. "Guess you saw me going down."

She covered him with a blanket. "You expect too much. It has only been a week or so since you arrived here."

"Can't help it. They need me at the ranch."

"Who has time for you there?"

"No one, I guess."

She bent over and kissed him on the mouth. "You answer your own questions."

He agreed.

He closed his eyes and whispered to her, "I love you."

"Oh?"

"Well, I do."

"Good. Yes, damn good, because your stay here has

made me find that I can't do without you. How I'll ever manage my parents and you with yours, I am uncertain. But I want to be with you—beat up or well."

"I'll find us a way." He closed his eyes and fell into sleep's arms.

Chapter 9

Two weeks later, on a Monday, Kathren drove him back to the —$\mathcal{C}$ in her buckboard. The morning sun was warm. They stopped for the mail in Mayfield and she went to Grossman's store and brought back a big sack of hard candy for the ranch bunch. The south breeze sweeping them was a harbinger that spring sat around the corner.

Chet hoped to talk to the Johnson brothers, who were taking his cattle to Kansas. He knew it was getting close to time for them to leave for the north. Most of the way back, his gut-roiling concern was about not getting that chance to talk to them.

"I'd ask you how you felt, but you'd lie to me," she said over the beat of the horses' hooves and the whirl of the narrow rims.

"I never said I was well. I'm better; that's it."

"If I didn't—love you so damn much, I'd take you back and keep you."

He blinked at her in disbelief. "You never said anything like that before."

"Well, I never felt this way about anyone in my life like I do about you."

"We been having an—yes, you call that an affair—that we've had for two years, and damn near got married once."

"We should have, the day you came back from Kansas."

"You want to get married today?" he asked her.

She relented. "Let me get things straight with my parents. Dad's doing some better. You don't have your plans straight either, to go or stay. I'll work on mine harder."

"I will, too."

He reached over and took the reins from her. The horses stopped; he put his arm around her and kissed her. For a long time. Then she sat up and drew in a deep breath. Without a word, she took the reins back and made the horses go faster.

He sat back as if he had won a major battle in a war. His complaining muscles never felt sore or anything— she had agreed to marry him. *Heaven help them.*

Chapter 10

Two days later, Chet sat on the nail keg and the two Johnson brothers, Rod and Elgin, squatted in their knee-high boots with their pants tucked into the tops. Reg and J.D. were both in that audience.

Rod was shorter, and the toughest man with a reata that Chet knew. Freckle-faced, he always grinned, and his rep as a ladies' man was true. Lankier Elgin looked much plainer, and was the business partner of the deal.

"I ain't giving you advice. I'm telling you what I know. Injuns want some beef for crossing their land, give them a couple of limpers. I figure most stampedes ain't set off by a lightning storm. They are caused by folks, Indian or white, that want to steal a few head and figure you won't get them all back.

"Let them rain-swollen rivers go down all you can afford before you cross them. And don't let your cattle get swallowed by another herd or yours do the same—or you've lost a week's worth of work sorting them."

"We had that the first year," Rod said. "Our herd got mixed with some guy's from Waco at the Red River. They wanted to drive them across and go on north to separate them on some plains in the Indian Territory. That was two weeks later, and we busted our asses for eight days separating them. It was a mess."

"Good luck, boys," Chet said. "Thanks for taking Kathren's cattle along, and your outfit for getting them up for her."

"No problem. Mr. Byrnes, we also appreciate the horses and the credit. Without your horses and the bar-C cattle consigned to us as well as the people you recommended, we'd have had a mighty small drive. This way we all can make a profit," Elgin said, as he stood to shake Chet's hand and the other two.

Chet felt glad he wasn't going north that spring. His body still ached and probably would for six more months—the sharpness was down to where he could handle most of it. He headed back for his room— a short siesta might make him stay awake a while longer after supper.

On his bunk, he stared at the ropes of the bed over him. The smell in the bunkhouse reeked of old socks with the windows closed all winter. Soon they'd all be open and the smell of horses and livestock would drift in. He rolled over; he'd be ready for spring. . . .

"Chet," Reg called him from the doorway. "Supper is on at the house."

"Oh, guess I overslept. I'll be there." He mopped his face in his calloused hands and shook his head as he sat up.

"Good."

They had waited, and he felt embarrassed finding them standing there, held up for him to arrive as he told them to bow for a prayer. His brief words of their gratefulness to the Lord ended with amen. Everyone sat down.

The bowls of food soon circled the table and everyone worked to select their choices. Susie joined them as the two kitchen girls refilled the bowls and poured coffee. It was good and bad for him to be home. He was eating food seasoned and cooked like he knew it—but Kathren wasn't there. He missed her picking on him. Little things. No way to explain—he simply missed her.

Mashed potatoes and rich flour gravy made a big hit on his palate. The rest was mouthwatering. The meal over, he lingered in the house while the girls cleaned up. Sipping coffee, he tried to lay out things the outfit would need to do before summer.

"I need to get some supplies this week," Susie said. "You want to go along?"

"I reckon."

"Good. We'll go right after breakfast."

That settled, he thanked them and started for the bunkhouse. The temperature outside was pleasant. He walked along thinking about what he'd need to do to be sure everyone was safe. Those other two gunfighters had vanished after Kathren shot the one at her place. He hoped she was doing alright. Too much to think about.

Chet's night was fraught with wild dreams and things he couldn't save—he dreamt they'd taken one of the females in the family as a hostage. But he couldn't see who she was that they kidnapped. He woke up in a cold sweat. His sleep was worse than reality.

After breakfast, he and Susie left for Mayfield in the buckboard. A leather scabbard on the dashboard carried a loaded Winchester, in case. Clouds were rolling in and the temperature was muggy. Some good rain wouldn't hurt the newly planted corn or the oats. That morning, the Mexican crew was busy planting Susie's potato eyes in the three acres they had broken for her garden. He left Reg in charge of that operation. J.D. and Heck were going after an orphaned calf to raise on a milk cow. Things were close to settled down again, and he was mending faster by the day.

Mayfield in mid-morning looked busy for a week-day. Two delivery rigs were at the store unloading. Both saloons had customers with hip-shot, un-groomed horses at their hitch racks. Two farm wagons were at the blacksmith's shop, no doubt repairing farm machinery.

"Gonna rain?" Buddy Fracker asked as Chet started to enter the store's open doors.

"Clouds don't look thick enough," he told the middle-aged man wearing a cowpie-looking wool hat as he headed out.

"See ya. Glad you're getting around better."

"Thanks. I'm about fine."

"Yeah, you's look it, Chet."

"Tell Ollie hi."

"Oh, I will. You be coming to the dance Saturday night at the schoolhouse?"

Chet considered it and nodded as the man went on out with his arms full of purchases.

Susie turned back. "Are we going?"

"Yes."

Walking up the aisle ahead of Chet, she rocked her head from side to side, obviously wondering about his change of mind. His order from months earlier was that the family should not attend the supper and dance because it was too dangerous, so they had stayed away all winter from the neighborhood affair. He stood behind her as she waited for a gray-haired woman who was giving the young clerk her order.

"What made you change your mind?" she asked under her breath.

"Our family has lived here for years. We should have the right to go where we want."

She agreed with Chet and smiled at the lady in front, arguing that the price for an elixir was too much. The poor youth was red-faced. "Sorry, but that is the price marked on it, ma'am."

Grossman, hearing the problem, came over and told him not to charge her at all for the medicine. He smiled and told her he was sorry things cost so much, and waved at Chet, then went off to solve another problem. At that point Chet knew he could never run a mercantile—he didn't have the patience for the job. Her shopping began to look lengthy, so he excused himself and went over to Casey's Saloon and spoke to the bartender himself.

"Good to see you," Casey said. "Missed you dropping in lately."

Chet agreed and ordered a draft beer. He turned and looked over the dimly lit card game. Several un-employed cowboys and a few gamblers around the table were making bets and tossing in hands. No threat in those men, he turned back to enjoy the beer.

"You miss not going to Kansas?" Casey polished the glass in his hand.

Chet looked at him and shook his head. "I miss it like I would a dog biting me and he let go."

Casey laughed. Chet saw the flicker in his eyes when the swinging doors creaked. Slow like, Casey cast a gaze at the two men who came in and then turned back to the polished glass in a stack.

"Who are they?" Chet asked, not recalling them.

"Kyle Denton and Dick Reckles," Casey said softly "They're kin to the Reynoldses somewhere." He moved down the bar to serve them.

"I didn't know you let shit like him in this place?" one of the pair asked.

"Watch your tongue," Casey said. "You don't like my customers, take your business elsewhere."

"By damn, we will. I ain't drinking with a damn boy-killer. Come on, Dick."

When they were behind Chet's back, the younger one challenged him. "You got the guts to draw on a real man?"

"You go for that gun, Denton, you won't live one second," Casey said.

Chet could see the saloon owner was already armed with a sawed-off shotgun pointed at Denton. The bartender's speed shocked him, but it might have saved him from being shot when he turned around.

"Casey, you chose the wrong side," the youngest shouted, and they hurried out the batwing doors.

Chet dropped his face. He couldn't even drink a

simple beer in peace in his own town. He slapped a dime on the bar and shook his head. "Sorry, Casey, I simply wanted a beer."

"Don't apologize. He ain't worth two cents. No loss for me."

He thanked the man and went back to the buckboard, but not before searching the street for any sign of them.

Susie came off the store porch, holding up her dress hem. "You get into something?"

"Two of them chose not to drink in a saloon I frequented."

"Who?" she asked, looking around as he helped her into the spring seat.

He glanced back, but saw no sign of them. "Couple of their kin or in-laws. Denton was one's name."

"You sure that we should go to the dance?" she asked under her breath.

He stepped up and took the reins. "We're going."

That said, he drove home.

The next days, the dance was on everyone's mind and purpose. Reg and Heck unrolled the large shelter-tent sheet and made sure the mice had not eaten any holes in it. Rolled up, it required J.D. and the stable boy to help them load it into the wagon. The canvas was suspended on a main rope that was tied high up from tree to tree. Then with poles that made the side walls and the ropes off those poles stretch skin-tight on large stakes.

Susie's crew made desserts that would not spoil. A menu was listed and the items needed were written on paper for loading in the two wagons—one would not be big enough. Reg volunteered to guard the home place. May was also staying behind to take care of the house, baby, and Rocky. Both the kitchen helpers were remaining, as well.

Chet wished he had at least a couple more ranch hands. The money outlay concerned him—their entire income rested on the five hundred steers headed north. If the brothers were successful, the ranch financially would be in good shape. In case of a total loss of them, he'd be at the bank borrowing money before another year would allow him to take cattle to Kansas. Lots rested on their success. Squatting in the shade, he watched Heck drive the Belgium mares around the large lot, walking behind them. He must have settled down under Reg and from being separated from his stepmother.

Reg and J.D. were driving the big mule teams they used on cattle drives, so they didn't act high all the way to the Warner schoolhouse and cemetery. They had taken the mules down the valley an hour earlier for a two-hour trip. Each team was hitched to a wagon. Reg and J.D. could do any chore on a ranch— Chet was lucky to have them.

"I guess everyone is pleased we're going," Susie said, joining him to watch the boys drive the mares.

"I imagine the Reynoldses won't be."

She gave him a glare. "Nothing will please that bunch."

"I don't aim to." He rose and put his arms over the fence. At least he was about over most of his soreness.

"Will Kathren be there Saturday night?"

"I plan to ride over tomorrow and invite her."

"Good," she said, pleased. "I better get back. Tell Heck it is lunchtime and to get washed up." She shaded her eyes with her hand to look around. "Those big boys coming back?"

"They should be back here anytime."

"I'm glad you're civil again."

He frowned at her, but she had already headed back to the house, holding her hem out of the dust. Maybe he needed to listen more. Nothing like his sister to line him up. Guessed it was her job.

The two older ones drove in during lunch. From the sounds of their shouting at the mules, they must have had a race or two. Both soon were washing their hands on the porch and laughing as they came inside to eat.

"Sorry we're late," Reg apologized as they streamed in the back door.

"Those mules snorty?" Heck asked.

"They'll be fine by Saturday."

"You didn't use them plowing the corn ground?" Chet asked, wondering why they didn't use the large turning-plow on iron wheels.

"No, they're too fast for our Mexicans. They like oxen better."

"Take you forever to get to Kansas with oxen," Heck said in disgust.

Reg agreed. "I know. We seen them oxen-wagon outfits last year going to Kansas. Can't hardly keep up with the herd."

"I have even seen some who used *caritas*," Chet added. "Those squeaking axles about drove me crazy."

Everyone had some fun with the ways to travel during the meal. Even Louise chimed in. "I like passenger trains, myself. That is how civilized people go about this country."

"You ever been on an ocean sailing ship?" May asked her.

"Once from New Orleans to Houston, and I believe we were farther there from the ranch than we would have been had we came up river on a paddleboat. Oh, Mark and I were both seasick the entire journey. No, I don't wish to sail the seven seas."

The men went to the barn after lunch and put up the work animals, satisfied they'd be alright for the trip. The orphan calf was bawling a lot, but the two younger boys told Chet they'd fed him plenty of milk that morning.

"Guess he misses his dead maw," the little one said.

Chet agreed. A nice warm spring day. He told the pair they could check on the cattle up Yellowhammer Creek on their ponies. The two rushed off to get them.

"Curry them down first," he shouted after them.

"We will, Uncle Chet," they promised.

Chet made certain the shower tank on the roof over the bathhouse was full and the second one was filling. He hoped the water would be warm enough to bathe in. Wintertime, they heated water with wood heat, but it had to be hauled in buckets to the tub. Solar and gravity power took over when winter wound down.

After supper he planned a bath and to shave for his visit the next day to invite Kathren to the dance. That made two baths in one week—he'd do the same thing over again to get ready to go to the schoolhouse festival. He looked forward to getting out and talking to his friends. Hell with them Reynoldses.

Chapter 11

In the morning, Chet saddled Fudge before he went to breakfast. A cooler wind had came up from the Gulf, and clouds were low and thick. He'd probably want his slicker before the day was out, going over to see Kathren. He wrapped the Winchester in an oilcloth and put it in his saddle scabbard—in case he needed it. That all settled, he hitched Fudge at the house rack and hurried inside. Hat on the hook, he heard Reg asking for grace and nodded in approval.

He waited until the prayer was over, then came into the dining room and took his seat. "Thanks, Reg, for the grace, and my apology for being late. I didn't plan well enough."

His words drew a few chuckles and Ray told him, "it will be alright, Uncle Chet," which added to the amusement. Chet picked up his coffee cup, anxious for a sip and knowing it was tongue-scalding hot. He blew on it and then tried a sip. Still too hot. He set it back down and went to doctoring his plate of flapjacks with butter and lick. Everyone was so engaged they barely heard someone calling from the front door.

"Chet, someone is here," Reg said as he wiped his mouth on his napkin, then rushed to open the door.

Chet wasn't far behind. He saw past Reg, Raul holding a bloody cloth to his head and trying to get his breath. "Bandits, señor. They've attacked us this morning with several men. They hurt several of our people."

"You know who they are?" Reg asked.

"One I think was Toby Brown. He has a pinto horse with funny markings."

"He one of them?" Chet asked Reg.

Reg nodded. "What should we do?"

"Get some medical supplies and take Susie and May down there. We need to send for the sheriff. We want this all to be legal."

Chet turned to Heck on the porch. "Saddle a fast horse, Heck, that you can handle, then ride to Mason and tell the sheriff he needs to come on the run. They've attacked the ranch and hurt several of our people. Louise, we'll hitch a buckboard, you go to Mayfield and bring the doc back."

"J.D., you're in charge here. They come here, you be sure everyone is safe, the children and the girls. Don't worry about fighting them. Just keep everyone safe."

"I can do it. I'll get Maw the buckboard and then I'll barricade the gate with wagons and hayracks."

"Good idea. We'll be spread thin, but everyone has a job."

"Raul needs stitches," Susie said, examining the man's wound.

"We need a wagon hitched to take you women and Raul back down there. He won't bleed to death. We may have worse-hurt ones down there to see about. Reg, get the mares, not the mules," he shouted after him.

"I will."

Outdoors, he swung onto Fudge as Heck came from the corral on the horse he chose. A big, leggy thoroughbred that could run and was a handful.

"Don't kill him going up there," he said.

"I won't. May I go now?' Heck asked as the impatient horse danced around under him, and he checked him severely to hold him there.

"Be careful," Chet said and nodded.

The big horse they called Run-Away lived up to his rep. Like he had been challenged by others, the muscled horse swooped out of the yard and his thundering hooves soon were out of hearing. Heck sat like a feather on his back, but he was jockeying him hard.

Chet dismounted to check the hastily thrown-on light harness while J.D. helped his mother onto the buckboard's spring seat. "These horses are fast, Louise, but don't have a wreck. We'll have enough patients as it is."

"I will be careful and have doc back here as soon as I can."

"Take him directly to the camp." Chet stepped back and Louise left, wearing a wide straw hat held on by a large ribbon tied under her chin and carrying a buggy whip in one hand. She slapped the horses with the reins in the other hand, then drove off sharply.

Chet kneeled down and told the small boys to stay in the compound until he came back and to help J.D. They agreed with grim faces. That done, he saw that Susie, May, and the house girls were loading the wagon with their needs. No way to make Raul stop from helping them either. The man was eaten up with concern about his people. Reg stood behind the seat, holding the reins and keeping the big mares in place.

"Get Reg a horse," he told J.D. "Susie can drive those mares."

Chet hurried over and used his hands as a stirrup for them to put one foot in, and tossed both women and Raul up into the back of the bed. Reins at last in Susie's hand, Reg bailed over the sides and took off for his horse that J.D. was saddling for him. He returned in a few minutes.

Chet, back in the saddle, gave a head toss to Reg and they rode hard for the village. There were some tall plumes of smoke that worried Chet. The cluster of small houses where his farm help stayed consisted of fifteen jacals spaced around in a semicircle and several squaw shades called *remadas*. Many people in Mexico and south Texas used them as their houses, especially in the summertime. These gentle people were part of the ranch. The families and their children all came from Mexico to the ranch during the growing season and to work on the farmland, crops, gardens, and the fencing.

Mother Isabella, the matron of the village, ran out, crying, to hug Chet. "They were vicious. They took one of the girls away with them. Two men are dead. Others wounded. They murdered a baby's mother." She closed her wet eyelashes as he held her in his arms.

"I am sorry. Help is on the way. Where is your husband, Oscar?"

Isabella dropped her chin and sniffed. "He is among the dead."

They had killed a good man and the notion stabbed Chet's heart. He hugged her tight. "Oh, I am so sorry. How did this happen?"

"They came in the night and they ordered all the men outside. It was dark, but once most were out there they went to shooting at them. Women rushed out and some were shot at. This place was a living hell. They kidnapped some women they wanted and raped them not far from here. One is still missing. I fear they killed her."

"Who were they?"

"Gringos."

"Did you hear any names?"

"It was still dark. I was afraid. I never heard any names."

Susie ran over. "Two of the men have gunshot wounds. Did she tell you about the women they hurt?"

"Yes." Chet handed Isabella to her. "Try to comfort her. She's lost her husband. I better go help them fight the fires that everyone is trying to put out."

He could see a chain of children and grownups in a bucket line as flames consumed four of the ramadas. Looking over the fires, he held his hands up to get them to stop. The fires would consume the roofs, mostly hay and brush. The covers could be replaced easier than their inadequate fire department, who faced a failure at dousing them out in these cases.

He waved his arms and soon had the exhausted ones stopped. "We can rebuild them."

Weary men, women, and children nodded in agreement and began to move about like defeated warriors. He went back to find Susie and Isabella.

"Has anyone eaten anything?" he asked them.

Isabella shook her head.

"Then lets get the women to start making food. They need to eat."

Isabella agreed and the two women began calling to others. Chet went looking for Reg. He found him squatted beside two men digging a second grave.

"There are several to bury," Reg said.

"You hear any names of the ones responsible?"

"Gringos." Reg shook his head. "They were so shocked by the attack they couldn't think. Can you imagine?"

"It was hell, that was for sure. Go look for the tracks of their horses. Maybe we can track them down. I want these killers rounded up."

Reg agreed and went for his horse. Still in a daze, Chet headed back to talk to others. May came carrying a baby.

"They kidnapped its mother and she has not came back."

"Are there other relatives here?"

"In Mexico." May looked close to tears.

"Go talk to Isabella, she will know who can help you with the child."

He closed his eyes. The clock was ticking and the

ones who caused this horrible attack were getting farther away.

Reg came loping back on his horse. "They all rode south."

"How many?"

"I figure four."

"We have things here under control. Let's go find them." He went and caught Fudge, who was grazing. The reins picked up, he swung into the saddle and rode over to where Susie was overseeing the food-making process.

She used her hand to shade the bright sun from her eyes. "You going after them?"

He nodded. "Tell Trent."

With a grim nod, she agreed. "You two be careful."

He promised they would and sent Fudge after Reg, who'd already set out. No telling what they'd find. These men were cold killers and needed to be stopped. If they did this to get even with him, they'd learn how tough he was. No, those Reynoldses had never been stopped by the punishment dealt to them, whether the law hung them or by those killed in recovering the herd up in Kansas. Not even the deaths of those three who tried to ambush him had halted their obsession with getting to the —*C*.

Thicker clouds moved in and the chance of rain looked closer. He and Reg, coming over a small range of hills, approached an abandoned farmstead on Gibson Creek. It was the old Nelson place, which had been left empty for many years after a rash of Comanche raids had struck the area. Through the live oak and cedar from the ridge, Chet could see the weathered house, outbuildings, and pens. He reined up and took out the field glasses to check out a horse's tail.

"You see something down there?" Reg came back and stood in the stirrup to better view the place.

"Yes, there's a horse in one of those sheds." He could see the black tail switching flies; then the horse went farther behind the cover, out of his view.

"Think someone's hiding him?"

"Why else put him in a shed?"

"It means there's at least someone down there." Reg took off his hat and scratched the thatch of brown hair on his head.

"Maybe four?" Pretty damn brave for them to den up this close to the crime. This could be another trap or simply stupidity. *Too easy.* Instead of running like hell, they stopped—why, they might not even be the raiders. No, it would be them—the incriminating hoofprints led there.

"Right. There might be four of them if they're all here." Reg made a grim face. "This is sure where they were headed."

Light rain began to soak through Chet's shirt. He and Reg shook out their slickers.

"Just remember, these men could be desperate when we move in on them. Keep your pistol cocked. We better slip in on foot, since we don't want them to know we're coming."

Horses securely tied, they started through the pungent cedars. The moisture enhanced the smell. A tick of the droplets on his hat sounded like small birds pecking on it. The way downhill proved steep. He could see the buildings clear enough through small windows in the cedar boughs, and he still had not spotted any sign of an individual since they had begun their descent. They reached the base and slipped to the west to where they could use the outbuildings for cover to get closer to the main structure.

Chet had been in the old house several times. The roof, made of clay tile, had shed Comanche fire arrows, and was the reason it stood this long. The only windows on the first floor were slits in the mason walls. An attacker could not get inside through them, but it was easy to shoot from them. So they must have come in from the south porch to the front door to enter. The staircase to the second story was inside. Undiscovered, he and Reg eased into the shed where four horses stood hipshot. The prominent paint was in there.

"Is that his horse?" Chet asked, already knowing the answer.

"It's Toby Brown's, alright. What're you doing?"

"Loosening their girths in case they get back to them and try to escape." Chet pulled the latigoes loose on the nearest saddle.

With a grin, Reg holstered his Colt and joined him. In minutes, the girths were loose enough so anyone who grabbed the horn to get on would fall on their butts. The job complete, Chet heard someone coming. He held out his arm and both men backed quietly to the wall as the man grumbled about something.

Obviously unaware of their presence, he came into the dark shed. Reg stepped over and stuck his Colt muzzle on the man's back. "Don't say a word."

"Oooh—" Trembling like a freezing dog, the short

freckle-faced man stood shaking in his boots. "I—I— didn't do any of this—"

"Shut up. What's your name?"

"He's Cliff Thomas," Reg said taking a lariat down from a saddle to tie him up with.

"Who does he work for?" Chet asked.

"Some of their kin."

"I never shot no one. I swear—"

"Shut up. Who's at the house?"

"T-Toby—Cecil—"

Chet frowned at him. "Cecil who?"

"Crown."

Reg shook his head. He didn't know the name.

Chet did. "He came from New Mexico."

"Oh. One of those three?" Reg shook his head.

"I think so. Is there a kid in there?" At Thomas's nod, Chet decided they were the two who had escaped from Kathren's.

"His name's Doolin."

Chet turned his head. "Did you hear some boots running?"

Reg drew his gun and went to the door; then he fired his revolver rapidly. Chet swept up his rifle and moved to join him. There was only one target when he got past the door and took aim. The Winchester spoke and the man went down. No others were in sight.

"Guard him," he said to Reg about Thomas and set out in a run. He stopped and took the Colt out of the fallen Toby Brown's hand. The man on the ground withered in pain. "Stay right there. You move and Reg will shoot you."

Brown gave him a garbled reply. Chet dismissed it and ran to the porch. He hugged the wall. Had the pair gone inside, or were they headed for cover? The drip off the porch prevented any small sounds from being detected.

Past two shuttered slits in the wall, Chet shoved open the front door with his boot and stepped back. Nothing. Notions began mounting. They might not be concealed inside. Still, he didn't dare risk them not being in there.

Rain had increased. His nauseated belly told him it was mid-afternoon. With stealth he stepped into the room and flattened to the wall. Nothing. He dried his right hand on the side of his pants and re-gripped the wooden stock. Nothing but the pitter-pat of rain could be heard, besides his heart beating in his chest and breath flowing in and out of his nose.

The staircase was obvious. He searched the various rooms—nothing but a scurrying pack rat that made his heart stop for a second. Then, believing he'd taken the wrong trail, he charged the stairs with his six-gun cocked in his fist. The upstairs was empty. He raced to the window on the east side, but there was no sign of the fleeing outlaws. In the thick brush without bloodhounds, they'd never catch them. Besides, the rain would soon wash out any tracks. At the glassless window, moisture dampened his face. Those two hired guns had escaped. Damn them. He'd get them—they wouldn't be that lucky next time.

Back at the shed with Thomas tied up, Chet and Reg, not too kindly, dragged the wounded Brown out of the rain and put him on a canvas groundcloth in the shed. The man begged for whiskey. Chet ignored him.

"What did you do with the woman you kidnapped?" he asked Thomas.

"I didn't have anything to do with her. I swear."

"Listen, if you don't want your ears notched, you better start talking." Chet drew out his sharp hunting knife from its sheath. "Tell me. Now."

"They stopped a ways back and I rode on. I swear I never touched her. They told me to build a fire and cook something when I got down here and they'd meet me at this place. There was no wood here, and I had no food to cook."

"What happened to her?"

"I don't know." He shook his head rapidly like it was uncontrolled.

"One more time, you damn sure know what they did to her."

"I-I asked them. They all laughed, and the Kid drew the side of his hand over his throat."

"Why did they do that?"

"How in the hell should I know?" he screamed hysterically.

"Reg, take the paint and ride for the ranch. The sheriff should be there by the time you get there. Tell him we'll need a search party to look for her body. Have someone bring a wagon by the road for these two prisoners."

"What about those other two? Will they come back?"

"I doubt it. They're damn good at running."

"But they don't have horses." Reg began tightening the cinch on the paint.

"I think they'll steal some mounts off someone and keep going."

"I hate to leave you here with them two alone."

"I'll be fine. You be careful. The road will be the shorter way back."

Reg led the gelding out in the rain and it circled around him. He ignored the pony's anxious ways and stepped up into the saddle. "I'll be back." With a sharp jerk on the reins, he set him down. "Helluva stout horse." Then he rode off into the hard curtain of rain.

Chet watched him disappear, and could barely see the house in the downpour. He found some dried jerky in one of their saddlebags and took a place to sit on the boards of the hay manger where the angled slats had been taken out. His rifle beside him, all he had to do was wait, and that would be hours.

The pair might circle and come back. Hard rain could be a real tough thing when a person needed to get somewhere and had no transportation. But if they came, he'd be ready for them.

"I've got to pee," Thomas said.

"Well, pee in your pants then. I'm not untying you."

"I-I can't do that."

"Listen, I'm not your friend. If I'd had my way I'd've already hung you, but we're doing this by the letter of the law. So if you think I'm doing one damn thing for you, think again. You can rot in hell. I don't care." He went to gnawing on the tough jerky. Rifle across his lap—*come on back you two, I'm itching to take you out as well.*

Chapter 12

The late winter sun had set. The slicker Chet wore proved no cloak of warmth. He had put a blanket over the moaning, wounded man on the ground. The rain still dripped off the eaves and he thought he heard horses coming. Then the jingle of harness and the big Belgium hooves clopping over the muddy ground.

"Hey, Chet are you still here?" Reg called out.

"What took so long?' Then he laughed when Trent got off his horse, produced a lantern, and came inside to light it.

"Reg said there were four raiders. The other two didn't come back?"

Chet put his rifle down. "Nope, they ran."

Trent handed the lantern to Reg and knelt to speak to Brown on the floor. "You'll be on your way to jail, shortly," he said and rose to his feet. Brown sat on his butt, head downcast after Trent spoke to him.

"I never hurt no one," Thomas confessed when Trent asked him. "They said we were only going to scare them *Messican*s off. I didn't know what they planned. I didn't shoot anyone or touch a woman."

Trent rose, shaking his head. "Did he say what they did with her?"

Chet nodded. "He said the kid showed him that they cut her throat when he asked them where she was at."

"I never did a thing."

Trent nodded at the prisoner's words. "But you're still guilty. We better form a posse come daylight and search for her."

Chet agreed. "Let's go back to the ranch. Is everything there alright?"

"Fine," Reg said. "Susie wanted to come down here and help you. I made her stay home."

"Good. You okay, Heck?" he asked, noticing the boy standing in the edge of the lamplight.

"Oh, yes, sir. Been some day for me."

"You did good. Let's load these two hombres, get back to the ranch."

Trent agreed with a wary head shake. "What did they hope to do?"

"To scare our farm help off, according to Thomas."

"Shoot down innocent men and women—rape women. Who in the hell leads them?"

Chet chuckled. "Now if they tell you who that is, you'll have someone else to hang. Sorry I laughed, but this crazy killing business has been going on too long."

Prisoners loaded, the extra horses on a lead line, Reg drove the wagon and Heck led the horse string. The dark night was hard to maneuver over the dim road, but Reg was a patient driver and managed to hold them in the shallow ruts.

Worn out, Chet rode ahead the three hours or so it required to get home. At the lighted front porch, Heck pushed in close to Chet. "Why does that damn Thomas smell so pissy?"

"Guess he had to go."

Heck nodded, then he shook his head. "I'll put the horses up. I don't want to have to unload him. Yuck."

"You can simply handcuff them for now," Trent said. "We can lock them up after we eat. I bet she's got lots of food ready for us."

"You can bet on that, sir," Heck said. Then he started off, leading his string.

"We need to do something for Brown," Trent said quietly to Chet.

"You want us to take him to the doc in Mayfield?" Chet asked.

"He's in my custody. I'm responsible for him."

"Let's eat first. Then Reg, J.D., or I'll take him there. Sorry I have no feelings for the man."

"I understand that, but I have a job to do."

"We'll help after we eat."

"Fine. Thanks. I know you could have shot them both. I appreciate your holding them."

"No, I'd have hung them right down there where you found them. You would never have had to worry about them. Killing unarmed men and children, raping women, they damn sure deserve to be hung."

"They're my worry now."

Chet agreed, and they went inside the house.

The women rushed about to put the food out. How

Susie and her crew ever put all this together after the day at the village, he would never know—but the food was spread out and he asked grace. Then all hands set in on the meal as the mantel clock struck eleven PM.

After the last bite was consumed, the menfolk headed out the door. Chet stopped Trent. "I'll drive the wagon into Mayfield for you."

"Thanks."

"You ain't going without me," J.D. said. "The rest can take care of this place. I've missed all the excitement."

Chet took his rifle, in case, and he and J.D. climbed onto the spring set and took off in the dark for town. The clouds had cleared out some and Trent led the way on his horse. By star and moonlight the way went easier. Near two o'clock, they woke Doc up and carried the groggy, wounded Brown upstairs and put him on a table. Then they went to Trent's deputy's house and woke Charlie Hat up. After that they drove back to the doc's place and left Hat to guard the wounded prisoner.

The rain had quit. They shook Trent's hand, ready to drive back to the ranch. He thanked them and said he'd be back up there with help to look for the missing woman's body. Trent parted with them, leading his other prisoner, Thomas, back to Mason to put in jail.

"Did that damn Thomas piss in his pants?" J.D. asked, shaking his head. "He sure stunk of it."

"I wouldn't aid him. I guess he had to. I had no use for him," Chet said, clucking to the team.

The two took turns trying to stay awake and not drive off into some canyon or ditch. The mares were good and knew the way. The jingle of the harness and the large hooves striking the soft ground made a song. But Chet found it harder and harder to stay awake. They pulled over and slept a short while in the back, then woke and drove on in, hearing the bell ringing when they splashed through Yellowhammer Creek less than a quarter mile from the homestead.

Susie came out to welcome them. "If you two ain't too tired, breakfast is on."

Stiff and sore, Chet jumped down and pulled his clammy britches from his skin and then hugged her. Good to be back. He wasn't sure he could eat, but a cup of strong coffee might clear the cobwebs out of his brain. She led him along to the dry sink and he washed his face on the back porch. Hands lathered, he shook his head. "Guess you and Trent had no time for a word."

"That was about it."

"You invite Trent to the dance?"

"No."

"He's coming back to look for her remains."

"We'll see." She looked across the dark pens and outbuildings.

"Damn, I shouldn't complain. I haven't asked Kathren either."

He stopped before they went inside and gazed hard at her. "Running a damn ranch ain't all it's cut out to be."

"I agree. Get in there, they won't eat till you say grace."

"Yes, ma'am."

Seated at the table, he thought about the pair of

killers who'd escaped him. Cecil Crown and the kid called Doolin. Blowing on the vapors over his cup, he wondered how far they'd run. He'd get word in a few days where they went through and he'd have a lead to chase them down.

"What are we going to do today?" Reg asked.

"Saddle me a horse and one to pack her body on. A sheet to roll her up in. I'll sleep a couple hours and be ready to ride."

"I want to go," Heck said.

"No, I'm afraid this will be a grisly job for anyone."

"But I saw Dad dead—"

Slapped by the boy's words, Chet nodded. "Alright. You and Reg can go along. Reg remembers the way we went, is why I'm asking him. J.D., go and see if they need anything at the village. Get it for them."

"I'll go with him," Susie said.

Chet agreed. Then he went to the bunkhouse and his room. He sprawled face-down and collapsed. A few hours later he woke, rose, went out, and washed his face. Heck jumped up from a bench outside the bunkhouse and told him their horses were ready and Reg would met them at the village. He and the boy rode to where he waited for them.

Upon seeing them ride in, Chet saw Reg doff his hat at some pretty senorita and remount his cow pony. Chet joined them.

"The girl's name they killed is LaLana."

Not expecting a good answer, Chet asked, "Ain't no one seen a sign of her?"

"I figured they killed her, from what Thomas told

us," Reg said. "I was hoping, since he supposedly wasn't there, they might have lied to him."

Chet agreed with a stiff nod. The search process proved slow, and he dreaded the results of their efforts deep in his gut. They rode up various side canyons and sidetracked until, in late afternoon, Heck spotted some turkey buzzards.

"They're up on the next ridge." Heck came riding in fast, reining up and setting his horse down hard.

In a quick agreement, they put Heck in the lead and tore out of the cedars. Hooves scrambled over the rock ledges and soon gained the overlook; then they rode off to the right. Chet decided this was where Thomas probably parted with them. He pushed in behind Heck as half a dozen vultures took off from the ground in a clearing and exposed her naked body.

Filled with rage over their eating on her corpse, Reg began to shoot vultures. He emptied his revolver at them, and several fell to the ground, squawking in an explosion of black feathers. Some wounded ones rushed for cover on foot.

"Sonsabitches," he swore and slapped his empty gun away.

Chet waved the boy back, carrying the sheet to cover her. "Bring a rope to tie this on."

On his knees to help and seeing the work of her killers, Reg swore again. "You're right. We should have hung them." Then he shook his head at the sight of the gaping cut across her throat. "Damn them, anyway. Chet, they don't even deserve a trial."

Chet stopped and steadied himself as they tied the sheet on with a lariat.

"Tough deal?" Heck asked, working beside him to tie her up.

No way Chet could swallow the lump in his throat. No way. He finally managed. "Yes."

With her body loaded over the spare horse, they started back. Grim-faced, the three came into a line. Only a short ways back they met the sheriff. Trent saw the body over the saddle, and in a hoarse voice asked, "That her?"

"What's left of her," Chet said and booted his horse on by him.

"Sorry you all had to do this, this is really my job," Trent said.

"No," Chet said. "This is every man in this county's job. Worthless trash like those bastards shouldn't live to see another sundown. That woman had a child who will grow up without a mother. Never recognize her. They don't deserve another breath in this world."

"The law will handle them."

"I know, Trent, but somehow, these things get swept under the rug somewhere. Hell, as some would say, they were just Mexicans. If the law turns them loose for this—their life ain't worth ten cents. Trust me, pard. Trust me."

"Word came this morning those other two had stolen some horses and saddles from a bunch of cowboys and headed west."

Chet simply nodded. "Let them ride. I'll find 'em."

"I'll swear out a warrant for both of them. You want to put a reward on them?"

"I'd pay a hundred dollars apiece on each of them."

"I can do that."

"Trent, I need three good men that aren't scared of being in a shootout or sleeping with a six-gun. Reg's going need them to help him run this outfit."

Trent pushed his horse in closer. "I guess that you're going looking for them two."

"I may do that, too, but I really need a new home for the bar-C and I better get to looking for it."

"Where will you go?"

"I ain't certain. Maybe look in Arizona. Heard the Apaches are about rounded up out there."

"I've heard it's an uneasy peace."

Chet checked his horse to look across the hills. "There damn sure ain't no peace here with them Reynoldses till they're all planted in the ground."

"I'd hate to see you go. I'd sure like to court your sister, too."

"Trent, I'm sorry you two haven't had more time together. But me personally, I'm loaded with family, babies, and I can't have them hurt. By God, there has to be some real estate somewhere that I can live in peace on. But I have no hold on Susie."

"She won't leave you in the lurch. She told me so. The old man in the condition he's in, she has her hands full."

"Kathren has the same problems, pard. She can't leave either. Life's dealt us some tough hands in this card game, but I know now there will be no peace for any of my kin as long as we live in this land."

"When're you going to take off?"

"As soon as I can find the men to help Reg."

"I don't envy your job. Any way I can help, let me know."

Chet dropped back and rode between the two. "Reg, we're going to hire three good hands to work for you. I'm going to try and find us a place where we can live in peace. They ain't going to stop harassing us. Somewhere there's a place, and by damn I'm going to find it."

"I want to go with you," Heck said. "I won't get in the way."

"I'll take that under advisement. I ain't promising you anything right now."

Heck nodded.

"Those Hascal brothers, Walt and Rope, I think would make good hands."

Chet nodded. They were Reg's age and might fit. They knew how to work, and he'd never seen them back down when they thought they were right. "Keep thinking."

"Utah Kline."

"I'd consider him. I understand him and Frank Rich, the new boss on the Anchor, don't gee and haw too well together."

"I bet they'll be at the dance Saturday night. I'll talk to them up there."

"Damn," Chet swore under his breath. "I still have to go see Kathren about that. Anyway, we'll talk to them over there."

No time to go back and clean up. Kathren'd have to like him as he was. Better let the boys and Trent finish up this deal. He explained his plight, excused himself, and then set out east for her place. Really he'd not forgotten—she was in his dreams, on his mind, and the very notion of her even made a knot form in his throat. The worst part was he'd have to tell her about his plans.

Mid-afternoon, he found her on a rocker under the porch roof, mending a pair of overalls that she wore to work in.

She looked up at him and her face melted into a smile. "You look like the cat drug you in."

He dismounted and looked over his clothing. "I just don't have my Sunday best on."

The overalls set aside, she rushed over to kiss and hug him. Then, tossing her hair back and smiling into his face, she asked, "What bucket did you fall into this time?"

"They raided my Mexican workers' camp. Killed two men, wounded some others—raped two women and then killed one of them."

"Oh, no." They both took a seat on the porch stoop. "Who did this?"

"Toby Brown, a guy named Thomas, and those two who came in here with the dead man—Crown is his name—and they call the other one the Kid."

"My Lord, you've been in a another bad scrap. Where are they?"

"I shot Brown. He'll live. Him and Thomas are in jail. The other two, Crown and the Kid, got away from Reg and me, then stole horses from some cowboys and rode away."

She hugged him and squeezed her eyes. "No wonder you look so bushed."

"I'm fine. Came to ask you to the dance at the schoolhouse Saturday night."

"Cady and I will be there."

"Good."

"I bet if you took a bath, I shaved your face, and cut your long hair, you'd feel a hundred percent better. I still have a clean pair of britches and shirt that you left when you went back home."

"Well, ain't I a lucky cuss." He twisted around and hugged her. Kathren could chase away more things in his life bugging him than any woman he'd ever known. Somehow he needed to include her in his life—somehow.

"Is everyone alright at your place?" She stood up. "I'm not rushing you, but we need to heat some water to start this process."

"Where's your daughter?"

"Delivering eggs to her grandmother. She'll be excited that you're here."

"Here, let me unsaddle Bridges. He's been a fair piece. We had to go search this morning for the young woman's body they'd dumped in the cedars."

"Sure, put him in the corral."

"If she's going to be here—"

"Cady is a big girl, she'll understand."

Chet shrugged. "Be easier if you'd marry me."

With a hard squint at him and her left eye closed, she shook her head. "It ain't that easy, Chet, but thanks for asking me."

"Again."

"Yes, now put that dang horse up." She was shoving him away with her flat hands on his chest.

"I'm going. But you remember, I asked you."

"I haven't forgotten the first time, either. Now go." She pointed to his horse.

He relented and put Bridges in the corral. Tossed the saddle and pads on the fence and set out for the house. Damn, all he needed to set him off was the closeness to her and she always stirred him up. He removed his hat and combed his too-long locks back with his fingers before he replaced it. Why in hell's name weren't they married?

Kathren brought him some cool, sweetened tea from a large hanging bowl. Some pottery from Mexico that sweated and kept liquid cooler than usual. At the first taste he nodded his approval.

Tea finished, he picked up both pails and went to the well to refill them. His muscles complained coming back with the full ones, but they were only faint reminders of his beating. She was stoking the range and smiled. "When did you sleep last?"

"Oh, a little this morning."

Her hand on his shoulder, she bent over laughing. "Chet Byrnes, you're a mess. Where were you last night?"

"I told you we had to take that wounded prisoner along with the other one into Mayfield for the sheriff, didn't I?"

"No." She was still laughing.

"What's so funny?"

She shook her head and wiped aside tears with her fingers. "Nothing. Just you and me. I get so I could kill you with me getting so upset about you not being here. Then you come and I fall to pieces."

He hugged her. "I'm the same way."

His bath went uneventfully. Then, with him dressed in his clean britches and tented by a sheet, she used the scissors on his long hair and the floor soon was covered in dark brown hair. This completed, Kathren let him look at himself in the small mirror.

"You look alright?" she asked.

"Of course."

"Shave comes next."

Chet ran a palm over his bristly cheek. "I need that, too."

The mowing process completed, with him dressed, she told him to go catch a nap. "I'll get you up for supper."

He never argued. Then they kissed and he in his stocking feet went over, laid down on her bed, and soon fell asleep.

He heard her and Cady talking. China plates were talking too as her daughter set the table. His new haircut was the first thing he felt when he sat up and tried to escape the dullness of his sleep-filled mind.

"Good, you're back," Cady said as he emerged.

"How's that?" he asked.

She wrinkled her nose and in a stage whisper said, "She'll be in a better mood."

"Cady," her mother said to admonish her.

Cady shrugged. "Well, she'll be better, anyway."

Looking at the ceiling for help, Kathren let out her breath. "Now she has help. Oh, heavens."

With each place setting, Cady arranged the silverware in its proper place. "I'm learning how to set the table for company. She says someday I will need it more than knowing how to rope a calf. I want you to show me how to do rope tricks."

"I'm not the best. but I'll try."

"Oh, you will do fine. I saw you one day in May-field, making a circle and jumping in and out of it. "

"Alright." He wondered if he'd been showing off that day.

"You feeling better?" Kathren asked.

"I feel fine."

"I've got some coffee."

Chet stood up and stretched. "I'd really like some."

"Mother said you had more trouble at the ranch." She delivered him his cup.

"Yes, we did."

"Cady, he may not want to tell you all that."

"Mother, he doesn't have to."

Kathren raised her eyes again, but he saved her. "Cady, some mean men raided where my farm help lives and shot two men to death, wounded some other people, then they murdered a young mother."

"Oh, that was terrible."

"We arrested two of them and two escaped."

"What will they do to the two captured ones?"

"Try them." Then he blew on his coffee.

"Will they be hung?"

"I imagine they will be. A jury will hear the case and decide about their guilt or innocence."

She nodded. "Thank you for telling me all this."

"Now," her mother said. "Let's talk about lighter things. He came over to invite us to the dance Saturday night."

"Really?"

"Yes. Should we go?"

"Why of course, mother. There is no reason not to go, is there?"

"Oh, there could be some."

"What would that be?"

"You might have to dance with boys who would step on your toes."

They all laughed. She put the plate of brown-crusted biscuits on the table, then they all three stood holding each other's hands as he asked grace. His words slow and soft: ". . . Lord, we are grateful for the rain, our togetherness here tonight, keep us in the palm of your hand, may this food feed us in Jesus' name, amen."

"Did you start saying prayers for a reason?" Cady asked as they sat down. "I never heard you pray before."

"No, it is alright, Kathren." He blocked her from stopping her. "I felt so many things in my life centered around the things that I wanted for my friends, family, and myself, I needed to lead them to Him."

She nodded she understood and they began to eat. Soon they finished the meal, talking about horses, what to plant in the garden as the days grew longer and warmer. At last, Cady went off to bed in her room.

The two of them talked in whispers. Kathren moved over to sit on his lap and her presence warmed him. The faint smell of lilacs in his nose, they settled into each other's closeness.

"Wouldn't it be nice to do this a lot of evenings?"

He agreed and kissed her. It wouldn't only be nice; for him this would be heavenly.

Chapter 13

Saturday came fast. Everyone at the —𝒞 was busy early that Saturday morning, loading enough food for an army. But Chet knew how many cowboys, young and old, would make a beeline to sample some of Susie's cooking. He called it "riding the grubline" for the —𝒞 camp and laughed a lot about it.

She separated him from the rest in the kitchen. "You and Kathren talk."

"We always do. But we don't ever get past talking. We both have our obligations. Mine to this ranch and her to her parents and the two places."

"No, that's not it. The boys said you plan on hiring hands tonight. That means you're going to leave the ranch."

"To look is all. I haven't fully made my mind up. But these damn killings are all pointed at us. I don't want to bury my own family with my own stubbornness."

"I see. Where will you go look?" she asked, her coldness in the air.

"I'm going to see if I can get a lead on those other two that got away. I can't find them, then I'll look around in New Mexico and Arizona."

"Heck wants to go along."

He nodded. "He told me so."

"You know he and May don't get along. When you were over at Kathren's recovering, Reg moved him to the bunkhouse and talked to him like a second father."

"He told me. But I thought things have been quiet since then."

"They have, but May feels she is his stepmother and has a right to tell him what to do. He resents it. To be truthful, he's a lot like his father, Dale Allen."

"Is it best he goes with me?"

"Well, he listens to you."

"I savvy that. It might turn dangerous; that's the only thing that worries me about having him along."

"Whatever you think. Trent promised if there was no trouble in the county he'd be there to dance with me." Her face brightened.

"Why, that's great news."

She blushed and agreed. "Now what will you tell Kathren?"

"She knows I have problems I have to solve. I think she'll understand."

"Such a damn shame. I know you still have some scars from the murder of Marla Porter. I knew that tore you apart for a long time."

"Marla wouldn't divorce him. I begged her to marry me. But I think her pride kept her from doing it. Like the divorce would be a stigma on her person.

Folks would talk behind her back how we'd had an affair for years." He shook his head. "They hung the Reynolds who did it."

"Your affair with her was the best kept damn secret in Texas. I didn't know. I knew you saw someone— but." She changed her tone; someone was coming— "I think we'll have enough food."

"Good," he said. The memories of Marla's death had stung him, but she was gone to a better place. Slaughtering brood mares, herding range cattle on the —$\mathcal{C}$, their attempted attack on Susie, Dale Allen's death in Kansas; he'd had it with those Reynoldses. The whole business made him sick enough to puke.

"Thirty minutes we pull out. Louise has already taken the buckboard and team to go on ahead. She wanted to visit a friend over there. I'll ring the bell to warn the rest." He put on his hat and smiled at the Mexican girl Juanita, who came in to ask Susie a question.

The bell clapper vibrating the signal to those going to the dance, he went on to find himself a horse. He found Fudge saddled, switching flies at the tackroom rack. Obviously the work of Heck—the want-to-go-with boy of a dozen or so years. The matter still wasn't clear in his mind about taking him along.

Both wagons pulled out. Reg hung on the porch post and waved them out the gate. J.D. was in charge of finding those three cowboys at the dance. May, with the baby in her arm, smiled and made her ward wave, too. J.D. drove the second team, Susie had the lead one, and Juanita, who was going along to help Susie, beamed as she rode with her. Louise had taken the buckboard and left before them, not to be in their dust.

Heck led two extra saddled horses in case they had a problem and needed to move fast. Chet and he rode in the rear, but they planned to cut across country after they forded the Yellowhammer. They could have a campsite located before the wagons' arrival. Beyond the creek, the two short-loped their horses and cut southeast—while the wagons had to take the lengthier road.

At last at the schoolhouse and cemetery, he and Heck rode downstream till they found the tall cottonwoods where they could string the large canvas. Heck took a lariat and climbed the first one to hang it over a thick limb where they could reach it and pull the tent up. Then he did the other side with Chet watching from underneath.

"That boy of Dale Allen's sure growing," Henny Price said, joining him. The gray-headed rancher came ambling up like most cattlemen that age with a limp from some former horse wrecks.

"He is. What do you know?"

"The Johnson brothers sent us word from Fort Worth yesterday; they'd not had a problem. Said they slowed down. They were ahead of the new grass."

Chet had thought so. "I was afraid they left a little early. But if they can find some feed and move slower, they'll have heavier cattle to sell. Those cattle they have aren't the old brush-popping critters we first drove up there. They've been handled all through their lives. Those old brush mavericks we first drove up there were more like deer."

"Yes, they were really wild." Henny slapped his right leg. "That's why I got a hitch in this leg. Boys set the bone, but I had to ride, no matter. We were so shorthanded on that crew."

Chet nodded.

"Things alright over in your country?"

"Nothing like what's happened over your way. Me and the missus said y'all are sure catching hell from them ignorant Reynoldses."

"I guess. I thought things would quiet down."

The old man shook his head. "No, I figure they took an oath against ya."

"Thanks. I miss your missus. Tell her hi for me."

"I will. You know I've got a good place, three creeks, plenty of open country. We've got three hundred mother cows under my brand. Millie and I don't have any kids. Our kin in Arkansas we ain't seed in years. Would one of them big boys of Louise's like to take care of us and the place? When we're gone they could have the ranch, lock, stock, and barrel. Don't owe a dime on anything."

"My Lord, Henny, I'd sure ask them. I'll let them talk it over."

"I ain't going to die no time soon, but we've talked and feel if there was anyone we knew, they'd be loyal. Ain't everyone in this world loyal anymore, you know that?"

"I know that well."

"I knew you needed them, but I figured you could spare me one of them. They got the right breeding in them. I knew Rock well. Guess he ain't no better?"

"No. He lives in his own world."

"Those damn Comanche took a toll on us. I figured after we whipped Santa Ana's ass we'd have it made in Texas. But we was broke when we got here and there was no money, so we joined the States. Finally got the Comanches out of our hair. That last damn war was stupid. But this cattle drive business has sure made us better off."

"It has saved us. I hear the wagons. I'll have them boys give you an answer or come talk to you two."

"No problem. Millie and I are fine right now." Henny waved at the folks in the wagons and ambled back toward the schoolhouse.

Chet frowned. What an opportunity for one of them boys. But what would he do without even one of them? And they'd still be in the Reynolds's part of the world. The big wagons were there. Kathren and her daughter should be arriving at any moment. Where was Louise? She should have already been there, driving the buckboard. She had left a half hour before the rest.

"You seen Louise?" he asked, helping Susie down.

"No, I thought she would be here."

"What's wrong?" J.D. asked, climbing down and coming over.

"Your mother hasn't came in yet. You see her on the road?"

"No, she never said nothing but that she'd meet us here."

"Good grief, where could she be?" He stood on his toes to see down the draw at the schoolhouse. Their matched team would stand out. Where was she?

"What's wrong?" Heck asked.

"Louise isn't here."

"What are we going to do?"

"Go backtrack and try to find where she went. Heck, you stay here. Don't shoot anyone. J.D. and I better go see where she went." Then he paused. "I hate for you to have to do things I should be doing."

"What's that?" His sister frowned at him.

"Explain to Kathren what I'm doing. I hate like hell for her to come here on my invitation and then find I've rode off."

"She'll be fine. She knows about emergencies. She'll be fine," Susie said. "You two go on, we can handle this part."

He and J.D. rode like the wind to follow the road back and look for any sign of Louise. They halted where the road went to Mason. Her narrow tracks went in that direction. But other tracks told him several riders had been around there at or near the time hers were made.

"Reckon they kidnapped her?" J.D asked as they circled the sign in the dirt.

"Damned if I know. But they went north here."

Chet in the lead, they flew northward, seeing the thin ribbons of the buckboard rims cut in the dust going in that direction. Then the tracks went off the road and forced them to rein up sharply. The horse under Chet slid to a sharp stop, and he booted him off into the cedars. The rig and team stood abandoned, hidden in the pungent boughs. Still in their harness, the horses had dried, so it had been some time since the rig had been deserted there. The heel marks of her button-up shoes were around it, but none led anywhere. She must have been packed off by the ones on horseback.

"Which way did they go?" Chet asked, impatient over the time they had already wasted. Both men were searching around on foot for any signs.

J.D. found some prints. "I think they went south."

"We need to split up here," Chet said. "I'll leave signs for you on my way. You go find Trent and you two follow my tracks. I don't want them hurting her. And also find someone to take that team and buckboard back to the ranch."

With a concerned frown written on his face, J.D. said, "They may plan to ambush you. This all might be a trick."

Chet vaulted into the saddle. "I know that, too, but these men are killers and I don't want anything to happen to your mother."

"Me, either. I'll bring Trent and get someone to drive the buckboard back home."

"Good." He booted Fudge through the cedars, seeing more horse prints and trying to imagine who had taken her. He thought the biggest share of troublemakers in the Reynolds outfit were either dead, in jail, or on the run. What family branch were these from?

One thing for certain: Louise wasn't taking being kidnapped sitting down. He'd bet good money they were getting her verbal abuse unless they'd gagged her.

Mid-afternoon, the riders had switched to back trails that ran southerly. He figured that was so no one would recognize her. Where would they come out, going this way? They'd soon be somewhere on the stage road to San Antonio. He crossed the well-used east-west route, nothing in sight, and found their tracks again—heading south in the brush.

Chet had not ridden this far south much, but knew that somewhere the Perdanales River ran east to west, south of the stage road. He turned and looked back— *Kathren, forgive me. Darling, I hate leaving you there alone.* Where were the others? Had J.D. found Trent?

An hour later, he descended into the river bottoms of the stream lined with towering, gnarled cottonwoods. The kidnappers had made a lot of distance, and he wasn't certain of much except the smell of smoke in the air, and he still could see their tracks. Unsure if they had halted to cook something or what, he decided to hitch Fudge and to scout ahead on foot. With care, he slid his rifle out of the leather scabbard. He levered a cartridge into the chamber and started forward as quiet as he could.

First he heard Louise's voice chewing them out and he made a small grin. Thank God, she was still alive. Then he spotted three men fighting to pin someone naked on the sandy ground. The exposed white flesh under them had to be Louise's. They had stripped her naked. The sight made him sick and he cocked the rifle in his hands.

His first shot sprayed sand all over them. "Stay put or I'm killing you."

"Who the hell?" One of them standing went for his side arm. Chet clinched his teeth, spun around, aimed from the hip and squeezed the trigger. The hot lead struck him in the chest and spilled him backwards. Of the wide-eyed other two, one raised his hands and the other struggled to pull up his britches and stand.

"Don't shoot," he shouted.

Chet came in close, his rifle ready for them to make a move, and jerked the handgun out of the younger one's holster. Not looking aside at her, he said, "Get dressed, Louise. It's over. Sorry I got here so late."

"I'm not. Why, your voice sounded to me like God talking to these devils."

He could hear her trembling, saying the words and gasping for her breath. He asked the bigger one, "Who are you?"

"My name's Curty—Curty McCurty. I'm sure my paw would pay you a big reward for me if'n you'd take me home." His hands trembled as he held them high.

"Alright, your name?" he asked the other.

"Josie Knight."

"Your daddy got a lot of money he'd pay me, too?"

"Naw. He ain't got shit, mister."

"Who's on the ground beside you?"

"Lithe Combs."

"His daddy rich, too?"

"No, sir. His daddy's dead."

"Who hired you to do this?"

"No one—"

"Come on boys, you could have bought all the flesh you wanted in Mexico or even closer. Why in hell would you kidnap and rape a woman like Louise?"

McCurty shrugged. "She was handy."

"No. How much did they pay you to kidnap her?" He fired a rifle shot at their feet that sent sand all over them. In swift action, he reloaded the rifle's lever action. "Next shot will be in your foot."

"A-a guy named Bent. We don't know his last name, I swear," McCurty said.

"That right, Knight?"

Josie Knight bobbed his head and swallowed hard. "He pointed her out to us coming in the buckboard and said here's two hundred dollars. You boys have all the fun you—ah, want with her. But be damn sure that she don't come back. Sell her in Mexico or bury her."

Chet frowned. "Did you see him, Louise?"

"Yes," she said from behind his back.

"Who was he?"

"Cleb Cleator."

"How did he meet you boys?"

"In a bar in Fredericksburg two nights ago. He said his name was—"

"Hell, he promised us a better-looking one than her. Lots younger, too." Knight wrinkled his nose and both of them laughed. Not a free laugh, but the kind someone under great pressure let out.

That "younger one" meant one thing to Chet: that Cleator had meant to show them—Susie. His finger tightened on the trigger. The two of them needed to be sent to hell on an express train. Cleator wasn't even kin to the Reynoldses. How did they get him involved?

"Set your asses on the ground," he ordered. "You can't outrun this rifle and I'm just itching to use it on either one of you."

He stepped back to where Louise was trying to brush the sand out of her hair. In a low voice he asked, "You sure it was him?"

"I'd know him anywhere. Don't you recall when your sister sent him packing two years ago?"

"Not really. You think he wanted revenge against her?"

"I think he wanted revenge against her and them Reynoldses gave him the money to do it."

"Where's the two hundred dollars?" Chet asked them.

Knight said McCurty had it.

"My daddy can make that a thousand." McCurty handed over the roll of bills.

"What are you going to do with them?" Louise asked, rearranging the skirt at her waist.

"Trent's coming. If you can't testify in court about them raping you, then I'm going to shoot them right here and tell God that they died."

Louise closed her eyes and he saw she still had sand on the fine lashes. "Oh, I can tell my story to a jury and judge."

"Alright. You have sand on your lashes."

"Shoot, I have it behind my molars." He hugged her shoulder with his free hand. "I'm so sorry."

"I am simply so glad that you found me. I won't ever again complain about your leadership of the ranch." She began to sob on his shoulder. "You won't ever know how grateful I was just to hear your voice a few minutes ago."

"We won't get back to the schoolhouse until the middle of the night, maybe later. This body may need to be carried into Fredericksburg." His gaze locked on the prisoners as he hugged her with his rifle hand as well. "It's all over now."

She continued to sob. He made her hold the rifle on them and ran to get Fudge. Back again, he tied them up, then secured their horses. The kidnapper he shot had no pulse. By himself, he struggled to get the dead body over the saddle. Once was enough to load him. So the dead one didn't fall off, he tied him up good. He put nooses around the other two's necks. Made plans to make them ride double and have a rope tied on to jerk them off the horse if they tried anything.

He helped Louise into the saddle, and she fought her dress down modestly to better cover her legs. With her settled at last, he gave her the lead on the two prisoners' horses and told her to go ahead. He'd bring the dead man and extra horse behind them. Headed north, she lost her way a few times, but he directed her back to the cow trail they had taken.

Chet felt half sick about abandoning Kathren at the dance. The matter made his empty guts roil. When he finally had things going right—all hell broke loose again. What would she be thinking—*oh, he's off again*. Going across the stage route, he looked west. El Paso was that way. His travels would take him there soon enough.

"See those tracks ahead of you?" he asked Louise, who had stopped on the far side and acted confused. "That's where they brought you off that hill."

"Yes, I see now," she said, and booted her horse off the road and onto another cow path.

"Take them two right on," he said. "Trent and J. D. will be coming to meet us."

He hoped they hurried. The sun kept dropping lower in the west. Still, there would not be enough daylight for the time they'd require to get back before dark. The four of them might be in nowhere land when the sun went down. What if they'd lost his tracks? Nothing he could do but look for some ranch to head toward before it turned pitch-black, if worse got to be worst.

They crossed a large, wide-open flat and he turned an ear to the sounds of horse hooves coming. He shouted for Louise to rein up. They could be reserves for those three. Pushing his horse up to the lead, he recognized a familiar hat. J.D. was bringing the good sheriff in a hot race.

"We've been saved, Louise."

She looked on the edge of exhaustion. At the news, she slumped in the saddle. "Good, I can use some relief."

"I bet you could. Well, your son and the sheriff are coming fast."

Trent reined in his lathered pony hard, and slid to a stop. "What have we got here?"

"Two alive and one dead kidnapper. They kidnapped Louise and assaulted her down on the Perdanales. I ordered them to surrender and one went for his gun. A fool move with a cocked rifle in my hands. He's dead. These other two can tell you the rest. They have some tall tale to tell how some guy hired them to kidnap a female in the family and take her off. I guess to sell in Mexico after they finished with her."

Trent frowned. "Who hired them?"

"They said Cleb Cleator."

"Ain't his daddy a big rancher?" The sheriff frowned in disgust.

"That's the one. But better yet, to start with, I think that Cleator really wanted them to kidnap Susie. He thought she'd be in the buckboard that Louise ended up driving."

"He any kin to them Reynoldses?" Trent asked, looking sour at the two of them.

Chet shook his head. "I don't know, but I'd bet a dollar to a cow pie that's where he got the idea."

"You must have made good time to catch them."

"I did. They thought they were beyond any pursuit when I found them."

"Sheriff, he did a superb of rescuing me." Louise said. "He certainly is the hero of the day."

"Mrs. Byrnes, I agree with you a hundred percent. It's going to be dark in a short while. Should we head back for the schoolhouse?"

"No," Chet said, shaking his head. "You take them two to the jailhouse, there's folks up there that would lynch them before this night was over."

"I agree. Can I borrow J.D. to help me get them back to Mason tonight?" the sheriff asked.

"J.D.?"

"Oh, I'd help him."

"Good, I think Louise and I can make it back to the schoolhouse before the last dance. Or do you want to go with them?" Chet asked her.

"I may look like a hen that's been rustling in the dirt, but I choose the schoolhouse."

"Trent, the big one is McCurty and the other one is Knight."

"We can handle this from here. Now, Mrs. Byrnes, you will file charges against these men, won't you?"

"Sheriff, I told Chet I would, or else he intended to hang them down there. But I want to see them get what they have coming. I'll be in your office mid-morning on Monday and give you my full story."

"J.D., get the prisoners and we'll put them in irons and let these folks go dance."

"Good." Chet wheeled his horse around. "Come on, Louise. I know a shortcut."

Short or not, it was long past ten when they reached the —$\mathcal{C}$ tent. Juanita came from the tent and blinked in disbelief at them in the glaring firelight.

"I will go quick and tell Susie you are back—already."

"Fine, we'll find some food while you go after her. She's probably worried about Louise."

"There is plenty of food in there," the girl said, like she was torn between feeding them and going to get Susie.

"We're fine. You go find her." He helped Louise out of the saddle and she kissed him on the cheek. Her action about shocked him. Last time she kissed him, he had been in diapers, he was certain.

She took his arm in the crook of hers, then grasped his hand and led him to the table and all the sheet-covered food. He ate a big slice of dried apple pie first. The sugar and the cinnamon made his mouth flood. Time for food later—he wanted something special.

Seated on the bench, he turned at hearing Susie coming running. He said, "Louise, I told you she'd be worried."

Grateful that Susie ran in and hugged her aunt first,

then he asked if she was alright. He watched the two, close to tears, pound each other on the back and shoulders.

"I am fine, thanks to your brother's quick action. He must have came at lightning speed to my aid."

Susie looked back at him in the orange light. "He is a real special guy."

"Have you seen Trent?" his sister asked him.

"He had to take those prisoners on to Mason. I feared they would be lynched if he came by here with them."

However, before Susie could even ask who the bad guys were, a crowd from the schoolhouse burst in to check on them. The tent turned into a madhouse of folks clamoring for what happened and who did it. Took over a half hour to tell them all that had taken place. Chet had read the anger in the crowd's eyes as the incident was spilled out to them. From his vantage point, he saw the angry notions cross the looks on their faces. Trent was right to take them onto the county jail—otherwise they'd never have been breathing when the sun finally rose the next day. He, at last, excused himself to go find Kathren.

Kathren stood outside the tent, and at the sight of Chet, came on the run to hug him when he came out to look for her. "I was so worried about you."

"It worked out anyway. I'm glad Louise is going to be alright, but I worried that you'd give up on me. I'd invited you to come and I ran off."

"I knew when they said you went looking for her, you had not ran away 'cause I was coming."

"Where's Cady?"

"Dancing, I think. She's giving Heck lessons tonight."

He kissed the side of her face and hugged her tight. "Wonderful. Louise says she'll be alright. The two alive kidnappers are in the Mason County jail."

"Did you eat?" she asked.

"A piece of pie."

"Let's go back in there and I'll feed you."

"Whatever—"

Chet followed her back inside the tent. How bad could things get in this war? Outsiders were even planning things against them. One more reason why he needed to find a new place for his kin. But Kathren's presence overshadowed his move plans and he simply enjoyed her company.

Later, with Kathren and her daughter ready to sleep in the tent with Susie, Louise, and Juanita, he set out to stake himself a place nearby under the stars and rolled out his bedding, after kicking the rocks and branches off his plot.

In his bedroll, he tossed all night. Sleep avoided him despite the bone-deep tiredness and exhaustion he'd suffered. They were still out there poised to do something harsh to him or his relatives. *Damn them, anyway.*

Chapter 14

Sunday morning, the two families went to church services early, except Susie, Juanita, and Kathren, who stayed behind in the camp to fix breakfast. They all sat in the midway section, and listened to Preacher Rankin lead the prayers and songs and deliver the sermon. They stood to sing the various hymns, and their voices rang out. "Nearer My God to Thee" filled the fresh morning air. Rankin spoke about Jesus and how he died on the cross so they could be saved. That their salvation was in accepting him in their hearts. He closed in prayer, and then they filed out shaking his hand at the door.

When Chet stepped into the broad daylight, he narrowed his eyes at the three hard-case men sitting on horseback. Burl Reynolds, the patriarch of the family, Tye Watkins, a cousin, and Blythe Campbell, another kin or an in-law. He signaled for J.D., who'd come back late in the night, and Heck to go on.

"Byrnes!" Reynolds shouted.

"I'm not wearing a gun, Burl. But if you came here

for war, I'll go get one. This is hardly the place to start. We've been to church. It wouldn't have hurt you none to have been in there, either."

People were hurrying to the side to be out of gun range. Concern-faced woman herded their children aside. Others were so shocked at the three men's appearance they went back inside the building.

Reynolds pointed his index finger at Chet. "You better attend church. 'Cause you're going to need all the help you can get to stay out of hell when I get done with you."

"Wait." Brother Rankin rushed by Chet, holding his hands up in defense. "'Vengeance is mine' saith the Lord. We are gathered here in peace and loving thy neighbor. Have you lost your mind, Burl? This is a place of God, man."

"I didn't come to kill you," Reynolds said. "I want him."

Chet noticed that several of the men were returning with arms. He hoped this didn't turn into massive shooting. Too many kids and wives were still in the area.

"Reynolds!" a rancher named Hurst shouted. "There are several of us here that want you to leave— peacefully. Consider us carefully. There will be no gunplay here unless you choose to die."

Reynolds rose in the saddle and looked around at the number of armed men, which had grown. He sat down in the saddle looking a tad more uncomfortable than before, and said, "Byrnes, you may live today, but you won't for long."

He gave a head toss that he was ready to leave. The

three filed out and then short-loped away. Several men spoke to Chet to apologize. He nodded that he understood and shook their hands.

One rancher asked, "What will he try next?"

"I don't know."

Chet walked back to camp, thanking his backers as he went. With this confrontation he knew, even stronger, that he needed to find new land.

Heck was at his side. "That sumbitch came asking for it, didn't he?"

"We better leave off the cuss words. Yes, he did."

"What will they try next?"

"Heck, if I knew that we'd all be better off."

"I savvy, I savvy good."

Kathren came running to meet him. He hugged her. "I'm sorry."

"Sorry? Why, he needed his neck strung up for coming to a church gathering and threatening you."

"I simply could not help it."

She wet her lips. "Makes me so mad. I wasn't that mad the day they shot at us at my place."

"You two come and eat," Susie called out from the edge of the tent. "We still have to break down this camp and get home today."

They agreed and moved to join her. He took one long look back and saw nothing but other folks getting ready to pack up. Shame those Reynoldses had ruined such a well-attended event.

After lunch, while the women washed the dishes, he noticed that Louise was even helping them. The men loaded the tables and benches, then took down the large canvas. Everyone was working. Things were taking shape quickly to make the move for home.

Chet watched Utah Kline ride up the creek bottom, dismount, and take off his weatherbeaten hat to speak to Susie. Interested in talking to him, Chet left J.D. and Heck to load the rest, and walked over.

"Well, howdy, Chet. I got the word you wanted to talk to me."

"I did, Utah. Did you get in on the tail end of that deal at the church?"

"I heard about it. Them Reynoldses won't let go of you, will they?"

Chet shook his head. "I need to hire some men that are willing to stand and not run to support Reg. Ain't for everyone to know, but I'm going looking for a new place. I figure I can tell you and not have it spread all over the country."

Utah nodded and beat his felt hat against his leg. "I can see your point. I'm not real pleased these days where I am. When can I start?"

"Whenever you can. I pay thirty and found."

"Fair enough." They shook hands. "I'll be there in a week."

"Utah, I'm not asking you to fight my wars."

"I understand, Chet, but when I work for someone I ride for the brand."

"Reg said that about you, too."

"Miss Byrnes," he said to Susie when she walked up. "I'll be looking forward to putting my boots under your table, too."

"Thanks, Utah, but I'm Susie at the ranch," she said and then told Chet they were ready to go home.

"Alright, I'll see you and Susie in a week." Utah mounted up and jog-trotted his pony down to the bottom.

Chet felt good. He'd hired one sure hand to back Reg. What the man's problem with Frank Rich at Anchor was, he'd probably never know—but he felt this was his gain and Anchor's loss. Later in the week, he'd run down the Hascal brothers. It was April already, and if he was headed west he wanted to miss the deep desert summer heat. So he'd better get to cutting.

After sending the crew for home, he and Kathren took a walk together and found a large rotting cotton-wood log to sit on.

"I'm going looking for a new place in the next week. This event today was more of the same old business. They have no sense, coming to places where women and children are and asking for a gunfight."

"I understand—" She swallowed hard. "I can't promise you to move anywhere. We will just have to see."

He held both her hands so he didn't lose her. "I won't ask you to do that."

"I know, but—" She wiped a tear from her cheek with a knuckle, then she straightened.

"Kathren, let's let things simmer. I have not found a new ranch yet, but this fight is not getting better."

She closed her eyes and nodded. "I knew what he wanted sitting on his horse out there, and I would have shot him if I'd had a gun."

"No need in that. Kathren, be patient with me.

Maybe—hell, I want it to work out. Not as an affair, but as a life for both of us."

She leaned over and they kissed.

"You be careful. I'll be here."

They rose and he walked her to her horse and boosted her into the saddle. His hand on her leg, he nodded. "I'll be back."

Kathren bit her lower lip and then turned the sorrel horse away. The knot behind his tongue proved painful to swallow. Damn, was he wrong? Would he lose her—again?

Chapter 15

They rode horses to El Paso. Chet and Heck with a pack horse carrying war bags and bedding. Drinking water got to tasting worse by the day, and the temperature soared higher. Lots of creosote bushes, a few jackrabbits, and some rattlesnakes thrown in. When they could even find a ranch, they stopped and offered to buy their meal. Only a few took their money and most wondered why the two of them were out there. In two weeks, they arrived in El Paso. Chet sold the horses and they boarded the stage line that ran to Tucson. They crossed more desolate land over New Mexico, and eventually somewhere into eastern Arizona saw their first saguaro cactus. Heck rode on top of the coach a large part of the way.

A gambler told Chet about the wild town of Tombstone, with all the fortunes won and lost down there. Chet had no time to take a side trip and swung though Benson on his way to Tucson. May heat was turning the winter growth of annuals to brown when they arrived in the hot, walled town of Tucson. Two dead burros lay in the street, hogs keeping cool in the depressions where the slop water was tossed out. Drunk, dark-skinned people were passed out on the walks. The two quickly bought tickets to Papago Wells and were on their way to Phoenix. A man on the stage out of El Paso had spoken about Preskit in the pines—but the stage agent in Tucson told him that the man had meant Prescott—and that there was a daily stage from Phoenix to there every day.

So far, the cactus-spiked desert didn't look like ideal ranching country to Chet. Maybe his entire search was going to be a waste of time. No telling. He hoped Prescott—or as the native folks called it, Preskit—would offer him a better-looking area to find a ranch.

Heck never complained. His eyes were wide open the entire time. He'd seen lots of Indians, and smiled at many dark-eyed pretty girls who, when they spoke to him, made his face turn red. Seeing this new world was exciting at that age. He'd asked Chet many times if someday he thought he could climb some of those lofty mountains and see as far as he could see. Chet promised him that he could—someday.

Road-weary, they climbed on the Black Canyon Stage Line coach in Phoenix, a dusty small town along the Salt River surrounded by low mountains. The driver let Heck sit on top, and they were off rocking in the coach. A woman in her twenties who wore an expensive dress shared the coach with Chet. She dressed like Louise, and made him wonder how much help his aunt was offering Susie.

"Are you a stockman?" she asked.

"In Texas, yes, ma'am." He took off his hat for her.

"What brings you to Arizona Territory?" she asked, trying to cool her smooth face with a small Chinese fan.

"I'm looking for a ranch."

"Going to Preskit?"

"Yes, as matter of fact, they told me the climate was much cooler up there than down here."

"Oh, yes, it is. My name is Margaret Christianson. We own the LYT ranch up there."

We, he wondered who all that was. "My name's Chet Byrnes. I live near Mason, Texas. Our ranch is the bar-C."

"Oh, how nice to meet you, Mr. Byrnes."

"Chet, please."

"Margaret is fine. How large a ranch are you considering buying?"

"As much as my money can afford."

She pasted on a smile. "That could be anything out here."

"I understand. I'm not familiar with the land market. But I am mainly looking for a place that suits me right now." The stage lurched from side to side, climbing a steep grade, and the four horses were reduced to a walk.

The hot air that flew through the passenger compartment felt dry. The steep rocky land on the side of the mountain, that he could almost reach out and touch, looked like a tough place to handle cattle. Those towering cactus and beds of prickly pear he recognized, but there were other plants that looked real stickery.

"Do you have a family?"

"Yes, my own family, but I have no wife. The boy

on top is my nephew. His father, my brother, was killed last year on a cattle drive to Kansas."

"Oh, how unfortunate."

He agreed.

"Well, our ranch is close to Preskit, so if you are around, drop by the LYT. It's easy to find."

"Thank you. I'd offer you the same, but the —*C* is outside of Mason, Texas and I doubt that you would ever come close to it."

"One can never tell, Chet."

"No, I guess not, ma'am."

"At least this trip so far, we have not been held up." She stuck her head out the side window as if looking for holdup men.

Chet frowned. "Is that a usual part of this business of stage riding?"

"I never carry much money with me. Once I said I had none to the holdup men and they, well—practically undressed me in the road to try and find some. I was very embarrassed."

Chet frowned. "They ever catch them?"

"The law?" She raised a shoulder and then shook her head. "Why, lands no. This is a very lawless place, this Black Canyon run."

"I guess you can expect anything then from these bandits?"

"In the case of a robbery, I always give them a small amount of money since that horrible incident."

There was something about her that made him wonder—he knew she was worldly, but most respectable women would never have talked to a stranger about such an ordeal—*practically undressed me?* Was she feeling him out? Or was she simply a very frank person? He might never know, but it passed the time of day better than with some drunk drummer or a gambler who was down on his luck. He'd shared the coach with both kinds earlier. The road became rougher again, and the ruts made the coach sway like a willow stem from side to side.

"Did you have some bad experience in your life happen?" Margaret asked, looking inquiringly at him before they were jolted again.

"What do you consider bad?"

"I am sorry. I was simply curious. You have no wife?"

"No wife."

"I can see that I am inquiring too deeply in your life, Chet."

"I run a family ranch in Texas. My father lost his mind years ago searching for two of my brothers and one sister that the Comanche kidnapped. My mother died in mental distress. My aunt lost a husband in the Civil War; she is in our family circle. My brother left several children from his first marriage and a baby by his second wife. I mentioned he was shot down last spring in Kansas. We have become involved in a Texas feud with another family over their son that was hung for stealing our horses."

"Oh, I'm so sorry."

"No need, these are my problems. But we thought a place in a new country might give us all a new start."

"I can see where you are going. Come by the ranch when you are in the area. If you have any questions, my father knows the ranching business in Arizona. His name is Harold McClure."

"Thank you, ma'am."

He looked across the hills and saw evergreens appearing that looked like red cedar on the hillsides. "What are they?" he asked her.

"With a rise in elevation the junipers begin to dot the land. A sign they get more moisture up here. Next we'll get into the pine country. Preskit is in the pine country."

"I see live oak, too. That and cedar is what's in my hill country back home."

"Chet, you will find lots of good ranch country at this elevation."

"I can see that, I can sure see that." For the first time he felt excited by the looks of the range land he could see from the stage.

Heck leaned over and shouted, "It's lots cooler up here, Uncle Chet."

"It's nice. I agree, Heck."

"Welcome to my land," she said, and recrossed her legs, swinging her button-up shoe back and forth from under the lace trim of her petticoats.

"Thank you." He did like the looks of the forage and could vision how a cow could eat it. After all that desert they'd crossed, he finally had found real range land. This country looked like home to him.

They arrived in Preskit after dark. He and Heck unloaded their saddles and pack gear on the stage line office porch. A well-dressed man with silver sideburns stepped out and welcomed Margaret.

"How are you, my dear?"

"Wonderful. I want you to meet a man looking for a ranch up here. Meet Chet Byrnes. This is my father, Harold McClure."

The two men shook hands.

"Good to meet you sir," Chet offered.

"Welcome to the territory. We can use more serious ranchers in this region."

"Thank you. I am enjoying this much cooler air. My nephew and I have been coming for several weeks across the true desert to get here." In the moonlight, Chet looked at the pine-clad hills around the town and the thumb-shaped butte on the west. "Very nice place."

"Come and see us someday," her father said. "Our ranch is east of here."

"Heck and I will try to do that," he said.

Next, he needed to park his gear there at the stage office and go find a room for the two of them. He signed in for one at the Brownstone Hotel across the street, and then they walked two blocks to a restaurant the desk clerk recommended. The temperature had dropped, and Heck was rubbing his arms.

"I bet it will really be cool by sunup," the boy said.

"But it will sure beat that old desert oven we've been in for weeks." Chet opened the restaurant door and let him inside the lighted business.

Seated in a booth, they ate pork chops, potatoes, green beans, and some French bread and apple pie. Sipping his coffee, Chet felt relaxed for the first time in days. This was the part of the land where he hoped to find a ranch suited for the family. Back on the boardwalk, he picked at his teeth as they headed for the hotel.

"What do we do next?" Heck asked.

"After a good night's sleep, we'll buy three horses tomorrow, and talk to some land agents."

"What will they tell us?"

"What ranches they have for sale."

"Sounds interesting. I'm proud you brought me along. I've sure seen lots of country."

Chet clapped the boy on his shoulder. "There's lots more to look at, too."

At dawn they found a hole-in-the-wall café, but the one row of stools down a long counter proved to be a great place to eat breakfast. Eggs as you like them, fried side meat, biscuits and thick gravy, rich coffee, too. They left full, and the blond woman who waited on them sent them to Frey's Livery to look for horses, saying he was honest.

At the stables, they found folks saddling their own horses, and a man hitching a buggy in front of the livery. A tall, lanky, red-faced man in his forties with freckles came out and introduced himself as Luther Frey.

"What can I do for you gents?"

Chet introduced himself and Heck. "We're needing two good saddle horses and a pack horse or mule."

"Where you from?"

"Texas hill country."

"My. You two have come a fur piece. He your boy?"

"Nephew."

Frey nodded and led the way, talking to his customers as his men completed the saddling process on some and boosted others onto their animals. They walked through the sour, horse-piss-smelling barn to look at the ponies in the corral.

"That roan is five. He's a ranch horse and you can rope from him. Sound as a drum. That bay," he pointed out a shorter horse. "He's four and I think he'd suit your nephew.

"But I've got more in there might work. I also have a well-broke mule for a pack animal. He's got some age on him, but good teeth and he knows the job. He'll keep up with your horses."

"If they suit us, how much do you want for them?" Chet asked.

Frye closed his eyes like he was thinking. "Roan's worth thirty, the bay twenty-five, and the mule twenty."

"I'll give you seventy for the lot if they suit," Chet offered.

"Oh, they'll suit. Saddle them up and try 'em. I'm not afraid."

"Seventy?"

Frey agreed.

Chet peeled the money out to the man. "Our rigs are up at the stage office."

"I have a buckboard hitched out front. The man won't need it for an hour. Go get your things in it."

"You're a might obliging man, Frey. They told us that down at the café."

"I'm in business. And I want to stay in business. What's yours?" He tucked the folding money into his vest pocket.

"We're looking for a ranch to buy."

"Good luck. And you ever need anything again, come see me. I've been here about ten years and know most folks."

"Thanks." Chet had judged the man to be honest as was promised, and felt in time they might build a friendship.

At last the saddles were recovered, along with their bedding and camp supplies. Chet took a lariat off the fencepost and roped the bay for Heck first. The gelding acted a little buggery on the start, but when he came up the rope to fashion a halter, he settled down. Sign of a well-broke horse, and he led him out the gate.

"He looks nice," Heck said, coming with a blanket in one hand and a saddle in the other.

"Guess we'll see," Chet said, and went back with another lariat for the roan with the split mane. The second loop he tossed fell over his head and he snorted, but like the bay, settled down when Chet approached him.

His legs looked splint-free, and no ringbone. The horse had some old dark scars that showed on his roan coat, but few looked serious. He took the bit and remained standing while Chet saddled him. Obviously he was ground-tie-broke, too. Chet liked that— most of the —*C* ranch horses had been trained when the reins were down to stay there.

"Can I ride him around a little?" Heck asked, finished saddling.

The three stable hands were standing at the wide-open back door, arms folded as if looking for something to break loose. Chet knew by the looks on their faces they were expecting some fireworks from either horse, or both.

"He may buck," Chet said, and caught the bridle as Heck swung up onto his back.

"Turn him loose," Heck said and spun the pony around. It was all the horse needed; he stuck his head down and went to crow-hopping down the alley. Heck rode him sitting tall, and even urged him on some. He came back pleased as punch while Chet finished his own saddling operation.

The stable men were nodding approval and joshing Heck about his horse bucking. They had no idea how much that boy had ridden. His ride must have satisfied them, but the onlookers soon turned their attention to Chet and Roany.

He stepped into the stirrup, threw his leg over and checked the horse as he found his right stirrup. Then he made him sit down and made certain the girth was tight enough. The roan had plans of his own, the realization came with the tightness of the gelding's body under him. Then Chet leaned forward and gave him some rein. Roan stepped out like he was walking on eggs, and Chet kept the reins tight enough to keep his head up. They went down the alley and back, practically dancing a jig. Stopped in his tracks, Chet patted the thick black mane on the right side. The urge to buck had evaporated from his horse.

The disappointed stable crew caught the mule, and the three men put on the cross buck saddle, and loaded the panniers and bedrolls in the shake of a lamb's tail.

Their leader, a man called Jasper, handed Heck the lead rope. "You boys damn sure know horses. Have a nice day. Come back and see us."

The mule did some braying about leaving his friends, but otherwise they jogged up the steep street headed east. The road let over the pine-clad hills to a wide-spread valley and past the ranch gate with the LYT brand nailed on top of the crossbar. The big house and outfit sat a good quarter mile down a lane from the gate.

"We going to stop by and see her again?" Heck asked.

"Maybe later." Chet wasn't satisfied he knew the lady's real purpose in inviting him to their place. Deep in thought, he wet his lower lip. But he'd find out sometime when he didn't have so much on his mind as finding the —𝒞 a new home. What was Kathren doing that day?

They rode east and saw several range cattle doing fine. Most of the outfits they passed, he decided, were hundred-and-sixty-acre homesteads. A few had planted orchards; others had large gardens, by his observation. He wanted a ranch, not a farm. But he might change his mind—he had both back home.

Chet and the boy put off dropping down into the Verde River Valley until they had more time. But Chet was glad to be back in the saddle, and knew Frey had sold them some good mounts.

By late afternoon they returned and stabled their horses. He sent Heck off to buy some candy and told him they'd meet at that one-row-of-stools café around five.

He chose the Palace Saloon in the middle of the

block of saloons facing the courthouse called Whiskey Row. He entered the two-story room and saw the ornate wooden bar and brass rail on the left. A lot of art and taxidermy was hung on the walls. The sawdust floor under his soles, he ordered a beer and took it to a table to appraise things. The beer was cold. They must have ice, Chet decided. In Texas, they imported some ice in places like San Antonio, but most of it was gone by May.

The barmaid came by with a towel over her arm. Still in her late teens, short too, she had a hardness about her that even her smile could not erase. Her name, he learned, was Jane, and she rubbed off the table with a towel and told him she didn't get off till midnight, if he was interested.

He said, "I'll pass, but thank you. Are there any land agents in here?"

She cut a glance at the men at the bar and then nodded. "Yeah, Bo Harold. The guy in the brown suit with the small-brim hat. Wanta talk to him?"

"He honest?"

She gave him pained look. "Honest as most men."

He smiled. "Tell him, if he gets time, to come over and talk to me."

"Sure, bet he'll be glad to. I never caught your name?"

"Chet Byrnes."

"Nice ta meetcha, Chet Byrnes," she said, and in a swish of her skirt headed for Harold.

The man soon joined him with a "What-may-I-help-you-with ah, Mr. Byrnes?"

"Have a seat, Mr. Harold. My name's Chet."

"Well, Chet, Bo's mine. What brings you to Preskit?"

"I need a ranch."

"Aw." Bo seated himself, pushed the felt hat back on his head, exposing blond hair, and nodded. "I have some listings. How big?"

"How big you got?"

"You must come from Texas?"

"I live in the Texas hill country."

Bo sat back in the chair. "I have a large ranch for sale down in the Verde Valley. Three sections of deeded land—that's big in Arizona. I can show it to you tomorrow. Good water rights, some irrigated land, and set up where you can run a thousand cows. What do you think?"

"Let's go see it tomorrow. I have horses at Frey's stable. What time?"

"How does six A.M. sound?"

"We'll be saddled and ready to go by then. Meet you at Jenny's Café."

"Very good, I'll meet you there. You'll love this ranch."

"What do they call it?"

"Quarter Circle Z. Best ranch in this country. Let me buy you another beer."

Chet shook his head. "Thanks, but I have to meet a man."

He left through the swinging doors and realized it would soon be sundown. Mid-April, it still went down early. Heck might worry that he had forgotten him. What did they price the ranch for? It could be more than he could afford. Still, he wanted to see it. Regardless of the asking price, he'd look at it anyway.

He spotted Heck waiting in front of the café. "How did things go?"

"Fine, Chet. You learn anything?"

"We're going to the Verde River tomorrow with a land agent named Harold and look at a large ranch." He held the door open for the youth to go inside.

"We going to buy it?"

"Look at it. Lordy, it may be too costly for us to afford."

"How much is that?"

"We'll see." He motioned for him to get on a stool.

The same broad-shouldered woman with her thick blond hair braided and coiled on her head waited on them. "Well, what did you two see today?"

"All the country we could see east of town," Heck said. "We must have rode a hundred miles."

"Where do you plan to go tomorrow?"

"Verde Valley," Chet said.

She nodded. "That should be interesting."

"You know anything about the Quarter Circle Z?"

"Hoot knows, he used to work down there." She waved to a short, nearly crippled cowboy for him to come over. "Tell my new friends here from Texas about Talley's ranch."

After introductions, the man took a stool beside Chet and nodded. "They've got it for sale?"

"A land agent told me they did. Why?"

"They don't live here. A bastard named Ryan runs it for them. He's a crooked sumbitch and I hate him."

"Where do the owners live?"

"St. Charles, Missouri. They seldom come out here. Ryan does what he wants out there. I'd sell it, too. They must be afraid to fire him." Hoot chuckled. "I bet that's why. He's a tough hombre. I broke my leg in a horse wreck doing my job. One of the boys brought me in here to the doc's and left me. Next day, Ryan came by Doc's office where I was in bed and fired me. Said if I couldn't keep from having wrecks he didn't need me."

"Did he pay the doctor bill?"

"Hell, no."

"Sounds like a real nice guy." Heck and Chet both agreed.

"What's the ranch like?"

"They've got forty acres of alfalfa. It's a good crop. And that much timothy, plus another forty in corn."

"Who farms it?"

"Some Mexican folks work for a guy who does the farm work. His name's Chandler."

"What else?"

"Ryan ain't supposed to, I know that much, but he still lives in the big house with some Mexican woman. They moved out of the house when the Talleys came out here last time. But as soon as they left for Missouri, he moved right back in. I heard old man Talley say for him not to live in the main house when he was gone. Ryan's ornery as a bull, I tell you. He may not even let you look at the place."

"Let me buy your supper," Chet said. "I appreciate you. I may hire you to show me all that place, if we like it."

"I'd be real proud to do that, Mr. Byrnes. Jenny

knows how to get hold of me. And thanks for the meal."

The man hobbled out the door and Chet nodded. "We learned something, Heck."

"Sounds like this Ryan may learn about us, huh?" Heck grinned.

"Yes. We better eat. We have to get up early to meet Harold."

In the morning, they met Bo Harold for breakfast and short-loped their horses to the edge of the great escarpment that overlooked the Verde River and the wide basin. Far to the north, another great wall rose up, and beyond that the San Francisco Peaks showed their snow-white tops. Before the breathtaking view, they started down the steep road that clung to the east side wall and practically dove off into the valley. Mid-morning, they reached the floor and rode west along the cottonwood-lined river. Red mesas rose in the north and the junipers were everywhere. Some had been burned out in grass fires in years past, and the grass had taken back the land. They spooked a few mule deer and even some cottontail rabbits. The day before, they'd seen plenty of big jackrabbits.

Harold had spoken about the water rights to this ranch, which gave them plenty of river water to irrigate the fields they had open. He reiterated what he'd said about the three crops, but he had a higher acreage total than Hoot. They soon saw the large house on the rise, windmills, corrals, and outbuildings.

"We going to get a chance to see this place?" Chet asked the agent.

"Why, of course. I'm Mr. Talley's agent."

"Folks say his ranch foreman Ryan don't want him to sell out."

Harold frowned. "He is a mere employee. He has no say-so about the sale whatsoever."

"I heard he ran some folks off."

"Not who I brought out here."

"Good."

"They were telling lies. Mr. Talley wants to sell this place. He lives in St. Charles, outside of St. Louis, and has no time or a quick way to get out here. He was promised a railroad to Flagstaff when he bought it, and that is why he invested in the ranch. But the rails are coming very slow, and some years they even stop building track whenever the stock markets get bad in New York."

"They do that all over Texas, too."

"Mr. Ryan will be no problem."

"Fine," Chet said and winked privately at Heck. He never believed that part of the man's conversation, but a land agent was allowed a few exaggerations. They reached the house and dismounted. A few stock dogs barked at them, and a pregnant Mexican woman in her twenties came to the door.

"Go away," she said. "My husband is not home. I have no time for you."

"Mrs. Ryan?" Harold asked her.

"Of course. I am his wife. But I have no time for you."

"I am the agent that Mr. Talley hired to sell this ranch."

"No for sale. My husband he say this ranch no for sale."

"Excuse me, I am going to show these gentlemen the house. Stand aside."

She tried to kick him, but with his hand on her forehead, he drove her backwards. Chet and Heck dismounted, trying not to laugh at Harold's plight. The two front doors they passed through were twelve feet tall, ornately carved, with brass door handles. Once inside, they saw him gently driving her off to the back. She had taken up cursing at him in Spanish.

The tile floors were gritty and cobwebs were everywhere. They found the bedroom that the Ryans must sleep in. A great feather bed, waist-high, with a shelf around it to get up on, and the headboard was also carved. The room smelled stale, like dirty socks.

Chet counted six bedrooms downstairs, and guessed there were more on the second floor. One room downstairs was an office with a large green safe that was closed, but, he could see, not locked. He sent Heck up the wide staircase to count the rest. The house looked big enough for his tribe. It needed a good cleaning, but other than that it should suit his family. The gentle spring wind would soon clear out much of the closed-up smells.

Ryan's wife and three other Mexican women were in the kitchen being contained by Harold. Chet decided that the spacious kitchen would please his sister. Large ranges and prep tables and running water from a tank—obviously Talley had spared no money freighting all that in there, plus the material for the house and the furniture from Mexico.

Heck rejoined him, out of breath. "There are six more upstairs, all full of beds and furniture."

This place was a palace—the problem was: could he afford it? The land, house, and the rest would bring a fortune in the Texas hill country. What he knew about irrigation would fit in a thimble. But the native Mexican people would know how—he wasn't a farmer at home, either, but he had learned what he needed to do.

"Shall we look at the outbuildings?" Harold asked.

Chet agreed, and they left the cursing woman in the house and went out through a once-garden that had been let go and out the gate of the walled area. For Indian defense, he knew about such areas. They had the Apaches there, like the Comanche had been in Texas. The windmills creaked and needed greasing. But like the many things that were unrepaired, like the wired-up once-hanging gates, he knew a new crew could have this place shaped up in a month. He liked the layout of the pens and saw that lots of alfalfa hay had been wasted. Several rails were missing in the corrals and pigs were running loose. At their approach, a sow and six piglets fled. All in all, it could be a real ranch headquarters.

They mounted up, and Harold shook his head. "I wouldn't even ask those sloppy housekeepers for lunch, even though it is long past that time."

Heck laughed. "Guess we'll starve, huh?"

"No, I'll find us some food. Let's ride upstream and I can show you the small dam and the diversion canal that feeds this place."

"They sure are wrecking his ranch, letting it fall into such disarray after he spent so much money building it." Chet said.

Harold twisted in the saddle. "It is a grand place, isn't it?"

"I like it. What does he want for it?"

"Twenty-five thousand."

"That include his livestock?"

"Yes."

"How many head will he guarantee?"

"Three hundred mother cows and a hundred head of horses."

"Where are they?" Chet booted his horse up beside Harold's.

"Out on the open range," Harold made a wide sweep of his arm.

"What if they aren't all here?"

"Oh, they're here, alright. Roundup up here is big business. There are lots of cattle out on these ranges."

"When is roundup time?"

"In May."

"How many men do I have to furnish if I buy this place?"

"Two or three for the six weeks, if it takes that long."

"They're going to start the roundup then, shortly."

"Oh, yes."

"Let's say I pay Talley ten thousand dollars down and all the cows are worth fifteen bucks, then the difference in three hundred head he credits me. Same on the hundred horses at thirty per head."

"I would have to ask him by wire if he would do that."

"Good. I can have my bank in San Antonio wire him the money once they can confirm he has signed the mortgage agreement. The balance I'll pay in two years at six percent interest. There are no liens or loans on this ranch?"

"None, but we can be certain by checking with the clerk in Preskit."

"Is Talley that afraid of Ryan?"

"What do you mean?"

"I had word that the man back east was so afraid of his foreman that he is selling it."

"Oh, I can't believe—"

"Yes, you can. He's walked away from it."

"Alright. And if I had that much money, I'd own it myself today."

"You aren't afraid of Ryan at all?"

"I brought you down here today, didn't I?"

"You sure did. Wire Talley and give him my offer. The Stockman's Bank in San Antonio will tell him all about me. I've never missed paying any note I owed."

"How in hell did you ever gather that much money?"

Chet shrugged. "Driving cattle to Kansas over the last few years."

Harold shrugged. "What made you think the cattle count might not be there?"

"The way the ranch is being run. I bet there ain't a quarter of the horses around there anywhere."

"Where did they go?"

"I bet the sheriff can find where Ryan sold them."

Chet twisted in the saddle to look back one more time at the large house.

"Ryan?"

"Whoever did it."

They rode for the small settlement at Camp Verde at the foot of the mountain which they must climb to get back to Preskit. Chet checked the sun time and turned back. It would be after dark before they found any food. They'd live—this day turned out special for him and Heck. He'd found a helluva great place where all the Byrneses could live—now the details were all that kept him from moving there.

Chapter 16

Well past midnight, Chet and Heck parted with Harold and made for the stables in Preskit. Heck proved excited. "I wanted to ask you all day, do you think we will get that place?"

"Good thing you didn't, they might ask for more money."

"That is a good price, isn't it?"

"Sure, but between Ryan and the fact that folks avoid him, it may not be such a bargain. I need to line up some tough cowboys, I figure, to take that place. I wonder why Talley didn't get the sheriff to evict him."

"That's strange, isn't it?"

"Maybe Talley couldn't hire any tough hands to back him. In a few days, we'll know the answers. Let's get some sleep."

"Why, I think even Louise will like that place."

Chet laughed at his words. "You might be right."

The next morning in the café, Chet asked Jenny to send word for Hoot to join them. She smiled, "You're going to make that old man's day."

Chet blew on his steaming first cup of coffee. "Good. We're going to need a half dozen good men as well. You think he can find them?"

"Sure, he knows every ranch hand in the territory that's worth his salt."

"Good."

The coffee was hot enough to make his tongue tender, but the first burst of it filled his mouth with saliva. The rich taste exploded in his brain and he savored Jenny's words. He needed the toughest men he could hire. Ryan would not go without a fight unless he was outnumbered, outgunned, and he knew they would wipe him out.

Chet regretted that Ryan had not been available so he could have studied the man in person. A bully was a bully, but this might be the toughest man he'd ever faced. Communication with the owner would take Harold some time. The ranch owner, Talley, might want to check with his bankers in San Antonio. No reason to think they wouldn't immediately answer him, but again that would take time. He'd have to trust that Harold was pressing for an answer.

Hoot arrived before he and Heck finished their breakfast. Chet asked if he had breakfast and the older cowboy said, "No."

"Put him on my tab," Chet said. "For three meals a day until I have to leave."

"Sure," Jenny said and smiled.

"I-I didn't come for a handout—"

"It isn't a handout. You're on my payroll. While we work on buying the Quarter Circle Z, I want you to find me a handful of good men with lots of back-bone."

"How many is that?"

"About four or five. I want real cowboys with lots of bottom. This may get tough if we have to evict Ryan."

Hoot agreed. "I know the men we need."

"Roundup is coming. We are going to need to do several things before that time."

"What'll they ride?"

Chet frowned at him, "You think the ranch horses are gone, too?"

"There haven't been many, I can tell you, in the year I worked there."

"This is the most serious thing I can think of. Bo Harold thought they were out on the range."

"We can go look, but I don't recall seeing many."

"Can we slip in and look for them? You draw us a map for where to look."

Hoot agreed. "I can get a good wrangler to go with you. He ain't working, and has a good horse or two of his own to use."

"Who is he?"

"Tom Flowers."

"Where does he live?"

"He's on a small place in Prescott Valley."

"Heck can find him?"

"Sure, I can fix him a map. Tom needs some work, like them others."

Chet stopped Jenny when she came by. "We need some butcher paper and a lead pencil."

"I'll get some soon as I set down these plates."

"Wonderful." He leaned back and sipped some coffee from his cup, pleased with the turn of events. Things were beginning to take shape. There were still lots of problems that could trip him.

"Heck, when we get the map I want you to invite Flowers to come in here."

"You bet."

"Tell him we have a good job for him if things work out."

"I can do that."

"Is he a tough man?" Chet asked the older man.

Hoot nodded. "He'll sure do to ride to hell with."

The old man neatly drew a map on the paper and pointed out the features where to turn off the main road. Heck was up in a shot.

"Don't run that horse into the ground," Chet said after him.

Heck nodded and went out the door.

"Can he deliver the message?" Hoot asked.

"A year ago, he rode back from the Indian Territory to get me when his father was killed by rustlers on a cattle drive."

"How old was he then?"

"Eleven. No, he can get your man back here in a few hours. Harold's cattle count is three hundred mother cows."

"Maybe half that many. Ryan has sold the heifers every year for the past three or four. Some of them cows haven't got a tooth in their head."

"Where did they go?"

"Died, I guess. He sold lots of calves right off the cows."

"Why has he sold them as calves? They ain't worth anything. You mean there aren't any yearlings?"

"Not many."

"A hundred head?"

"I don't know. Ryan's been working with only a few ranch hands, so some may have escaped. We were working some yearlings up in the north canyon country. He said he needed them to pay for his expenses."

"Who bought them?"

"Some dealer named Young up at Ashfork."

"Isn't that a strange place to sell them?"

"You tell me." Hoot shrugged.

"I'm going to try to see the sheriff today." Chet tossed the idea out to see if Hoot might know if it was worth his time to talk to him.

"I'm not sure. He's an office man who sends out deputies to do his field work. He might give you a deputy or two, but I doubt it."

Two men came into the café and nodded at Hoot. One asked, "How are you making it, old man?"

"Fine, without the likes of you."

"Hell, it wasn't our fault Ryan fired you." The thinner one adjusted his gunbelt around his waist and searched around with a hard look, acting mean. "You seen that damn Bo Harold? He upset Ryan's wife yesterday. I think he must have tried to rape her."

"So?" Hoot said.

"He sent us to teach him a lesson. That damn land agent needs to know he has no business stepping on the Quarter Circle Z land."

Hoot nodded and the pair started for the door. Chet

rose and drew his six-gun. "Real easy, drop them gunbelts on the floor and then get your hands up high."

The sound of the click of his hammer being cocked made both men start, then reconsider. They reached carefully for their belts and let them fall to the floor.

"Who in the hell are you?" the skinny one asked over his shoulder.

"I was there with Harold yesterday. She was not raped or even manhandled, despite her mouthy charges."

"You taking sides with him?"

"I guess so. I don't want a hair on him hurt, and if I learn you did anything to him you better go to wearing your Sunday clothing 'cause that's what they're going to bury you in."

"Who in the hell are you?"

"The man that is going after you if you don't beat it out of town."

"Can we have our guns back?"

"Hell, no." Chet gave him a shove out the door. "Get out of town and be quick about it."

"We're going, but you ain't heard the end of this. Wait till Ryan gets word of this. Mister, you're a dead dude."

"Tell him my name is Byrnes, Chet Byrnes, and maybe he'll think better about going to his own death."

"You'll see. You'll see." In the saddle, they rode out and turned left on the main street and went east. Chet watched them. *Good, they went east, meant they were headed for the ranch.*

His head stuck in the doorway, Chet told Hoot, finishing his breakfast at the counter, that he'd be back in a short while. He needed to find Harold and warn him to be ready. At the Palace, he asked the young barmaid Jane where the man's office was.

"Oh, he's gone to the telegraph office. Said he had lots to do today."

"I can find him there?"

She shrugged. "He should be there."

"Thanks." Chet headed for the swinging doors. The incident at the café had upset him. He needed Harold in good health to make this deal. Ryan would increase his pressure when he realized the ranch might sell and he'd lose his stranglehold on the thing that was his golden goose.

The Western Telegraph office had several people inside. He found Harold reading the latest copy of the Preskit Miner newspaper.

"What do you need?" Harold asked.

"I just disarmed two of Ryan's cowboys down at Jenny's Café who came to town claiming you raped Ryan's wife yesterday."

"What? Were they crazy?"

Chet shook his head. "You better get a gun or hire one, 'cause Ryan is going to send them or some others back. Have you heard from Talley?"

Harold looked shaken. "Not yet. I sent it early this morning. What did his men say about me?"

"Something about teaching you a lesson for messing with his wife. I know you didn't do much but push her into the kitchen. You had the right to show me the house."

"I did—wait, they have a telegram for me." He rushed over and straightened out the paper they handed him.

"What did he say?"

"That he does not want to sell it that cheap."

"What else?"

"Ask the sale prospect for more money. Stop. I need at least twenty-five thousand for the ranch."

"You tell him the ranch livestock has been rustled by his own foreman. The house is in ruins according to the buyer, too."

Harold nodded. "I can do that."

"Tell him that I would guarantee him twenty-two thousand, but I want the livestock count up to his numbers. Those he can pay for out of the final ten thousand."

Harold nodded. "That may help."

"We don't have much time to act. You tell him things are going sour at the ranch. If he accepts that, then have him send approval for the buyer to take charge of the ranch at once, before they destroy it further. I'll be at Jenny's Café."

"It may take hours to do."

Chet clapped him on the shoulder. "The clock is ticking, my friend."

"Oh, I can sure use this sale." He hit his forehead with his palm.

"Get a new telegram on the wire." Chet expected his new plan to work.

"Chet?" Harold waited for him to turn back. "Thanks. I will be armed from now on."

"Good." Chet left the telegraph office and headed back for the café. Coming down the hill, he saw Heck's bay horse hitched with another in front.

Tom Flowers was a medium-built man with clear blue eyes. Chet guessed him to be in his mid-thirties. He had a slight smile and a nod when they shook hands.

"Hoot says you have work?"

"I'm in the process of buying the Quarter Circle Z. I need to hire a crew. Right now, this animal count interests me the most. Hoot thinks you have no respect for this Ryan."

"Hoot underestimates my hatred for the man. What are your plans?"

"Bo Harold is negotiating an agreement on the price. I have asked Talley to give me control of the ranch so I can run Ryan and his men off. We have not heard on that yet, but Ryan doesn't need to know that. Tomorrow, I want to look for the remuda he counts as a hundred head."

"Count me in."

"I pay thirty-five and found. You won't make less than two months' pay."

"Fair enough."

"If the deal goes through, I will need to go back to Texas and settle my business there. That may take a year. I want some honest men to work for me. Hoot, I figure, can cook, and we'll get the rest of our crew I guess from former ranch hands who all seem to hate Ryan."

"They won't be hard to find."

"Good. This ranch buying business is getting tough. Let's make a three-day hitch covering part of the range and look for the horses. Meet us on the road to Camp Verde early tomorrow. Heck, you, and me. Hoot can keep an eye on Harold. I'll get enough supplies to feed us."

"Sounds good. I better go home and tell the wife that I'm working again and get everything fixed so she don't have any trouble."

Chet agreed and they shook hands, then Tom left.

"Like him?" Hoot asked.

"Yes, you did good."

"The other two are doing day work this week for a rancher over east, but they should be back here by Sunday."

"Good. I better get us some grub." He looked over at Heck. "You coming?"

"If I can ride my horse."

"Sure." They left the café, waving at Jenny, and went to the big mercantile on the square. The place buzzed with business, and a young clerk finally waved them to the counter. "How can I help you? My name's Franklin."

"Mine's Chet Byrnes and my nephew's Heck."

"Pleased to meet you. What do you need?"

"A slab of bacon, five pounds of rice and five pounds of brown beans, five pounds of flour, baking soda, two pounds of sugar, coffee, and two pounds of raisins. Plus a can of lard." He turned to Heck. "Anything else we need?"

"Some dry apples."

"Put them in, too."

"Where're you going?" the boy asked.

"Bear hunting."

The clerk swallowed. "Grizzly?"

"Yeah," Chet said.

"Whew. Be careful. They can be mean."

Heck nodded matter-of-factly and finally spoke. "We go all over doing this."

"Glad to meet you," the clerk said, and shook his head as if amazed.

Chet paid him, snickering about Heck's remark when they went outside to hang the goods on the bay horse. "You can take it to livery and put it in the panniers. I need to check on Harold."

Heck really laughed. "That clerk in there thought we were real bear hunters."

Chet nodded with a chuckle. "He's a town kid."

"I'll take it to the stables so we can pack it on that mule," Heck said. "I sure like her food. We going to eat supper at the café tonight?"

"Yes. I'll meet you over there later and we'll sure need some sleep tonight. We're going to put some miles on our ponies the next few days. If there aren't any horses, we'll need some, and soon." The notion that he didn't have enough horses for the roundup made his roiling stomach sourness rise up behind the root of his tongue.

Chet had found the ranch he really needed, but he might have bought a dry well. Tom should know the range well enough, and if there were any ranch horses left, he would find them. It would be hard for him to sleep, knowing he was going on such a mission. *Damn.*

Harold bolted up from his seat on the bench when Chet came into the clacking office. He looked wide-eyed. "Where have you been?'

"Getting supplies to make a quick ride over part of the ranch's range."

"Talley said he'd take your deal. You have his authority to take over the ra—"

Chet put a finger over his mouth to silence him. "No one needs to know that."

He took Harold outside by the sleeve. "No one needs to know this—yet."

"I know. I know. Here's Talley's last telegram."

Chet read the lengthy telegram. "Tell the buyer to take control of the ranch. I will wire the Arizona Territorial Bank to stop Ryan's use of that account. I will need the ten thousand as soon as is possible. I understand the money is in his Texas bank. They said on the buyer's word they would transfer it to me."

"You get Talley's signature on a deed to me. Make it to Chester Byrnes and he can have that money. I want him to release the brand, too."

Harold nodded and sagged against the wall of the brick building. "At this distance, what you and he expect of me . . . it is hard to do that quickly."

"The bank is still open. Who handles his account?"

"Mr. Tanner."

"Let's go talk to him."

Harold sighed and moved along beside him, shaking his head. They hurried to the bank and soon were ushered into Albert Tanner's office. The gray-headed man in the brown suit rose and greeted them. After intros and handshakes, he asked them to be seated.

"Mr. Byrnes is buying the Talley operation. Talley has agreed to sell him the ranch. I have his wire right here."

Tanner took the paper and nodded. "We were notified today not to honor any more of Ryan's checks. What is wrong out there?"

"We—Chet here—is buying the ranch. He thinks the property is way short on livestock that has been sold off by, well, Ryan."

"My goodness, the man has been in charge of that operation for several years."

Chet sat back in his chair. "And the owner being absentee, Ryan's had lots of opportunities to remove livestock, according to some previous workers that I have interviewed."

"I understand. I have already sent a warning to all the people he deals with in town not to take his checks."

"Fair enough. I will start an account in your bank in a few days for the new ranch."

"I would appreciate that. When are you taking over?"

"I want to make a survey of the livestock and then I'll oust Ryan. I have Talley's permission to do that, but I want that confidential until I do it."

"I understand. Welcome to the Arizona Territory. Any way that we can help, call on us, Mr. Byrnes." He rose and shook both men's hands.

"Chet's fine. Nice to meet you, sir."

Once in the street, Harold about collapsed. "These transactions—mercy me, I am going crazy sending

wires, making deals with bankers, owners, and I don't
know what all—"

"Let's go find my boy and eat supper."

"I think you must get cooler under stress than I do."

"Perhaps I do." Chet had no answer for the man.
Doing business was much easier than being pinned
down in a cedar break and three killers shooting at
you. Poor Harold didn't know real stress. If the ranch
deal closed without many more hitches, he'd be satisfied. Perhaps in twenty-four hours he'd know the
livestock situation better. Then he could go turn
Ryan out.

During supper with Harold and Heck, Chet noticed
that Harold hardly touched his food, jiggled his coffee
cup picking it up, and generally acted shook. Until at
last he reached over and grasped the agent's wrist.
"Settle down. This deal is going through."

Harold collapsed on the stool. "I damn sure
hope so."

After supper, he and Heck had parted with the man.
The youth laughed and then said, "Man. He was sure
nervous."

"He'll settle down when he gets his commission."

"I bet he does, too."

The two of them went on to their hotel beds and
Chet tried to sleep a few hours. Instead, he tossed and
turned and woke up several times. At last, when it was
time to get up, sitting on the edge of the bed, he regretted not sleeping more when he had the chance. In
the predawn, they slipped inside Jenny's Café—she'd
told them to come by and she'd open early for them.

Breakfast was scrambled eggs, fried side meat, and

a large stack of pancakes with butter and maple syrup. Jenny slid onto the stool on Heck's side and asked them if they needed more to eat. Both told her no, and Chet thanked her.

"We owe you for opening early," Chet said.

"No, taking on Hoot was plenty of thanks. I love that old man, and I've hated how Ryan treated him. I'll be glad to see Ryan get what he deserves." Then she asked Chet, "You ever been married?"

He shook his head. "Never had time. I'm going with a lady back home—don't know if she can come out here. How about you?"

"Me? Lands, I've been married three times. First one run off. Second one got kicked in the head by a mule. Number three, I divorced." She wrinkled her nose. "Guess I wasn't meant to be a wife."

"Maybe you need to be more choosy."

"To tell you the truth, you're probably right."

"Don't get married too soon and quit cooking," Heck said, with a triangle of pancake on his fork. "We like your cooking."

They all chuckled.

"You guys be careful up there. I need the business." With a wink she was gone.

Chet considered her ample frame going into the kitchen. Maybe she was the German girl Susie had been talking to him about needing—no, Jenny was too worldly for that role. The notion made him think about Kathren, and the consideration made him half sick to his stomach. If it wasn't for those damned Reynoldses, she'd already be his wife.

They rode out in the cool predawn for Tom's place.

He was ready, kissed his wife good-bye, swung into the saddle, and they were headed in a short lope for the escarpment off the mountain. The pack mule kept up, and aside from his braying, did well. On the brink, the first purple in the eastern sky appeared far off, and they rode down the steep grade in the dim light of dawn.

After the shallow Verde crossing, they headed northwest with Tom guiding them. He'd spoken of some country where the horses might be. Ranch horses usually stayed in contact with each other. Being geldings, they were soon run off from any wild mares by the stallion in charge. By mid-morning, they'd covered lots of country.

The discovery of horse apples made some hope rise in Chet. If they weren't simply mustangs they might be ranch horses. In the other case, they'd only find a band of wild ones. Tom rode up a rise while Chet and the boy dismounted to vent their bladders. He came back off the loose gravel slope and nodded. "I saw some horses I knew."

"How many?" Chet asked, remounting.

"Maybe thirty."

"Good. How do we send them back to the ranch?"

"South. We aren't that far west yet."

"Sounds like news I can stand. I don't want to drive them in to the ranch today."

"Whatever," Tom said.

"I am worried, as spiteful as Ryan is, we'll have to watch the place so he don't burn it down in revenge. We get them close they will stay there long enough to recover them."

Tom made a face, nodding. "Be just like him to do that."

"I'll head for the far side and swing around them," Heck said, and Chet agreed. The boy left the mule's lead with him. In the distance, the various-colored horses looked alright. This deal might work. With enough horses and workers, they could find the cattle left on the range with the ranch brand on them. This place would be no bargain, but he liked the range grass he'd seen, and there was some live water. Nothing like the hill country. Arizona was lots drier.

Getting to the horses, they rode past a small group of cows and calves who scattered at their approach. Chet frowned at the black, mostly longhorn bulls trailing them. That hatchet-assed stud should have been worked as a calf. How many more of them did he have?

"How did you like that two-hundred-dollar bull?' Tom asked, riding stirrup-to-stirrup with him.

"Ryan paid two hundred bucks for him?" Chet shook his head in disbelief.

"Great Hereford stock, wasn't he?"

"He have pedigree papers for a Hereford bull?"

"Sure, bet you find them in a desk drawer at the house." Tom took off to bring up the drag as the horse herd began to gather and move south.

This Ryan had figured out all the angles on how to embezzle money out of the ranch. Longhorn stock was getting harder and harder to sell. That bull wasn't worth fifty bucks on the market—his offspring would sure be docked. Damn, he had a hornet's nest to straighten out. He booted the tough roan after the horses, who soon settled into a dust-raising trot. Riding to the side of the bunch, he twisted and saw Tom cut a rebel back into the herd beginning to form. The man was a pro.

Standing in his stirrups, Chet began to count them, waving his lariat at some fools wanting to break off, and sent them back into the herd. Heck was holding the west side and Tom had the drag. The horses settled into a more broke way, except for a few hardheaded ones. But they soon learned they could not escape, and fell in with the rest. Mid-afternoon, Tom indicated that the level land ahead might be a place where they could leave them.

Chet waved his hat at Heck and he came around them. The horses acted satisfied. A few took the opportunity to lay down and roll in the dust. Chet's count was thirty-three. Were there any more? He looked back at the tall mountain range north of them. He'd know in a week or so. At least he had some horses, though two or three looked lame. Not bad, though, to have this many usable horses.

Heck soon joined them. "Them horses don't look bad. One of them must have got bit by a rattler. His ankle is really swollen."

"Let's hobble Jack here. We don't need a braying jackass to wake them at the ranch."

Heck dismounted and took the hobbles out of his saddlebags. Then he busied himself strapping them onto the mule's front legs. Before he left him, he checked them until he was satisfied the pack animal wouldn't go far. Heck slapped him on the neck. "Whoa, Jack, we won't forget you."

"Good job, Heck, you'll make a packer yet," Chet said, and then turned to Tom. "Think we only have part of the remuda?"

"There may be more in the west," Tom said. "It wasn't all we had last year for roundup."

Chet nodded his head. "I hope they didn't see our dust down at the ranch house."

"We're higher up here than the ranch. That's why I stopped here. What now?"

"We ride in and evict Ryan along with his crew."

Tom agreed with a grim set to his lips. "That might be fun."

"We can look this bunch over when we get Ryan and his bunch off the ranch."

Tom reined up his horse sharply. "Oh, I heard the other day he's sold the first cutting of alfalfa to some guy in Cottonwood."

"That's interesting." Chet shook his head in dismay, and swung down to get his pants out of his crotch and get his legs some more circulation. "No end to his business deals. Let's take a short break to loosen up, then go get him out."

The other two did the same.

"Man, this is different country than Texas," Heck said, walking around some. "I like it, but those mountains look tough to get over."

"You'll get used to them," Tom said. "There's trails all over to get up them. You simply have to know the way."

"I guess so. Chet, are we going to have to kill that bunch down there at the ranch?"

"Heck, I hope they leave peacefully, but that's their

choice. Don't be gun-happy with that .30 caliber you're wearing."

"Oh, I won't. Just curious."

"We aren't looking for trouble, but we may get some."

"Wonder if them two that you stopped and disarmed at the café got new guns?" Heck asked.

"More than likely."

Chet and his crew mounted up and rode south. When they came to the next edge, high above the ranch, the alfalfa field sparkled like a green-painted patch. The timothy made a lighter stamp and the corn was too short to notice. As for the big house in the cottonwood grove, they could only see the tile roof. Chet used his field glasses and saw little activity around the place. Coming in from the north might fool them. If no one noticed them, they would be a surprise, but the long hillside they rode off was devoid of much brush. It had been cleared at one time to grow more grass, no doubt. Also to have it open so the Apaches couldn't easily sneak up on them.

Then Chet saw the small form of a woman, using her hand for shade in the fenced garden and looking up at them. Screaming, she left for the house on the run. Her wails sounded frantic above the wind in their faces. Soon a hatless man came back with her, and she pointed in a reckless manner in their direction. Chet handed the glasses to Tom. "Know him?"

"When you get done, let me see him," Heck asked.

Tom shook his head and handed the glasses to the boy. "He's a new man Ryan must have hired."

"I sure never seen him before," Heck said, handing them back for Chet to put in his saddlebags.

"Guess we won't be any surprise." Chet shook his head at the loss. He reached behind into the scabbard and unlimbered his Winchester .44/40. A quick-action lever opened and shut, and the rifle in his hands was loaded. He set the hammer on safety and put the rifle butt on his right leg.

"If they shoot at us, head for some cover. Spread out."

They soon were forty feet apart, their horses dropping down coming off the steep slope, and no shots had been fired. Chet felt any shooter would come to the back fence to get as close as he could before he shot—but there was no telling.

His roan acted like he knew something was about to happen, and bobbed his head a lot, making waves with his thick, split mane. The pony was sure-footed, and Chet had the notion that if he needed him to bolt, he would in a split second.

The house drew closer. A Mexican woman came out, looked at them, then in Spanish said something loudly to the ones in the house. She disappeared back inside and reappeared, exposing less and less of herself, and her Spanish words became more audible to Chet.

"*Sí. Those hombres are still coming.*"

Yes, they were still coming. With a head toss, he sent Heck and Tom off to the side, and, expecting the report of a gun, he sent Roan after them. In a few minutes, Heck and Tom were among the thick trunks of the cottonwoods. Chet told the two, "Stay here and back me."

Then he sent Roan in a hard run around to the yard gate where he reined him up.

"Who the hell are you?" a tall, unshaven cowboy asked, looking hard-eyed at him.

"Is Ryan here?"

"Naw, he's in town on business."

My, my. The man might have already learned his credit was no good. Chet reset the roan down with a jerk on the bridle. He could hear the Mexican women all talking a mile a minute behind the single man Ryan had probably left behind to guard the place.

"Unbuckle your gun and drop it gently on the floor, then kick it across the porch. Any wrong move and you better be wearing your funeral clothes." Chet leveled the rifle at him.

A woman tried to stop the cowboy from disarming, but he shrugged her off and did as he was told.

"Now, all of you come out and stand with your faces to the wall. Hands pressed on the wall. Anyone tries anything will be shot. Otherwise you can live, if you listen. Now get down on your knees. Good." Four women, one pregnant, one a teenager, and two in their thirties knelt with their hands on the wall.

What's your name?" Chet asked the cowboy.

"Ralph Keyes."

"Ralph, go hitch two horses to a wagon and don't try anything. Bring it up here."

"What for?"

"Oh, you all are leaving today, didn't I tell you? Tom, you accompany him. Shoot him if he tries anything. Who else is on the payroll?"

"A cowboy named Doug and another they call Cal. I don't know their last names."

"Where are they at right now?"

"I don't know. Ryan told me before he left to guard the house."

"Tom, you and Heck watch for them coming in. When's Ryan coming back?"

Keyes shrugged. "Tonight, I guess. He didn't tell me. Maybe these women know."

Chet had dismounted and Heck took his horse. "Put those three horses out of sight. Then come back to the house."

"Yes, sir. I'm sure glad they all weren't here."

Chet nodded. This mess wasn't over yet, either. He sent Keyes with Tom, then climbed up the porch steps and spoke to the women in Spanish. "You have a short while to get your personal things. Don't steal anything belongs to the ranch, or you will go to prison. I will check all your things. Now *mucho ándale*."

"Where will we go?" the older woman asked.

"Wherever you came from."

She swore at him, going inside the house, shaking mad.

Chet shrugged her words off. One thing he wanted to avoid was having to slap a pregnant woman around, but he wasn't taking much more of her bad mouth. He went inside to oversee their packing. He noticed no rifles on the wall rack. That was why Keyes hadn't gotten one down. No doubt he didn't know where either the guns or the ammo for them were at, or he might have tried to hold them off.

Ryan had made a mistake leaving Keyes in charge. One of those other two cowboys might have defended the place stronger. This had worked slick—but Ryan wasn't home yet, either. Then a notion struck him. If Ryan had made so much money selling off ranch assets, where was it hidden? One of those women knew where he hid it. But it would be like pulling teeth to get them to tell him.

With them out of the room, Chet knelt before the cool hearth and reached inside on the ledge above the front opening. Nothing but soot in there. The fireplace was bricked, and he saw none that looked loose. Chances of him finding the hidden loot were slim, but the notion intrigued him. What could Ryan have spent it on? The amount of money he stole off the ranch must be a fortune. Where was it?

The first woman came lugging a large blanket wrapped around her possessions into the main room. He told her to sit down on the tile floor. The teenager obeyed him.

"What's your name?"

"Maria."

"Good, Maria. You just sit there."

She nodded.

Chet had a mess on his hands with four women to evict, but that wasn't his fault. Whatever they did or where they went was not his problem. In less than a half hour, Keyes would be driving them all off the ranch. Fine, then he'd have that solved and he could wait for Ryan's return, if he thought he had to come back after learning his check writing was closed. Maybe he'd meet his women on the road and think better about coming back. Not likely—he might even mount an army to come back with him. Something Chet needed to think hard about.

Heck stuck his head in the door. "The wagon's hitched. I'll go get Jack and try to bring in the horses, huh?"

"Yes, then we can start checking them out. They should come on down here for you. There's plenty of hay in the barn to feed them lot."

"I'll get them."

"Fine, be careful. We don't know where those other two goons are." What was taking those women so long? Heck left the doorway, and Chet turned to see the older woman, who had been crying, coming in with her things in two blankets.

"The wagon is ready. Go load up." He made a head toss at the open door for those two. They acted deaf, but soon moved to the opening.

"Get down here now!" he shouted up the staircase for the missing ones.

They appeared, and bounced their possessions down the stairs, two-handed. He stopped them at the base and made them take out the brass candlestick holders and a few other items he felt came from the house.

They angrily complained in Spanish, speaking a mile a minute that those were theirs. He shook his head and pointed to the doorway. "Vamoose!"

They obeyed and dragged their remaining loot down the front steps to the gate. Keyes loaded them and their things into the back of the wagon.

"Deliver that wagon to Frey's stables. Tell him that

this is my wagon, and he is to take care of the animals until I can get back there. If you don't, the sheriff will hang you for horse stealing."

"Ryan owes me money," Keyes said, sitting on the spring seat.

"I'm sure he'll pay you out of his own pocket. Now get the hell out of here. And don't come back."

The pregnant woman, standing, had to get in her last cusswords and threats in Spanish. She about fell down when the horses jerked the wagon to leave, but she never missed a word in her thorough blessing of him.

Shots came from behind the house. Chet rushed inside and grabbed his rifle—were they after Heck? Damn them. His heart pounded in his throat as he tried to get outside and around to see the source of the shots.

Chapter 17

Chet and Tom rounded the house in time to see Heck, his horse, and the mule making a run across the hillside to get off the slope, and two riders shooting their pistols at him. They must be the other two, he decided, taking a sight down the barrel. The riders, seeing him and the long gun, took wings for cover.

"I hate to shoot damn horses," Chet said, shaking his head, glad he didn't have to. "But I feared they might get lucky and hit Heck with one of their six-guns. Let's go see where they went."

"There was nothing else to do, if they hadn't turned tail," Tom said, running beside him.

Heck slid the bay to a stop and Jack put his four feet down in stiff-legged jumps. "I had taken Jack's hobbles off when they came charging down out of a draw. I had better forget the horses and get my butt down here."

"You did alright, son. In fact, you did wonderful." Tom looked where the two riders had disappeared. He shook his head.

Chet nodded. "I've been wondering where Ryan kept his money."

Tom shook his head. "Danged if I know."

The safe in the one room. Chet'd noticed that the day before, when they inspected the house. He wanted to kick himself.

"Heck, head for the house, go in back, and check that safe." He had never thought about Ryan using it. "If it's been cleaned out, those damn women took it."

Heck raced for the front door, and in a flash was back in the doorway. "They must have got it, Chet."

"You two watch for the others. I'm going after them." He jumped on Heck's bay and charged off after them. There was no way they were getting away with that money. When he hit the road, he could make out the wagon's dust ahead. Topping a rise, he saw the women look back, and the one sitting beside Keyes began beating on the horses. But it wasn't even a horse race. He was soon beside the team and drew the near horse, down by the bridle, to a halt.

When Chet dismounted and tried to get on the rig, the pregnant one went to trying to beat him with a buggy whip. But he had no mercy, and jerked it from her hands. When he climbed up to save being hit again, he pulled her off the seat while she still struggled with him. Tired of her fighting, he let her fall to the ground. No way to treat a lady, but she wasn't one. He brought out his large knife, and the other three screamed and backed away to the tailgate. Hers first, he slashed the blanket open and the paper money fluttered everywhere.

"Now open yours. You got any money in them, you'll go to prison, too."

"No money, señor! No money," they screamed and tore open their blankets to show him underwear, Sunday dresses, a towel or two, and some toiletries.

"Fine," he said and told them to sit down in the back. He used one of the woman's slips by tying the top end, and began to gather the money. By the handfuls, he stuffed it inside his "bag." By then, Heck and Tom, who had saddled horses, were there to help him.

Heck jumped in and whistled. "How much money is here?"

"A lot of money."

"How did you figure he had so much?"

"He's been stealing for a long time from Talley. No one checked on him. He had the run of the house. Before Talley came to visit, I bet Ryan cleaned it out, and when he left, Ryan went back to using it."

"Why was it open?"

"The women wouldn't dare touch it, and they'd tell him if anyone else did so that they didn't get the blame. He probably had it shut, but the combination wasn't locked. That's what she went after instead of her personal things."

"She says you broke her arm," Tom said.

"Load her up. Keyes can take her to a doctor."

Tom and Heck boosted her up in back, and she cried out, holding her right arm. Chet decided that was better than her cussing and hitting him. "Take her to the doctor, Keyes."

The three rode back to the ranch with the money-full slip tied on Chet's horn.

"How much you reckon all that money's worth?" Heck asked, riding his bay alongside.

"I have no idea, but we can count it and wait on Ryan."

"I never counted that much of anything before," Heck said.

'We're going to improve your math tonight," Chet teased. "And no taking your boots off to use your toes to count." All three laughed.

Where had those two shooters gone? No doubt to find Ryan and tell him that Chet had taken charge of the ranch. More troubles.

Chapter 18

Chet went upstairs with his rifle and kept an eye out for any sign of dust on the road or movement, while his helpers fixed the meal. No sign of anyone in his field glasses. But he felt certain it was only a matter of time before Ryan and his force came back for their loot. The sun soon began to melt in the west. Supper consisted of biscuits and beans with fried, smoked side meat to season them, and they wound the meal up with sweetened rice and raisins that Tom concocted. Not half bad, Chet decided, recalling his sister's fine cooking.

With a few candles lit after supper, they began to count the recovered pile of bills. There were so many bills, they looked like chicken feathers at a fowl dressing party. Lots more money than Chet even imagined. Stacks and stacks of it in large bills—fives, tens, twenties, fifties, and hundreds piled in a mountain on the long dining-room table. Tom had only seen a few hundreds in his life, and it was Heck's first time to stretch one out and look at it. As they worked into the night counting and recounting, Chet began to realize that Ryan would not sit still and simply lose this much money. No way he'd let it go without a fight.

At long last, their tally showed ten thousand, four hundred and ten bucks. In the candlelight, seated on the floor, they shook their heads at one another. The great ranch robbery loot all stacked neatly on the large table, Chet decided there was no telling how much more Ryan had taken and used for himself.

"Guess he didn't have lots of places to spend this money out here." Tom said. "Why, I couldn't have spent that much in my lifetime."

"What do we do next?" Heck asked.

"We'll get a bank count on the amount to certify it. Then we'll have them put it in a safety deposit box until we can work it out with Talley who gets what."

"That means we need to move it to Preskit?" Heck looked upset.

"That means, yes, we need to take it to the bank in Preskit."

"You figure Ryan's going to be blocking that steep road up that mountain?"

"Heck, he may be standing anywhere he can to stop us. I'm not afraid of Ryan or his men. I understand your concern. But there are things that you must do in this world. This money is not ours simply because we took it from Ryan's wife, but we have a claim on it."

Heck screwed up his face. "Things can sure get complicated—fast, huh?"

"I agree. Right now, I hate to leave this ranch and have Ryan come back and burn it down in revenge."

"There's some other trails that can get you up on the mountaintop and on to Preskit," Tom said.

"How dangerous are they?" Chet asked.

"I've been over them before on a sure-footed horse like your roan."

"He's a good mountain horse. Could you get all this money to the bank?"

"I could, I'm pretty sure."

Chet used the edge of his front teeth on his chapped lower lip, considering the plan. He needed to remain here. With his experience, he could hold off any drunks that Ryan rounded up in the bars to attack the place.

"When do you want to leave?" he asked Tom.

"Right now. I want to be at the base when the sun comes up, or partially up the trail."

"Ryan may already have guards stationed around the ranch."

Tom shook his head. "I can avoid them. They'd expect us to go out by Camp Verde."

Chet agreed. He simply hated sending someone else on such a dangerous mission that he should be doing. Tom knew the trail; he didn't. The roan was the most sure-footed horse he'd ever ridden except for a few he owned in Texas.

"Alright, we'll put this money in a canvas cover so it looks like a bedroll."

Heck rushed over to get his, and unwound his ground cloth to spread it out on the floor.

"Deliver it to the bank president, Albert Tanner, in the morning. Have him get a count of the money and put it in a safety deposit box. It isn't mine to trust a bank not failing while the loot is in there. I want a receipt for it, too."

Heck was shaping the stacks in the center of the roll. They brought him handfuls of money until the dough was wrapped much like a bean burrito about four feet long. Then they folded in the ends and tied it every foot with leather strings. Heck shook it several times and nothing opened.

"It'll work," Tom said. "They won't know it's money."

"When you come back, bring along four more cowboys. Hoot, who's eating at Jenny's place, will help you find them. I want all of you armed with rifles—get some and ammo at the big store. I'll pay him when I get back there."

"I know Mr. Newman. He'll let me have them."

"Good." Chet blew out the candles. "I don't want them to see our moves if they're around the place."

In a small voice, Heck asked, "Do you think they're out there now?"

"I have no idea, but we're not taking any chances."

"Yes, sir."

"Grab my rifle," Chet said to Tom.

Tom frowned at them in the dim light. "But you and him will need it."

"We'll figure it out—some way. You try to be back by dark tomorrow with guns and hands. We'll hold them off till then."

Tom agreed. "Fast as I can."

Roan was saddled and the bedroll tied on. Chet listened and peered into the starlight outside the dim-lit grove of cottonwoods where they stood. All he heard were some crickets and frogs. At last, with the rifle in his scabbard, Tom took the reins and set out on foot.

Chet understood his method. The man wanted to be certain that he didn't run into any resistance out there, and he knew the place well enough to avoid them. Chet crouched to listen to the night insects, and thought he heard a horse cough that was not one of their animals. He crouched and Heck followed suit. Both soon had six-guns in their hands.

"See anything?" Heck asked in a low whisper.

Chet, creeping toward the house, stopped and listened. Then he shook his head. "I don't believe they're close right now. Let's get inside and bar the doors."

"I'm right behind you. I bet you never thought buying a ranch would be this damn hard."

"Heck, I had no idea."

Inside, they barred all the doors and shuttered the lower-floor windows. Taking turns sleeping with the other one standing guard, they spent the night upstairs, ready for anything. Before dawn, in the coolness of the night air, Chet smelled smoke. It came from the south—then he saw the red flicker of flames. The fire was near the gate, and someone was clanging some iron kettles. He really wished he had the rifle back. But Tom might need it worse if he got into a gunfight going over the ridge.

Chet hoped his man was well on his way upward over the range. No telling. He sat down on his butt beside the open window. They were out there blocking their escape or working up their nerve to attack. Maybe simply sizing up Chet's force in the house—

big force, him and a twelve-year-old. He closed his eyes, hoping for tears to ease their dryness. Once again, he had himself in a real tight corner and needed to hang on until help arrived.

Tom could gather men, guns, and horses and be back before sundown, if he was still alright. The man had to be that, or him and Heck would be in a hornets' nest when Ryan figured out there were only him and the boy inside. Still, for the ranch to be worth anything to him, he needed to save this large house.

Oh, well, time would tell. He'd whipped the Comanche a time or two as little more then a teenager. This crook couldn't be any slyer than a Comanche warrior.

Chet would never forget crawling on his belly for a long way in the underbrush with the nine-pound Walker Colt in his fist. Expecting to hear a rattler any minute, 'cause he was in the Willow Creek bottoms near water, and they liked such places. A situation developed rapidly before him when some near-naked buck bent over to scalp Jim Cross, who was lying face-down in the grass—Chet could see the face-down man's spur rowels from his cover. Then the buck straightened up, holding the blood-dripping hair, screaming like a madman. Chet shot him in the back of the head where his braids came from, and he could recall the greasy eagle feather tied in his hair. Chet still had that as a souvenir—at home among his things.

He heard a horse in a gallop coming down the lane toward the house. Hard to make out in the starlight, due to all the shadows under the cottonwoods. Then a bullet report slapped the adobe plaster on the side of the house. Chet stepped to the window and took a steady shot. The .44 bucked in his fist. The rider went off the other side—hit. *We ain't sleeping, Ryan. Your decoy was shot. What now?*

Heck was up and in the room, keeping low. "Who was it?"

"Some dumb gunman who thought he was invisible, I guess. He wasn't."

"Are more of them coming?"

"I don't hear anything but his horse running away."

Heck made a puzzled look on his face. "Did he think we wouldn't shoot him?"

On his knees reloading the chamber, Chet shook his head. "I'm not sure of anything, except we took out one of his hands."

Heck silently agreed.

Then a rooster crowed. There had been some hens and males around the house and pens, but he had never paid them much mind. Chet sat down on his butt on the pine-board flooring. "It's going to be a long day ahead of us."

"Yes, sir."

"Heck, I appreciate you. I didn't aim to get you in a mess like this, but you take in life what life wants you to have. Right now, it's us against them."

"I know and I know why. It's that money. That's the glue going to keep them out there trying to recover it. Ain't that it?"

"Good way to put it. I know little about Ryan. Many people hate him, but I don't have any inclination how he thinks. Why he sent a man up here shooting like that, I'll probably never know for sure. He damn sure knows now that we're here, if he had any doubts before.

"Bring us some of those leftover cold biscuits up-stairs for our breakfast and some water. With that pitcher pump in the kitchen, we should have water enough to hold out."

"Right, I'm on my way." The youth scrambled to his feet and he heard him rush down the stairs.

Chet used his field glasses and could make out the wagon and team parked down by the end of the drive. In the lens, he could see several women were busy cooking. The sharp smell of their cooking fire carried on the wind. He saw a shorter man remove his hat and wipe his forehead on his sleeve. That could be his man—a fifty-caliber Sharps buffalo gun might have brought him down, but Chet didn't have one of those, or any rifle for that matter.

"Chet," Heck called up. "In the front hall closet I just found a Spencer rifle and tubes of ammo. There's two shotguns and brass shells for them, twelve-gauge."

He took a quick look outside and at their camp. No movement. "I'm coming down."

In minutes, Chet was working the action on the Spencer. A good, well-kept firearm; and when he looked inside the closet he saw a canvas bucket full of loaded tubes. Plenty of ammo. He should have searched the place better. They had fire power. He and Heck totted them upstairs. The boy went back for the biscuits and soon rejoined him.

The rifle, loaded by a tube that slid in the butt sec-tion, sat close by. He loaded both shotguns, too. One was a double-barrel Greener made in England, twelve-gauge. An expensive firearm, but accurate as any scattergun. The other, a new pump Winchester with a goose barrel. It probably had as much kick as a Missouri mule, but a powerful load of buckshot from it would damn sure stop anything.

Chet and Heck sat cross-legged and chewed on the dry biscuits, and washed them down with cool water. The firearms discovery evened the playing field.

Between bites, Heck said, "I'm sure glad I looked in there."

"Hey, you may have saved our hides. Lucky break—" His speech was shattered by the crack of a rifle and a bullet shattering some wood on the window frame in their room in the southwest corner of the house.

"He must have a sharpshooter down there in the trees."

The youth looked bug-eyed. "How're we going to get to him?"

When Chet edged to the window, he could see the remains of gunsmoke in a treetop about halfway to the gate. Grateful the wind had not begun to disperse it, he dropped down and drew Heck a map in the dust on the floor.

"That shooter is right here. I saw a large dead limb pointing east out of that tree. Take the Greener and go in the next room. Have the butt against your shoulder when you fire it and shoot high over that tree top where you think the main trunk is at. Then get down. I'm going to shoot at him, too. The range is long, but if we hit him, he may fall out of the tree."

Heck made a serious nod. "I think I recall seeing that dead branch."

"Simply stand up, aim, and fire where you think he is at, then get down. No hesitation or another sniper may shoot you."

"I will."

The youth left the room with the loaded Greener. Chet used the pump to put a high brass cartridge in the chamber. He asked the boy in the next room, "Ready?"

"Yes, sir."

"Get down fast after you shoot, but keep your finger off the second trigger."

"Yes, sir."

"Ready, shoot." Chet had the Winchester to his shoulder and drew a bead over the tree. The shock of the recall slammed into his shoulder. Then Heck shot and someone screamed. A falling rifle clattered out of the tree, and then a body hit the ground like a ripe watermelon thrown off a bluff.

"We get him?" Heck asked.

"Yes." Though he had not dared to look, in case there was a second rifleman in place. "Stay down."

"I am. Whew, this gun sure kicks."

Chet crawled over to the other front window in the room. "You think that one's bad, this one's worse." He dared look out from the east side edge, moving in more to see what was out there. There was a man sprawled on his back on the ground beside the lane. Two down and how many more to go? The body didn't move, and he was satisfied he was dead or dying.

Chet lifted his field glasses and saw the panicked

women in their colorful attire climbing into the wagon. He counted three men running around to load them.

"What are they doing?" Heck asked, coming into the room.

"Here, take the glasses. You can see them." Chet unslung the glasses from over his head. Then he reached for the Spencer. With it laid on the windowsill, got on his knees and raised the sight as high as it would go, lined up the horse and rider, then squeezed the trigger. A short time passed in the gunsmoke-filled room, and all at once Chet saw the horse bolting, tossing his rider.

"Damn, you must have got real close," Heck said. "He threw that galoot off like a sack of flour—oh, oh, that guy's running bareheaded after the wagon. Now, he got to the tailgate and the women are pulling him in. That horse that threw him is coming to the house. Must be one of ours that belongs here."

"Good, we can add another horse to our tally."

Heck sat down cross-legged on the floor. "This has been one helluva morning."

"You better drop the cusswords or Susie will use lye soap on your tongue when we get home."

"I will."

Chet reached over and shook his shoulder. "We better go see about those loose horses, pard. This has been one tough deal. We've earned a siesta."

"I was thinking about something to eat."

Chet nodded, considering a boy's appetite. "We can do that, too."

Shouldn't be long until Tom and the reserves arrived. The smell of spent gunpowder still burned his nose. He blew it into the kerchief from his pocket. His shoulders gave a small shudder under his shirt and vest. Their threat was a good thing to have behind him.

What a damn night and morning.

Chapter 19

Both loose horses at the corral gate carried the ranch brand. Chet learned that letters he found in the pockets of the first man he shot were from Willard Duck. His sister Alma lived in Springer, Utah, and she wanted him to come home—she thought the new law wouldn't prosecute him for past things. She needed his help to run the farm and cattle. The second man had a perfumed letter from a dove in Mesilla, New Mexico. Her name was Rosa, and she wrote part in Spanish and part in English. She called him Randolph McQuire.

Rosa told Randolph he was a grand lover and how each night she cried for his return. Sounded very sad, and she offered to meet him in Tombstone or Tucson. Then Chet and Heck dragged the bodies closer to the house and covered them with a tarp so the buzzards wouldn't eat them. They probably needed to be taken to the sheriff in Preskit.

"Them sonsabitching buzzards must be starved— oh, I'm sorry," Heck said, and took off his felt hat to beat his leg. "There's a lot up there circling, ain't there?"

"More than enough." Chet chuckled over his error and retraction. The sky was full of the big black birds floating on updrafts, anticipating a meal. "Let's go find that food."

"Yeah, my belly is growling at my backbone like a bulldog."

Chet chuckled.

"Now it's over, I'm sure tickled you brought me along. Why, we've had more adventures and seen more country than most folks do in a lifetime."

"We have, indeed. Do you like Arizona?" Chet looked at the towering mountain that rose in the south and wondered about Tom's success.

"Long as them Reynoldses don't find us. Guess we've traded them for this Ryan, huh?"

"If he's all we've got for an enemy, he can be eliminated."

"I'll get a fire going in that range. Guess we'll have frijoles, huh?"

"That's about it. In a day or so we'll be back and have some of Jenny's cooking. After you get that range going and beans on, there's some paper and a pencil in my saddlebags. You can write Susie a letter, but kinda keep all the shooting stuff down. I don't want her alarmed."

"Yeah, women don't need to be upset and they'll sure get that way when they hear about the details."

"Right, tell her about the house and the mountains and how nice it is up here."

"I can do that."

"Good, I'll fix the beans."

Chet found two pans: one, a large kettle to fix a mess for the incoming crew, and a smaller one to cook faster for him and Heck. He'd noticed several chickens running about. "You know, Heck, we might have an egg hunt after lunch. I've heard enough hens cackling. We might have some scrambled eggs for breakfast tomorrow."

"Yeah, shame we don't have them boys along to gather 'em."

"I bet we can find enough fresh-laid ones to feed that bunch in the morning."

"Be like home, huh?"

"No, we don't have Susie to head up the cooking team."

"How long's she been the cook?"

"Since she was twelve and your grandmother's mind began to slip."

"Shame, but I don't ever recall Grandma ever being what I'd call—well, right."

Chet chewed on his lip and nodded. Neither she nor Rocky had been alright for the biggest part of Heck's life. Rocky lasted longer than she did, but he was a vegetable now. Always worried about the damn Comanche, and all of them penned up on a reservation in the Indian Territory. No telling what those long, depleting searches for the kids were like for him. It was a wonder he even survived them.

The frijoles were slow to cook, and Heck found a large bowl of eggs he considered good. There were some hens with new chicks Heck told Chet about, but they nested a ways from the house.

Dear Susie and crew,

*We found a nice ranch in the Verde Valley
north of Preskit. That is what folks call
Prescott. Ranch is kinder run down but it
belonged to a rich man who lives in St.
Charles, Missouri and he didn't check on it
enough. But you will like the big house. It is a
two story house. A pitcher pump in the kitchen
and water tanks with windmills—except they
creak a lot—need greasing is all. Plenty of
chickens, lots of shade. Big mountains all
around us.*

*We ~~mess~~ miss your cooking most. Even
beans don't taste the same. Chet says we
cannot say when we will come home. There is
lots to do here. New hands supposed to show
up this evening.*

> *Our best,*
> *Chet and Heck*

Chet finished reading it and nodded. "You did
swell. Writing good letters is important if you ever
have to run a big ranch. I'm proud of you. That's a
good letter."

Heck beamed, and then at the sound of horses, he
ran into the front part of the house. "They're coming.
A mess of them. I see Tom in the lead."

Chet came in to join him. "Won't they be surprised?"

"I bet so. They don't know what we've been busy
doing."

They went out to greet them. Men stepping down,

pulling their pants out of their crotches and then shaking hands.

"Did they ever show up?" Tom asked, looking around. "Oh, Chet, this is Roamer. He's a deputy sheriff."

"Nice to meetcha."

The deputy nodded.

"There's two under the canvas over there were part of the raiding party. The rest ran off about noon today."

"You and the boy ran them off?" Roamer twisted on his handlebar mustache like he couldn't believe them.

"One came tearing up here about sundown, shooting at the house. I cut him down. He was riding a ranch horse and his name was Willard Duck. I read his mail."

Roamer nodded like he knew of him.

"The second one is Randolph McQuire. He was up in a tree down the lane, shooting at the house with a rifle. We got him out of the tree with two shotgun blasts of buckshot."

"You two are a tough bunch. I'm glad I didn't have to go up against you. We better take those bodies back to Preskit tomorrow. There will be an inquest held. If you can ride in and appear, I'd appreciate it."

"I can do that, now that my hands are here."

"Hoot is driving a wagon out here that I rented, loaded with supplies,' Tom said. "He'll be here later."

"Good idea. Introduce me to the crew."

"This is Hampt Tate." The tall, broad-shouldered cowboy stuck out a mountain-size calloused paw and shook his hand. "Proud to meet you, Mr. Byrnes. I worked here last year."

"Good, you know the lay of the land."

"Most of it. Appreciate the job."

Wiley Combs was short, but bowlegged enough that Chet decided he'd never send him to trap hogs. In his late teens, Wiley looked tough enough to react to any threat.

Next Chet shook hands with Bixsby Stone, a medium-built cowboy who had a rusty voice. "Good to meet you, sir. I got clotheslined once, my voice is about ruined."

"I can understand you fine, and fellars, my name's Chet."

"I'll remember that," Bixsby said.

The last man was no doubt from the cavalry. Shoulders back, he stepped in and they exchanged a handshake. The man's blue eyes were the color of a pale sky, and Chet figured they didn't miss much.

"They call him Sarge." Tom said.

"You were in the army?" Chet asked him.

Sarge nodded. "Ten years. And I got so tired of gritty beans and moldy bacon half-cooked, I resigned."

"I'd agreed with that. You have to work, they should feed you well."

A smile cracked his tight face. "Sounds like a man with my heart. I'm glad I made the muster."

"Good to have all of you. This place needs lots of elbow grease. Those windmills in the morning need the gears cleaned and new grease. When you men are out riding and see a seep of water, make a map. We need to improve the range with more water development. I intend to hire a contractor to build us some tanks, too.

"Water is the secret to keeping cattle closer to the house and getting the far range pastured as well." The men nodded.

"We've found some of the horses. There may be more. The ones we brought in need to be checked out and culled. That's a start, and the cattle come next. These longhorn bulls need to be made steers and some British breed bulls brought in, that's all down the road. Glad to have you on the ranch, and the beans are about done."

"Thanks, Roamer, for coming out. Heck and I were dreading them charging us before you all got here."

"Can we make any charges against Ryan about his stealing here?" Roamer asked.

"Might be hard to prove," Chet said, considering the question. "He can say he was told to run the ranch. By the way, how tall is he?"

"Oh, five-six, looks like a bulldog."

"I saw him in the glasses when they were down by the head of the lane. I'll know him next time."

"He's damn sure tough and crooked as a snake. I'd like to slam him in prison." Roamer shook his head in disgust.

"Let's work on that, then." Chet herded them all into the house.

Heck had made one dutch-oven batch of biscuits and was refilling it with new ones. The new hands shook his hand and bragged on his cooking, as they filled their tin plates with steaming beans and took on some of his fresh bread.

Before he went inside, Chet looked over the valley bleeding in sundown's last moments. His new land—maybe Kathren would share this vast place with him. He sure hoped so.

Chapter 20

Chet woke before dawn on the hard floor in his bedroll. He planned to take over one of those beds to sleep in after he ant-hilled the bedding on it to get rid of any bed bugs. The cooler night air soon reached him. Hands on his hips, he stretched his sore back muscles and then pulled up his pants and sat down to get his boots on. A bath and shave wouldn't hurt him, but his clean clothes were back in the hotel.

During the night, Hoot had arrived with the rented wagon full of supplies that the crew unloaded late the night before. But Chet could hear him opening the lids on the cast-iron stovetop downstairs and building a fire in the range. Things would turn around soon in this ranch's operation—but things never went as fast as Chet wanted them to.

The sleepy-looking Hoot shook his head at him in the candlelight. "I forgot how much work this was."

"You can handle it?"

"Sure, but you ever had a camp cook before that didn't complain?"

"Only my sister. We'll find you some help when I'm in Preskit."

"Thanks, I'll get by till then."

"You have any idea where Ryan might have gone?"

Hoot shook his head. "All I've known about him was he was here running this ranch."

"Since he became my enemy, I need to know all I can about him."

"Talk to Hampt. He worked for Ryan for some time. He might know more than I do."

"Now, how can I help you?" Chet asked.

"Crack me enough eggs to make some flapjacks." Hoot turned up his lip. "Some may be fertile. Watch them."

"I will. How many good ones do you need?"

"Six will do."

"I can do that."

"What can I do?" Heck asked, sweeping his hair back and looking like he'd been dragged through a knothole.

"Chop more firewood," Hoot said.

"I'll get it."

"Don't chop a finger off," Chet teased as he went out in the first glow of dawn.

"I won't." He forced a smile and went on.

"Arizona's a tough place," Hoot said.

Chet agreed. "I had no idea we'd get into a tough war out here trying to buy a ranch."

"He's a tough kid."

"Yes. Last year he must have rode five-six hundred miles by himself to get me when they shot his father."

"Damn, that was a man's job."

"And it worries me. I never had a boyhood myself. I've always felt cheated and I hope he doesn't miss his, too." Chet shook his head at the thoughts of that happening to Heck.

"Aw, you get this ranch straightened out, he'll have a great time making pack trips to hunt elk and bear. There's lot of pretty girls to dance with on Saturday night in Camp Verde. He won't miss a thing."

"I hope you're right. Here's the good eggs you needed." Chet put the bowl of cracked ones down on the table.

"Thanks, better get the crew up. This food is coming together. Coffee's made."

With a hot holder on the handle, Chet raised the pot to get some for himself. It steamed up as he poured it. "I'll get them up."

Smelling the first pancakes cooking on the sizzling grill, Chet went upstairs to stir the crew. Mounting the stairs, he met Tom coming down. "Go back and wake them. Hoot about has it ready."

"Sure. I can smell it up here. Heavenly, isn't it?"

"We may need to give him a hand, but the old man is trying hard."

"You bet." Tom went right back upstairs.

Chet took his steaming cup and went out the front door to listen to the mourning doves. What was Kathren doing? She probably was up and checking cattle. He could imagine her leaning slightly forward in the saddle as she urged her stout horse up the hillside on a cow trail. He missed her and his sister. Susie was his conscience. She reminded him of things that needed done. Keeping him from getting too angry over mistakes and generally pushing him on. Two great women, a thousand miles away, and he missed both of them.

"Going to be a nice day," Hampt said, coming outside. He checked the sky like most folks did, appraising the weather in the morning.

"When will it rain again?" Chet asked.

"June. That starts the monsoon season and is near a month away. If we do get any then."

"I understand it's a dry land. Who took care of the hay and watered it?"

"A man named Chandler. He usually has some Mexicans do that."

"From nearby?"

"Hoot was the last one of us to work up here. He might know."

"I'll ask him. Thanks."

"We better get in there. That hungry bunch may eat the plates."

Deep in laughter, Chet followed the big man back inside. There was some humor left in this world— he'd about forgotten all about it.

"What's so funny?' Heck asked.

"Hampt was worried you guys would have it all eaten up, including the plates," Chet said, and most looked up from feeding their faces, then smiled. "Maybe."

Then they dug in again. Hoot made more pancakes on his grill and then poured another round of coffee from the big granite pot. The boys were down to thanking him. Finishing up, they turned to Chet.

"What are we doing today?"

"I want two men to go west and look for the rest of the ranch horses. We covered most of the north part, Tom said. The rest of you will cull and see about the ones we brought in. One thing you'll draw straws for—two of you are going to help Hoot and do his dishes. This cooking for you all is hard work. We'll have to pitch in till I get him some help."

Everyone moaned, but it was mild.

"By the way, who's the windmill mechanic in this bunch? We get the bodies loaded in the wagon for Roamer to take back and then you all get the horses checked, then start on the windmills. They'll need all that old grease cleaned off the gears and new applied."

No one had raised their hand—most cowboys hated windmills except when thirsty. "Heck, you show them how we do it."

"Yes, sir."

"I better go in town and see my land agent, set up an account at the store and hopefully settle this business about Ryan. If I'm not back by bedtime, you'll be fine. But everyone keep their gun handy."

They all agreed that would be necessary until the Ryan problem was settled. Chet decided he'd talked enough for one morning. Hands soon fit in and knew what to do. The corpses were loaded. Roamer drove the light wagon and hitched his horse on behind. Chet rode his roan that Tom had brought back, bragging on his surefootedness.

At Camp Verde, they had a beer in a small bar and let the horses rest before they climbed the mountain. The bartender asked them who was in the back of the wagon. Chet told him their names and he nodded, "Part of a tough bunch from out there. They were no-account."

Chet agreed, paid the man, and they left. Standing outside in the bright sun, he pulled down his hat brim, facing the towering mountain. What had he said? Part of a tough bunch. Worthless bastards, he called them.

On the road again, he and Roamer wound their way up the side of the canyon wall, with the team hitting the collars and digging hard to make the grade. The steep grade was a tough one, and so narrow in places as to only allow single passage. Luckily some freight wagons had stopped on a wide place in the road for them to get by. Riding by them on his roan, Chet thanked them.

At last on top, they pulled off the road and let the sweating horses rest. Chet looked across the wide valley at the faraway peaks. Vast country, and he could see for miles.

"Tom said you were moving your whole family out here," Roamer said as they stood on the lip of the world over the Verde country.

"I hope to, in a year. No way I can close out all my business back there any sooner."

Roamer nodded. "Good to see real ranch folks taking over that ranch. Absentee owners usually end up in a mess like this Ryan deal. You know this country is going to grow, too. There will be more folks like you moving in. Solid family folks."

With the Apaches no longer a problem, more settlers would sure come. They did in Texas. Chet simply hoped he would have all his land and business settled.

Then it would be time for them to move out here, so they could enjoy the vast country before him.

When they reached the courthouse square, a crowd had gathered, shouting questions at Roamer about the bodies in the wagon.

Had Injuns done it? Who were they? How did they die? Where did he find them? What was law doing about it?

At last Sheriff Sims came out, spoke briefly to Roamer, and then told everyone to hold their horses. He shook Chet's hand and said he was sorry they were too late to prevent the raid on his ranch.

Chet dismissed his concern and sat on his horse to listen.

Roamer stood up in the wagon. "These dead men were part of a party that attacked the new owner of the Quarter Circle Z. Led by the ex-foreman, a man called Ryan, they charged Mr. Byrnes and a twelve-year-old boy who were in the house. These men were shot during the raid. One's name is McQuire, the other is Willard Duck. Ryan and some others escaped. That's Mr. Byrnes on the roan horse. Why don't you welcome him to Arizona?"

A round of applause as Chet dismounted, took off his hat, and went to shaking hands. Folks acted proud to meet him and glad he'd taken care of those raiders.

Chet offered to buy Roamer's lunch, but the deputy backed out. He needed to go home to check on his pregnant wife. He excused himself.

"The other deputy will take your wagon back to Frey's after he leaves the bodies at the funeral home," Roamer said.

"Good enough. I'm going to eat, get a bath and shave, and then join civilization."

In a hurry, Roamer waved and rode off on his own horse. The sheriff walked over. "Any more about Ryan?"

"I wasn't sure that Tom had told you, but there was lots of money in the safe. We thought it was loot from Ryan's shady dealings. It is at the Arizona Bank in a safety deposit box. I'll resolve that with Talley."

"Fine, but how can we build a case against Ryan?"

'I've thought about it. Might be tough. He can say he collected the money as the manager, huh?"

The lawman agreed. "I see a smart lawyer doing that."

"Maybe after I clean up and have some food, I'll be able to think more on all of it."

"No idea where Ryan went?"

"He took the Mexican women, a ranch wagon and team, and I don't know how many hands—not many—and left after we shot a sniper out of a cottonwood tree."

"When was that?"

"Yesterday morning, oh, about nine or ten. And I was glad. By then, Heck had discovered some arms in a closet and we were better armed. A Spencer rifle and two shotguns."

The lawman was looking hard across the street at the saloon fronts down Whiskey Row. Then he nodded. "You were lucky and brave."

"At first, we only had two revolvers, but had they rushed us, we'd've gotten part of them. I've fought Comanches and had less odds."

"I bet you have. Be glad General Crook rounded up all the Apaches around here."

Chet nodded. "I damn sure am proud of that. I've been in a blood feud back home in Texas and lost my brother. I want to move out here to simply live and ranch in peace."

"I understand."

"What about a hearing? I'd like to get back to the ranch tomorrow."

"If I need you to testify, I'll send word. I hope things cool down for you."

"They will. They will." And Chet left Sheriff Sims.

Bo Harold caught up with him at Jenny's, where Chet had barely finished explaining the shooting business to her. He motioned for the agent to sit down as Jenny's helper delivered him a heaping plate of food.

"Say, you're some kinda hero around here, ain't he, Jenny?"

"I'd say a big one." She slowly smiled and bobbed her head in agreement, resting her butt on the counter behind her with her arms folded. "I always heard them say don't mess with Texans, they'll bite you."

"Yeah, yeah, well, I have wired Talley," Harold said. "He wants to sign the deed and brand over to you."

Chet looked hard at his man. "For twenty grand, with three hundred mother cows and a hundred horses guaranteed."

"He didn't say that."

"I'll pay him ten down and the balance in eighteen months, minus the shortage in cattle and horses."

"What about the money I heard that you found?" Harold asked.

Chet set down his fork and reached for his coffee cup. "I guess you heard about that, too. I can take the money for stock out of it and send him the balance."

"That sounds alright to me. I'll wire him and let him know you have agreed with the deal."

"But if someone impounds that money, his part about replacing the cattle and horses that are listed on the inventory comes out of the place money that I owe him."

"How short are they?"

"We found about forty horses. I have men out looking for the rest." Chet sipped on the hot coffee and nodded in approval at Jenny.

Harold shook his head, as if a little lost. "At say thirty-five to forty bucks a horse, that's from two-thousand to twenty-five hundred dollars. How many cattle are gone?"

"That looks to me like the big loss. We saw one or two small bunches after the horses, and I've even seen my first brown-faced Hereford bull."

"Huh?" Harold swallowed hard.

"The inventory you gave me called for twenty head of purebred Hereford bulls—all I saw were some longhorn bulls. I'll bet Ryan never bought one white-faced bull, but Talley paid for them."

"Damn, he was slick, wasn't he?"

Chet nodded. "He was a damn crook, and not smart."

"That's another twenty-five hundred. So we're up to five thousand or so."

Chet pointed with his fork to make a point. "I bet good young cows will cost a hundred bucks, with everyone wanting to stock these ranges now the Apaches are gone."

"If you're missing a hundred head, say, that's ten thousand." Harold shook his head. "You're driving a hard bargain."

"He'd have had nothing at all if I hadn't taken it over. Most locals were as scared of Ryan as Talley was," Chet said.

"What if he agrees to give you that money for the stock that's lost—you pay him ten thousand now and ten thousand in eighteen months for the ranch?"

"If I am as short as I think I am on cattle, I'd be a fool," Chet answered.

"But"—Harold screwed up his face—"you'd still be giving a cheap price for three sections down on the Verde, a nice home place, and some good grazing country."

"I'll consider it."

"Would you agree to that?"

Chet recalled the bank's figure on that sheet was only a hundred dollars off from their count at the ranch. He could make that all work. Whew, he'd been figured out.

"If he agrees to that, are you going on with the deal?" Harold asked.

"Tell him not to mess around. I need to get back to Texas."

"Sure. Sure. I'm going to the telegraph office

right now." Harold patted him on the shoulder and rushed out.

"Well, big man, you've kinda woke everybody in town," Jenny said.

"How's that?" he asked her, reaching for his piece of apple pie.

"Margaret Christianson."

He paused for a second with his fork suspended. "I met her on the stage. What did she want?"

"Lot's of information about you." Jenny rocked slightly with her arms folded.

"Did you tell her?"

"Didn't figure it would hurt to tell her what I knew. Besides, I was curious why she wanted to know so much about you."

"Figure it out?" He wiped his mouth on his napkin. "Good pie."

"Glad you like it. Margaret isn't my best friend unless she needs me." Jenny wrinkled her nose, "But she sure has set her hat for you."

"I ain't eligible. Unless a lady in Texas says no to Arizona. I have a woman back home."

A smile crossed her lips. "Well, I've warned you."

"Thanks. Hoot's doing fine. I'll find him a boy to help him. I'm sure the old man will make it."

"Good. I thank you for hiring him. He was too old to cowboy, but Ryan never treated him right. He was sure proud when he told me about his new job."

"He's what I needed. Total up my bills here. I imagine you need your money."

"Margaret paid them. I hope that don't make you

mad. She acted like she was doing it for you and you knew all about it."

"Well, how much was it all together? "

"Twelve-fifty for Hoot's bill, plus what you two ate here."

Chet pushed the hat on the back of his head and shook his head in wonderment as he rose off the stool. "That might be interesting to know—why she did that."

Chapter 21

Chet soon learned his livery bill was paid, too, when he rode the roan to the livery. Frey came out of his office and told him he sure had a pretty partner.

Chet stopped and frowned at him. "What partner? Tom works for me."

"I know Tom. Mrs. Christianson said you were busy out at the new ranch, and she was settling what you owed. She's sure a nice-looking woman."

Shaking his head, he dismounted. "She's fine-looking, but she isn't my partner."

Frey cocked his hat to the left, and scratched his brown thatch of hair. "She sure acted like you and her were partners."

"How much was it?"

"I'll go look."

"Thanks." Chet went to stripping out the latigoes on his girth to remove the saddle.

"Wagon and team rental plus the board for your horses came to nine-fifty."

"Thanks, I can handle that." A stable man took his horse and said he'd grain him.

Chet thanked him and waved at Frey. "I'll find out."

The livery owner nodded his head. "Then tell me."

They both laughed.

So far, he owed her twenty-three dollars. Why was Margaret Christianson doing this? The good Lord only knew. He went into the Chinese bathhouse. They soon had a tub of hot water ready for him to climb into, and the little man took all Chet's clothing with him. The room smelled of sour water and old soap, but he was getting the dirt out of his pores. Then he sat in the tub and about went to sleep, simply soaking.

"*Wince* you off?" the Chinaman asked from the doorway.

"Fine, whenever."

He came back shuffling his wooden shoes and stood on a chair to dose away the soap. "You *velly* good now."

The large towel he handed him was no flour sack, and soon he was dry. Mr. China soon brought him the Miner newspaper and lighted a lamp for him to read by. He also found a robe for him to wear.

"Clothes soon be *weady*," he said.

"Good."

The newspaper spoke of a large silver strike in the area. The interview was with a mine superintendent at the Lucky Star Mine, and he really went on about the possible silver in that mountain and how much they expected to extract.

One man was shot in the back and left to die in his backyard. The city police had no leads, but were interviewing neighbors and his close friends. Someone unknown was lynched down by Dewey. Parties unknown were blamed. The dead man was suspected of appropriating horses that he did not own in the region.

Sounded like back in Texas to him. The little man entered with his clothing all pressed and folded.

"Thanks. How much do I owe you?"

"Oh, no owe me. You are the new man on Verde ranch?"

"Yes."

"Yes. I think so. Pretty lady pay me for when you come in."

"How much was it?"

"Fifty cents. But you have three more baths coming she pay for."

"Are you serious?"

"Oh, is so. She *velly* nice lady."

The new total he owed her was twenty-five dollars. Dressed and ready to go find a barber, he thanked the man and then strapped on his gun. *Margaret, what are you doing?*

He slipped into the barber shop. The barber was lighting a lamp and turned to nod. "You must be Mr. Byrnes, I presume."

"Do I have a free haircut here?"

"Matter of fact, someone did come by and paid me for one."

"Was it a lady in her twenties or so?"

"Yes, it was."

"Did she tell you to be on the lookout for me?"

The barber, who called himself Johnny, swung the sheet of cloth over Chet and pinned it at his throat. "She said if you don't come by to keep the money."

"Generous enough, at thirty-five cents."

"You must have done her a big favor, I decided."

"No, we merely met on the Black Canyon Stage coming up here."

"Oh, my, that's funny then. Unless she's set her hat for you."

Chet slumped in the chair. "Beats me."

Johnny paused clipping with his scissors. "Maybe you should stop by and ask. She lives on a place—"

"Oh, I know where she lives. She told me."

"So what else did she pay for?"

"Everywhere I've had charges. Livery, café, I guess the hotel where my things are at."

"Does she think you're broke?"

"Close to it. I'm buying a ranch down on the Verde."

"Which one?"

"The Quarter Circle Z."

"Interesting place. You keeping Ryan as your foreman?"

"No, why?"

"He's run that place several years, just wanted to ask." He was using the hand clippers that pulled hair going up his neck.

"Lots of folks didn't like him."

"Kinda gruff. Folks said he was wanted somewhere. But there's several of them living up here."

"Really?"

"Yeah. There's even an ex-marshal from Wichita,

Kansas. Earp's his name. Raises hogs up here, says a man could make a fortune arresting them, but it was so damn hard to get them to pay them rewards on them handbills."

At last his whiskers were scraped off, and he knew all the scandals and city problems in town, when Johnny rubbed some alcohol product on his face as an aftershave. Then the man swept the sheet off and thanked him.

"Don't thank me. Thank her." He laughed, and headed for the hotel in the twilight.

"You're finally back," the room clerk said.

"Guess you saved my room?"

"Oh yes, and someone paid your bill."

"Let me guess."

"I don't know who paid it. The day man took the money."

His gritty soles ground on the stairs as he went up to his room. At last inside, he smelled something; then he lighted the lamp with a torpedo match from his vest pocket to see by. Roses filled a vase, and a note was hung on them. He picked it off and held it to the light.

> *Darling,*
>   *When you get time, stop by and see me.*
>   *Your best friend,*
>   *Margaret*

Well, so much for the suspense of who this rich woman was—she even sent him flowers. Guess it was the first time anyone ever bought him flowers. He figured there would be some at his funeral someday. Of course, he didn't expect to smell them. He went and opened the windows. A little stuffy in the room, anyway. The cool air soon came in to flutter the curtains. Undressed, he went to be bed.

Strange woman who went around paying his bills. . . .

Chapter 22

The next morning, Chet moved his and Heck's war bags to the café to take back to the ranch later on that day. Jenny greeted him where he sat on a stool among the working men wolfing down their breakfast. In her usual good-natured way, she paid attention to all "her men." Sashaying up and down behind the counter, there was a little more woman there than he wanted. Maybe she was the one Susie had recommended. "Go find some German girl over at Fredericksburg, marry her and she will be your wife, have a bunch of kids, do the gardening, and keep your clothes ready," she'd said.

"You look so nice all cleaned up," she said, putting his *unordered* breakfast before him. She looked it over. "Did I miss anything?"

"The food looks fine to me."

"Coffee is coming. I ran low. Too many big drinkers this morning." Her laughter was like a silver bell, and she told another man his order would be out next. He looked at his platter heaped with biscuits under gravy, browned German potatoes, ham and scrambled eggs.

That might actually be the man's plate who she just promised his meal was next. Maybe Chet would stay single. Pleasing a wife might be more than he could stand, except Kathren, but that might be the most impossible thing in the whole wide world. How would he ever get her to come to Arizona? Big question.

"You going back to the ranch today?" Jenny asked, pouring his coffee.

"Yes, there are several things I want to resolve up there before I go back to Texas."

"Sounded complicated yesterday." She paused for a minute. "But I don't understand that kinda business."

"Everyone simply needs to understand the deal. Buyer and seller."

She smiled coyly at him. "I'll leave that to you. Tell Heck I miss him, too."

"Oh, I will." He blew on his coffee.

"You hiring, Mr. Byrnes?" a man asked from behind him.

He put down his coffee and turned. Hardly more than a boy, he looked pretty shabbily dressed. But he did look like a prospect to help Hoot.

"What's your name?"

"Cory Winfield."

"How old are you?"

"I ain't real sure. I guess fifteen or sixteen, best I can tell."

"You have any folks?"

"Naw, they got kilt by the Injuns. So did the rest of my family."

Chet frowned in disbelief at him. "How have you been living?"

"Doing chores for folks. I quit my last job. The man went to beating me two days ago, he said for messing with his wife. I swear I never touched her."

"My cook needs a helper. Pays fifteen a month and found."

The boy's face lit up. "Sounds good to me."

"You had breakfast this morning?"

"No—sir."

"Get on a stool, Jen will feed you. Here's two dollars, go take a bath at the Chinaman's bathhouse, then go buy yourself a pair of new waist overalls, suspenders, and a long-sleeve shirt and a hat."

Chet glanced down at Cory's dirty bare feet. "A pair of shoes. Be sure they fit."

"Yes, sir." The youth looked overwhelmed. "I ain't never had no new clothes in my life."

"Time you had some. I have some things to handle today."

"Oh, I can get to your place, alright. I'll be there this evening."

"Fine. Tell Hoot that you're his new helper."

The boy was chewing on his lower lip. "I sure appreciate all this."

Chet gave him two more dollars for the rest. He nodded to his latest employee as tears ran down his freckled face. "Go get some breakfast."

With Cory gone to take a place down the counter, Jenny came by. "You take on lots of strays, don't you?"

"You know him?" he asked with guarded words.

"He'll work." She shook her head ruefully. "He's never had a real chance."

She glanced down the corner where he sat on a stool. "You might make a man out of him, otherwise he'll be nothing."

"That's how I figured it. Better go find Harold and see what's new in our dealings today."

She smiled. "Watch out for Ryan, he's a back-shooter."

"I will." He didn't doubt her warning one mite.

Thirty minutes later, Chet found his agent Bo Harold at the telegraph office. The man had several yellow sheets in his hand.

"How is it?"

"Talley agreed to the money situation covering the stock loss. I really think he's relieved this is over. I am sending him a deed and a mortgage that you must sign today. Once we get a bank to certify that he's signed the deed, then you need to have your bank transfer the money to him. Ten thousand. And I will then get my fee."

"How much is that?"

"Five hundred, and I get the same amount when you settle the second part."

"A little nerve-shaking, but it all worked out and you weren't even shot at."

"Shot at?" The man jerked to attention.

"Yes, Ryan had a sniper shoot at us."

"Yes, but you're a Texan and they don't care."

"Texans die, too. Good, now the brand deal?"

"I'm certain that we can handle that transfer at the courthouse, too."

"Why don't you go try to find who in Arizona has the —𝒞 brand for me? Then you can contact them and buy it for me. I'll have lots of horses and maybe some cattle coming under that brand. I'd like to have it registered here to my family."

"How high are you willing to go to buy it?"

"Two-fifty?"

"That should buy it. And what will you pay me?"

"Fifty bucks."

"I'll start on it tomorrow."

"Good. When do I sign the mortgage?"

"Courthouse at one PM in the clerk's office."

"I'll be there."

"Maybe we can finally close the deal." Harold looked worn out and close to collapse.

They both walked out into the bright light. Harold made certain they were alone before he asked, "You courting Margaret?"

"Not really. I have a woman at home that I hope will marry me when I go back and come out here."

"Oh."

"You tell me. I only met her coming up from Hayden's Mill on the stage. That's near Phoenix, I guess."

"The word's out that you and her are very serious."

Chet shook his head. "Who was or is this Christianson?"

"Her first husband, you mean?"

"I guess. It must be her married name. I met her father, Harold McClure, at the stage office."

"Walt Christianson was a handsome cowboy. Smooth

talker, came in here a few years ago. Folks thought he had lots of money. I showed him some places, but we were having lots of Apache trouble. He said that was why he wasn't ready to buy. That made me check on his credit in Fort Worth, where he said he hailed from. None of the banks I wrote knew him.

"There was a bank in Denton who finally answered me. Said he'd made some cattle drives to Kansas and had a respectable reputation, but he had no deposits in their bank at that time."

"What happened to him?"

"Margaret had been married to a Yankee officer who killed in some battle in Virginia during the war. His name was Fulton. So when her and her father moved here from Kansas—at the end of the war—she wore black and cried a lot. She met Christianson at some dance, and he must've swung her around. Soon they were taking buggy rides and became engaged. They had a big wedding and he became the ranch foreman.

"Two years later a horse threw him, broke his neck, and he died that evening. So once again she was a widow. She must really like you."

"How's that?"

"She sent you roses, I heard."

"And I'm still wondering why."

Harold clapped him on the shoulder. "My amigo, to my notion there must be lots of real woman under those satin dresses of hers."

"There might be. I better do some business while I have the time."

Harold shook his head warily. "If she's got her

mind set on having you, she's an awful persistent woman."

"I have one of those back in Texas right now."

"I'll see you at the courthouse at one o'clock."

Chet closed his eyes for a moment. A persistent woman, huh? No time for that. The store where they got supplies and rifles. Two blocks away. He smiled and tipped his hat to ladies on the boardwalks. Got lots of smiles back—like oh, you're the new man in Margaret's life. He made it to the mercantile unscathed.

Ab Morton owned the large store, Yavapai County Mercantile. A tall, bearded man who did look some like Abe Lincoln, but perhaps not as rawboned a face.

Chet met the man and Morton showed him into his office that looked very neat. The door closed and shut off the noisy store.

"Welcome to Preskit," Morton said. "They tell me you're buying the Quarter Circle Z. Good to have someone real out there to run a ranch."

"I'm going back to Texas soon and close out my business there, which may take some time. But I have the money to run this ranch while I close my Texas business and will pay my bills monthly, if that is satisfactory. My address is Mason, Texas."

"I've heard lots about you and all good. I'll have the account listed in your name if that is satisfactory?"

"No problem. The man I make foreman while I'm closing out in Texas will be the party to deal with here."

"You picked one?"

"Not yet, but I'll do that before I go home."

"Fine, I'll be glad to do whatever I can to help your manager."

"Thanks." They shook hands and he left, headed for the Palace. Maybe the barmaid Jane who had steered him to Harold had some information on Ryan as well.

She saw Chet come in the batwing doors and trailed him to a table. "I hear Harold found you a ranch."

He nodded. "You know anything about this foreman Ryan?"

She looked around as she stood beside him. "I heard someone trying to recruit a guy the other night for him. Ryan seldom ever comes in here. He was always secret-acting."

"Any idea where he might be now?"

"Horse Thief Basin. That's what I heard someone say."

"What did they want him to do?"

"Never said, but I know it was something illegal. Ryan's a cheap little bastard."

"I trust you, thanks." He put a ten-dollar gold piece on the table. "Keep your ears open."

"Holy shit—I don't get that much for laying on my back—never mind."

"Bring me a beer and a sliced beef sandwich."

Jane took the coin, dropped it down into her small cleavage, and rushed off. Soon he had a draft beer. Then she came back and assured him his lunch was coming on fresh hot bread. The mug of beer was cold and tasted like honey. Plenty of foam on the top. He sipped it and sat back as the lunch crowd began to file in. She brought his sandwich and she was right. The sourdough was still warm and the meat tender.

Jane came back and took his mug to refill it. Chet paid her for it all with fifty cents, which left her a dime tip. The new beer came with foam lipping over the side and she smiled big. "See you later."

"Yes, ma'am."

He sat back and watched her sashay her way back to the bar. Horse Thief Basin. Where was it at? If things settled down some more, he might ride down there and check it out. Maybe Roamer, the deputy, in the meanwhile, would figure out an excuse to arrest Ryan.

Chet crossed the street to the courthouse. Inside he found the clerk's office and told the young man at the counter he was there to meet Bo Harold. The man had not seen Harold and told him to have a seat.

Fifteen after one, Harold busted in with several papers in his hand. "Sorry, I have been hurrying."

They filed the mortgage and the clerk charged them two dollars. Chet paid—obviously Harold was short on the funds. Their business completed, they went outside into the courtyard.

"Where's Horse Thief Basin?"

"Why? What's going on down there?"

"I heard that Ryan might be hiding down there."

Harold blinked. "Don't go down there without an army. Tough place."

"I'll try to remember that."

"Oh, yes. You can get killed down there. Lots of outlaws are hiding around that place."

"What else? I want to get back to the ranch."

"Nothing more that I can do now."

"Thanks. I'm going to the ranch."

"You stopping to see her?" Harold paused for an answer.

Chet frowned and then shook his head. "No."

Harold shrugged. "But she's rich."

"I'll handle my own business, thanks."

"Oh, yeah. Sorry."

"I'll be at the ranch if you need me. I want things straightened out there." Chet parted with him and went to get the roan horse. The whole Margaret thing had gotten under his skin. It was no longer funny to him.

With the two war bags hung on his saddlehorn, he headed for the Camp Verde Road. He passed her ranch gate and kept going. And by sundown he was going off the steep road to the Verde Valley. With only starlight to guide him, he never met or passed anyone making his descent and was grateful to at last have found the bottom.

It was far past midnight when he reached the ranch. A cowboy armed with a rifle met him short of the house.

"That you, boss?" the rusty voice in the night called out.

"Yeah, Bixsby, I think. Got a late start home. You boys expecting trouble?"

"Tom ain't taking any chances. All of us that know Ryan expect him to want some revenge. You heard any word on him in town?"

"No. He's gone like smoke." Chet dismounted and found his sea legs. With him leading the roan horse toward the corral, Bixsby offered to put him up.

"I'll accept your offer," Chet said, took the war

bags down, and carried them to the house. When he found his bedroll by moonlight, he removed his boots and pants to lay down. The night's coolness made the blanket feel good. In a sea of snorting and grunting, he quickly sought sleep.

Dawn and the wakeup call came too early. He could smell breakfast clear upstairs. Then he recalled that except for some jerky from his saddlebags, he had not eaten since noon the day before.

The usual cowboy bantering went on when he went downstairs. The young man he'd hired, Cory, was fresh-faced, looking busy, helping Hoot get things out. He nodded.

"How did you get out here?" Chet asked him.

"Like I usually do. Walked, Mr. Byrnes."

Chet nodded. He did look better cleaned up and wearing fresh clothes—but still barefooted.

"You buy some shoes?"

"Yes, sir. But I ain't used to them yet."

Chet nodded. He would be, in time.

"Shoot," Hampt said. "That boy's feet are so tough, he could run over flint stones and start a fire."

Everyone laughed. Chet didn't doubt it. "Any problems?"

"Naw. Wiley found another dozen ranch horses yesterday," Tom said. "We've got another problem."

"What's that?"

"Injuns."

Chet frowned at him. "What are they doing?"

"It ain't what they're doing. They're starving." Tom made a sour face.

"Why ain't they feeding them? Isn't the government supposed to do that?"

"They had some supplies to give them the first of the month. None now. It wasn't much then."

"Is the army in charge?" Chet asked.

"No, some agent has them now. I mean, they're starving." Several of the crew agreed, obviously upset about the matter.

"You give them anything to eat?"

"Some beans yesterday."

What was Chet supposed to do? "If a couple of you boys can round up one of those big longhorn bulls this morning, drive him down there where they are and shoot him. We need those worthless studs gone, and there ain't a big market for them anywhere."

Everyone around the table brightened up and the thanks rolled in.

Chet looked over his crew. "You all are really worried about them?"

"Boss, there were little babies up there crying for food," Hampt said. "Even Injuns shouldn't starve."

"Take another full sack of beans with you, too."

"I know right where that bull is this morning," Bixsby said.

"Good enough. Don't any of you get hurt working him. Shoot him if you have to, and they can come get him."

"They'd do about anything to get to eat," Hampt said between bites.

The rest agreed.

"It was real bad yesterday over there at their camp,"

Heck said. "We were all taken back by what we saw. How was Preskit?"

"Fine. Jenny said to tell all of you hi."

Next time he was over there at Camp Verde, he'd see that agent and find out what was wrong. Maybe report him to the authorities. No way they'd keep those people from going back to war if they didn't feed them. Unless starving was the plan—surely not.

Tom divided up the hands and everyone, except Hoot and his helper, started for the horses. Recalling he had not told Heck much about the ranch purchase, Chet called him back.

"I wanted to tell you this ranch is going to be ours in a few days. Talley agreed to pay us the money we recovered for the livestock shortage."

"We're damn sure low on cattle. Ain't no three hundred momma cows that I've seen."

"Keep looking. We'll figure it out. How do you like it here?"

"Swell, these are sure enough good hands and they treat me like I'm a man."

"You deserve that. Have a good day."

"I will, Chet."

Wiley must have drawn a fresh horse 'cause the pony he was aboard was bucking and farting like a steam engine. The boys were throwing lariats under his hooves to make him buck more. Chet decided the big bay could have tossed a tick off easier than that bronc buster. The excitement sure livened up the crew.

Tom rode back from the pens. "A little excitement to make the day. Heck tell you we haven't found many cows and calves?"

"Yes. How long will it take to make a good estimate of the numbers?"

"Five or six days."

"By the way, the ranch will soon be in our name. You can tell the crew."

Tom smiled, "Guess that means job security?"

"Yes, it does. Ride easy and thanks."

"No, it's all mine." Tom saluted him and then rode off in a jog.

A man drove up in a one-horse buggy. A tall man in a suit, probably fifty years old. White mustache and all, he had to duck under the roof to get off the rig. John Chandler introduced himself.

"I'm the man who bought the alfalfa hay from Ryan. I planned to cut it next Monday."

"Did you pay him?"

"Yes. Ten bucks an acre. Did you get the money?"

"No, but you're a man of your word. He sold it to you, then you may have the first cutting."

"I don't want to get in a war with you on our first meeting," Chandler said briskly. "But I understood that when I paid him that I'd bought all the hay for this year."

"No, I'm sorry. We'll need the rest of the hay for our operation. Mr. Ryan obviously had different plans than I do."

"I suppose you want the hay equipment back."

"That what belongs to this ranch, yes, I do."

"I have it all. The two horse-drawn mowers and two twelve-foot-wide dump rakes, three wagons, and the stacker. See, Ryan hated making hay."

"Come inside. Hoot will have some coffee. You no

doubt have the machinery in good repair. You have a hay crew?"

"The machines are in good shape and I do have a crew hired."

As they entered the house, Chet called for Hoot to bring them some coffee. He showed Chandler to a chair and took one opposite him. The man sat down and looked around. "I was never inside this house in all my dealings with Ryan."

"Strange. Now what all did you and Ryan do together?"

"He didn't tell you a thing?" The man looked upset.

"No, we ran him and his bunch off. I even shot two of his men who tried to take this place back."

"My heavens."

Hoot arrived at the table with cups and a pot. "How are you, Mr. Chandler?"

"Why, Hoot, I see they retained you."

"No, sir. Chet rehired me." He poured them each some coffee and offered them sugar. "I can crack open some canned milk if you need it."

"No, thanks." Chandler went on. "I didn't realize there was such a stir going on up here. To explain my part in this. My man, Adrano, does the irrigation and takes care of those fields."

"Fine, then you buy the hay?"

"I have been paying Ryan ten dollars an acre for the alfalfa each year."

"There's timothy, too?"

"I always stack a portion of it for him to feed horses for the use of the machinery."

Chet blew on his coffee, too hot even to sip. "Ryan

hasn't been on the level with Mr. Talley. In many cases he's been pocketing the money, and we're trying to straighten things out after we ran him off the place."

"I really don't have any hay equipment of my own, since I have been using yours on the shares. It would no doubt take some time to get my own equipment and to get it out here. Could we make a deal that I'd supply the mowing and putting up the hay, and also use your equipment to do my other places where I put up hay down the valley?"

"I do think we can make such a deal. You keep it in good repair and I'll saddle some of that, if it is major. I need to get back to Texas and close out my business back there. My cowboys, I bet, have no desire to be hay hands, and you have workers. Besides, they have plenty else to do."

Chandler nodded. "That is sounding reasonable."

"I'll meet your payroll when you put up my hay."

"That's more than fair. Now, about this first cutting. I have some customers I promised hay to."

"We can split it. You take half and I'll take half."

"Now, about my man watering it?"

"These cowboys won't fight him over that work. I'll pay him to do that for me."

Chandler reached over and shook his hand. "This should be a good partnership. Thanks. When do you leave?"

"Soon, I hope, when things are straightened out here. Tom Flowers will be in charge."

"I know him. You made a good choice."

They shook hands and the hay deal was made.

* * *

A couple of hours later, Heck and Hampt rode in together, smiling. Heck bailed off his horse when Chet came out to greet them.

"We fixed them starving Injuns. Gave them the sack of beans you sent. Boy, they were really starved. Then we went and drove them in a big fat longhorn bull. Hampt shot it and they butchered it in no time at all."

Hampt leaned forward in the saddle. "We also found about thirty cows and calves, plus several un-branded mavericks up there in what we called the High Meadows."

"You boys had a good day."

Heck shook his head like he was still impressed. "Them Injuns really were starving. I'm glad you're feeding them."

"Thanks. You boys won't have to put up hay this year. Mr. Chandler is to be our partner in that business."

Hampt looked gratefully up at his hat brim and went, "Whew. Thanks."

All three laughed. Maybe this Arizona ranching was going to work out for him. Still, he couldn't get over worrying about what Kathren was doing back in Texas. He hoped she was fine—but his guts roiled over his concern.

Chapter 23

Early Saturday morning, Chet took a bath under the sheepherder's shower and then got some hot water and shaved. Next he went back to the house and had breakfast with his crew. They were busy talking when he walked into the dining hall and gave him some greetings.

"You going to the dance at the schoolhouse tonight, Chet?" Wiley asked.

"Hadn't planned on it. Many of you boys going?"

"We kinda hoped to wind up everything here by noon, then head that way," Tom said. "'Cept me. I planned to run in and check on the family. Be back Sunday evening 'less you want me to change my plans?"

Chet agreed. "Sounds fine to me. I could stake you all to a few dollars apiece if you're broke."

A couple of faces nodded.

"Now, who's in charge here at the ranch?"

"Me and the two boys can watch the place," Hoot said. "I don't expect no troubles."

"Well, I'll be here. That's fine. Have a good time."

With those words, everyone went back to a normal conversation. The flapjacks were mouthwatering, and Chet liked Hoot's own sugar syrup.

"Now we've got that all straight," Hampt said, "what're you going to be doing?"

"Working on my books, I guess."

"You should come in and join the celebration."

Chet looked over the crew and they all agreed. "I will—one day. Right now I need to figure this operation out on paper. Thanks for asking me."

After the noon meal, the crew cut out. Chet was busy in the room he set up as his office. The long table was made of planed lumber on sawhorses. Everything was in neat piles of papers with smooth river rocks holding each stack down. From the open windows with the red curtains flowing from the strong winds, he could look down the lane that led from the road.

Chet heard the rumble of a light wagon and team coming, and looked up from listing his figures about the cattle count from the small pieces of paper turned in by each crew. Who was it? Then he saw the wide hat the woman wore driving it—Margaret Christianson in a deep red velvet dress. What did she want?

He put down the pen he'd been recording with and rose. Hoot stood in the doorway with his frosty-looking beard stubble. "Hey, we've got real company."

With a nod, he went by his cook and smiled. "What did we do to deserve this?"

"Damned if I know."

The same thing that he knew about her arrival— why? When Chet came out of the house, she'd reined up her smart team. She tied them off and climbed down, looking excited. "Why, Chet, I hardly expected to find you at the house."

"Doing book work. How are you, Margaret?"

"Oh, fine. This is some dwelling for a ranch house. I'd never been here before. Have you purchased it?" With the hat brim held up by her right hand so she could better examine the front of the house, she nodded in approval.

"Yes."

"Then we are neighbors." She held up her dress and advanced into the yard where he stood.

"We live in the same county, anyway."

"Oh, my. There are some big rumors about your bravery in Preskit."

"I had no idea. Heck and I held some attackers off."

"Modest. Oh, I expected that from you."

"Come inside. I am sure we have some coffee."

"Very kind of you. Thanks."

Her lilac perfume filled his nose when he let her pass him. Not irritating, but powerful. He wasn't used to women who wore more than a hint. But he wasn't her keeper, and he had no ambition to make that even a probability.

Chet showed Margaret to the table, then spoke to Hoot in the kitchen doorway. "Mrs. Christianson would like some coffee."

"Do you use cream?" he asked her.

"If you have some." She paused to smile at Hoot.

Chet held her chair, and she swept her dress under and sat down with a soft thank you.

"Canned only."

"That would be fine."

"Where is your nephew?" She looked around for sight of him.

"He and the new cook's helper have gone fishing in the river."

"What does he think of the territory?"

"If I was twelve and the rest of the hands thought I was eighteen, I'd think I was in heaven. He likes it here."

She laughed, sounding more at ease. "How funny."

"If you aren't lost, Margaret, you must have a purpose coming here." What did she really want?

"There is a dance in Camp Verde tonight. In the past, I have attended it. I thought perhaps I might invite you and introduce you to your close-by neighbors."

"Many of my hands have already gone there. I had not considered going there tonight."

Hoot brought the two cups of coffee, a can of milk, and a sugar bowl with a spoon to the table on a tray. "This is fresh," he said, setting down the punctured can, then handing out the rest.

"Oh, thank you so much," she said. "So Chet, what do you think about joining me?"

"I'll consider it."

"Good." She acted relieved and reached over to squeeze his forearm. "I guess I am rather bold, coming here and asking you, but I feel we have something in common."

He leaned back in his chair to study her and tented his fingers. "First, I have a list of items you paid for me."

"So I'm trying too hard to make a friendship. Can you forgive me?"

"After I repay you."

She made a face like a child having been caught doing something prohibited. Her shoulders raised under the dress that hugged her figure and made a window to see her cleavage, and then she dropped them down in surrender. "Whatever will make you happy."

"I can pay my own way. I thank you for your concern, but I wonder what people think. 'He doesn't have money to pay his debts and is leaning on her to stay here.'"

She chewed on her lower lip. "I never thought of that."

He decided that she'd agree to anything that coaxed him into going to the dance. What was the use? Unable to find himself enough gall to throw her out, he slumped in the chair. "I'll need to iron some clean clothes."

"I can iron." He knew he'd rewound her spirit.

"We need to find an iron," he said, and tasted his coffee. "There are lots of things here we have found. In fact, when they tried to attack the house, Heck and I found firearms to turn the tide."

"What were they after?"

"The money in the safe I recovered from his wife after I threw them out."

"Sizeable?"

"Over ten thousand dollars."

Her hand went to her mouth and she frowned at him. "Oh my. Was it theirs?"

"If it had been, they could have hired a lawyer. I think it is proceeds from Ryan's sale of ranch assets."

"Can you prove it?"

"I have several witnesses who talk about Ryan's secret sale of stock."

"My, Chet, you have had troubles here."

He nodded to reassure her. "We're getting things back to normal again. I better go look for an iron. Hoot," he called out. "Do we have some clothes irons?"

"I saw some in the pantry," Hoot said, coming to the door.

"Heat them. I'll go get my best shirt and pants out of my war bag. Excuse me."

"Of course," she said, looking relaxed for the first time since he'd met her on the stagecoach. "I can iron. I'm quite domestic."

"Between us, I guess we can do it." He left the room to find his best clothing. She still mystified him. If she thought she was such a seductive person to capture his heart, she might be overshooting her charm—she was way too society-struck to appeal to him.

When he returned with his clothing, she had removed her hat and found an apron to wear over her dress. There was a blanket on the kitchen table, a bowl of water to sprinkle on the items to be ironed. She did his white shirt first, and he stood by. Her hard-pressed efforts to take out the wrinkles were successful.

Alternating irons and placing the cooler one on the stovetop to reheat it, she pushed back the wave of hair from her face and attacked his britches. He could see lots of things about her as she fought the wrinkles— she worked with what he saw as a deep-set determination either to impress him, or such actions were a usual part of her nature.

The weather had warmed, but the open house swept by the wind wasn't that hot. When she finished, he thanked her, and Hoot asked if they were staying for supper.

"No, there will be plenty of food at the affair," she assured him.

"So it's set," Chet said. "I'll go saddle a horse to tie on behind your buggy so I can come back afterwards."

"Oh, I can bring you back."

"Then I suppose I should offer you a place to sleep."

"Not necessarily. But I would accept the invitation."

"You are invited. Hoot, have the boys sweep out the first room at the head of the stairs for our guest tonight when they get back."

"I can do that. Nice to meet you, ma'am."

"Oh, yes." She agreed.

"I'm going to water your horses," Chet told her. "Then I'll change to my clothes and be ready to go into town."

"Thanks for thinking of them. While you do that I shall freshen myself some."

"You can use that room I mentioned. Wait." He dug in his pockets, counting out the money he owed her. "Now I think we're even."

She hesitated for a few seconds, then she swallowed hard and gathered the money. "If I caused you any—"

"That's over and done for my part."

"Thanks." She hoisted her dress hem and took on the stairs.

Chet went outside to water the team. With the reins

in his hand on the seat, he found them well broke, drove them up to the large tank and let them drink. Much easier than unhitching them, and when they had their fill he returned them to the shade. So far, he had obligated himself to go with her to the dance. Obviously she had shoehorned her way into his life. A place where he felt uncomfortable, but he'd try to show her a good time. Maybe she had only good intentions. He hoped so.

They reached the schoolhouse near sundown, about the time for things to start. Plenty of activity going on. Several outfits had set up large tents much like they did in Texas to stay overnight. Others served meals under the shade. Margaret directed him to a setup and Chet recognized her father's brand when he reined up.

A young Mexican boy beamed at him, ready to take the team. "Good evening, Señor Byrnes. My name is Leon."

"How are you, Leon?"

"Very fine, sir."

Chet gave the youth the reins and went around to help her down. "So you have tricked me," he said under his breath, as he guided her around the buggy.

"No. This is my father's camp," she said under her breath.

"How did that boy know my name, then?"

"My father must have told him. Don't you believe me?" She looked ready to cry.

"Alright, but you better be more honest with me."

"I will be. My father is coming."

He nodded, still hot under the collar over his discovery.

"Well, good to see you, Byrnes." The distinguished-looking gray-haired man said, approaching them. "We have the food ready. Will you two join us?"

"Of course," he said, as if he had expected such an arrangement.

She held him back a few steps. "If I had planned this, wouldn't I have hurried you along to get here?"

"At this moment, I'm not sure of anything."

"Good." She squeezed his arm. "I did not plan this."

"Accept my apology."

"Accepted," she said and laughed, guiding him to a table and a two-person bench.

Margaret soon introduced him to several people at the table, obviously the more powerful ranchers in the region. Alan Gates, a man in his fifties, with his much younger wife, Madrid, who owned the CXT ranch; Thomas Hanager, who ranched at a place called Holdenville; the woman with him was his daughter, Cayleen, a girl in her teens. Floyd Kent in his early forties, with wife Kay and their three teenage children.

"Chet Byrnes is buying the Quarter Circle Z. He's bringing his family from Texas here to live on the ranch."

Chet nodded, said he was glad to meet them, and held the chair for her. Obviously, these were all powerful men on the scene. Maybe he could find a purebred breeder among them to supply him some working-age bulls to replace Ryan's longhorns. Seated beside Kent's wife Kay, who passed him a platter of steaks.

"These are from Hereford," Kay, a short blonde, said under her breath with a sound of pride.

"Good. Do you raise them?" he asked, selecting a T-bone cut.

"No. We usually order our bulls out of Kansas. Do you need some bulls?"

Chet nodded and passed the platter on to Margaret. She chose a small fillet and passed it on. The mashed potatoes were steeped in melted butter; he spooned some off onto his plate. Then fresh green beans came by next. A girl brought a selection of bread by and another waiter poured coffee.

He found the dark whole-grain bread delicious, and buttered a second slice halfway through his mesquite-smoked steak. Susie would love this—not that she was a snob, but the fancy ways they served it would impress her.

"Are you enjoying the food?" Margaret asked quietly from beside him.

"I will be eternally grateful for you inviting me here. Very good food."

"Did you want some wine?" She looked concerned, as if they'd left him out of the serving going on.

"No. I want to be alert. I have no idea who might be one of Ryan's men."

"You are serious, aren't you?"

"Yes. He's not an ordinary cowboy, and he doesn't think like one. I'm not afraid of him, but he might spring out any minute and try something."

"I think you are a tough adversary. Sorry the situation will dampen you from having a good time here."

"I'll try to not let it bother me and in turn ruin your evening."

"Well, that sounds perfect. I can hear the music has started." Her long hand reached over and squeezed his.

The fiddles sawed and he waltzed with her around the smooth floor, slick with soap shavings. They managed to find a seat after the third dance and Kent's wife, Kay, asked him for a dance. Obviously, her husband was busy talking to others.

"Does Kent dance?"

"No. I have to beg his friends," she said cheerfully, as he swung her slender girl-like figure around the floor.

"Well, you dance very well. Why doesn't he dance?"

"He says he has two left feet and refuses to try to learn."

"He's missing some good times."

She nodded. "That's not all."

"Oh," he said, not interested in hearing of any more of her husband's shortages in social skills.

He felt her exhale with his hand in the center of her back. "I'll bite my tongue. You're not married?"

"No, ma'am. Never have been. Too busy running a large ranch."

"I see."

"A couple women have been in my life. One was ruthlessly murdered. Another at home is very close to me, but we have many obstacles."

"I'm sure you'll find a woman. You have danced a lot with many partners. You are a very easy man to dance with."

Chet took her back to the bench and Margaret was on her feet to claim him. They swept off to a polka, whirling around in great circles. At the end, they were out of breath, and she guided him to the open doors for a breath of the cooling evening air outdoors.

"Did Kay tell you about her problems?" she asked, backed against the wall of the building and holding his hands.

"She said he wouldn't learn how to dance."

"That is not all."

"Oh."

She looked around to be certain she would not be overheard. "He won't even sleep with her."

"Oh."

She nodded. "I think it is killing her. She's hardly past thirty."

"What caused that?"

"No one knows."

"Ah, the problems of the world are all on our shoulders."

"Good thing you have strong ones."

"I tell you, since I was in my teens I have had to run a ranch. My father and mother both went near crazy over the kidnapping of two of my brothers and a sister. So I never had a chance to sow many wild oats, look for a new land for myself. I have always been in charge. I wouldn't be here tonight if a family hadn't started a feud with my family. It cost my other brother his life, and others as well."

Margaret nodded and pulled Chet close enough to quickly kiss his cheek. "Thanks for the dancing. I have not felt so free in a long time."

"Hey, as good as you dance, no problem."

"I want to polka again with you before the night is over."

He noticed the broad shoulders of Hampt standing off in the night, away from the crowd as if waiting for a split second to tell him something. "Excuse me, one of my men has something for me."

"Certainly."

Leaving her, Chet walked over to his man. "What's happening?"

"They say Ryan has been here tonight. Sarge, Wiley, and Bixsby are checking around to see if they can learn anything about where he is."

"Thanks. Don't any of you tangle with him without me. I can leave on the drop of a hat and join you."

"I'll tell them. You know, there ain't no love lost between the three of us and him."

"You do anything, you come get me."

"Yes, sir." And the big man was gone. Chet watched him fade in the dim light from the big blaze illuminating the school yard.

"Is everything alright?" Marge asked.

"Alright enough. Let's go dance."

"I can see you are upset. Don't you trust me enough to tell me?"

"It isn't your war. Hampt thinks Ryan is around here somewhere. He's gotten some competent word on it."

"And?"

"I told him to get me before they plan to do anything."

"Boy, who do I thank for all this?"

He hugged her shoulder, feeling guilty that he was spoiling her event. "Let's just go inside and dance, and forget this mess out here."

"Amen. I'm willing."

Before Chet went back in, he looked over the orange-lighted men and woman standing outside. Nothing he knew about showed up. Maybe it would all blow over— but somehow he doubted it.

Chapter 24

After the dance broke up, Chet and Margaret stood holding hands. He felt like a bashful sixteen-year-old boy, standing facing her, gripping her long fingers in his own calloused ones. The campfire's red glow shone on her face and her eyes danced with excitement.

"Thanks for the evening," he said. "It sure beat reading the Police Gazette for the fifth time."

"Maybe we can do it again—sometime. I know you're trying to get things settled so you can go back to Texas."

"I have to do that. My family isn't safe back there."

"I hadn't polkaed in such a long time, I thought I had forgotten how. Whew, I am still dizzy. But don't you dare feel sorry for me. That was great. Dad has a place here for me to sleep tonight. I'll either come after the team or send a worker. It won't stain your reputation like me sleeping at your house might."

"My rep ain't that good. Why don't I drive them by the ranch Monday morning when I go in to Preskit? I can tie a horse on behind."

"Do you like fried chicken?"

"Sure. Why?"

"Come by the house about noontime and I'll have some Southern fried chicken ready for you to eat."

"Sounds great. Do they always call you Margaret?"

She cocked her head to the side. "You can shorten it to whatever you like."

"Is Marge alright?"

She leaned over and kissed him on the mouth. "Wonderful. I loved the entire evening. Thanks for accepting my invitation."

Chet let go of her fingers. "My pleasure. Now I need to go get the team."

"My fault. I talked you out of bringing your horse."

"No problem. I see some of my hands are ready to ride home with me. So I won't be lonely after all."

"Lonely? Why, Chet Byrnes, I bet you haven't been lonely for a day in your life." Then she laughed until she looked embarrassed, and then patted his arm. "Sorry, it simply sounded too funny."

"No problem." He could see the young stable hand had the horses hitched and ready. Hampt rode up about then, and dismounted.

"Take my horse," he said. "I'll drive that rig."

Chet frowned, but he knew the big man had a purpose—only he wasn't certain what it might be. Margaret hugged him, and on her toes, kissed him softly in front of his ear. "It turned out wonderful."

"I'll be there Monday to eat chicken," he promised her.

Margaret waved, and he fell in with the crew

member. When they were a good distance away, Chet turned to Wiley. "What's the deal?"

The cowboy twisted in the saddle as if to make sure no one was close. "We think Ryan is going to try and stop you tonight."

"You hear anything to make you suspicious?" Chet frowned in the starlight at the three of them.

"Roamer warned us earlier. He was trying to arrest him, but never connected. Ryan had bragged somewhere that he'd have that ranch back in a few days. And Roamer figured the only way that could come true was for him to kill you. He said that tonight might be his best chance since it was common knowledge that you drove her over here in that fancy surrey."

"Why's Hampt driving it instead of me?"

"His head's clearer than yours. You kinda took a shine to her and we didn't want you distracted. Me and the boys think if you can't convince that gal to come from Texas, well, Margaret might not be such a bad deal."

"Hmm," Chet snuffed out his nose. "I sure have a different impression of her now from the one I had riding on the stage with her."

"You need anyone to go along with you to Preskit Monday?' Bixsby asked in his hoarse voice. "We figured the fried chicken she offered you will be some of the best in the land. It'll damn sure be better than any you've had lately."

Chet held his hand up to stop them. In the half moonlight, all he could make out was a man's outline ahead of them. His right hand sought the butt of his gun.

"Boys, don't shoot," Roamer said aloud.

"It's Roamer," Wiley said, checking his horse.

"What're you doing out here?" Chet asked the deputy.

"Trying to keep a rancher friend alive."

"I appreciate that, mi amigo. You have any trouble up here?"

"Naw, but when Ryan's bunch figured I was watching them, they lit a shuck."

"Come on to the ranch. Hoot will have some food ready, and we can find you space to sleep."

"Might as well. I won't make it back to town tonight. Thanks," Roamer told him.

"No problem. I have to go in to Preskit Monday morning and check on a few things myself."

"Good, I'll go back with you then. Beats riding alone."

They rode home with the crew teasing Bixsby about some plump widow woman he'd taken a shine to. Chet guessed that he must have danced some with her and then they disappeared for some time, which brought on much suspicion about what they might have done out of sight. Bixsby was shedding their words like a duck did water on the subject of his involvement with Mrs. Kelly O'Brian, and simply rode along.

"She'd sure keep you warm snuggled up to her in the winter," one of the men said, and they all laughed at the man's expense.

"Why, she'd be like having a big furnace all to yourself," someone else promised him.

No matter how hard they tried, Bixsby never gave them one word of satisfaction to settle their questions or his guilt. Chet mused about how the cowboy had simply Indianed up on the matter.

At the ranch, Hoot had a big kettle of hot beef stew on the stove and welcomed them all back. Heck and the new boy, Cory, got up and joined them. The crew was waving spoons around eating stew, still intent on Bixsby's romance, and also told the stay-at-homes about the threat of Ryan's that had never emerged.

"What are you going to have to do about him?" Hoot asked. "Ryan, I mean. I know you can't break up this romance with Bixsby." His words drew a knee-slapping laugh from the rest.

Chet simply shook his head. "Can't do much about either one."

The funning crew finally dragged themselves off to their cots and found Roamer one, too. On his back on the bed Chet'd chosen for himself, he stared at the dark ceiling for a long while. What could he do about Ryan? How was everyone in Texas doing? Could he ever bring Kathren out here? His chances looked slimmer and slimmer. Not that he didn't want her, but he worried about all the problems she'd have over leaving the hill country. Damn.

Chapter 25

Sipping coffee, Chet talked to the kitchen crew, Hoot and Cory, as they worked around getting breakfast ready before sunup. He went outside the back door with his cup and studied the stars. Cool air swept his face. So far, the crew's estimate was about a hundred fifty mother cows with maybe ninety calves on them. Either they'd had lots of wolves, cats, and grizzly predator losses, or theft. His cowhands had not developed any theory that explained it. He decided he needed to really take a look at those things when he settled more of his town business.

The horses they found later were mostly crow bait, and Chet told them to take the starving Indians the ones suitable to eat. Like the horse bitten some time before by a snake, with a front ankle that was twice normal size, and nothing reduced it. In good flesh, they led him off to the camp along with other animals that bore problems too big to ever be usable again.

The number of good ones was down to forty-eight sound-enough horses. Chet would need to find at

least thirty more head for the coming roundup—the
men felt they had all the ranch horses they could find
on the range. More headaches to keep him in Arizona. This morning, he was going back to Preskit and
eat fried chicken with Marge—he'd promised her.
Oh, well, it would work out.

Chet and Roamer left out, sharing the buggy seat
on Marge's fine rig and leading their saddlehorses
behind. Since they had the buggy with a lid, it would
be easier to talk together.

"Your wife ever have that baby?" Chet asked.

"A big boy. We named him Ralston. She's doing
fine now. Her younger sister came over to help her
while I'm out chasing outlaws."

"How many kids you have?"

"Four."

"That's a nice-size family."

"My wife don't think so. She wants a dozen."
Roamer laughed.

"My lands, Roamer, why so many?"

"She comes from a big family." He put his dusty
boots on the dashboard. "Says she wants lots of company."

"Good luck."

"I'll need it. Do you have a big place in Texas?"

"Not by Texas standards, but it's a good one. Live
oak and cedar, like your juniper on the small hills,
and clear water in the creeks. Usually have lots of
water, springs, shallow wells. It's a great country. I
hate to leave it. But in the case of a feud, you have to
jerk up roots and move on."

Chet flicked the team into a faster trot. Good horses, no telling what they cost. He could almost taste the fried chicken, cooking miles ahead.

"The Texas law couldn't stop them?"

"No. He's tried. They came from all sides of their kinfolks. Before I left, three of them cut me off out riding the range. Me all cold and hunkered over in the saddle. Lucky I busted my horse into a cedar thicket and we had a shootout on the south end of my land. I rode home alone in the end."

"Whew, even sounds tough to me."

"They ambushed my brother a year ago, way up on the Indian Territory with a herd of steers headed for Abilene. Heck hurried back and got me. He rode two horses to near death coming for me. Maybe rode five hundred or more miles."

"Damn, I believe I'll stay here."

"Good idea. I aim to." He could look up and see the mountain's face and some buzzards on the updraft.

"I figured I'd have Ryan run down by now. He can't hide for long."

They let the horses breathe and had a beer apiece in the same small saloon before they climbed the mountain. Roamer asked about Ryan being around there and the man shook his head. No answer there. Chet paid the twenty-cent bill, and they climbed back on the seat and drove up the steep road.

Near noon by the sun, they came down the lane to Marge's father's place. It was a neat enough outfit. The rambling one-story was made of logs and rocks. Impressive enough place. The Mexican boy Chet saw at the dance came out and took the horses. Calling him Mr. Byrnes politely, he drove them to the corral and promised to water their mounts as well.

Bareheaded, Marge came from the house in a blue dress with lots of ruffles, smiling big as all get-out. She nodded to Roamer and hooked her arm in Chet's. "Nice to have you two here. Lunch is about ready. Me and Malinda have been slaving over the meal all morning. Dad had to go to Dewey on business, so he's missing the best part. Eating hot fried chicken.

"I heard you have new baby boy, Roamer?" she asked.

"We named him Ralston, and him and her are doing fine."

"Congratulations."

"Thanks, ma'am."

They washed their hands and faces on the shady porch; then after Chet took a good look at the wide rolling valley, he nodded. "Nice place."

He took the towel from her and dried off. "You been alright?"

"Certainly. Are you hungry?"

"Near starved to death."

Marge poked him. "We'll see."

The great table was set for three. The woman she called Malinda had brown skin, with black-as-coal hair in a bun. Her droopy eyelids looked sleepy, but her dark pupils danced when she smiled. He guessed her past twenty and tall for a Hispanic, with a ripe body. She welcomed him, and then took both of their hats from them. "We are so glad to have you here."

"Our pleasure," Chet said, and put the chair under Marge at the table. "We're sure anxious to enjoy your ladies' chicken."

Malinda began serving the bowls of food on the table, and the aroma of the freshly-fried bird parts filled his nose and tickled the taste buds on his tongue. Mashed potatoes and flour gravy, new peas, and sourdough bread a bear could have smelled from a mile away. There was little talking by the men until Chet realized Malinda had joined them with her own plate at Marge's invitation.

"Whose recipe?" he asked, chewing on a drumstick.

"We both cooked it. We do lots of cooking as a team. I help her when I'm home."

"And señor, I miss her when she is gone. She really does help me."

"Your father have many hands to feed?"

Marge wiped her fingers on a cloth napkin, then she looked up. "We usually have half a dozen besides dad at every meal. They carried their lunch today. They're catching some colts."

Chet didn't feel as comfortable being with her as he had at the dance. Something wasn't as smooth, but what did he expect? They hardly knew each other. One night at a dance was nothing, but the notion bothered him. Maybe he'd read too much into their relationship. Still, things were not right, and he had no answer for his feelings.

The women served them each a big wedge of sweet cinnamon-flavored apple pie from dried apples grown on the ranch. After they finished, Chet wiped his mouth on the napkin and thanked her.

"I guess you are here on business today?"

"I'm sure Roamer is, and I have lots to do in town. So thanks for the great food, and it was delightful chicken."

Roamer agreed.

Marge showed him to the doorway and let the deputy go ahead. "I'll get the horses," Roamer said over his shoulder.

"Fine," Chet said after him.

"Did today disappoint you?" she asked with her arm linked in his, standing beside him.

"I guess I have lots on my mind. Ryan, closing the deal, and what's happening in Texas with me gone."

She nodded. "Will you be at Camp Verde schoolhouse next Saturday night?"

"I'll do my level best to be there."

"Good. Come and bring your crew in for supper with us." She stood on her toes and pecked him on the cheek. "I'll see you then."

"Thanks, Marge."

"You take care. Remember that Ryan is a killer."

"I will." And he hurried to his horse that Roamer brought in. Chet waved and mounted, then they left in a long trot.

When they reached the end of the lane, Roamer looked over at him. "Something wrong?"

"No. Guess I wasn't feeling real friendly today."

The deputy nodded like he knew enough, and they rode on in silence for a long ways. Crossing over the pass at the end of the valley deep in the pines, Chet looked back and tried to put everything about her into a new perspective. What wall had came between them?

Once in town, after shaking Roamer's hand and parting with his companion, who was headed for the sheriff's office to give his boss a report, Chet went on to the post office to mail Heck's letter to Susie. He'd added a few lines about his ranch purchase and the lovely Verde River that flowed by the place.

A letter from Susie awaited him as well. Everything sounded alright, so he hoped nothing was wrong that they were keeping from him. Reports from the Johnson brothers taking their cattle north were all, so far, good. *J.D. was stiff from the gray horse throwing him. But everyone said he made a good ride. Gray was turned out until you come back.* He laughed, folded up the letter and put it in his vest pocket, then mailed Heck's letter with the clerk.

"You enjoying Arizona so far, sir?" the stoic clerk asked.

"Yes sir. It's a fine place."

"Too close to hell for me."

"Where are you from?"

"New York."

"Hey, what's wrong with Arizona?"

"Those drunk Indians lying all over. They say they are the harmless ones."

"They probably are."

"Why doesn't the government dress them different so you can tell them apart, the harmless from the harmful ones? Then you would know for sure which ones to avoid."

"I don't know a thing about that. Thanks." He left the post office before he started laughing and was two blocks away, still chuckling about a dress code for Indians when he went inside Jenny's Café.

"What's so funny, big man?" she asked.

"Oh, Lord. The postman wants the government to dress the mean Indians different from the harmless ones so he can avoid the bad who are passed out in the street."

Jenny laughed, and two cowboys on the stools eating joined in. They passed it on to the cook who came out wiping his hands on his apron to learn the humor going on. He shook his head in disbelief. "That's a dude for you. Always got some damn answer to everything."

"What can I get you?" Jenny asked.

"Kinda early for supper, but bring me a plate."

"I've got it." She put a steamy cup of coffee in front of him and some silverware. "How are things going on the ranch deal?"

"Fine, I guess. I need to find Bo Harold and talk to him."

"He's at the Palace Bar."

"You talked to him today?"

"He had breakfast here and said he was flush with money from some land deal and was going to play poker there today. So if his money is still holding out, that's where he should be. He even paid his long over-due bill here, so I know he has money."

* * *

There were times Chet really enjoyed the big woman's friendly company. She was open and had a free way about her. He simply felt easy being around her. Maybe that was why he headed there at four o'clock in the afternoon—looking for some relief.

She was back in a short while with his plate of food and some sourdough biscuits. The butter melted on the opened ones and his mouth flowed with saliva. When the two cowboys left, she came and stood with her back to the screened pie safe, her arms folded. "How is the boy doing?"

"Good. He's riding with a hand every day and having fun. He even laughs a lot."

"I guess he misses his dad?"

"I'm not certain. He never talks about him. But Dale Allen turned his back on his family when his first wife died. He and Heck only renewed knowing each other a few weeks before they left for Kansas." He put down his fork. "I guess that's why I brought him along out here. Him and his stepmother were having a row. Reg, my other nephew, was in charge while I was recovering from a beating I got from some hired thugs. Part of the feud deal. Anyway, he moved Heck to the bunkhouse, and we thought he was doing better there."

"He's nice and polite."

"Supposed to be. Jenny, I wonder though how much he's scarred inside. Standing by his father when he was shot down."

"Bound to be some."

"I don't probe into his mind. But I'd really like to know how he feels."

"Maybe one day he'll open up when the right time comes."

"You have any kids?"

"A daughter."

"What's she do?" In an instant, her blue eyes flooded with tears and he knew he'd opened up a nest of hornets.

"I'll tell you sometime—" Then she ran off to the back, crying.

He put down his fork and went back to the kitchen. He found her sobbing with her face to the wall where the calendar hung. The cook turned up his hands at him—he didn't know anything to do.

Without a second thought, he put his arm on her shoulder. "I'm sorry. I didn't mean to jab you about something that upsetting."

"It's not your fault." Jenny shook her head and turned her wet face toward him. "Birdy is working in a brothel in Tombstone, last I heard from her. She wouldn't listen to me."

Chet hugged her and she sobbed on his shoulder. Holding her, he wondered what he could do to help her—probably nothing but comfort her.

At last she straightened and took a towel the cook gave her to mop her face. Her blue eyes twinkling, she shook her head. "I didn't mean to burden you with my baggage. Sorry."

He nodded, then re-hugged her. "I guess we all have our private wars to fight."

She shook her head as she began to relax. "Why in God's name don't you have a wife?"

"What brought that on?"

"You're too nice a guy to simply be by yourself."

"Aw, come on."

"I'll join you in a minute."

"Good." He knew she wanted to reconnect with herself, so he went back and picked at his food, tasted the cooling coffee, and considered the imperfect world he lived in. Things should be easier, buying a ranch, solving the barriers that held Kathren in Texas, and maybe reaching into his nephew's mind to somehow help him.

She soon came back, fresh-faced, and refilled his cup. "Ready for pie?"

"I guess. Sure, what's new?"

"Rhubarb."

"What's that?"

"A tart-tasting dude."

"I'd like to try some."

"There's plenty of sugar in it," she assured him and put the piece before him.

He nodded and cut a bit off with his fork. "Tastes grand."

"Figured you'd like it if you ever tried it."

The sharpness of the slick fruit brought out the flavor, and he decided he would plant some whenever he moved there. "Hard to raise?"

"No, it comes up every year. Has big leaves and you only use the stems."

He'd put that idea away for a while. Finished, he paid her and then leaned over to kiss her on the cheek.

With her fingers covering the spot, she looked wide-eyed in disbelief at him.

"Just a thanks for being yourself." He winked and was on his way out.

"Chet Byrnes—you're a real rascal."

"Everyone needs one," he said over his shoulder, and headed for the Palace. His mood was upbeat and he felt alright—if Harold had some good news on the deal going through, he'd even be better.

Chapter 26

With his hat cocked on the back of his head, the land agent smoked a huge cigar and waved his hand around like a fan. Before him, a large pile of money indicated his success with the paste cards.

"Hey, Chet, do you play poker?"

"Sometimes." He'd stopped behind the backs of other players and nodded.

"Get in this game then."

"No, I'll have a beer. Do we have any problems?"

"No. Our business's going alright. Okay—" He turned his attention back to the game. "I'll raise you ten dollars."

"Why, you no good sumbitch—" A short man bolted out of his chair, drawing his gun. "You've cheated on me for the last time."

Without even thinking, Chet grabbed an empty captain's chair, and in one swing raised it over the man's head and crashed it down before he could shoot Harold. Instead, the bullet went through the table and the shooter's knees crumbled into the darkness. The percussion of the shot put out the lights, and the gunsmoke-filled barroom was dark save for what light came in the front doors.

Men scrambled around on the floor. Money must have been scattered from the upset table, and the bartender ran about trying to relight his lamps. Chet had the would-be shooter by the collar and dragged him to the lighted door. The man had lost his hat, and was bleeding from a cut on his forehead and moaning aloud.

Someone of authority was coming on the run from the courthouse. Out of breath, the man, armed with a shotgun, drew up before the two of them. "Who's shot?"

"The table," Chet said. "This man tried to shoot Bo Harold."

"What happened to him?" The lawman indicated the man on the ground.

"I broke a chair over his head before he could shoot Harold."

The deputy tried to see past him. "What else is going on?"

"They are trying to fix the lights and pick up all the money that spilled on the floor."

"Holy shit. Any more in there want to shoot someone?"

"I don't think so. But take this man here." Chet pulled him to his feet. "And stick him in jail."

Sheriff Sims was there by then. "What's going on?"

Chet shook his head, shoving his man at the deputy. "They were playing cards. This man jumped up, drew a gun. Before he shot anyone I busted a chair over his head."

"Quick thinking."

"Take him to the jail and have Doc come look at his head. What's your name?" the sheriff asked the would-be-shooter.

"Buff Yearns."

"Well, Buff Yearns, you are about to learn all about our justice system. It does not take kindly to gun-shooting incidents."

"That Bo Harold guy was cheating!"

The sheriff frowned him down. "I doubt that. But we'll see. Thanks again, Byrnes."

"Damn, oh damn, you saved my life," the out-of-breath Harold gasped, staggering out the batwing doors into the bright sunlight and blinking. "He was ready to shoot me."

"Find all your money?" Chet asked.

"Most of it. That man is crazy, sheriff."

"He's going to jail, Bo. Take it easy. I may need all the card players as witnesses at his trial."

"I'll damn sure be there."

"I'll get a list of them." the lawman said, and left them alone on the boardwalk.

"Damn, Chet, I'm still shaking inside and out."

"Let's go back in there and have a beer."

"Sure, but I'm having whiskey—beer ain't strong enough."

Jane waited on them at the table and fussed some on Harold. "You better choose your card players more careful from now on," she warned him.

"Yeah, yeah," He reached out and swept her against his chair. "I'll sure do that, honey."

She shook her head in disbelief and went after their drinks.

"You know her?" Bo asked.

"Yes, she's how I found you."

"Oh, yeah. Damn, I am still shaking inside. I never been that close to death before in my life."

"You'll get over it."

"Yeah, you've been in a range war. You don't worry when men shoot at you."

"A man would be a fool not to worry about being shot at, no matter how many times you're facing down a gun."

"Have you ever done that chair act before?"

"No. It was the first thing I reached for to stop him."

"Oh." Harold slumped in his chair. "I am so glad it was there."

Chet asked about the brand business, but Harold had no answer from the owner so far. Good enough. He watched his man sorting out the money on their table from his pockets which were full of bills and coins.

A cowboy came by and stopped. "Your name Byrnes?"

"Yes."

"There's lady out front in a buggy that would like to talk to you."

"Thanks."

"No problem. She's sure a looker."

"Who is it?" Bo asked.

"I imagine Mrs. Christianson."

"Margaret?"

Chet reset his hat. "I may not be back."

"Ah, ah. I don't blame you. Breakfast at Jenny's Café early. Say seven?" Harold said after him.

Chet stopped and nodded. "Make it six. I need to get back to the ranch."

In the bloody light of sundown flooding the street, Chet saw Marge under the buggy roof, sitting stiff-backed on the seat in her red velvet dress, holding the reins.

"How are you this evening?" he asked. "I guess you wanted me?"

"Get in. We need to go somewhere and talk. In private." Marge never even looked his way.

What did he do now? She couldn't kill him. He agreed and climbed in to sit beside her. His weight getting in made her shift hard as the buggy leaned to the right, and he took his place beside her. The rig righted, he sat with both hands in his lap, and she softly chucked to her team.

He bent down and checked the sky. "Better not go far. It'll be dark soon."

"I know when the sun sets."

She must have driven four blocks up a steep street. At last, she parked in an overlook of the town as the last orange glow shone on Thumb Butte. She tied off the reins and then turned to him.

"What went wrong with us today?" she asked.

Chet took off his hat and scratched an itch over his right ear. "I don't know. It was like a wall was holding us apart."

"Did I do anything wrong?"

He replaced his hat and shook his head. "No."

"What was it?"

"Honestly, I was not sure. Something came over me."

"Was it the lady waiting in Texas?"

"Maybe, but she wasn't a strong force on my mind then."

"I know I am playing second fiddle—"

"Did I ever say that?" He looked hard at her in the twilight.

"No. But I know you want her to come here and you said it was hopeless. If she can't come, I want to be on your list."

Chet nodded very slowly. "I had a long affair once with a married lady. Her husband ran around on her, but she couldn't face the disgrace of a divorce and live in that same country. But when she finally had the courage to leave—three men who hated me rode in, raped her, then they murdered her. I found her dead, and also found her note to her husband telling him that she was leaving him that he never saw."

He could make out her shocked face in the dimming light—nodding. Then she blew her nose in a kerchief and swallowed hard. "That would hurt anyone. I'm sorry."

"I don't think about it much now. But I was uncomfortable when I went with her behind his back. We only dared to dance one dance each week at the local schoolhouse. But he was gambler and went off leaving her at home for days alone to run things while he consorted with a rich widow."

"Did they catch her murderers?"

"Yes, she left the name of the ringleader written in

her own blood on the sheet. They all three hung. I was there and saw justice served. I just hated how they smeared her name so at the trial about our affair."

"I could see that."

"Marge, I guess I'm not ready to be committed to any woman. I really in my heart doubt that Kathren can move to Arizona, but I left her with a pledge I'd come back and marry her if she would or could come out here to the new place."

"I understand. I'm trying to be very frank with you tonight. I want you to understand that what I am about to say to you I have deeply thought about all day. I have never said this to any other man in my life. Would you consider having an affair with me?"

Chet collapsed on the leather-padded bench. His eyes closed in deep concentration.

"I'd have to think about the consequences. My life is so filled with unfinished deals. I really should be back in Texas running things—being certain my family members are not going to be murdered. I expect a sad letter every time I go to the post office. The choice you have given me is very generous, but—"

She unpinned her hat and tossed it into the back. Then her face loomed over his and she kissed him. Her lips were hard and demanding, but he didn't dare respond. At last he gently set her back upright.

"Marge, I can't promise you anything. But I will dance with you, and I promise to stop by. But give me some time to think. I promise you, whatever I decide, you will be the first to know."

"I am not sure I can wait that long."

"I understand. But I am being sincere as I can with

you. Let me have enough rope to see things clear. You're a wonderful woman, but I'm not ready to choose."

In a little girl's voice Marge asked, "You will forgive my boldness?"

"I will. I understand you have needs. And desires. But for now I need more time."

She rearranged her dress and straightened it. He climbed down and retrieved her hat. Handed it to her, then he got back on the seat.

She nodded to him and then drove the horses off the hill and let him off at the Palace.

"I shall see you at Camp Verde Saturday night. Come by for supper. I'll even feed your ranch hands."

"They'd love that."

"See you then." And she drove off in the gathering darkness.

He walked across the street to the hotel, took a room, and went upstairs to try to sleep. It was before dawn when he left his bed, went and took Roan out of the livery, then rode him over to Jenny's.

Harold was ten minutes late getting there. He apologized and sat down beside Chet on a stool. "Damn, this is too early."

"I guess you haven't heard anything more?"

"No wires. I have no idea what is happening. How's the ranching going?"

"We've found maybe a hundred and fifty momma cows."

"Oh, yes, you mentioned that. A man down at Congress has two three-year-old Hereford bulls. He'll sell them for fifty dollars apiece."

"Haul them up here?"

"I guess. He says they're sound and highly-bred stock."

"Tell him with delivery to the ranch included and they're sound—I need them."

"That's a helluva long ways to haul two bulls," Harold said.

"You working for me or him?"

"You."

"Good, make the deal."

Jenny brought them eggs, German potatoes, big slices of ham, biscuits and gravy on two platters.

"I heard about a man has three yearling Hereford bulls for sale." She refilled their cups.

"If they are sound I'll buy them for the ranch."

"Good, that might make me ten bucks." She winked at him and went to put the pot up.

When Jenny went back to the kitchen, Harold asked under his breath, "Where did you go last night with her—Margaret? I was just curious."

"Our business was short and I was tired, so I went to bed by myself."

"Oh, I see."

Chet didn't need to share his personal business with Harold. No telling who'd know about them next. He finally parted with the man, told Jenny good-bye and headed east. He rode past her gate and went on. He'd see her at the dance, anyway.

On the road from Camp Verde, close to the ranch, he spotted a hard-faced stranger armed with a rifle who stepped out of the willows and aimed it at him. Chet's hand went for his own gun. The rifle belched out a shot from a ring of gunsmoke and the roan reared on his hind feet. The bullet sounded like it had hit a watermelon, and Chet felt something had struck the roan. In the confusion, the roan fell over backwards. Only in his quickness to shake his boots out of the stirrups was he able to fall aside and away from the wounded horse's striking hooves. The sharp cries of pain came from his horse, thrashing his legs as Chet came out of the boiling dust, shooting wildly at his attacker. When he shot the man's hat off his head, the ambusher quit the country. Then others busted out of the willows. Chet's eyes burning, he emptied his gun at the five retreating riders.

"You no account back-shooters. I'm going to run you down for this horse killing," he mumbled, reloading his handgun with shaky fingers. Bullets in the cylinder, with a sad heart, Chet shot the roan in the forehead to end his pitiful misery.

He'd have to come back and get his saddle. Setting out for the ranch on foot, he saw his first buzzard circling high in the sky. That sight of death-on-the-wings only drove the nail deeper in his chest. Those worthless lowlifes would pay dearly for this interruption and his loss.

Hoot must have seen him coming up the lane and ran out, wringing his hands in his apron. "Why are you afoot, boss man?"

"Shot my horse out from under me between here and town."

"Cory, go ring that bell until I tell you to stop. We need the boys all in here right now."

"Yes, sir." The barefoot boy raced for the large bell in the yard and began making the bell ring hard by jerking the rope. In a short while, Hoot told him to stop.

"There's cowboys coming. Go hitch that team to the farm wagon."

"Yes, sir."

"Who was it?"

"A short, hard-faced guy with a Winchester. Roan reared up about the time he shot at me, and he hit him instead of me."

"That sounds like Ryan. But he shot your good horse?"

"He might have shot me, but Roan was in the way. Others were there, too. Then they all lit out like shucks."

"Where did they go?"

"They rode west."

"What are you after?" Hoot asked from back of him, as he rummaged in the front closet.

"One of those shotguns."

"They're all cleaned and oiled out in the kitchen."

"Shells there?"

"Yes. I planned to have one of the boys make a gun rack to put them on."

"Good idea. I'm going to borrow a saddle and go after them."

"By yourself?" Hoot asked.

"They only send one Texas ranger to settle a tough town down where I come from."

"Yeah, but they might kill you, too."

"I doubt it." He turned as Tom busted in the open front doors.

"Who shot your horse?"

"I reckon Ryan. He stepped out of the willows down there where the road runs along the river. Roan reared and he shot him instead of me. Then they ran like hell. Pick me out a tough horse to ride and let me borrow a saddle and bedroll. Hoot's fixing me some grub. I'll be ready to leave in thirty minutes."

"The Dyer horse is the one. He's tougher than rawhide and you'll appreciate him. I'll get him ready. We'll go get your saddle and gear. Damn shame. That Roan was a great horse. I rode him that night over the mountain. Dyer's okay, I've shot deer off his back."

"Good, let's get ready for me to leave. You boys hold down the ranch. I'll be back when I get them."

"You don't know that country to the west," Tom said. "It gets wild and western out there. I don't know where they'd have a hideout. There's some ranches out there, but they're small and there may be some outlaws hiding in them besides Ryan. They won't all be friendly."

"Fine. I'm going to find that bunch and make them pay for killing Roan."

Chet made a boot leg for the double-barrel Greener, then planned to load one of the new .44/40 rifles in the scabbard under his right stirrup. They soon had the horse saddled out front. Sarge and Bixby came in on the run and they were told about his incident and plans. Hampt and Heck were still out, and he felt bad about not being able to wait on Heck and tell him all about the deal. But Hoot could do that for him.

Loaded down, Chet short-loped the big bay horse for the road and, leaving, waved good-bye to them. A tough enough horse under him, he soon located the familiar fresh hoofprints on the road and took them up. In his mind they were only a few miles ahead of him. If they didn't think he was after them, they might ease their pace.

Chet met a Mexican on the road, driving a squeaky *carita* pulled by two white oxen, who told him the five riders weren't over a half hour ahead of him. He rode on hard to cut that lead down. The day was waning fast when he topped a ridge and discovered that they had turned off the road—somewhere a ways back. He shut down the big horse among some large rocks in case they were going to try an ambush. Sounds of men chousing their horses were coming off the mountain above him. They must have chosen a steep side trail. There was lots of scrambling, cussing, and small rock-slides way above him. Obviously, they had not known he was that close to them or they would have am-bushed him. His luck was holding. Chet turned the big horse around and soon found where they had left the road to enter the big pine timber. The tracks were easy to follow, but the trail hardly more than a game one.

They must have crossed over the top by then, for he could no longer hear them scrambling. Undecided about whether to spend the night lower down and not ride directly into their camp or go on foot to check on them, he hitched the horse and removed the saddle. There wasn't any graze anyway, where they were at. On his hike upward, he'd look for some.

Chet took his Winchester with him and set out in the orange glow that flooded the steep trail above him. There was a large, open-rock slide area they had crossed over about a quarter-mile long. Not only was it steep on both sides, but it was a wonder they didn't lose some of their horses crossing it to where two tall rocks made a wide enough V for them to pass through. Chet entered the open-slide area, and in the twilight, crossed to the opening. The rocks held under his boots, but with a horse all that would be much different. He could see where some of the animals had spooked and they'd almost lost them.

At the V, he discovered a better trail that went off the north slope. Not as steep, and no sign of the bush-whackers. They'd no doubt rode on. Damn. Where were they headed? Undecided, still he didn't want them getting away. Could he get Dyer across that broken rock to the V in the dark?

Nothing to do but try it. He backtracked to his horse and the twilight dimmed more on him. He sad-dled Dyer and started for the loose-rock trail. Coming out of the pines, there was more light on the fractured rock, but not daylight. Dyer was a calm enough animal, and also tired enough not to be jittery. Chet felt sure he would not panic if he slipped a little.

The crunch under his shoes sounded loud as they began their trip. He talked to him softly so he wasn't shocked by any misstep or slide underfoot. Then Dyer lost his front footing with a small slide.

"Whoa. Whoa." The horse replaced his hoof on a solid place and came forward.

Next a back hoof sunk, and Chet clapped him on the neck with soft words until the gelding found his footing again. "Steady, big man, we're going to make this."

With his heart pounding in his throat, he put his

own feet down gingerly and brought the horse across this gap in the sky. He sure hoped there was another way out of there besides this one. When at last he passed through the rock V, he stopped to relax. Hands on his knees and bent over to recover his sanity, he let Dyer stand for a few moments on solid ground. The horse shook hard enough to rattle the stirrups.

Chet led the gelding farther down the trail and found a small, grassy meadow in the starlight. Dyer put his head down and went to grazing, with his bridle clacking on his molar teeth. The saddle stripped off the horse, Chet sat down on the ground and gnawed on some jerky. The most disturbing things to him were that he didn't know where he was or how he would get out. Worse than that, he didn't know where the ambushers were, either.

When Chet awoke before dawn, he could smell faint wood smoke, and saddled Dyer in the dark. Then, cautiously, he led him down the tracks left in the game trail as the gentle lamp of dawn began to purple the skies. Mounted up, he crossed through some open timber. At any time, he knew he might ride right into the middle of them. Then, as the light began to spread over the land, Chet spotted the source of the smoke. A small cabin and ranch setup was in the valley beneath him. He reached back for his field glasses in the saddlebags. Then, careful that no glare off his lens reflected at them, he searched the pens. Men were saddling horses at the corral. He made out the short man who had shot Roan ordering them around. They were moving on, and he wondered who owned this station and had obviously put them up for the night.

In a short while, Chet would face that person or persons who aided them. The gang rode north, and he came off the mountain as fast as he dared. In a short while, he rode up on a woman busy hoeing in a fenced garden. When she straightened up, looking surprised, he dismounted with his hand on his gun butt.

Maybe in her late twenties, with a willowy figure, she was an attractive woman. Who was with her? He searched around. "Who else is here?"

She shook her head. "Oh, they left a half hour ago."

"You have a man?"

"Yes."

"He with them?"

"No, he's in Utah."

"Utah?"

"I see you don't understand. I am a member of the Church of Latter Day Saints—have you ever heard of Mormons?"

"You're a polygamist."

"Yes. My name's Edna. Are you the law?"

"No, ma'am. My name is Chet Byrnes. Those men shot my horse out from under me yesterday. He was a great horse, and they need to pay for him. The law in Preskit wants them for suspicion of theft from the ranch I bought."

"Oh," she said and leaned her chin on the hoe handle. "So you're the Texan they spoke about."

"Guess they think I'm bad."

She looked at him, troubled-looking. "They said you shot two of his men."

"Ryan's men said that?"

She nodded.

"Me and my twelve-year-old nephew held them off and yes, we shot two of them who charged the house."

"Twelve years old? He must be brave."

"I'm very proud of him."

"I don't have any coffee or I'd offer you a cup. I don't drink it." Edna shrugged her shoulders under the nice dress—too nice a dress for her to work in, but she no doubt dressed that morning for her company.

"I have some coffee. Tell me why a young woman lives out here by herself who has a husband in Utah."

"Life has its twists. We own this claim and we run our cattle in this range. We would like to make it larger. Without someone living here we fear that outlaws might roost here. So I was chosen from my sisters to come up here."

"Sisters?"

"Yes, we call each other sisters. His wives, I mean."

"Do you hide outlaws?"

"No, not on purpose."

"You did last night."

"How could I know they were outlaws? They had no handbills showing their crimes. I thought they were lost ranch hands."

"Did you know any of them?"

"Yes."

"Who was that?"

"Ryan. He had been here two times before."

Chet walked with his horse outside the fence to the gate, where she unlatched the leather loop and opened it to let him in. The gate closed again, and she hitched her hem up enough for him to see she was bare-footed.

The cabin was neat, but sparsely furnished. She filled the kettle half full of water from the canvas bucket and put it on the small stove. Then she fired the kindling under the utensil to get things going.

"You make the coffee. I've never made any."

He nodded. "I will, when the water boils."

"Oh, have a seat. I am not very society-conscious."

Chet wanted to laugh at her simplicity. Was she a little *tetched,* or was she simply not accustomed to company? No way he could figure out the woman's problem. He got up to add the coffee grounds that Hoot sent along.

Edna rose and watched him closely as he spooned it into the boiling water. "I think I could make that."

"It isn't hard. Did they say where they were going?"

"Utah, I guess, but the Grand Canyon will block their way. They will have to swing way east to the Navajo Country and go way up to Lee's Ferry."

"There is no way to cross it short of there?"

"No, it is a long ways and lots of desert."

"How far north is there a road?" The pungent smell of coffee soon filled the room. Chet rose and found two cups. From the kettle that he moved off the burner, he dipped her out one, and then one for himself.

She tried to hold her handleless cup, but soon set it down and went for a rag to protect her hands. "Hot, but it tastes good."

"Too hot to even taste," he said to her. "Wait till it cools."

She shrugged. "It smelled so good I couldn't wait,

I guess. Do you know why good things are always the prohibited things?"

"I don't understand why coffee isn't good for you."

She smiled and shook her head. "I've been reading the book of Mormon and I don't know, either."

"Is there a road north of here?" he asked her again.

"Yes, the Marcy Road is maybe a day's ride north of here. But it runs east and west where the railroad someday will run."

Chet blew on his coffee, anxious to drink it. At last he dared a sip and agreed, despite the tongue bit, it was a rich-tasting concoction. There was nothing she did or said, but he felt wary about the spaces in their conversations. Like she acted as if she had something to tell him and didn't know how to broach the subject. He didn't know what, but he wanted to get on his way in pursuit of the horse killers.

"You know, it gets lonely at times down here."

"I imagine it does."

"I've had lots of company this week."

He rose and went to refill his cup. "Plenty more. You want another cup?"

"No, you drink it. I'm not supposed to. You married?"

"No. But I am engaged to a lady in Texas."

She bobbed her head like she heard him. "At times it gets real lonely up here."

"I bet it does."

"Mister, would you consider staying over a few days. Here with me. I ain't a wanton woman, but—"

"Edna, I simply can't. Those men shot my horse

and tried to kill me and my nephew. I want them arrested. They're getting away."

Edna made a pained face. "Then simply hold me for a few minutes."

"I could do that. But don't expect more."

"I won't."

"When is your husband coming back with supplies for you?"

She pressed her face in his vest and hugged him. "That's why I feel so sad. I don't know."

Sobs wracked her body in his arms, and he felt a knot he couldn't swallow behind his tongue. How did he get into these sticky deals? That bunch was getting farther away. Was she simply stalling him from catching them? Damn, it was uncomfortable as hell holding a vibrant woman against his body. Lord help me.

At last Chet excused himself, and she collapsed on a chair and swept the wavy, dark hair back from her face. "I'm so sorry. I must have lost my mind. I'll be fine. Thanks for what you have done here now. I won't forget you. I had no right to ask you to heal me."

Then she buried her face in her arms and cried. He made her look up at him.

"You need to be strong. This won't last forever. When I get home, I will send a man over with some supplies and to check on you."

"But what if Howard is here?" Her brown lashes flooded with tears sprung open. "No, no, you better not send him."

"If your husband is here, he'll ride on like nothing has ever happened."

"Thank you. You will be my best friend forever."

Edna hugged his arm possessively and followed him out to Dyer, who was busy grazing on the new wild oats. He kissed her on the forehead, mounted up and wondered what Kathren was doing in Texas. Then he waved good-bye and rode off.

A half day later, Chet had been tracking them eastward on the Marcy Road when a crude sign said PEACH SPRINGS—FIVE MILES. They'd turned off there and went north. The country was rolling, with lots of grass and sagebrush. Junipers and groves of pines dotted the country.

Peach Springs looked like some fresh-cut, rough-board buildings lining a short street that Chet knew, if it ever rained, would turn into a sea of mud. From a distance at Edna's place, he'd seen their horses. He recognized the bay, a paint, and two that he recalled. All stood hipshot outside a bar called the Eagle Saloon.

Chet checked his Colt. Five of the cylinders loaded. And an empty under the hammer. Then he decided to go in with the Greener cocked. They might have given up on him following them. He rode Dyer around to the back. Most such places had a rear exit for customers to go outside and vent their bladders. There he found a door half-open. He hitched Dyer, then drew the double-barrel out of the boot and loaded both tubes. Dodging the heaps of discarded brown bottles, he climbed the three steps quietly. He listened. He could hear a slur or two, like they'd had enough to drink. Good. Drunks were reckless and usually poor shots.

The hall gave a clear shot down a short way to the main part, where Chet decided they were all standing at the bar. He eased inside, and on soft footfall was soon in sight of the five men.

Was that all of them? Chet had to be certain. When he stepped inside the barroom, the bartender saw him first and his blue eyes widened in shock. Then the others.

"What's going—"

"If you ain't wanting buckshot in you, put your hands on the bar. One wrong move and you're going to meet your maker. Bartender, you get around out here, too."

They obeyed, and so did the white-shirted man.

Ryan twisted some. "You ain't the damn law, you can't arrest us."

"Face the back bar, and move again like that, I'll kill you. I don't need to be the law, I'm taking all of you in. Not you, bartender."

Shotgun in his right hand, Chet went down the row, disarming them. Their handguns on the floor, he kicked them aside. Then he drew another from the next man's holster. At last he felt they were partially disarmed, and herded them to the doorway under a barrage of questions about how he was getting them back and what for. He ignored them and used the Greener for a prod. He made them lie on the ground outside. With care, he tied each man's hands behind his back with his own neckerchief.

Chet had drawn a small, curious crowd. He spotted a boy in a one-strap pair of overalls, looking over things. "Come over here. I want you to go down to that store and buy me a hundred feet of light chain and five padlocks. Here's the money. If you can get back here in five minutes with it, I'll pay you two dollars."

"You the law, mister?" The youth peered hard at Chet.

He nodded privately at him.

"I thought so. I want them two bucks." He left on the fly.

"Hell, anyone would have gone for that much money," a bystander said, and spat tobacco off to the side.

Chet nodded at him.

"Let's talk deals," Ryan said from his place lying on his belly. "I've got some money I could pay you."

"You mean pay for my horse?"

"I mean pay you to forget this entire thing."

Chet's mind went to work on how he'd ever get them back to Preskit. "No deal. Anyone got a wagon and team? I'll pay a hundred dollars for them to carry these men to Preskit."

No one moved or offered him any help. Then a tall, thin man with gray hair stepped out. "Make it two hundred, and me and my boy will go with you."

"Go get him and the rig. I'll pay you half now and the rest in Preskit."

The man nodded. "I'll be back in an hour."

"Bring your bedrolls. I'll get us supplies."

With a store clerk helping him carry it, the boy came back with the chain. Chet made a tight loop in the chain and then locked it around the first man's throat; then he did the next one with about eight feet between them. Ryan started to protest, and he rapped him hard over the head with the barrel of his .44.

"One more move like that and they'll have to carry you." Chet clicked the brass lock shut and Ryan coughed, but he didn't try anything else. Their hands tied behind their backs, he soon jerked each one to his feet. They looked downcast as he jammed their hats on their heads.

"Now the rules are, if you try anything I'll shoot you, and maybe the man beside you as well. So you will have to make everyone behave or risk your own life. Do you understand me?"

Their dull yeses told him it would be a long trip back to Preskit. And he would certainly miss the Saturday night dance in Camp Verde—maybe Mrs. Christianson would understand. But he really needed to get back to Texas. This business of him buying the ranch must surely be over soon.

Nick Donaldson and his eighteen-year-old son Troy were back with the wagon and team in the time promised. Chet had ordered enough food from the store to keep his bunch fed for a week. They only had to load the supplies into the wagon and then get his prisoners on board. With the chains in place on each of them, Chet untied their hands, but promised them that any slipup or incident, and they'd be bound hand and foot. The bartender brought him their guns and, in a tow sack, he hung them on his saddlehorn.

Nick said he'd drive the large team of black Shires. Troy would ride and lead the outlaws' ponies. Nick, wearing his best felt hat and a new pair of overalls, clucked to the big horses and they were underway. Chet wondered what Edna was doing. She'd sure been surprised to learn how swiftly he had caught them unaware and had them in chain-gang fashion, where they'd stay until they got to the Yavapai County courthouse in Preskit.

Nick explained they'd have to go east to the base of the San Francisco Peaks and south on the military road to Camp Verde. Then go up over the hump to Preskit. He judged the trip as requiring five or six days and waved away Chet's offer to pay him half of the fare. He'd get it all later.

The big horses made lots of miles, and Chet bought grain for them at an outpost to keep them churning up dust. His prisoners drew some stares at the isolated places where they stopped. Chet had a chance to see this higher range country, and liked the grass and grazing conditions. Maybe summer stock in this country and winter them in the valley. Nick said many years they got too much snow this close to the peaks, and if he left them up there, he would have to feed them hay.

By Chet's count they had been on the way three and a half days when they headed south for the valley. Nick promised they'd be in the valley in another long day.

After dark, on schedule, they pulled up into the ranch yard. Hoot came out with a lamp. "Where in tarnation have you been? Boys been riding looking all over for ya. What'cha got with you?"

"Ryan and his gang."

"Uncle Chet? Uncle Chet, you alright?" Heck came blazing out of the house and tackled him around the waist. "I was plumb worried they'd kilt you."

The rest of the boys were up and busy peering at the prisoners, using candle reflectors.

"Why if it ain't ole Ryan," Bixsby said, looking hard at his ex-boss. "They've got you going right where they ought to have you. In jail."

Chet introduced Nick and Troy, then told Hoot they all needed to be fed.

"If I had some slop and moldy bread I'd make that sumbitch eat it. I really would. Cory, you go stoke the stove. We've got some food fixing to do."

"Yes, siree. You hear the boss arrested all them outlaws hisself?"

"Ain't nothing he ain't done before. Now quit palavering, we've got work to do."

Tom asked Chet what they needed to do for him.

"Guard the prisoners and let us three have a night's sleep. We've been on the road a while."

"We can do that," Bixsby said. "Mrs. Christianson sure asked about you Saturday night. Couldn't hardly believe we didn't know where you were."

"Nothing I could do about that. I trailed them to a place called Peach Springs, then Nick and his boy hauled them back from there."

Wiley closed his eyes and stared in disbelief at him. "That's way up on the Marcy Road, isn't it?"

"Yes."

"Heavens, you were a couple hundred miles away from here. No wonder we never found you."

"Where's Hampt tonight?"

"He took a pack horse and rode west to look for you two days ago."

"Sorry, I had no way to tell anyone anything."

"Bet Bo Harold will be glad to see you. He's been out here almost every day, asking where you were. Think he was scared you were dead and so was his deal."

"I'll see him in town tomorrow. Thanks. Are things going alright?"

"Good. We expect to find a few strays during roundup, but I bet that count you have is close to being right."

A big yawn overtook Chet. "Thanks, Tom. You want to foreman this place while I'm in Texas?"

"I'd be proud to do that. Could I move my wife and kids up here?"

"Move her into the big house for now, and we'll build a bunkhouse and one for you and your family this winter."

"Wow, she'll be tickled."

"I don't expect her to feed the crew either. Hoot can do that. My family gets here, we'll spread out some more."

They shook hands and Chet knew his selection of Tom would be a good one. Maybe he needed another place up near the peaks for Reg and J.D. to work. He really liked the high country he saw coming down from up there.

After his supper, Chet climbed into his own bed and slept like a log. In the morning, Tom asked to ride along with them and then drop by and check on his wife and family. Obviously, he was going to tell her about his new job.

Chet felt so grubby and whiskered that he took a

bath and shaved. Then put on his other clothes and ate breakfast as the boys were finishing their meal.

"Fed them oatmeal," Hoot said meaning the prisoners. "They won't get any better in jail. You know them boys with him?"

"After I took them prisoner, I talked to some of them on the road. Some of them probably ain't as bad as Ryan, but they ain't innocent of nothing. I figure a judge will sentence some of them to ninety days in the local jail."

"Ryan can go sweat in Yuma for a long time," Hoot said. "For my part."

Tom rode along with them, and smiled at his boss when Chet turned the black colt the boys had chosen for him to ride down the road to Marge's gate. "See all of you in town, 'cept Tom. He needs to go home and count his chickens."

Nick and Troy laughed and told Chet they'd be fine and would see him later at the courthouse. To get ahead of them, he took off in a short lope. The father-son pair could handle the prisoners. Chet wanted to stop and apologize to Marge on the way into town, and Tom could back them.

A few hours later at her ranch gate, he jogged the black up to the front-yard hitch rail.

Marge shouted, "Chet Byrnes, where have you been forever?"

"Peach Springs," he said dismounting. "Rounding up outlaws, woman."

She was in his arms in a flash and hugging him. "I

have been so worried about you for the last week. What now?"

"I need to catch up with my wagonload of prisoners headed for the sheriff and meet them at the courthouse."

"No time for lunch?" Marge stuck out her bottom lip in disappointment.

"No."

"Well, then we'll hitch up the team and I'll go with you."

"Sounds good to me, but no dressing up and all that. I have to be there when they get them delivered to the jail."

"Go hitch the team." She left him on the run for the front door.

When Chet returned with her rig, Marge had on a different dress and a hairbrush in her hand, a wide summer hat under her arm, and was running hard to get to the rig. He reached over and pulled her up. She raised her eyebrows and smiled big. Sweeping her dress underneath her, she settled on the leather seat and then squeezed his arm.

"I was so worried that they had killed you. No word, nothing."

"I knew I'd beat the mail. Have you ever been to Peach Springs?"

"No."

"That's where I got the drop on them in a saloon. I hired a nice man with a team and wagon as well as his son to haul them back here."

"Who are they?"

"Ryan, for one. A big man who calls himself Carter. I bet he's wanted somewhere. A follower named Trigger and two kids who are scared to death. Kent and Swann."

"I don't know any of them."

"I got to meet all of them on the ride back. I could see Ryan and Carter were the kingpins. Trigger is an ex-convict, I'm certain. Them two kids were along for the excitement. They'll tell the authorities anything they want to know."

"Did they try anything?"

"No. I locked a hundred-foot chain around each one of their necks every eight feet, and they're still wearing it. They know if any one cuts up that others could be shot."

"How did you ever think of doing that?"

Chet shrugged. "There I was holding a shotgun on five men, and knew I needed some restraint for them. The store had a chain and five padlocks. It worked."

She narrowed her eyes hard at him. "You are amazing, do you know that?"

"No, but when you get backed into a corner you need to find a way out."

Marge leaned her cheek on his shoulder. "I about cried when they told me you were gone after them and they'd shot your good roan horse."

"I hated that, but I had no way to send you word."

"What are we doing at the jail?"

"Unlocking the padlocks I put on them. I have the keys for the locks. In my pocket."

"What will you do after that?"

"Maybe take you someplace to eat, then?"

"That would be nice." Marge stretched her button-up shoes toward the dashboard and then snuggled back to his arm. "So you are unharmed."

"What do you know about Mormons?"

"You thinking about joining their church?"

"No, but I met a Mormon woman who lived alone way back up in the mountains tending a ranch."

"No doubt she was handling stock that needed the re-brands to heal."

"Are you serious?" Chet looked over at her hard.

"Yes, there is also a secret outlaw trail that comes down from Montana, and these isolated ranches serve as hotels and hideouts for felons on the run."

Had Ryan used her to hold cattle for him that the brands had been changed on? He'd never thought about her being involved in rustling. Maybe he had discovered another loophole in this business of stealing from the Quarter Circle Z.

In a short while, Chet drove up and met Sheriff Sims on the Whiskey Row side of the courthouse, with the five seated on the ground, waiting to be unlocked.

"How are you today, ma'am?" the lawman asked, taking off his hat for Marge.

"Fine, Sheriff." She remained on the buggy seat as Chet went from prisoner to prisoner, unlocking his padlocks. The job done, Troy gathered up the chain and put it in to the back of the buggy. A lot of neck-rubbing went on by the prisoners as the shotgun guard drove them inside the jail's side door.

"Nice haul. These are the men who shot your horse?" Sims asked.

"Yes."

"Where did you catch them?"

"Peach Springs, in a saloon."

"My heavens, you did really track them down that far. I'd offer to buy you a beer, but you have prettier company than me."

"What happens next?" Chet gave a head toss toward the disappearing outlaws at the back door.

"I'll interrogate them, then I'll visit with the prosecuting attorney, Sam Yates. He decides on the charges."

"Good enough. I need to go back to Texas as soon as possible."

"I understand. We may need a deposition from you about the other crimes you know about."

"None of them said much on the road, but put those two boys in a cell by themselves. They're so scared they'll tell you anything you need to know."

"Thanks, and thanks for running them down."

"I wanted them prosecuted. Guess that will have to be my repayment for the loss of a good horse."

"By the way, if we prosecute them and the jury finds them guilty, you get their horses to keep. Only way I can pay you anything."

Chet shook hands with the lawman, and then he paid his haulers and shook both of their hands. "Is there enough food left to get you two home?"

"Don't worry about us," the man said. "We've sure enjoyed your company and hate to part with you. You don't need a farmer, do you?"

"I may. I guess I can send a letter general delivery up there?"

"You sure can. Me and Troy would consider it an honor to work for you, sir."

"Chet," he reminded the man.

"Yeah, Chet."

Chet hated to part with the pair. They'd worked hard making the transporting easy for him. Good, real folks. He waved good-bye, then climbed in the buggy and about knocked his hat off on the roof.

"You alright?" Marge asked, sounding concerned.

"Fine, just too damn tall. We need to leave my horse at the livery."

"Certainly."

After boarding his horse at the stables, Chet and Marge found the Brownstone Hotel's dining room near empty. It was way past noontime.

"Can we still have a meal?" Chet asked the waiter.

"Certainly, sir. What do you and the lady wish to eat?"

Chet closed the menu. "What do you suggest?"

"Oh, sir, the fresh elk steaks are tender, and come with sides of mashed potatoes and green beans fresh from a grower down in the valley. You should be quite content."

Marge nodded in agreement. "I'll take the same."

"Coffee?"

"Yes, we both want some."

The waiter left with their order and Chet nodded to Marge. "I hope to get things wound up here soon. So with Ryan out of the way, I'll head back to Texas. It will be a year, I imagine, before I'll be able to close out my business in Texas and get back up here."

"I know you will be busy. Will you write to me?"

"My letters are brief."

"Hi, good-bye, so I know you are alive, is suffi-cient."

"If you find someone else, don't wait. I don't know what my future holds or what anyone else will do."

Marge raised her chin up. "I accept that risk."

"Fine, so we have all our cards on the table."

"Yes and thank you." She wet her lips. "What will you do in Texas?"

"Put the home place on the market. My family has lived there since shortly after the Texas revolution. My parents and grandparents came down there from Arkansas. We fought the Comanches for that land. My brothers and sister were kidnapped by them and never heard of again. My parents lost their minds over those events."

"Will it sell?"

"Yes, I think so. The Kansas cattle market has made many men rich in the state."

The waiter returned with their coffee, and Chet and Marge drank it slowly. Alone in the red-velvet-draped room, even the sound of their china cups on the china saucers sounded loud.

Chet reached over and caught Marge's wrist to squeeze it. "This is not the end of either of our lives. Simply a break—a short lapse in time."

Marge formed a slight smile. "Yes, I realize that. On that stage coming here with you, I was really taken by you. I'm spoiled, but you've taught me some lessons—'be patient, Marge.'"

Chet nodded. "And you know the rest."

"Yes." She chuckled in her throat. "That you do things with zest. You ride off against large odds and bring in a wagonload of outlaws."

"I was lucky."

"Hell, no. That's your way, Chet Byrnes." Marge put her fingers over her mouth and looked around to see if anyone had heard her swear. No one else was in the room.

They both laughed.

After lunch, Marge drove herself home, but they had a hard time parting. She reminded him about the dance—he promised to be there. When, at last, Chet watched her buggy take on the hill a block away, he turned and headed for the Palace to find Harold.

The agent was deep in a poker game, but excused himself from behind the next hand. They moved aside to talk softly.

"Everything is going smooth," Harold promised. "I had a wire from Talley and the paper thing has begun. You don't have to do a thing. What about this prisoner deal I heard about?"

"Ryan and his men are in the jail. I captured them at Peach Springs and had them hauled back here."

"I knew who you got. Do you have a badge?"

"No, but a citizen can make an arrest of a criminal in this country. The Constitution says so."

"You sound like a lawyer. Couple of days and the matter may be settled. Still no luck on that bar-C brand deal."

"You're doing good. Get back in there and win some more."

Inside the Palace, Jane brought him a beer and Chet dug two dimes out for her. Standing aside of the table, he watched them play. It was good to be back. Sleeping on the ground and the march with the grumbling prisoners had been no fun at all.

Chet's obligation to Marge was taken care of. He finished the cold beer and made a high sign to Harold that he was leaving. The man caught his signal and then turned back to his cards.

In the post office, Chet found two letters from Texas.

Cattle had arrived safely and sold in Kansas. Money in San Antonio Bank. Proceeds: thirty-six thousand and some dollars. He'd paid a ten percent fee for driving them up there. A smile crossed Chet's lips reading Susie's letter. The ranch's share of the cattle that the men took up more than paid for all their expenses. Maybe he should have gone. No.

The other letter explained that Reg, despite his mother's fits over the upcoming event, was going to marry the kitchen girl, Juanita. Obviously, Louise thought the brown-skinned girl was beneath her son's station in life. They planned to wait until he was back in Texas to tie the knot.

Must be no sign of trouble; Susie never mentioned a thing about the Reynoldses in either of the letters. Maybe she was concealing what was going on back there. No way they could go for months without an incident between the Reynoldses and his family.

Too late to ride back to the ranch. Chet chewed on his lower lip. And there would be too much temptation for him to ride out to Marge's place and spend the night. No, he'd played the game straight—despite the notions in his head that passed through from time to time. Marge was a very tempting woman.

Still full from the magnificent late lunch he had with her, he went by Jenny's and drank some coffee. Told the bunch of hangers-on and her about the arrest deal, since the town buzzed about it. Several people walking on the street going over there stopped and thanked him as well.

Arms folded over her chest and her butt against the back counter, Jenny shook her head in amazement. "You're a jim-dandy kind of guy, and we've been needing you around here for a long time. When're you coming back?"

"I figure it will take a year to close out my Texas business. Tom Flowers is going to run the ranch here. I should be back next spring with my family and outfit."

Smiling like she was pleased to the core, Jenny laughed. "We get lots of big deals that move out here. They don't pan out. But my, my you've done good here."

"Hey, you've been a big help. Hoot takes care of the ranch boys and found me the crew. I won't leave for a few more days. But I need to get home."

"Sure you won't eat?"

"No, Jen, I'm going to catch some sleep and head back in the morning. But I'll see you at breakfast."

"We'll sure be here."

Chet walked back to the hotel and took a room. Bigger fools than him in this world would have invited themselves to Marge's for the night. Damn. He undressed, then drew back the sheet and blanket.

Windows open, he'd sure appreciate that blanket by dawn, for it really cooled off up here at night.

Better head back to the ranch at first light. What was happening in Texas? He tossed and turned, concerned about his family.

Chapter 27

Past lunch time the next day, Chet was back at the Quarter Circle Z. Hoot came out on the porch and smiled at him. "No problems?"

He dismounted and shook his head. "Not even a whisper of one."

"None here, either." The older man looked at the passing clouds. "Sure ain't rained either. Getting dry."

Half-turning to check the sky, Chet packed his saddle to the porch. "None today."

"Right. What else did you learn?"

"I saw a sign in town that they're planing a big picnic on the 4th. They're having roping and bronc-riding competition."

"The boys will want to attend. Some may even enter. It's a big show. Folks come from everywhere to attend. Bigger than the county fair. The ranchers all bring in the saltiest broncs they've got for the cow-boys to try to ride them."

"Who runs it?"

"Ah, some town folks do part of it, and the rest just

happens. The sheriff puts on two dozen extra deputies. You know them boys. They get drunk and then they fight. But they're all pretty friendly."

"They do something like that down at Mason, Texas. Fire an old cannon off to celebrate the nation's birthday and boy, do the horses break reins if you ain't there to quiet 'em down."

Hoot laughed. "The planners usually come around and ask for a fat yearling to barbeque. I bet they hit you up at the dance for one. Why, there's more cooks at that deal than you can shake a stick at."

Chet agreed with a bob of his head. "As many as want to can go. Ryan in jail, it should be pretty quiet up this valley."

"Sure. Boss, would you ride up to the Indian camp and tell them there is a crippled yearling up on Beautreau Creek that they can have to eat? He's got a star in his face. Boys said he must have got his hoof caught in a crevass and he tore half of it off. They asked me to do that this morning, but I'm busy baking a cake for Wiley's birthday."

"I can do that."

"Ride due west along the Verde. You can't miss the camp."

"They know where that creek is at."

"Yeah. They know this country like the back of their hand."

"Alright, I'll get a fresh horse and go do that right now."

"I better see how it's baking. I've still got to put frosting on it."

In a short while Chet was headed west, and in a few

miles he could smell the wood smoke of a campfire on the wind. Next he dropped down on the flat and rode closer to the river.

Some females screamed and before he knew it, bare brown butts were gathering up their clothes and running to the willows for cover. Most of them looked like teenage girls. Chet reined the big dun horse back up the bank to the next level to avoid any more scares. The camp wasn't like the Comanche ones with their tall, colorful tepees. They had small brush huts with pieces of canvas over them to shed rain and sun.

A tall Indian woman appeared. She stood much taller than the rest. Dressed in a white woman's blue dress, she acted in charge. Her dark hair was in thick braids that looked like they pulled on the corners of her large eyes.

Chet nodded to her and tipped his hat. "Good day. My name's Chet Byrnes."

"Yes, you own this ranch. We are very grateful that you let us stay here. There is a sweet spring comes out upstream. The water is cool and healthy. Do you need a drink?"

He stepped down off his horse. "You did not tell me your name."

"My name in English is Mary Green, but my people call me Tall Pine. The Indian Service gave us those names when they put them down on the rolls."

This woman was educated. "Are your people Apaches?"

"We are Yavapai."

"Are you part of the Apache family?"

"We have been." She used the side of her hand to shield the strong sun from her eyes.

"May we go in the shade and talk?" Chet wanted her more at ease to visit with him.

"Yes." She spoke the word so correctly he could hardly believe it.

At a safe distance, small children dressed in rags watched this white-eye with his cold, suspicious ways. The disturbed bathers or swimmers giggled from behind lodges. And a few old women with shrunken faces like dried apples and no expression watched their show.

"Are the men gone?"

"They went looking for game today, and took the boys along to show them how."

"I see. There is a crippled yearling on Beautreau Creek that you may eat. I could go up there and rope him for you since your men are gone. Do you have a horse to ride up there?"

Tall Pine shook her head, standing under the leaf-rattling cottonwoods. "We have no horses. But I can run with you up there."

"Run?" Chet frowned at her.

"Mr. Byrnes, if you don't have horses, then you learn to run."

"I guess you do. Please call me Chet."

"I will get the girls you obviously chased out of the river coming to see us."

"I didn't know—"

"I am, how you say, teasing you."

He laughed. But in a few minutes she had over a

half-dozen girls, each carrying everything from old gray canvas to wrap the meat in to baskets to transport the entrails. Tall Pine pointed to the west and set to trotting with her army behind. Chet had to spur the dun horse to keep up on their heels.

Tall Pine pointed out the tree-lined creek coming out of the north. Chet nodded and then shook loose a lariat, setting the dun on a lope headed up the bottom. He had gone some distance when a dark brown yearling jumped to his feet. He might have been three-legged, but he could move. The dun soon closed in on him and Chet threw the rope over his knobby horns, then pressed the horse to pass him, and whipped the lariat over the calf's hip. The rope wrapped hard on the saddlehorn, Chet went straight left, and the steer did a somersault in the air to land on his back. To his shock, the woman and her assistants rushed in to keep the steer down. In the process, she cut his throat before he could even hardly bawl. As the last of his life ran out of him, her helpers avoided his thrashing legs.

Chet rode back and asked her, "Want to hang him in a tree to skin him?"

Tall Pine shook her head. They were already starting to skin him on the ground. Chet coiled up his rope and tied it on the saddle. These people were dead serious about supper.

His dun busy grazing, he went over and squatted down to watch them. "You have a good crew."

"Your crippled horses and the big bulls have been very important for us to eat. Has the agent complained yet?"

Chet shook his head as her workers stood the steer on his back. With a sharp knife to cut the flesh away in his flank, another girl with a hatchet stepped in and cut off his hip bone. The skinned hind leg was soon wrapped in canvas. Two other girls were putting his entrails into a great basket. Another skinned leg was detached and wrapped up. Then the calf's head was detached with an axe, skinned, and also wrapped.

"We can tie some of that meat on my horse."

Mary looked at first like she would decline his offer, then she spoke, "That would be very nice of you to loan him to us. To carry it would take us many trips to get it back to camp."

Mary rose, and he saw the blood had dried on her hands and forearms. She went to the shallow creek and knelt down to wash them. Soon others, with their work complete, came to do the same thing.

Flinging the water off, Mary smiled. "See, not bad for lazy Indians, was it?"

"I never called you that."

"Others have. Has Mr. Swartz been to see you?'

"No. Who's he?"

"The agent who is over the Camp Verde reservation."

"No. Should I have met him?"

"He sent an Indian Police man named Gill to tell us if we did not move back to the reservation, he would put us in chains and drive us back there with whips."

"When was that?"

"A week ago."

"I will ride up there tomorrow and ask to see the food he has to feed your people."

"There is none. His so-called month's supplies only lasted us for a few days. They were moldy and rotten. We were given two old toothless cows for a month's supply. They were piles of bones."

"I will go tomorrow and see him."

"I hope he does not harm you."

"Mary, trust me, he won't."

She nodded her head as if considering him. "Your cowboys say that you are a tough hombre. I can see that you are one. But don't let him hurt you because of us. I can tell you if he is at the fort by Preskit, go see Nan Tan Lupan, who is a friend of the Yavapai."

"Who's he?"

"General Crook."

"If I have to, I'll go see him. Let's load my horse."

"Yes." She clapped her hands and the girls fell in, almost without words. One of them took the reins from him and then pointed at her chest, then the horse. She intended to lead him back to camp.

Chet hoped they all did not run back, and he felt certain that they could outrun him.

At last, everything and everyone was back in camp. Mary very eloquently invited him to stay for supper, and he thanked her but said he needed to get back to the house. Besides, he wasn't too interested in eating raw liver and heart, an Indian delicacy.

"You must come again to our camp, Chet."

He agreed and noted that all the blood from the meat had been scrubbed from his saddle leather. No doubt at her insistence.

How old was she? Twenty, maybe more. She wasn't

bad to look at either. A very much in-charge, well-educated woman.

Chet short-loped the dun. They must be getting closer to the longest day in the year. In the morning he'd go see this Swartz. *Drive them home with a whip, his ass. He'd see about that, too.*

Chapter 28

The crew was all at the ranch when Chet got back. Bixsby took his horse to put him up while Chet washed up on the back porch with Heck asking him lots of questions. What had Chet heard from Aunt Susie and a million more things. Chet dried his hands and smiled. "Everything is fine, they say."

"They say?" Heck frowned at him.

"Yes, they don't want to worry me."

"I bet that's right."

"We'll head back there as soon as we get the deed recorded and things set here. I may speak to a banker. We need about a hundred more cows or some young stuff to grow out."

Heck agreed and they went to eat. The conversation during supper turned to building a bunkhouse.

"We need a bunch of logs cut this winter and hauled in here. Any of you fellars part loggers?"

Wiley said he knew how to use a double-bitted axe. The others acted like cross-cut saws were poison. Chet finally smiled while blowing steam off his coffee. "I bet there's some loggers up by the San Francisco Peaks that would cut the trees down and you could haul them down here. Tom will need a residence for his family. You all will need a bunkhouse when my family gets here. My Aunt Louise will probably need a cabin of her own. The list goes on and on."

"Charlie Simpson and his brother Archie are real mechanics with wood and building. They can build anything, and last I knew they were short on work." Hoot said.

"What would they cost?"

"For lots of steady work oh, thirty and found a month."

"Who can you send to get them?" Chet asked his cook.

"One of the men can ride over there and get them."

"Do that, then. But it will take all of you helping them."

The crew agreed, and looked relieved that part of the job was off them. Chet was satisfied that with hiring some craftsmen, he'd have better buildings.

No one was expecting the birthday surprise. Hoot brought out the frosted cake, and they really razzed Wiley about how old he was getting. Twenty-seven sounded like rheumatism was right around the corner for him. They laughed and ate the whole cake at one sitting.

Afterwards, Heck told him he had mixed thoughts about staying there or going back to Texas with him. But Chet explained that he needed Heck to go home and help him close out the Texas ranch deal. The boy agreed. They parted, with no time set for their leaving.

After the men had gone to bed, Chet sat out on the porch as the evening cooled down, and listened to some coyotes wailing at the moon. Hampt joined him.

"I been thinking about you. On my journey, I met a woman named Edna. I can't tell you where she lives, but I can draw you a map to her place. I figure I owe her a sack of pinto beans for her troubles in steering me onto their trail. Also, take her two pounds of coffee and a small sack of sugar. Hoot can fix you up. She may even need some things fixed around her place that she can't handle. May take you a few days to get it all done."

Hampt nodded. "I can handle it. What's her last name?"

Chet shook his head, "Edna is all I know." He made sure they were alone before he said, "Don't tell the rest of them."

"Oh, trust me, I won't."

So Saturday morning, Hampt rode out on a mission for the boss man. He left leading a pack horse, whistling "Yankee Doodle Dandy," and had assured Chet he'd be careful crossing the rock slide. Also, if her man was there, to simply ride on. Chet was pleased that the matter was in good hands and he joined the excitement about the dance.

On the road to town, Chet wondered how well his big man Hampt and Edna would get along. Smiling to himself, he straightened and went to trotting his dun horse. Looking forward to the evening, he decided Marge would be good company to distract his attention from worrying about how things in Texas were going.

Heck was even going along with them. Cory and Hoot stayed home to watch the place. The crew left in mid-afternoon, planning to eat with Marge's bunch. She'd know better next time than to invite the entire Quarter Circle Z outfit to eat with them. They'd all show up.

When they arrived, Heck strung a picket line up for their horses, and soon Marge had Chet under her wing and swept him away. Her father, Harold McClure, spoke with him about the outlaw chase, and they had a double shot of Kentucky whiskey together to chase off the dust.

"Is it always this dry in Arizona?" Chet asked, with his throat cleared by the liquor.

"Sometimes it rains and you can't stop, too." Marge's dad chuckled lighting his pipe. "Rains usually starts in June and we have scattered afternoon showers most every day somewhere in the mountains the rest of the summer."

"I'm ready for some."

"Oh, it'll come."

"Tell me about bankers in Preskit. I met one at the Territory Bank where I stashed the ranch money. Are there others? I need make some improvements and to buy some more cattle."

McClure took out his pipe. "How much money do you need?"

"Cattle and buildings and all? Oh, I'd say twenty thousand, and what I have should do the rest of the things I need done."

"I'd loan you that on your livestock as security."

"That's a lot of money." Chet looked hard into the man's steel-blue eyes.

"I agree, but you have the livestock as your collateral, and that should get better with your herd additions."

"What interest rate?'

"One percent under the Territory Bank's rate."

"You have a deal. Thanks." They shook hands. So his plans to build and add on more livestock sounded on the move. He wanted to find some more cows, but with not much time left before he went home, he'd be pressed to buy them. Maybe someone at the dance had some for sale. No matter, Chet liked her father—considered him a man who shot from the hip.

Marge and her help made a fancy spread—linen tablecloths, and silverware. The cowboys about jumped back like a rattlesnake was about to bite them from the shock of seeing the setup under the tent. She kind of herded them on inside and told them to act like they were at home. Pleased, she introduced herself to each one and they acted very grateful to be her guests.

The cowboys ate everything brought to them from the soup on. Though a few of them slurped it too loud.

"They really can eat," Marge whispered to him as the roast beef, mashed potatoes, green beans, and fresh-sliced sourdough bread disappeared and were replaced by her help.

"Sorry I didn't warn you. Hoot spoils them."

"No, I love it, they are dandies."

Chet made a face at her. "Don't tell them that. They might misunderstand your usage of the word."

They both laughed. Chet noticed that Marge's father and Heck shared lots at the meal. The boy didn't act as stiff in the situation as the men did.

At last, Bixsby stood up and swallowed hard, then said thanks to everyone from the crew. "Best damn meal we've had in our lives." And the rest agreed. Then he offered for them to do the dishes, but Marge thanked him and said they had that task handled. A big relief swept over the faces of some of the hands. The dance came next.

"Do we need to stay and help clean up?" Chet asked her.

"No. I came to dance with you. The women will do it in a short time. Now I hear the fiddler playing."

"Yes, ma'am." Chet rose and gave her his arm.

And they waltzed. They polkaed and square-danced. He couldn't recall in years having that much fun or doing that many dances. Marge danced with some of the ranch hands. Chet danced with some of the ranch wives, including Marge's friend Kay whose husband ignored her. It was a shame J.D. wasn't there; he and the shorter woman would make a pair to dance together.

The dreamy night went on until a drunk made a scene on the dance floor. The couples began to stop and back away, in silence except for the man's threats.

"You're a worthless bunch—the whole lot of you. Some of you been stealing my stock." He waved a whiskey bottle around in his left hand. "I'm goin' to kill the next sumbitch steals a calf from me."

Chet was to him in a few steps. He spun him around

by the arm and gave him an uppercut with his right
fist that raised him on his dusty boot-toes. He crumpled to the floor. The whiskey bottle didn't break, but
some poured out on the floor. Wiley snatched it before
much ran out on the floor, and nodded firmly at his
boss. "Thanks, boss. You beat me to that filthy, mouthy
rascal."

"What do we need to do with him?" Bixsby asked.

"Haul him outside and tie him to a tree until he
sobers up."

The men crowded around nodding, and the moaning man was carried feet-first for the door. By then
Marge was at Chet's side and drew his fist up to examine it.

"You break anything?" Her blue eyes looking serious at him.

Chet dismissed her concern. "He'd not been so
drunk I'd talked him out of his business." He forced a
smile. "Guess he went all over me—cussing in a crowd
like this."

"I saw that before you even stepped up to him."

"Sorry."

"Don't be," Marge's father said. "You did all of us
a favor. That was Erv Holmes. He's a real loser. You
need to be on roundup with him someday. He mouths
all day and is always saying someone is cheating
on him."

Others pushed in to shake Chet's stinging hand and
thank him. He hid any discomfort.

"Let's make the musicians play," he said. "No sense

in someone that stupid ruining a dance." Marge's hand in his, Chet led her off at the first note.

"I saw a mountain lion move fast one time. You were like one. Wow, it don't take much to tick you off."

"If he wasn't raised any better than that—" He glanced over his shoulder to be sure it was clear to spin her to the left. "Then he needed some lessons in manners."

"I'm anxious to meet your family. They must be something."

Marge whirled around the floor at his lead. Chet felt the anger drain out of his body and with his hand in the middle of her back, he felt her muscular, smooth movement. Chet could hardly wait to be back in this country as a resident. The fiddler sawed away as their feet took wings. He wondered how she learned to dance so well. Perhaps her late husbands had shown her, or he figured, as rich as her father appeared to be, she probably learned that in finishing school.

"You ever attend finishing school?" he asked softy.

"Do I show it?"

"Sometimes."

"Oh, I was supposed to be a lady and marry some well-to-do sissy. Actually I wanted to ride horses and jump. Which I still do, but not publicly."

"I always see you in a buggy."

"I guess they reached me that far. Ladies drive, not ride, except on hunts and such."

Chet laughed. "You're full of surprises."

"So are you. Everyone stood around in shock, and

you jumped in and solved the problem before it broke up the dance."

Chet hugged her a little tighter. "I'm glad I did."

"So is everyone here but Holmes? Let's get some fresh air." The dance set over, he herded her toward the door. The bonfire blazing to light up the yard, he saw a young man step out in it.

"Mister, that was my dad you knocked out in there." Feet apart and armed, he stood challenging him.

"I don't know who you are, but there won't be any gunplay in this yard. There's children and women all over. You want to settle anything, I'll meet you tomorrow in the daylight and we can continue this."

"No. I want you now. You have a gun, go for it."

"No." Chet moved Marge back. "I said there were too many people here who could get hurt."

Then Chet saw someone step behind the boy and smash him over the head with a gun barrel. Disarmed by the force of his attacker, who jerked the gun away from the boy's holster, his knees crumpled and he hit the dirt face-down. Then Sarge waved everyone back. "Sorry, Chet, I didn't think he had that much backbone to challenge you. We'll tie him up with the other one."

"Who's he? The one who did that?" Marge asked from behind him.

"One of the ranch hands."

"Whew, they sure back you."

"I'm grateful, too."

Chet reached back and took her hand. They swiftly crossed the yard to escape the questions and then were alone behind a wagon, standing in each other's arms. Before he could explain anything, she put her finger to his lips and then kissed him.

She buried her face in his shoulder. He could feel her trembling in his arms.

"You alright?"

"I will be. I could see him shooting a dozen people and killing you."

"It was a tight place. Not a spot for gunplay, but there seldom is. Ignorant people like those two are the reason I'm having to leave Texas."

"Oh, hold me. I usually don't get this upset, but that was close."

Chet hugged her face to him. "Part of life. It ended well."

He kissed her and let her composure return before they went back for some lemonade.

"Getting late, isn't it?"

"You tired?" he asked, before sipping the sweet-sour. icy drink.

"No, I could stay up till dawn in your company, but I know you have things to do."

"They'll get done."

"Fine. I hope I'm not confining you so much you can't stand me. I simply can't resist holding your arm or hand. I enjoy connecting with you. I steal some of your strength."

"I understand. I feel the same way, but I also have obligations."

"I hope you can find your way back here. And I will treasure the fun and the excitement we had and how polite you are to me, as silly as I must be."

"You are excused," Chet said and laughed.

Marge jabbed him in the side with her hand. "What shall we do?"

"I'll walk you back to your camp and then I'll go find my bedroll. It has been a lovely evening."

"Yes, I seldom have shared such company. You are a real gentleman."

"Just me," Chet said to dismiss her compliment as she swung on his arm, heading through the camps for hers.

"Breakfast at seven?"

"Sounds excellent."

"Tell the crew."

"You sure?"

"Positive."

"Alright, it's your problem."

Then, at the large tent under the stars, he kissed her and stepped back with a bow. "My pleasure."

"Go." Marge pointed away. "Before I cry."

Chet laughed and strode away in the starlight shining through the tall cottonwoods. Damn, he'd boxed himself in. One woman in Texas, another out here. Heaven help him if he had to make a decision—maybe he'd join the LDS church and marry both of them.

No, that would not be an answer. Chet hoped his family in Texas faced no tougher decisions than he had to make out here.

Chapter 29

In the cool air of the early morning, Chet was dressed and ready to go. He set out kicking sleeping hands in their rolls and telling them they could have breakfast with a lovely lady.

Heck grumbled and told Chet he was coming. Sarge agreed and turned over. Wiley mumbled he'd sleep, and Bixsby wasn't there. He must have found a bedroll to share with some widow woman. Shame he'd miss all the food Marge's crew stirred up.

Seated at the long plank table under a white linen cloth, Chet sipped rich coffee as the crew arrived. He wondered if Heck had imbibed any the night before, for he acted like the rest. Maybe just worn out from all the things that went on. He'd noticed the boy had even danced some with young ladies.

"Good morning," Marge said, with freshness, to the crew. "Be seated. We have some wonderful things to serve you."

They obeyed. Some stared in wonder at the boneless

trout served after the canned peaches. Then came the
scrambled eggs with spinach, fried ham, sourdough
bread, and fried potatoes, followed by Danish pastry.

Chet about laughed when Wiley elbowed him.
"Wait till Hoot hears what we ate."

Heck made a serious face when Marge excused
herself to go check on something. "Whoever ate fish
for breakfast before, save on a camping trip?"

The boys shook their heads. Sarge spoke up. "I'd
dang sure take it over army beans."

They all laughed.

Politely, they each one thanked her after the meal.
Chet was glad that Heck was thoughtful enough not
to ask her about the trout. He let them go to pack their
things and smiled big at her. "Well, my hands are all
ready to quit me now that you've spoiled them."

"Oh, Chet, at times I can't help myself. I love them.
I never saw that Sarge do anything but stand back.
Last night he stepped out of nowhere and handled
that boy like it was nothing."

Chet slapped his leg with his hat. "Those boys know
what is supposed to be right, and I trust them."

"Where was the big one?"

"Hampt was helping a widow, I guess."

"Oh—"

Chet bent over and kissed Marge. "Thanks, *mi
amiga*." With that he slipped his hat on his head and
went for his horse.

"When will I see you again?"

He stopped and showed her his hands with a shrug.
"Some time this week."

"Good enough. I'll be home."

* * *

At the ranch, Hoot came out on the porch wiping his hands on his apron. "Fine-looking lot you all are. What mischief did you all get into, and where's Bixsby?"

"He's been delayed," Wiley said, stepping down.

"Yeah," Heck said with mischief written all over his face. "Maybe derailed would be better."

Everyone laughed. Then they began telling him about the excitement, and Chet went inside for a cup of coffee.

He heard Hoot ask them, "She served you fish for breakfast?"

Cory came in carrying an armload of split wood. "A big tall Indian woman was here asking for you earlier."

"She say what she wanted?"

"Nope, wouldn't tell me or Hoot anything."

"I'll ride up there and ask her." Chet couldn't imagine what she needed, but it must have been serious or she'd not have come and asked for him.

He rode upstream to their camp and saw it was empty, save for some things they couldn't carry or didn't want. Where had they gone? He found some tracks and rode his horse up in the hills to the north. They were sure being careful and not leaving much sign.

Chet crossed a long meadow surrounded by pines on the slopes. Some movement in the timber and then Mary appeared, coming on the run. He booted his horse out to meet her. Sliding him to a stop, he swung down. "What's wrong?"

"They put my brother in irons at the reservation and some other men. Then one of the police said they were going to drag us back to the reservation like dogs."

"I haven't had time to meet this agent. Sorry. What can I do?"

"Nothing I guess, but there is no food here. Children and women will starve."

"Can you lose their trackers?"

"I think so. Why?"

"Gives me time to go speak to the agent and if he has no answer, I'll go see General Crook."

"I will hide them long as I can."

"Two fires means it is okay to come down. Three means stay up there."

"I will watch for the smoke. Chet, thanks. We will repay you."

"No need in that. I'll try to find out what I can do."

Then Mary hugged him and stepped back as if embarrassed by her boldness. "May your God be with you."

With his nose full of campfire smoke from her closeness, Chet nodded. "I hope so, too."

He watched her run through the knee-high brown grass, then swung up in the saddle and headed for the ranch. He told the boys about what happened and they were all on his side—how could that agent expect them to return and starve?

By dawn, Chet was at the agent's house, pointed out to him by an old woman. He knocked until a sleepy man answered.

"What in hell's name do you want at this time of day?"

"You the agent here?"

"Yes, why?"

"I want to know some things—"

The man tried to shut the door, but Chet blocked him and moved him back with a shove. "Not so fast. Do you have any food for the Indians on this reservation?"

"Of course, they get monthly rations."

"No, they get little but spoiled food, and now you want that small band on my ranch to come in here."

"They aren't supposed to be out there."

"Listen, Swartz, I am going to have the U.S. Marshal and General Crook down here looking over your shoulder and seeing how bad you are treating these poor people."

"Bring them. Crook has no authority over me."

"By damn, someone does, and I'm getting to the bottom of this. You better have everything in order or you're going to Alcatraz for a long time."

"Who do you think you are, busting in here threatening me?"

"I ain't threatening you. I'm telling you what I'll get done. Now you want to talk or hear from higher authorities."

"I'll do as I'm—"

"Listen, you come or any of your police come on my ranch without the proper papers, my boys will shoot for trespassing. So come prepared to die."

"Who is this man?" a woman in a robe demanded.

"A wild man obstructing the business of a duly appointed Indian Agent."

"What is he saying?"

"Ma'am, I'm sorry, but your husband is abusing people who are under his care. They are starving and that's not right."

She raised her face and double chin, shaking it like a wattle on an old hen. "You, sir, are a liar and a troublemaker."

"When you ride the boat out to Alcatraz to see him you won't think so."

"Can he do this?"

"No." He shook his head at his wife.

Chet used his finger to point at him. "If you're so sure, go right on. I'm going to the authorities this morning. You might ought to pack and run cause I'm bringing the federal law back here."

"You are absurd. No one but Washington, D.C., or the Indian service can remove me from office."

"Alright, you won't cooperate. Wait until I get through with you. You'll wish you'd listened."

Chet started to leave. "And don't send those Indian Police after the band on my ranch. They won't come back alive."

He left the huffy agent shouting after him, and rode for the military base nearby. With a sharp nod, he went by the two black soldiers guarding the door to headquarters.

"I have business here."

The non-com nodded to him. "And your business, sir?"

"Who is the commander here?"

"Colonel Carr; he's not here."

"Who is next?"

"Major Brown. He is not here."

"Who's after him?"

"Lieutenant Granger."

"He here?"

"Yes, sir. What do you wish to speak to him about?"

"Starving Indians."

"But sir, the army is not in charge of them. They are under—"

"May I help you, sir?' A young man in an officer's uniform came to the door.

"Yes. My name's Chet Byrnes, and the atrocities being laid on these Indians is criminal. They are given little food and are starving to death. We have been feeding a small band of mostly women and children on my ranch. Now the agent is demanding they come back and starve here."

The young man folded his arms over his chest. "We have heard this report before, but we are not in charge of the Indians any longer. They are wards of the Interior Department, and there is nothing we can do."

"What happens if a bunch of them go on the warpath?"

"I guess then they'd want our help. But I have not heard or seen of any trouble with them."

"Then you'd have to take charge of them, right? Why don't you wire General Crook that there is a band of Yavapai off the reservation who will only surrender to him?"

"You know General Crook, sir?"

"No, but I can lead him to talk to this band, if he is willing to come down here."

"You know, he is a very busy man."

"These Indians respect him. They don't the agent."

"You know, I could be court-martialed for this if it turns real ugly?"

"This is serious business."

"I will wire Whipple and see what the general says."

"Good, I'm finally getting some action."

"This will require several hours, I am certain. Do you wish to wait?"

"I'm going to sit right here until we hear from him."

"Your name again is?"

"Chet Byrnes. I own the Quarter Circle Z ranch just west of here."

"Thank you, Mr. Byrnes."

About that moment, a red-faced Swartz rushed into the office and demanded that the lieutenant arrest Chet on the spot.

"Agent Swartz, this man has filed a report with the U.S. Army that due to your lack of proper care a band of Yavapai have fled the reservation."

"They are nothing but some discontented women and children."

"I am wiring General Crook and asking his advice."

"That's stupid. Here is the troublemaker. He encouraged those people to leave the reservation, and now you are doing an equally stupid thing asking for military help. My tribal police will have them back here in a short while."

"You don't even know where they're at." Chet rose to his feet, ready to throw him outside.

"Gentlemen," the officer said. "The General or his staff will tell me what to do."

"Stop that wire. I need to wire Washington instead and have them tell you and this cowboy who runs the Indian affairs here."

"I won't stop the wire. It is an army telegraph; usage for other business is not allowed unless an emergency. The army business comes first and until I hear the reply from Whipple the line will not be used."

"You'll be peeling potatoes when I get through with you!" Swartz stormed out of the office.

"Will you need some ranch help when he gets through with me?" The officer grinned big, and then shook his head to dismiss any concern on his part.

Two hours later, the wire came. The lieutenant called to Chet, who was sitting on a wooden folding chair, looking at his calloused hands and wondering if they would even answer.

"General Crook is sending his best negotiator this afternoon. He expects his man to arrive here by sundown."

"Who will that be?" Chet asked.

"I'm not certain. But he has some good staff members. There's lots of bad blood these days between the Army and the Indian agents. But I am sure anyone he sends can advise you on what to do next."

"Lieutenant, thanks. How many will be in the party coming?"

"Maybe a dozen, maybe one. Probably a few Indian

scouts. General Crook counts on them to help him get through these matters."

"Could you direct him to my ranch? West about two miles on the river road. It's the Quarter Circle Z. And my name is Chet Byrnes."

"I will do that, sir. And thank you for being so calm in all this."

"If Swartz tries to take those poor people, they may find my ranch hands are tough, too. They're mad as I am about the conditions for those people."

"Try to be calm. General Crook has many supporters in Washington, D.C., that can get some things done up there."

"Thanks. I will be at the ranch and have a meal waiting on whoever he sends."

"Thank you, sir."

Chet rode his horse home in a short lope. Still mad about the agent, he wondered how many more Indians were being treated this badly. No wonder Indians went on attacks.

"Any sign of the Indian Police today?" Chet asked Tom when he met him.

"They coming?"

"General Crook is sending a negotiator."

"Who is that?"

Chet dropped heavily out of the saddle. "Danged if I know, but the young officer at the camp says he'll be a good one."

"Meanwhile, they won't find the camp easily." Tom gave him a sharp nod. "We hid them."

Chet rubbed the back of his stiff neck, and then

smiled. "That agent Swartz has a lot to learn in this world."

Near sundown, an army officer and three Apache scouts rode up the lane. The man in charge was in his thirties, with a short mustache. He reined up at the yard gate where Chet waited for him.

"You must be Mr. Byrnes?"

"Get down, Lieutenant, we have hot food ready for you and your men."

"You sound very serious, sir. We won't turn that offer down." They all dismounted and the ranch hands took their horses to the corral. The three Apaches, wearing knee-high pointed-toed boots and loincloths, squatted on the ground with their Spencer rifles over their legs.

"Let's go eat." Chet waved for them to follow and he shook Chet's hand.

"My name's Jim Hulbert."

"Nice to meet you." Chet noticed the scouts had stopped at the stairs. "Won't they come inside?"

"I doubt it. They fear large houses might fall in and kill them."

Chet shook his head. "Cory, fill three plates and feed them. They don't like roofs."

"I can do that." The barefoot boy went off to get them food.

Chet showed the man a chair and took one opposite him at the large table. He indicated for Hulbert to help himself to anything on the plates Hoot had prepared. Sliced roast beef, mashed potatoes, fresh green beans, fresh bread and butter. Hoot had learned lots about local farmers and available items. They came by twice a week and sold him fresh things.

"How are the scouts doing out there?" Chet asked Cory on his way going back with a granite coffeepot.

"Hungry as wolves."

"Good."

"Mr. Byrnes, tell me about the Indians you are concerned about."

"Call me Chet. My ranch hands came across a camp of starving Yavapai a few weeks ago up on our land. Mostly women and children. They told us the food the agent gave them for supplies was moldy and rotten. The two cows were just old bones. There was nothing for them to eat. So we gave them a fat bull and a few crippled, but fat horses to eat. Also some beans and flour.

"They were afraid the Indian Police would come drive them with whips back to the reservation. I went to reason with the agent Swartz, and he shouted I was making them hostile and belligerent. No way. They're polite, gentle people. As I said, most are women and children, some are real old."

"The Indian Service hates us. I know how crooked most agents are and how they buy sorry products that are cheap and pocket the difference."

"What can we do about it?"

"We can scare Swartz into giving them the staples by law he is required to give to them. There are some inspectors who have to cover too many agencies that have some power of enforcement. I can try to wire for one of them to come up here."

"If they're slow, these people could starve."

"The government took the care of these people away

from the army. People like Swartz are going to make enough Indians mad enough to have more trouble." Hulbert took up his coffee and blew on it. "You set a great table, Byrnes. No wonder those Indians want to stay here."

"What can I do to help them?"

"I'll put my three scouts to guard them and call them runaways. The tribal Police won't mess with my guards. Then I'll try to get an inspector up here to look over the conditions. I can't guarantee to do much more than that."

"What can the General do?"

"Raise cain in Washington."

"Will they listen?"

"Sometimes. But it isn't at lightning speed."

"Will you go up and talk to the woman in charge? She's very serious. You want to go tonight?"

"In the morning will be fine."

Chet looked him straight in the eye. "I know how I'd handle it. But that would probably draw me some time in a federal prison."

Hulbert nodded. "Don't go that far."

"Will your men need a place to sleep tonight?"

"No. I have a bedroll on my horse. I'll sleep with them."

"Breakfast is at dawn."

"We'd appreciate that." Hulbert shook Chet's hand. "The general sent his regards."

"When you get back, thank him for me."

"I will, sir."

After Hulbert went outside, Chet and most of his crew huddled.

"What's he going to do?" Hoot asked.

"Try to get an inspector of Indian agents in here. Otherwise, the Lieutenant is making them his prisoners so the Tribal Police can't take them back."

"Good," Wiley said as if satisfied.

"We've done about all we can for them, boys."

"You did well," Bixsby said. "You must have seen what we saw up there when we found them."

"Boys, we're doing all we can for those poor devils. Let's get some sleep."

"Night, boss man."

"Night."

But Chet didn't find sleep easy. So many unsettled things beyond his control in this world. But no matter, he'd still stand up for them or anyone else in that shape.

What was happening at home?

Chapter 30

Hoot's bell woke the dead. Cory could make it ring. Chet opened his eyelids, and finally his pupils began to focus. If he could wind up his business, he should be on the road to Texas—shortly. Maybe not soon enough. His gut feeling was there were things going on back there that he needed to attend to—that they simply weren't telling him everything. Dressed, he went downstairs and found the blue uniform already at the table and eating. Hulbert raised his coffee cup. "Your food is excellent."

"They feed your scouts?"

"Oh, yes. We'll be on our way in a few minutes. Thanks again."

"One of my boys need to take you up there?"

"No, one of my scouts made contact last night with Mary. She is expecting us."

"Wonderful. You're organized. We'll get on with ranching. All my men have been concerned about their welfare and the state they're in."

"Very generous of them. We can handle it from here."

"Good." Chet would take the man at his word.

The lieutenant soon excused himself, then shortly he and his men rode out.

Wiley said, "Imagine that. One of them scouts found them and made contact with her. I never thought much about them soldiers before except for Sarge here. But there are some sharp folks in our army."

"They ain't all as dedicated as he is," Sarge said.

"I guess you'd know," Chet added.

The ex-soldier nodded and went back to eating.

In an effort to get the ranch deal closed out, Chet saddled Dyer and headed for Preskit. When he stopped at Marge's place, she was jumping rails with a young horse. Dismounted, she came in her riding clothing and knee-high English boots to greet him. The fresh look on her face under the large Western felt hat brim made his guts roil.

"How are things going for you today?" she asked.

"Better. General Crook sent one of his staff up to the ranch to help the starving Yavapai. I think he can handle a sorry agent and get those people some provisions."

Marge shook her head in disbelief. "What else do you do?"

"I'm trying to get this ranch deal settled, so I can head home and sell out."

Marge stepped in and hugged him. "I never cease to be amazed at you, Chet Byrnes."

The whisper of her perfume ran up his nose and

began to intoxicate him. He pressed his forehead to hers. "I don't know anything else."

Then Chet stepped back and smiled. "I only came by to say hi. Maybe if I have time, I'll stop by, going home."

Marge started to walk toward his horse with him. "Do that. I can hold some supper for you."

"Better not hold that. I don't know when I'll come back—tonight."

"No problem, I will have something for you to eat."

"Good-looking leggy colt that you've been riding. He's taking to the jumping business?"

"Oh, yes. He's got plenty of jumper in his blood-lines and he shows it."

He gave her a peck on the cheek and then swung into the saddle. "See you later."

"I certainly hope so. Be careful, too."

He touched his hat brim and sent Dyer off for town.

In the Palace Bar, he found Jane, and she said Bo Harold had been up all night playing poker and was sleeping in her room in the Duffle Hotel. Her directions were go out the back door, take the bridge over the small creek, and go up the hill to the gray building on the right.

Chet did all that and twisted the knob on the front door. A bell rang, and a stout woman in her forties came in the living room, dressed in a corset. "What may I do for you, sir?"

"Bo Harold is sleeping in here?"

She gave a tug up on her underwear to get the top end higher, then pointed to the stairs. "Second room on the left. My name's Clair."

"Nice to meet you ma'am. Mine's Chet."

"Now Chet, you need anything, simply whistle." She looked him over from head to boot-toe and then smiled. "Just whistle, darling."

"I'll remember to do that."

He found Harold half-undressed, laying across the bed, face-down and snoring. He shook him by the shoulder.

"Huh?" He sat up and blinked his eyes. "Oh, it's you."

"Where are we on the ranch business?"

"The papers are in the mail from back there."

"How many days will they require to get here?" Chet squatted on his haunches.

"A good week, maybe longer to get here from there. What do you need me to do?"

"Tell me I have no worries and can go back to Texas and settle things there."

Scratching his rumpled blond hair, Harold nodded. "I can do all that. Brand deal is done. You have the Quarter Circle Z in your name. Don't have the bar-C deal made yet."

Chet pivoted back toward his man on his boot sole. "A few more things settled, and I'm going back to Texas."

"You figure it will take a year to get that straightened out and sold back there?"

Chet shrugged. "I'm allowing that much. It may be quicker."

"There's talk about an Indian uprising—"

"No, the agent's starving the Indians and I've got General Crook to intervene."

"Good. I don't need any more Indian wars around here. Bad for my business."

"I'll let you sleep."

"How did you find me anyway—oh, oh, you know Jane, I forgot."

"You better take her more serious. She looks out for you." Chet rose to his feet. He would soon be Texas-bound. He better go get Heck cleaned up and some new clothes for the trip. He had a new family headquarters on the Verde River. All he had left was settling out back there and hauling his tribe out here.

"Oh, I take Jane serious enough." Harold yawned and stretched his arms over his head. "Sometimes. But you're right, I should be more serious about her."

Chet left the agent and took the stairs two at a time. Clair opened the front door for him. "Don't run off the next time. We might find something interesting to do."

He winked at her going out. "We might."

The counter stools were full when he reached Jenny's for lunch. So he stood back of the eaters. When she looked up after delivering a lunch plate to a customer, she frowned at him. He smiled back at her and said he was fine.

At last he was seated; she brought him a plate of barbequed pulled pork with fried potatoes and hot bread on the side. Then she filled a coffee cup for him. "Everything going alright?"

"I'm close to being wound up here and headed home."

"I'll be caught up in a minute then you can tell me all about it."

"I'll be here."

"Good. What was it you needed?" She asked a man down the row. "Oh, more bread. Coming up."

"She gets any busier, she'll be feeding some of us in the street," the short man beside him said.

"She may have to."

They both laughed.

The crowd soon thinned and she came by, writing down charges on a small tablet to hand out. "You okay?"

"Fine."

"I heard about an Indian uprising in the Verde Valley. What was that about?"

"I wired General Crook for help. That agent was starving them to death."

"Oh, it was you on the warpath." She laughed until she cried. Shaking her head and dabbing at the tears, she smiled. "I should have known. You're sure going to brighten up this country."

"And I will be back, the good Lord willing."

"You going back to Texas already?"

"Plan to, as soon as I can."

Jenny crushed her lips together and shook her head. "We're gonna sure miss you. Who will give jobs to all my unemployed customers?"

"By spring, I hope to be back."

"Good, and be careful, we want you back here."

He talked to Tanner at the bank, the man at the store, and even went by to shake Frey's hand. The livery man promised him another roan horse or two as good as Roan when he came back. Then he left town and went to Marge's place even before suppertime.

When Chet rode up, Marge rushed out to hug and swing him around in a green velvet dress. Out of breath when they stopped, she beamed up at him. "You're back early. I wish we could polka one more time."

"Da, da, da," he began the beat and they did two whirls in the dust.

She laughed so hard he had to let go of her to cough as well.

"This is all very crazy."

"Who cares?"

"Not me." She tackled him around the waist, and hugging, they barely made it up the front steps. On the porch, she pushed him against the wall of the house and straightened. "You are something I never thought I'd find. You are one fun guy. And if you have to do whatever, I won't forget you."

"You are sure on a high today." He put his arm on her shoulder.

"And I don't drink."

He sobered up for a moment. "That's good."

"I don't. I had some drinks one time and didn't like how I felt or acted." She looked at the ceiling for some help.

"I'm not that well behaved, but it doesn't have any hold on me."

"I know that. Come on in. We're eating alone. Dad has gone to the lodge. I had a husband that drank—too much. I felt he never could stand his own place in society, always had to be better, do more things, and he crawled in a bottle."

"Bad thing when you can't stand the world you live in."

She agreed. "Let's quit talking about bad things. I want this evening to sparkle. I have you alone all to myself, and I just want to enjoy it since you are running away from me."

He seated her and then at her request took the head seat at the table. The Lone Star flag waved in his mind. It would be hard to leave her and return to yesterday. More things to fret over. If he knew what Kathren would do, he'd tell Marge right that minute. But short of a miracle happening, he'd come back alone. And he could have lots of laughs with her. What would Susie think of her?

The kitchen help brought them their food and poured freshly made coffee in their gold-rimmed cups.

"Kinda fancy," he said, "to drink out of these, isn't it?"

She wrinkled her nose. "Not for you."

"Well, I can tell my sister she can have tea with you out of gold-rimmed cups."

"Would she like that?"

"She'd be impressed."

"What is she like?"

"She works night and day to make the household right—food right—clothes right—you name it, she's a whiz at it."

"No wonder you don't have a wife."

"No wonder she doesn't have a husband. Doesn't have any time for herself. But my Aunt Louise, who's a widow, now she would be impressed. Really so."

"Who else?"

"I have my brother's widow, May. She's the most tender-hearted woman in the world."

"Would May be impressed?"

"I doubt it, but she'd be polite."

Marge sat back in the chair, wiped her mouth on a napkin. "You will have your hands full bringing them out here."

"Oh, I'm not through. My oldest nephew Reg is waiting for me to get back so he can get married to one of Susie's staff—Juanita. A lovely Mexican girl who's been working at our house over a year. She's sharp and a good soul. But his mother doesn't approve of her—Louise is hard to please."

"Well, you do face many problems. But I will be here."

Chet reached over and squeezed her wrist. "I thank you. I'll be careful and you do that same. You are lots of fun to be with."

When they finished, they rose without a word. She chewed on her bottom lip.

"Now don't plant your feet in the mud," Chet said. "As much as I'd like to, this is not the night for us to lose ourselves. If I make a commitment to a woman I try to keep it. Besides, if what we have is worth anything, we can wait."

She nodded and held on to his arm going for the front door. "I don't think I'd regret it."

"You might." He hugged her around the neck and kissed her hard on the mouth. Then he dropped back and held her fingers. "Don't fall off your jumper. I want to see you soar over those fences when I come back."

"Will you stop before you go out on the stage?"

"No. It would be too damn hard."

Marge buried her face in his vest. "Thanks, anyway. I have some wonderful memories."

"Good night."

He rode Dyer on home. He'd get Heck ready and they'd head east.

Chapter 31

Chet and Heck sat on the bench under the light coming from the smeared office window over their shoulders. The boy on his right with a short haircut and new clothes looked handsome. Night mountain air had cooled on Chet's windburned face.

Before them sat the Black Canyon stagecoach, without horses, in front of the office. Canvas sacks of mail were ready to be loaded. The express box, under lock, had been loaded with gold bullion and mounted in the floor of the coach. A shotgun guard stayed alert, standing in the area of the passenger door.

"Did the ticket man say I can ride on top?" Heck asked.

"Just so you don't fall asleep and roll off."

"I won't do that."

"Good. 'Cause I need you to keep me straight going home."

"Ha, what could I do?"

"I figure you learned a lot cowboying up here."

"I did learn some things. There's two kinds of girls in this world."

"Don't share that with your aunt."

"Oh, I won't. I learned I could dance with girls, which was nice. I can rope good as most cowboys. And when I get older I'm going to ride broncs. Real tough ones."

"You should do well. I want you to get some more book-learning so you can make a living with your mind as well."

"I'll try that."

"Good. They didn't say much in that last letter, did they?"

"No. I hope things are going that well."

Chet drew a deep breath. So did he. The jingle of the harness on the dancing teams coming from the stables behind the office told him they were near ready to head south.

Three men hooked them. The agent brought a nicely dressed woman out and loaded her into the coach, and then waved the two of them over. "Get aboard, gents. Now don't you fall off the top, young man."

"I won't, I'm too excited to do that." Like a circus monkey, Heck mounted the side and was soon sitting cross-legged on the roof.

Chet thanked the man and waved at his nephew before he joined the woman on the seat facing the back. Two more drummers came out of the office and took the back seat. They grumbled a little about how the stage should be leaving at a decent hour, and one of them coughed hard once he was seated.

The woman's name was Olive Ramsey and she

spoke like she came from the piney woods, despite her fashionable clothes.

"We's barely got space for two people to sit 'chere," she said to Chet.

"Ain't no room and no comfort in these dang coaches," the fatter man complained.

"If'n my mama weren't dying, I'd never got on this rickety thang," she drawled.

"Oh, I'm sorry to hear that," Chet said.

"Well'n I'm going. I hope I survive this one."

The driver rocked the rig, and then the guard did the same thing getting up into his place as well. They left Preskit with the man on the reins shouting at his teams and cracking a whip. They were off for Phoenix and then places east.

Chet even managed to sleep some. Then somewhere in between his dozing off and waking, a shot shattered the night.

"Hold up or die!" someone ordered.

The driver applied the brakes and whoaed them.

"Oh my Gawd—" the woman said, sucking in her breath. "Don't you let them rape me," she pleaded with Chet.

"I won't." He wondered why she thought they'd do that to her. Most holdup men wanted money, not sex.

She clutched his arm. "Say I'm your wife. Maybe they won't do it to me then."

What time was it? Close to dawn, by his calculation. He heard a familiar voice demanding they get down and not try any tricks. The voice cued him. He knew that person. It was the Kid. Where was his part-

ner? What was his name? Cecil Crown was it. They'd
gone from stealing horses in Texas to robbing stages
in Arizona. Chet stepped out under the stars and then
helped her down. She was trembling.

The Kid took Chet's six-gun out of his holster and
pushed them a few feet away from the coach.

"You all get down on the ground." That was Crown's
voice, and there were two more sitting on horses,
wearing flour-sack masks. "Don't try anything."

One of them got off his horse and unhitched the
back team, then did some more unhitching. Crown
climbed into the coach and shot the lock off the strong-
box. The boiling gunsmoke made everyone cough and
their eyes smart. It burned Chet's to the core.

"Damn bullion, boys," Crown said in disgust, holding a candle. "No, there's some coins in here." He began
filling his pockets while the Kid searched everyone. He
found some money on Chet, who appreciated that, in
the darkness, they had not recognized him.

The woman screamed when the Kid intentionally
felt her breasts.

Chet halfway stepped toward him. "Unhand my
wife."

"Sure. Sure, I'm looking for where she's hiding it."

"She has none. You have my money already."

"Damn sure ain't much," the Kid grumbled.

Chet again felt grateful for the darkness. He still
had not recognized him. Good.

"I've got all the coins. Here, take some of these gold
bars." Crown handed out some. "We can sell them
someplace."

"You boys ready?" he asked the others.

"Yeah."

"Take that boy along, so they don't get the urge to follow us. We can leave him off on the road somewhere."

Chet's heart stopped and fell out. Not Heck. . . .

Chapter 32

The riders shot off a few shots in the air and spooked the horses. Then the outlaws thundered off in the night.

"Oh, thank God, mister. I am so grateful to you. I was raped once by some highway men and my husband divorced me for letting them do that to me. I ain't none too sure this one I got now wouldn't do the same gawdamn thing to me."

Chet agreed, and asked the guard if there was a loaded rifle up in the boot.

He nodded.

In a bound, Chet was up there and had it in his hands. He checked and found, in the growing light, it was loaded. He swung down.

"Where you going, mister?" the driver asked.

"I'm going to catch a horse from the teams and follow them. That's my nephew they took."

"They said they'd leave him in the road somewhere if we didn't follow them."

"Bullshit. Those two I know are killers."

"But you ain't got a saddle. No provisions. You're going on a wild goose hunt."

"Tell the sheriff I went after them. My name's Chet Byrnes. He knows me and will send help." At that, he took off running down the mountain to find himself a horse. The purple of sunup was coming over the tall range to his left.

Where were those outlaws headed? He spotted two horses in the road still in harness. From a sheath behind his back, he took out his large knife and began to stalk them. They looked wide-eyed and ready to spook some more.

"Whoa. Whoa," he kept coaxing them, getting closer and knowing they were still in a high state of fear. They bolted away and then stopped again, fifty feet from him. Out of breath from his run off the slope, his heart pounded like a hammer under his rib cage. He swallowed and found himself about to shake from all the tension. Talking quietly to his goal, he slipped closer. This time putting down the rifle and gathering a trailing rein, and setting his heels in the gravel.

When they tried to take off again, Chet brought the left horse around. Moving in between them, he slashed the harness loose and cut the strap holding the left horse's collar off him. The animal spooked backwards when it swung off his neck and fell at his front feet. But he had the bridle rein and soon led him over to pick up the rifle.

In a fast swing, he was on the horse's back. Not once had he even thought that the horse might not be broken to ride. He urged him on, and the horse left, crow-hopping. Holding his rifle and reins plus a hank of his mane, Chet needed two more hands to draw his head up. Instead, he shouted at his mount and the horse broke into a run.

His green-broke horse soon settled into a short lope and he wondered how far ahead the highway men might be. He didn't need to burst in on them. They might blow him to kingdom come or kill the boy.

Mid-morning, he saw them way off, or at least their dust, headed for the Bradshaw Mountains. He wondered if they could see him. He eased his big horse down to a walk and settled in. He had their hoofprints memorized. If he overran them—it would be too bad for him. But if he waited till the sun went down, he'd have half a chance of getting Heck back safely.

Chet wished he knew this sparse country where the tall cactus began to appear. And where they were going.

At the next crossroad under the stair-step range, he saw the sign HORSE THIEF BASIN—TWELVE MILES WEST. HAYDEN'S MILL—SIXTY MILES SOUTH. PRESCOTT—the miles weren't plain—to the north. The temperature felt over 100 degrees.

Chet watered at a small ranch. The stern woman of the house held a .22 rifle on him the entire time the horse drank and he washed his face. He politely thanked her and rode on. The day was finally going down. The sun was beyond the range and he could see their tracks plain as day. How far would they go?

On a flat bench at last, with several tall juniper trees spotted across the near-level land, he discovered a horse. It had a wet spot on its back where the saddle

and pad had once been. They must have stopped. He
went to hide his own horse in a cluster of the trees.
Was it them or someone else simply stopped for the
night on the dim ruts some might call a road? No
telling. His horse hidden and grazing, impatiently he
waited for dark. His stomach barked at his backbone.

The smell of their campfire gnawed at him. At last
with the sun down, he crawled and ran, low like an
Indian, to get closer. At last he could hear their voices.
Resting on his belly under a pungent juniper, he heard
the Kid laugh.

Chet buried his face in his arms. No sound of
Heck's voice. Did they still have him?

Damn, he better be there. Chet's wind came back
and he edged closer. He found his hands were shaky,
holding the rifle stock and edging closer. Somehow
he must stop that weakness.

Still no sign of Heck as he viewed them in the
campfire's light. They were busy eating and had no
guard out. Cussing and fussing about the lack of much
loot, Crown was standing up telling them every robbery wasn't perfect.

Right. Including that last one.

On his knees and ready with the rifle in his hands,
he told them to put their hands in the air. He shot
Crown, first in the upper body, then took out another
fool who went for his gun belt. The third man was running and he cut him down. The fourth man rose,
screaming, "I give up!"

Chet advanced on him. Gunsmoke burning his
eyes, he came toward the firelight one step at a time.

"Where's the boy?" he demanded.

"He ain't here."

He could hear the man's voice trembling. Damn, what had happened? Heck had not been on the road that he followed them on. "Where in hell is he?"

"I don't know, I told you."

Chet jerked the .44 out of his holster. "What happened to him?"

"I don't know."

"Yes, you know." He turned the six-gun over in his hand. Just another cap-and-ball gun, with caps on the nipples. "You better tell me, or I'm going to shoot you in the left foot, then the right one. Then in the knees and then in the hip, until you tell me where my boy is at."

"Way back there the Kid done it."

"Did what?" Chet jammed the muzzle of the six-shooter into his guts.

"I-I-I didn't do it. I swear, mister, I never had nothing to do with it."

"What did they do to him?" Chet raged. He stuck his own gun in his waistband, then he jerked the man's revolver out of his holster. To press his point, he forced the man backward with the muzzle of the Colt. Hammer cocked, his trigger finger twitched.

"They cut his throat and threw him over the cliff."

"Tell me one more time what they did to that boy." His teeth were so tightly clinched that his jaw hurt.

"They cut his throat and threw him off a cliff."

"Damn you!" Chet pulled the trigger with the muzzle in the man's chest.

Gunsmoke boiled up. The man screamed, "No!" He

staggered backward each time that Chet pulled the trigger until the last bullet struck him as he lay on the ground. Shaking, Chet clicked the trigger two more times on empty. He went to Crown's body and jerked him up to his face by a handful of his bloody shirt.

"Did you kill that boy?"

No answer.

Disgusted, he went to where the Kid lay, rolled him over and knelt on the ground to draw him up to his face. "So you killed that boy, huh?"

The Kid's eyes looked glazed over, his face white as marble. His head was loose on his shoulders and rolled around when he shook him. "Did you?"

No answer.

He went to the last man he had shot in the back, and turned him over. "Tell me how they killed him. Where is he at?

"A long steep side—off a . . . ." The man's life escaped him and he went limp.

Chet staggered back to the fire and cried. The pain in his chest was like a knife stabbing him over and over again. He hurt so bad he wanted to shoot himself and be over with it all. How could he ever tell the family?

How could he go on living—letting them kill that innocent boy? *Oh, dear God please forgive me for bringing him out here. For letting these worthless bastards kill a boy who'd had enough hell in his life.* He tossed more fuel onto the fire.

No way Chet could eat. No way he could face anyone or anything. The cross he must bear was to find that boy's body come daylight and have a funeral for him. Oh, did he even have the strength? This must be one of those nightmares that ruined his sleep. No. He could feel the heat of the fire on his face. No, Heck Dale Byrnes was dead. But where?

Haggard, without any food or sleep, at first light, Chet saddled and rode one of the outlaws' better horses and searched off both sides of the route that they had taken off the far range to their camp. Then he saw the gathering buzzards circling high in the sky in the distance. Way down the road—he swung into the saddle and raced the horse to beat the scavengers to Heck's body.

Maybe he was still alive—no, he couldn't expect that. Whipping and lashing the horse over and under with the reins, he thundered off the mountainside. Skidding him to a ruthless stop, he bailed off the horse in the road and looked straight down the steep side into the canyon. Good grief. It was too great a dropoff to simply go down it. He'd need to take the side down. Then, hand over hand, he let himself down the bluff, looking for sight of it. He lost his footing. A juniper branch he caught in the nick of time tore into his palm, and soon blood began to appear. The way grew easier to descend and he could see the corpse. When he looked up, the way back was too steep to go up. No matter, he would have the boy's body and they wouldn't.

Chet rolled the limp body over, and beneath the dirty face he saw the wide rip under his chin. Sonsabitches! A shame Kathren didn't kill them all. Or the night in Mason when they beat him up that he didn't kill them then. He gently took Heck up in his arms and looked for the best way back up to the road.

It was a long, grueling hour or so for him to get back up to the top. He found the horse grazing, gathered the reins, and stepped up into the saddle, holding the boy in his arms. Then he headed east for the stage road.

An hour later, Chet met Sheriff Sims and his posse. The man dismounted and came over to look at the boy. "We can take him for you."

"No, I'm going to do that. Those men you want are all dead. We had a shoot-out up on that road to Horse Thief. They told me that the Kid cut his throat and threw him off a bluff. I found him about an hour ago. The gold they robbed is up there. So is one of the stage line horses with the rest of theirs."

"Thanks. Some of us can go with you. We want to help you. We're sorry they killed him."

"No, thanks. I can take him." He swallowed hard. "I'm sorry he's dead, too."

Chet booted the horse on before he cried.

Two hours later on the road, he saw a buggy coming from Preskit. The dust about obscured it, but he saw it was Marge's rig. They soon met in the road. Chet's vision was blurred and his mouth too dry to hardly talk. She was in tears when she took the body from him, and collapsed in the road with Heck sprawled over her lap.

Chet tried to jump down, but ended up falling from the saddle to the ground. The sun was blazing in his eyes. He crawled on his hands and knees.

"They killed him." He was on his knees, half blind, too groggy to think. Maybe like Rocky had been, out there looking for those siblings that the Comanche took.

"I can see that. Oh, Chet, what will you do?"

"Find a preacher—take him to the ranch. That's Byrnes land now. We can bury him there. He fought for it like they fought for the bar-C and was the—first to die."

In the dust, Chet began hugging and kissing her. My God, where was he at? How did she know to come for him?

"Chet. Chet, you fainted. Can you help me put him in the buggy?"

"Sure, sure," he slurred. "How did you know about this?"

"Harold came and told me you had gone after the robbers. The posse was already gone. Did they get them?"

"Yeah, that's another story."

"You can tell me later." She struggled to get the corpse into the buggy, and finally he found his sea legs and helped her put him on the floor between the seats.

"Now you get in."

Clumsy as a bear cub, at last he was on the seat. She ran around to get on, and took control of the team. They made a wide turn and headed north.

"My gosh, Chet, how did this all happen?"

"Stage robbers in the night stopped the coach. Some lady riding with me was so afraid they would rape her, she wanted my help."

"Why did she need your help, for Heaven sakes?"

"'Cause the last time she was held up, the bandits

raped her. Her first husband divorced her over letting them do that and she was afraid this one might, too—"

He was hysterically laughing and so was she. To handle the horses, she slowed them to a walk, then dried her eyes.

"That's as bad as my experience holding out my money from them."

"Yeah. That bad," he cried, and went back to his foot-stomping laughter.

Chapter 33

Close to the head of the Camp Verde Road, they met most of his ranch hands and stopped in the road. They removed the cover as they rode up close and looked in at the boy's small body. Many a tough hand had tears in his eyes.

Tom dismounted, holding his hat. "Word was out early today that you'd gone after some holdup men. We were coming to back you. We'll make him a casket. Guess you'll want to bury him on the ranch. We hope that suits you."

"Thanks. That will be just fine. Let's go home—" Chet swallowed hard and nodded for her to start on. As he looked off the dizzy heights at the vast valley beneath them, he wondered how his family would like his choice. Maybe this incident would draw them all together, closer. He simply dreaded to tell them about this loss. He closed his eyes as Marge fought the team to hold them back on the grade.

When they reached the next flat spot, he made her stop and give him the reins.

"I can drive alright," she protested.

"That isn't the problem, Marge. I can see on your face how strained you were driving. Let me do this. I'm going to have to go on living and face this loss like I have others. This is much easier than seeing my parents wilt away from life day by day, and them still alive."

She hugged his shoulder and buried her face on his sleeve. "When did you eat last?"

"I'm not certain."

"One of you boys have a canteen? He needs a drink."

Wiley rode in and handed her his. Leaning over his saddle horn, he asked. "You making it, boss man?"

"Yes, Wiley, I'll be fine." He reared back to slow the team. "Easy boys, easy."

Marge removed the cork and held it up to his mouth. Some sloshed down his dirty shirt and vest. But his dry mouth absorbed most of it. He swallowed and thanked her.

It was the longest trip off the mountain he could ever recall. Like looking down on ants to him, there was the small village, the army camp, and the cottonwoods along the Verde. Again, he leaned back on the reins to slow their pace. Tossed from side to side on the seat with her, he wondered if they'd ever reach the bottom. But eventually they did, and the wheels whirled up dust again, headed for the river road to the ranch.

There was plenty to do when they got there. Hoot had a fat yearling steer in the pens for the men to slaughter. Several ranch families were already camped there and helping the old man get things arranged and cooked.

With some help to get Heck out of the rig, Chet carried the limp body to the house. The anxious face of Marge's friend Kay met them at the door, and she led Chet to a bedroom set up to lay Heck down on some raw boards over sawhorses.

The corpse there, Kay told Marge to take him out of the room. She and some of the others would prepare the deceased for the funeral. Like a spent person, he let Marge take him out of the room.

More rigs began to arrive. Jenny rushed into the house to hug him. "Oh, Chet, I'm so sorry—" Then she burst into tears and they huddled in the middle of the room, holding each other up.

"Take him to the table," Marge whispered. "Hoot made him some chicken soup. He hasn't eaten in two days."

Chet caught the concerned look on Jenny's face, who led him over to sit down at the long table. "My gosh, why haven't you eaten?"

Warily, he shook his head at her. "I haven't had time." He looked over the growing crowd in his house. "I need to welcome all these folks that have come—"

The two women shook their heads at him.

"You need to eat," Marge insisted and Jenny backed her.

What could he do? His head was in a whirl. He was lost. Better obey them.

He slurped soup off a spoon they used to feed him. Somewhere this scene had happened before—some time in his life. Then he knew the time. It was when the two rangers brought his father Rocky home in a buckboard. They'd found him miles to the west, face-down with no horse or water. Chet's fifteenth birth-day had just passed.

But the boy was dead this time. Chet would have to recover despite his dizziness. The salty soup slid over his tongue and he blinked his eyes to clear the vision. With rest, that would clear up, too. He hoped. Be-tween spoons of soup, he sipped on coffee. His world was beginning to emerge.

"Why don't you take a nap," Marge whispered and Jenny agreed with her.

Chet didn't argue. Everyone in the room was look-ing at him like he was naked. He could feel their eyes on his gritty skin.

"Can he make it to the shower?" Tom asked them quietly.

Marge shrugged.

"We can bring the water to him outside the back door. You two tell all the womanfolks to turn their backs. We'll shower him down and we've found a knee-length nightshirt in his war bag to dress him in. He's so dirty he'd never rest in those clothes."

"Guess that's why he hired you as foreman," Jenny said with a laugh.

"Yes ma'am. We can handle this from here."

Folks exited the house quietly and Chet held up his hands to ward off Hampt and Tom. "I can walk that far—out the back door, right?"

"Yes."

Chet stood bare as Adam in the garden, outside the

back door on the tile walk, as they began dousing him down with water. All of their sources were not as warm as the others. But he lathered up and then let them rinse him. He felt much better, and dried himself with some help from Tom. Then he put the nightshirt on over his head and he thanked them. Barefooted, he crossed the tile floor.

"It will be cooler upstairs," Madge said. One woman on each elbow, they delivered him to the room. When he dropped to his butt on the bed, he smiled at the two of them.

"Don't let me sleep forever."

"We won't. Now get to sleep," Marge ordered as he lay down.

The last thing he heard were those two talking about him in low voices going out of the room. A soft breeze came in the window, and he slept.

Chapter 34

Lots of things in Chet's body hurt when he awoke. It was dark and he could hear some guitar and fiddle music in the night. At the window, under the stars, he could see lots of parked rigs and small campfires. How many people had come? No telling, but they were there for Heck and him, too.

The small, flickering candle on the dresser showed him his clothes were clean, pressed, and laid on the ladder-back chair. He set into dressing, grateful his latest haircut made him more presentable than he'd been before it. Pulling his suspenders up, he decided that all he needed to do was shave.

He came down the stairs and saw Marge, Jenny, and Kay. All face-down, sleeping with their heads on the table. He quietly went past them. He found hot water on the range—hot enough to shave with. Straight-edged razor, hog-bristle brush, and the enamel pan. He took them out on the porch. Then a candle lamp the wind wouldn't blow out. He took the kettle with hot water outside, too. In a few minutes, his face was scraped clean and feeling better; he quietly returned all the items to their places. Then he slipped out on the front porch and sat in a straight-back chair, letting the cooler night wind sweep his face. Things began to come to him. The clockwork in his skull began to work again.

He ran a calloused hand over his mouth and winced at the sharp pain. That was the hand that had almost lost its grip and a branch had torn it up.

"You woke up already?" Marge asked from the lighted doorway, holding her hair off the back of her neck.

"Why don't you girls go use that bed?"

"What do you need?"

"I'm fine. Take them up there and sleep some."

"You do look and sound better."

"I'm fine. Now get them and go upstairs."

"I will. I will—bossy."

Chet laughed. Fair was fair, they'd been ordering him around for his own good.

Hoot shortly showed up and offered to make him some coffee. He accepted the offer, went inside, and then leaned back on two legs of the wood chair. Cory came next to check on him.

"You alright, boss man?"

"Doing fine. Hoot's making coffee."

"Glad you're better. I just finished digging his grave. Thanks for letting me do that. I'll really miss him." And he left before Chet could thank him.

The camp before him began to rattle iron ovens and cough themselves back to life. Fires flared up and hungry babies cried for momma's milk. His biggest red rooster crowed even before the sun purpled the eastern sky. Mules brayed and made him smile.

Chet considered the three women, doing all that work for him. He'd have to repay them and all these people who so sympathetically had came to share his grief. He was in the right place. All he had left to do was bring the family to Arizona.

When the sun came up, Marge came down, brushing her hair, and joined him on the porch. He fetched her a chair.

"How is this going to work?" she asked.

"Eight o'clock we'll take his casket up where Cory dug his grave. He asked to do it himself. I'll ask the boys who rode with him if they have some words to say about him. Then we can sing a hymn that most folks know and I'll deliver him to the Lord."

Marge reached over and squeezed his forearm. "You are revived. Thank goodness. I knew if you ever cleared your head you'd know right what to do."

"Glad you had the faith."

"Oh, come on. I have all the faith in you a woman can possibly have for a man."

"I wasn't—"

"You were being Chet Byrnes, is all." She beat the top of his leg with her brush. "Don't stop being him."

He closed his eyes. "I'll try not to lose it."

Then she stood up, bent over, kissed him, and left to do something. He wasn't certain what she was up to.

The casket was shut, the ranch hands carried it up the hill, and the procession followed them. "Now we gather at the river," they sang clear as they toiled up the hill.

The wooden box so painfully made by some of his men was lowered into the grave.

Chet asked for the men to step up and say what they knew about the lad.

There was lots of throat-clearing, but their voices rang out loud.

"Wasn't a better hand ever rode a bucking horse or threw a lariat at a calf. Why, he shared every box of cookies his aunt made *fur* him with us." And Bixsby was through.

"That's no boy we're putting away. He earned his spurs with us. God take good care of him." Then Wiley stepped back.

Sarge moved up next. "A boy, I thought, when I came here to join this bunch. The boss's pet no doubt. But a longhorn bull charged my horse one day and this man who roped it and saved me was Heck Byrnes. I never looked back. He'd earned his manhood for my part."

About to tears, Hampt shook his head and excused himself.

Chet agreed, and asked them to pray with him. He started the Lord's Prayer and everyone joined him.

He told them about Heck's bravery, riding alone back from Kansas to tell him about the cruel people who had murdered his father. This young man was no coward and didn't deserve what they took away from him. A marriage and children of his own one day, a ranch to ride over, and a good life.

"May God take him in his palm and care for him in heaven. Amen."

They asked Chet to shovel the first dirt on him. He did, and heard the stones and clods hit the wooden top like someone knocking on a door. *Open it Lord, your man is waiting for your embrace.*

He went down the hill hugging both Marge's and Jenny's shoulders, concerned how Kay was coming along behind them. When all things were settled, he wanted to go back and look off that hill where they had lain him. To see that last setting where some day a granite stone would mark his grave.

Chet never sent a wire to Texas. He'd bear the news to them himself. He left Preskit five days later for home—well, at least his former-to-be place. The stage rattled down the Black Canyon Route for Phoenix. He sat back and wondered what had happened to the lady he had saved, according to her. Her tale and concern still amused him, and he would have kicked her husband in the seat of his pants for divorcing her if he ever met him.

No problems with robbers this trip, and the oppressive heat of the desert set in on him when they spilled out on the saguaro-clogged floor of the desert. His ride included Tucson, the walled city littered with dead livestock; then to Benson, another small town waiting for a railroad. From the railhead in Lordsburg, Chet took a seat car and rode it to El Paso; then taking the rails on, he soon arrived in San Antonio. The mail buckboard service to Mason let him sit on the spring seat beside their tobacco-spitting man, who drove like a crazy idiot with a whip and a short list of cuss words he called the horses and the road surface.

When word got out in Mason he was back, Sheriff Trent joined him in the cafe.

"You find a place out there?"

"Have a seat, It's a long story." Warily, Chet considered what all he must tell Trent.

"I have all the time you need. Didn't you take your nephew with you?"

"That's part of the story, too." Chet nodded.

Trent scooted into the booth across from him and ordered coffee. "What happened?'

"I found a place . . ." Then he told him the entire story.

Then they discovered the café folks were past their usual closing time and Chet apologized. They went to Trent's office to finish their conversation.

Trent acted taken aback by it all, and shook his hand when they rose to part at the end.

"You've damn sure been tested. I hope the new place works out for you and your family. I'm sorry I couldn't control folks around here any better."

"It wasn't your fault."

Chet slept in a rooming house that night, and in the morning he rented a horse to ride out to the ranch. It was noontime before he came up the bottoms. Someone had spotted him and came riding hard to meet him.

J.D. rode in, beaming, and slid his horse to a sharp stop. "How are you? Hey, where's Heck?"

"Better brace yourself, I'll have to tell the others next. Heck is dead. I'm sorry, and it is part of a long story."

"Oh, my God." J.D. sunk in the saddle. "I can't hardly believe it. How?"

"I'm saving it to tell everyone. It isn't a pretty one and it goes back to Texas even, but I'll tell everyone how it happened."

"Oh, Chet, I'm sorry, but what about you?"

"I'm over a big part of it. Won't get over it all. But we do have a wonderful ranch up in the Verde River. Good rangeland and room for lots more cattle. How are the rest of you?"

"Fine. Well, mostly fine."

"There anything wrong here?"

"We've had some more run-ins with them, of course. I'm just glad you're back."

"All the hands still here?"

"Sure. You have a crew out there in Arizona?" They turned their horses for the house. Chet could see everyone was in the yard waiting on them.

"Yes, some good ones too. Tom Flowers is the foreman in charge. He's level-headed and a good man. You'll like him."

"Why, you may not need Reg and me."

"Don't you go to getting cold feet on me. I'm planning to buy another place when we get out there for you two to run in the high country."

"How high?"

"I'm not sure of the elevation, but it's at the foot of the snowy peaks."

He reined up and dismounted to hug Susie.

"Oh my gosh, Chet Byrnes, we thought you'd never come back," she said in his ear.

He straightened and told everyone to have a seat. He wanted to talk to them.

When they had seats on the edge of the porch or the chairs on it, they buzzed about what he was going to tell them. He'd shaken hands or hugged them all.

"Now I know this is going to hurt. Heck's not coming home. He's with God." Chet paused and then began, piece by piece, to tell them about his demise and about the place he'd bought. Wet eyes and crying, they listened. When he got down to his last words, they nodded.

"We're tough people. The Byrneses fought in Scotland and they fought in Ireland when we were sent there. Our people been fighting something or someone for ages. Now I say it is time to take our flag staff to Arizona."

They nodded in silence.

Susie, red-eyed, told them to go in and eat.

Chet excused himself and told her he'd be back. That he had one more person to tell. She hugged him and then agreed. "Go, but wait a minute and take a sandwich with you."

At that she ran inside, and soon came back with two slices of sourdough bread full of sliced beef. He thanked her and rode off eating on it. He needed to tell Kathren before she heard it all from someone else.

The sun was far in the west when he came off the hill to her place. She came out at the stock dogs barking and shaded her eyes with her hands. Then she called out his name and he waved his hat at her.

Dress hem in her hand, she ran toward him. He put the horse in a lope and they met on the hillside. He dismounted on the fly and caught her by the waist. Two hungry mouths fed on each other—seeking the deepest honey.

He swung her up in his arms and started for the house, with her protesting for him to put her down. With a shake of his head, he dismissed her concern that she'd break his back. He set her down on the porch and she squeezed his face and kissed him.

"Gods, Chet, I've missed you so much."

"Where's Cady?" He looked around for her. Then he saw her leading a short buckskin horse under a saddle toward them.

"Where are you going?" he asked.

She shook her head and looked at the sky for help. "To Grandma's. You two don't need me here."

"Cady."

Chet put down her mother's arm and said, "Tell your grandma I said thanks."

"Oh, you two are in cahoots," Kathren said after her. "How old is she?"

"Not that old." She herded him inside the house, and once behind the door they went back to kissing.

An hour later, he told her about Arizona. Laying on the bed, squeezing her hand from time to time, as he told her all about his long journey. He studied the cedar shingles sliced off one at a time from a block of cedar.

She cried about the death of the boy. And then she sat up and looked down on him. "Damn, you've been through hell."

"That's the road I must have taken way back at the start of my life."

Then she buried her face on his shoulder. He could feel her tears spilling out on his bare skin. Damn, where to next?

Chapter 35

Chet rode back home the next evening. Though they never broached the subject, he and she both knew their situations. There was no way she could up and move to Arizona. Her father's health was no better. Her mother probably wouldn't leave, either. But kicking the bay horse into a lope, he knew all too well the answer. No.

Susie had kept a plate of supper for him when he arrived. He agreed to be right there, and put his horse up. Then he hurried to the back porch and washed up. May was washing dishes.

She looked red-eyed from crying. At the sight of him, she burst out bawling. He hugged her to him to try and stem the sorrow.

"Damn it. I tried, honey."

"I don't blame you, Chet. I know all you did. It was just so sad. I'm sorry I argued with him. I hate that worst of all." May wiped her face on her dry forearm and sniffed big time.

"Hey, he'd understood. He grew up a lot out there

riding with those big guys. Thought he was one of them. Roped a bull one time and saved another hand's life. He was sure enough one of them. They cried, too."

"Oh, if I only could take back my stubbornness."

"You can't lick up spilled milk, May. He's in a better place."

"What about you and Kathren?" Susie asked.

"Madly in love. But—" He shrugged his shoulders at her.

"But what?"

Depressed over the matter, he shook his head. "It simply won't work. She can't leave and I have to."

"Eat," May said, indicating his food.

"That's stupid." Susie said.

"I agree, but I've cut that trail and now the two of us will have to live with it."

Then he had two crying women to hug. *Oh, my God.*

Next day, Chet returned the rented horse to Mason. Reg and Utah had left the ranch before sunup to check on some cattle they'd seen the day before that didn't belong on their land. He wondered if Reg was avoiding him, and where was Juanita? Reg wanted to—or was supposed to—marry when he got back. Chet didn't bother to ask anyone. Some things were better left unasked than to stir up a hornet's nest.

He left the horse at the livery, paid his bill and went to eat lunch across the street. The usual noontime crowd was in the room, and he found an empty stool. Things were buzzing in the place.

A rancher named Dailey from Ash Creek stopped and asked if he'd found a place out west.

Chet nodded. "Northern Arizona on the Verde River. Some irrigated land and lots of range."

"What's that near?"

"Preskit. It's Prescott on the map, but the locals call it that."

"Land cheap out there?"

"They ain't giving it away."

The man laughed, then wished him good luck and went off to sit at a table.

What did you tell men like him? That he was moving to the Garden of Eden. There wasn't such a place in the west that he knew about. Lots and lots of rough country. Drier than the hill country. It at times was dry enough—maybe too dry. Chet left the café and mounted the ranch horse for the ride home.

Late afternoon he came up the valley, and met Reg riding to meet him.

"Thought we should palaver some before you got home," the dark, tanned-faced nephew began. I'm going to marry Juanita tomorrow. Mom ain't going, she's so damn mad. But I don't have to please her."

"What then?"

"Well, Henny offered me his place. I reckon we'll settle down over there when you get this place sold."

"They're getting up in years and have no one to inherit it. They wanted someone who would tend them, I guess, in their old age."

"That's the deal. He's got a lawyer drawing up the papers right now. You weren't here and we had no time to talk." Reg shook his head as if to clear it.

"Reg, remember the men shooting at me will shoot at you with us gone."

"I'm going to watch my back."

"Just remember now, there are several of us they can choose to shoot. All of us gone, you will be a single target."

"It sure looked like a good chance for me to have my own outfit."

"I won't stop you. What time is the wedding?"

"Ten AM. Saint Peter's Catholic Church.

"I'll be there."

"Thanks, I knew you'd understand."

"Reg, you ever need me, you know where I'll be."

"And I will."

"What did you and Utah learn?"

"Bunch of cattle wandered in from the south. We sent them toward home."

Whose were they? Chet wondered.

They rode on to the house. It was supper time. After the meal, he caught Louise headed for her quarters and acting huffy. He stopped her.

"You can cut the being mad at me. By damn, your son is getting married in the morning and after breakfast you have the dress that you want to wear to the wedding on. I'm taking you over there. You aren't cutting that boy off like that if I have to tan your hide with a rope."

"Who do you think you are?" She shook her finger in his face. "Why, that little slut coaxed him in her bed."

"Louise, that ain't none of your damn business.

That's their personal business. Now I rode to hell and back for you. I'm calling my card in."

She reared up like a fat toad. Then she deflated herself. "Alright. Alright. You saved my life. I'll go with you." Then, furiously shaking her head, she said, "I don't have to like her."

"But you will be pleasant."

"Alright."

That settled, he rode off to see Kathren. There had to be something bright in his life. In Mayfield he stopped and went in to Casey's bar and had a beer. He'd forgotten the ice would have run out by this time, and the tepid beer hardly cut his thirst. After telling Casey part of the story about Arizona, he went over and talked to Grossman at the store.

"I heard you were back and that young boy was murdered. How did such a thing like this happen?"

"You recall those three guys you warned me about? That Kid and a guy called Crown. There was one more named something. Kathren shot him. Well, those two were in the outlaw gang that held up the Black Canyon Stage—they kidnapped and killed him."

"Where are they at?"

"In unmarked graves."

"Good enough for that kind. What do you need?"

"A nice gift for a wedding."

"Does she have a dutch oven?"

"That sounds wonderful."

"You don't have one, you need one, right?" The man went to get him one.

"Right."

Chet decided after he made the purchase that he'd

wait and see Kathren later. He felt sick about what would be the eventual outcome of their affair. Maybe he should send the family out there and stay here.

No, they'd need him out there as well. A no-win situation, and nothing would change it.

Back at the ranch after dark, Chet stowed the present in the buckboard. Someone had put a second set of seats on the rig. Susie must be going as well. The oven in under the back row, he rode on to the corral and put up his horse.

At breakfast, he learned that May and Susie were going with him and Louise. Them all loaded up in the rig, he slipped into the seat beside Louise, who was well dressed for the occasion.

"Who is the dutch oven back here for, the newlyweds?" May asked.

He was driving the dun team and nodded. "It's Louise's gift for the two of them."

"Why I . . ."

"Yes, you did. You forgot." He clucked to speed up the team.

Louise slumped in the front seat, obviously pouting to herself. No doubt she was scheming on how to kill him. No matter. She'd better act nice or Chet would thrash her. He hoped all the church business might bring her around to acting civilized.

At the last moment, when he stopped in front of the church's front doors, Louise began sniffling. Bawling women were not his high card, but her crying was. He tied off the horses and went around to help them all down. He hugged her shoulder and whispered. "I knew this service would get to you. You aren't as hard-boiled as you act sometimes. Wait, I have to get the oven. They'll need it."

Susie winked at him when he rejoined them with the large oven. "It will cook lots of frijoles," he said.

"What do you do when you go in a Catholic church?" Louise asked him under her breath.

"If you're a man, take off your hat."

"No, I mean . . . never mind, I won't get it right."

They found seats near the front and he let them file into the pew, then took his place beside them.

A man came and whispered in Spanish, asking if that oven he brought in was a gift for the couple. "Oh, *sí*, it is a gift from his *mamacita*."

"Oh, I will put it with their other presents in the hall next door."

"Certainly."

Then he reached past Chet and shook Louise's hand. "My name is Carlos and I am so glad to have that fine boy in my family now."

She stammered something and nodded. "Me, ah, too."

Chet wanted to laugh. The man had meant what he said and she did not know how to take it.

The wedding went smoothly and the two made a handsome couple. The tall cowboy in his new black suit and she in a snow-white gown exchanged their vows before the rail, since he was not Catholic. Then, throwing streamers and colored-paper snow on them, everyone went to the hall next door. The food was beans, barbequed something, and flour tortillas to use for plates and silverware.

The music was lively, and the new couple danced around the room. Chet wished that Kathren was there. Then he watched Carlos invite Louise to dance with him, and she accepted.

"That's her father," Susie said. "His wife died a few years ago."

The man swept her away. One thing he could do was dance, and one way to her hard heart was a man who could dance well. They were locked up hopelessly into doing every dance. Then, when they were ready for the couple to open the presents, she stood beside him. Carlos Romano and Louise Byrnes, obviously out of breath. But she was not uneasy or out of place. Damn shame he didn't know about this man and how he could change his crappy aunt so easily.

"How did you know about him?" Susie asked in his ear.

"I didn't. I got lucky."

She shook her head. "I believe he has impressed her."

"Damned if I don't agree."

Since Chet and Kathren had talked about everything during their reunion but the dance, after the wedding he rode over to the schoolhouse, in case she had gone there. He left his horse hitched on a neighbor's picket line. They had not seen her. Walking under the tall trees that shaded the stars, he was beginning to regret coming here. No sign of her.

Then he heard a rustling in the leaves behind him,

and carrying her hem high, Kathren came on the run. Out of breath, she drew in some air.

"I thought—"

"No, I thought—"

They both laughed and hugged one another. He rocked her back and forth in his arms. What a heavenly deal. "It don't matter one little bit. You're here and so am I."

"Oh, Chet, I had to see you."

"I don't have a wagon or my outfit. Reg and Juanita were married today."

"That's the girl who worked for your sister?"

"Yes, the pretty girl."

"I heard his mother was very upset."

He wrinkled his nose. "Not anymore. She danced with his father all afternoon at the reception."

"She did?"

"Never mind Louise. What do you want to do?"

She looked around to be certain they were alone. Then she stood on her toes and whispered, "Did you bring your bedroll?"

"Yes."

"Good, we can dance a few times, then we can go get lost."

"What shall we eat?"

"Oh, some of the women are selling box suppers."

"Good plan."

They did that, danced, and then later they got lost.

Chapter 36

The sun peaked over the hills behind him as Chet short-loped for home. He wasn't thinking about much of anything except the past evening, when a shot rang out and he felt his horse trip and go down. Sprawled off over the cow pony's head, he skidded face-first to a tough stop in some briars. He felt for his six-gun. The grasp of the cedar grips made his heart quicken. He possessed five bullets in the cylinder and several more around his waist in the beltloops. The .44/40 was in the scabbard, no doubt under the dying horse who he could hear gasping and thrashing for his life. No time to eliminate a hurt horse. He knew blood was running down his face in a stream from the fall. But not a big enough leak to kill him. That could be stopped later.

Where were they? The birds, silenced by the first shot, had begun to twitter again. A distant mourning dove went back to cooing. How had they discovered him? Had they tracked him and Kathren from the dance? Chet was so intoxicated with her, no way he'd even thought about his enemies. But they must have thought about him. He made his way, snakelike, under the boughs of a cedar tree, and once inside it he tried to listen for their move. Obviously, they couldn't have seen him, or they'd have shot at him again.

He could be grateful they were such poor shots. Damn, he liked that gelding, too. Smooth-riding pony. Where were they?

"He's between you and me," someone said. He tried to match the voice to a face. Blythe Walker. He was married to Burl Reynolds's sister's girl. Burl, the oldest living Reynolds who was not in a cemetery or prison, must be out there, too.

A horse north of his location clattered over some rocks. That had to be the number-two man.

"Reckon the horse wreck killed him?"

"You see the horse yet?"

"No. but I'm close to it."

Good, get even closer. Chet dried his sore palm on the side of his pants and took the grips back. The horse drew closer.

"I found—"

Using both hands to stabilize his aim, he shot Blythe Walker twice in the face. He was pitched off his horse, who bolted to the side, and the man lay kicking on the ground. The throes of death were doing that to him.

Where was Burl?

He heard a horse galloping away. Then he climbed to his feet and went by the man's still body. With a little coaxing, he caught Walker's horse and mounted into the saddle. Burl had gone north. He sent the big sorrel in that direction. When he and the cow pony rode out into the open country, he saw the dust and the rider. They were headed north hard.

You ain't getting away this time. Chet sent the sorrel after him. Of course, if the man got into the brush, he might lose him, but it was a chance he'd take. He hoped Reynolds was panicked enough to keep running and wouldn't stop to ambush him.

He holstered the Colt and jerked the rifle out of the scabbard, never losing a stride on the big horse. It was loaded, he discovered, when he started to open the action with the lever and, seeing the cartridge, he drew the lever back up. He tried aiming, but he knew the rocking gait of the horse would spoil most shots. Anxious to shorten the distance between them, he spanked the pony on the butt with the barrel.

Burl headed for some cedar breaks on his horse. In a few short minutes, Chet drove into the woods and spotted the man's bay horse hobbling in circles, his front leg broken. He reined in the Walker horse. Where was the big man at? No way he could have gotten far after his horse went down. He circled to the south, wary that his enemy was out there, not too far away and in a tight fix with no horse.

The horse began to act uneasy. He couldn't see any sign of the big man. But still, he rode around feeling he must be close to him, knowing he might any second be the target of a man who wanted him dead. He dried his hand on his britches and re-gripped the long gun. At a time when he needed eyes in the back of his head, he kept twisting in the saddle to look for him.

After a fifteen-minute search, he turned the horse around and rode out of the canyon. No sense in making a target of himself. Damn, he needed to go see Sheriff Trent. Not home any time at all, and he was back to the old feud-fighting mode with those Reynoldses. One dead, and he'd lost a damn good horse. He pushed the Walker horse for Mason in a hard run. He let the big sorrel walk the last mile and cool off. A good horse, but he didn't have half the sense the pony he'd lost earlier had possessed.

"You look like a man who's been in trouble," Trent said and met him at the door of the courthouse.

"That's Blythe Walker's horse. But he won't need him. Him and Burl Reynolds jumped me coming home from the dance early this morning. They shot my horse from ambush, and I shot Walker. Burl got away, but his horse broke his leg and he must have slipped off on foot. I couldn't find him in the brush."

Trent dropped his chin. "How long have you been back? Two days?"

"Not long enough. But there is not much hope for finding any peace around here."

"Draw me a map. I'll send a deputy down there to get his body."

"I figure when Burl crawls home, he'll go back for the body."

"I'll beat him there."

"Whatever. I need some breakfast. Want some? I'll buy."

"You might be too dangerous to eat with. They may try to poison you."

"They may. Suit yourself," Chet said, leading his horse to Han's Diner across the street.

"I'll flip for who pays," Trent laughed, walking with him.

"Good. Gives me a fifty-fifty chance of not having to pay."

Trent shook his head. "Didn't take them long, did it?"

"Two or three days is all."

"And I already have a new body count."

"Anyone shot at you lately?" Chet asked.

"No, and I'm not all scratched up, either."

"When they shot my horse, I landed in some brambles. I guess I'm not bleeding by now." He had no idea how bad he looked. His horse hitched, he looked at his reflection in the cafe window—looked like a cat clawed him.

"Not much. Same old war, huh?"

"I have a solution. It's on the banks of the Verde River. In a year I hope to have it all there, lock, stock, and sister out there."

"And I'll be upset. I hate to see her go."

"Then you better get busy."

"What will you do about Kathren?"

"If I had that answer, I'd tell you, and damn quick." Chet dropped heavily into the first booth. His empty stomach rolled over. No way he'd forgotten about his dilemma over how to have both—his new ranch and Kathren together.

"I'm sorry," Trent said. "It's no fun being shot at by idiots on Sunday morning."

"You're excused."

"Thanks. You like the country out there?"

Chet bobbed his head. "But it's a dry place. There's

grass and forage, but there isn't lots of water. Water development will be hard."

"Every Eden has some cactus. I was sorry when I heard that you had lost the boy."

Chet nodded. It was hard for him to talk about Heck. "Arizona has some bad things, too, but the high country is a lot like here. Trent, I swear, this morning I was coming back from the dance minding my own business when they jumped me."

They were interrupted by the waitress and gave her their orders. Then they turned back to each other.

Trent nodded. "I know. They're crazy."

"I simply wanted to be sure we were on the same plate."

"I'm going to send for a deputy. Excuse me. I've been thinking about what you said about Burl getting that body." The lawman went outside, and waved a youth over on the street. Chet saw him give the boy a dime and he raced off. With a nod, he came back and finished his breakfast with Chet.

Chet returned to the ranch after noontime. Seeing him coming on a different horse, Susie ran out, drying her hands. "Whose horse is that?"

"Blythe Walker's. I traded him for a couple of cartridges and my pony."

She frowned hard at him. "He attacked you?"

"Him and Burl. It's why we must move to Arizona."

"What happened besides Walker?"

"Burl rode off. His horse must have broken his leg,

but still he got away from me. I rode to Mason and told Bob what happened."

"How is he?"

"Fine. He sent a man to get Walker's body."

"Fine Sunday morning, huh?"

He hugged her and rocked her back and forth. "You and I never talked, but you know we're going to lose Reg?"

She nodded. "I knew that would hurt you."

"I want him to succeed, but hate to lose him. And I fear them damn Reynoldses will pounce on him as soon as we're gone."

"Maybe he'll change his mind. Did you find Kathren last night?"

"Yes."

"I won't ask any more of you."

"She's fine. But I'm walking a tightrope these days and I don't dare fall. She's the greatest sunshine I ever found in my life. But I know in here . . ." He pounded his chest with the side of his fist. ". . . she can't go and I can't stay."

"Will you simply ride away?"

"I'll tell you when that day comes."

Susie nodded. "Other folks don't have all this turmoil like we do."

"It's the hand we drew, I guess. How's Dad?"

"You saw him since you've come back. He don't know any of us anymore and lives in yesterday."

"I know." He nodded. "I'm going to the bunkhouse and take a nap. Wake me up in an hour or so."

"I can do that. You better talk to those younger boys later on. They've took Heck's death real hard."

"I know he was a good big brother to them. I'd have given them my life if they hadn't killed him."

"No one's blaming you. You're just good at bucking up people that are in the ditch."

"I will speak to them." He started for the bunkhouse. Would it do any good to go talk to Burl face-to-face? At one time they got along. No hate, no killing. Lived like neighbors. Loaned each other harnesses, farm machinery, harvested crops together, traded day labor. Nothing left but the blood spilt on the ground, and it had soaked in deep.

Chet fell asleep easy, and woke up in a short while with a new plan. If he couldn't do anything else, he might as well try it. Burl had an interest in a woman who lived on Terrapin Creek, Lupe Mariono. More than once, he had heard others say, don't mess with his woman up there.

He needed to catch him at a place where Burl couldn't compromise the situation. But could he even trust him if he did promise amnesty for his part? He could try that, and if it didn't work, he could mark it off as a bad experience.

Where could he go up there and wait for him? He knew the entire area well enough. All he needed was to make the right choice on the right trail. If he was wrong, Burl would never step in his trap. Then his time would all be wasted.

He went by the main house. Somewhere in there was a black rubber rain coat. One mention to Susie about his needs and she went for it.

"What are you going to do?" she whispered.

Chet shook his head. "A secret I can't tell you."

In the kitchen, he took some leftover biscuits and filled his vest pockets. She was right on his heels and talking under her breath, "Tell me what you are going to do."

"Can't."

"Where can I claim your body then?"

"I'm not sure."

In the corral, he roped a quiet horse named Angel. Sure-footed as a goat, but nothing too fast. Hardly over twelve hands, he made a good pony to ride over hills and up craggy canyons. One he could step off and be right on the ground. They'd shot lots of deer off him, so he wasn't gun-shy. Everyone was off working when he left the ranch by the back way. He went the way he used to go to duck folks when he went to see Marla. By the time he drew close to Terrapin Creek, he hobbled Angel deep in a canyon and mounted the ridge on foot. From high on the hill, he used his field glasses and spotted her, busy hoeing her well-kept garden. She was a full-figured woman in a tan skirt and red shirt that showed off the treasures of her chest. At one time she had been a very voluptuous woman, but she showed some of her age. A widow for many years, she seldom left her small place. The gossip about her affair with Burl wasn't even news anymore.

Years before, he'd heard many stories about her entertaining some rich men, but as her looks and youth faded, she became dependent on and, so they said, loyal to Burl.

Chet found a seat in the dense cedar and live oak and waited. His man might not even come this night. It all depended on things at Burl's place. The death of his son-in-law might postpone him coming to see her for days. But when he did, Chet would be there waiting on him. He slowly masticated a dry biscuit. And he washed it down with spring water that tasted metallic.

Day two, Chet came back in the morning, resuming his post. And he watched her look, a little concerned, to the south where Burl would ride up from. He watched her undress and take a sponge bath through the lacey live-oak leaves. The sunlight splashed on her brown skin and flecked like glitter on her gray-streaked hair. Lupe was quite fastidious about herself, and brushed her hair with a hundred strokes a day. She picked things from her garden and when it was real hot, she hoed bare-breasted. He wasn't there to spy on her—he waited for Burl.

The third day Chet was there, she butchered a young milk-fat goat and cooled his carcass under a wet canvas which used evaporation to take the heat from his pink-white body. The small skin she saved, and she also shut up a hen with her fluffy black-and-yellow-feathered new chicks in a small A-frame coop so a coyote would not feast on them.

Late that afternoon, Chet could hear a horse coming. His hooves were clacking on the loose gravel of the trail as he climbed up from the creek below the house.

She ran from the house with colored ribbons in her hair. "My darling! My darling! I have missed you so."

Burl swung to get down, and Chet could see his bandaged right foot when he dismounted. He probably had hurt it in the fall from his horse. He hobbled to her. "Darling, I have been so busy. They killed my son-in-law, those bastards. I cannot say the misery they have caused me. They shot him in the back."

She hugged him and they kissed furiously. "Oh my darling, why do they do this to you?" she asked.

It was time for him to move in. They thought they were all alone. With his double barrel in his sweaty hands, Chet crept closer to the house. When he swung around the corner of the jacal, he could hear them plainer. Burl held her on his lap. She was singing some ballad about a wild horse, and her sleepy dark eyes flew open in shock at the sight of him and his shotgun.

"Don't move or you will both die." One-handed, Chet leveled the shotgun at the two of them. "No need to scream, Lupe."

He swung a empty crate around and took a seat on it with the sun behind him.

"Don't consider going for that gun in your holster," he said quietly. "Reach slowly with two fingers, then remove the Colt and drop it."

"I will—"

"You won't do anything. Today I am determined to do some trading. If you try to kill or kill any more members of my family you will be the first one to die. You won't know when I will strike, but I will strike and you will die a slow harsh death. I will use rattlesnakes to strike you many times. Then you will be naked, staked on an ant hill with honey poured on your crotch, and after you have screamed for a day, then I will hang you over a fire ring upside down and boil your brains."

Burl hugged her and looked shocked. "I—I can't control everyone—what if—"

"If even one person in my family is so much as bruised," he said softly. "Your life is over. I will find you like I did right here, and your last hours on this earth will be screaming until you are too hoarse to even whisper."

No reply.

"I don't think you understand me."

"I savvy. I savvy." Burl held out his hands. "What will you do to us?"

"That is why I came here. You have not answered my questions. What will you do? Die screaming or hold your peace?"

"Hold my peace, of course."

Chet sat back, set the shotgun over his lap, and folded his arms. "What will you give me to prove that you are saying the truth?"

"What—what do you want from me?"

Lupe looked ready to cry. "For God's sake, Burl, tell him what he wants."

"Alright, I promise to do nothing to you or your family and I will tell everyone the same."

"Tell me what I said will happen to you."

"That you or someone will ant-hill me, have snakes bite me, and then boil my brains in my skull."

"You have the picture. Now get down on your bellies. I am going to tie you both up."

"What will you do to us then?" Burl asked, looking wide-eyed.

"Get on the ground."

"Do it. Do it," Lupe said, looking worried at him.

"Alright."

On their stomachs, they put their hands behind their

backs. They watched for him to step over and tie them with some rope he brought with him. He made sure they were tied securely. Then he put a small glass in front of Burl's face. The top was sealed with a piece of paper tied by string on the side to keep the contents inside.

"See those red ants?"

"Yes."

"You know what they'll do to you?"

Burl nodded.

"Lupe, you want to keep him for a lover, every time he comes here you tell him what those ants will do to him."

"*Sí. Sí,* I will."

"You have enough. Don't forget what I or my relatives will do to you. Burl, you will be the first one treated like that."

There were no more words, but Lupe was crying, sobbing in the dirt when he left them. Chet took his time climbing the hill, and caught his hobbled horse to free his legs. He removed the black slicker he'd used to hide with. Then he mounted Angel and headed for the ranch.

Would his plans work? The Lord only knew, but he had showed the family king what he'd do to him at a place Burl considered his private kingdom. Only time would tell. All he needed was time enough to sell the ranch properties and move to the Arizona territory. He booted Angel into a trot.

He ate a late dinner with Susie accompanying him in the kitchen.

"You look more rested tonight. Did you get something settled?"

"Tomorrow, I'm going to speak to some land sales offices about the value of this ranch and see if they would try to sell it for us."

"That sounds so sad." Susie looked downhearted.

"Not as sad as burying a family member."

"Oh, you are right, but this is the only place I've ever lived. I thought I'd have a family here and someday be buried here."

"Things change."

She agreed.

Chapter 37

On the square in San Antonio, across from the tired-looking adobe former mission of Texas fame that warmed in the summer afternoon heat, Chet sat at a café table in the lacy shade of some mesquite trees. The man in the white suit across from him was Carl Rankin. He worked for the Stockman's Bank, and they waited for a prospective buyer who wished to discuss the ranch property Chet had for sale.

Albert Fine, in an expensive suit, and his son-in-law, Tony Doone, dressed in cowboy clothing, arrived by coach. Fine was a expansive-acting man who looked upset that there might be bird shit on the table. Both Chet and Rankin rose and shook their hands then invited the pair to have a seat.

A waiter came over and took their orders for drinks. Fine ordered some special scotch to drink, and his son-in-law said he'd have the same. Chet said he didn't need anything, and Rankin said he couldn't drink while representing the bank.

The matter settled, Rankin gave them the size of the ranch as 1800-plus acres.

"I want that surveyed and a proven deed, if we decide to buy it, sir." Fine said, using his index finger like a stirring stick.

"That can be handled," Rankin said. "There are three hundred mother cows with a normal calf-crop percentage, replacement heifers, and yearlings. All these cows are outcrosses with either Shorthorn or Hereford bulls. That is very important. The native longhorn cattle not showing British crosses are being discounted in Kansas.

"The owner will guarantee a remuda of eighty working horses. These are not mustangs, but well-bred horses."

"What colors?" Doone asked.

"Sorrels, bays, and some roans," Chet said.

"I'd like some claybanks."

Chet nodded. "I have two of those colts from a young Mexican stallion. But they're not a portion of the ranch sale."

Doone sprung forward in his wicker chair and gripped his knees. "How much apiece for them?"

"Five hundred a head."

"Kinda high, aren't you?"

"They are out of a closed line of horses. I own one of the only stallions outside of the Barbarousa Hacienda down there."

"Is he on the place? The stud?"

"He's not for sale."

"I'd like to see him."

"Come to the ranch."

Fine frowned at his son-in-law. "We can see them when we go out there to look at his operation."

"Oh, yes." Doone sat up straight and restored his composure.

Chet decided Fine didn't want Doone to act over-excited about the ranch or the horses. It was all part of his role—much better in the rest posture.

"What is the price?"

"There are a hundred acres of good land that they grow corn and oat hay on," Rankin said. Then he shuffled the pages. "The price for the acreage and buildings is seventy-five thousand dollars."

"This must be the highest-priced place I've ever heard of in that region," Fine said, standing up as if he was ready to leave.

"Best-watered ranch in the region," Rankin tried to tell him. "More shallow wells will produce plenty of water with windmills."

"I'll let you know what we think later. Good day, Mr. Byrnes."

"Same," Chet said, considering the big man's poor manners. Fine's son-in-law jumped up and thanked them like he didn't know his father-in-law was halfway to the buggy. They were leaving.

Rankin kept folding his hands and unfolding them. Chet wondered if he was going to explode, he was so worked up. "I hate that sumbitch."

Chet about laughed. "I can't say he's a very nice person."

"Oh, he'll buy your ranch and those high-priced horses, but he has to show his superiority."

Chet frowned and then slumped in the chair. Fine'd

do what? Pay that much money for his place. Rankin must be long on money and weak on good sense. Considering the strange meeting, he could hardly believe Rankin's words.

"I have sold him three large ranches in the past year and a half. He does this to me every time." Rankin gritted his teeth. "Get ready, he'll come back and buy your ranch with some wrangling in a few weeks. Are you packed?"

"No, but I can be. Easily." That was crazy. He'd have a million things to pack. He couldn't believe the man from the bank. He'd have enough money for another ranch. With all this talk and fretting about all those long days how he'd ever drive his herd out there, if this sale went through it looked like he'd only have a handful of stock to move. No killing newborn calves every day before they started out—he'd need some sort of a letdown from all this whirling-mind business.

"You better go home and pack. I'll send a telegram before he's coming out there to buy it."

"You can't be serious?"

"Yes, I am dead serious."

"I'll go home but—I can't believe this. Why, he acted like—"

"Trust me Mr. ah, Chet. I know him."

Chet shook his head in disbelief.

Two days later, he rode in to the ranch. Chet's arrival back at the ranch caused one of the young boys to ring the bell. He dismounted heavily, and let his sea legs catch up before he released the horn.

"You look like a man who's lost his best friend." Susie said.

He waited to answer her as the rest around the ranch house came to join them. Then he began to speak. "My banker in San Antonio says we've sold the ranch."

Several jaws sagged in disbelief. Susie's knees about buckled. "But—but I thought you only went to list it."

"I did, and they had a ready buyer who came to ask a few questions."

"How will we ever move all this?" Susie looked bewildered.

"Some things we have to leave or sell at an auction."

"When is this buyer coming?"

"I expect him in two weeks. Until then, start sorting things to save or leave. We can't take over a half-dozen wagons out there in a cavalcade. I'd be short on drivers with that many. Get back to work. We'll talk some more later."

May stood in the doorway, biting her lip and rocking baby Donna.

"You hear me?" Chet asked going by her through the door.

"We both did."

"I know it's scary. But you'll like it."

"I hope so."

The next two weeks dragged by; then a wire finally came from Carl Rankin, delivered by a teenage boy from Mason.

Chet read the contents to the women. "Fine plans

to buy the ranch. He made a down payment of $29,000 to hold the deal. Sending Doone out there to look at those special horses to see if he wants to buy them as well. He won't back out and lose that much money. Consider returning to San Antonio with Doone so we can close this sale. Rankin."

After that, Chet saddled a good horse, and without a word to any of them, he rode for Kathren's place. All the way, he fought a sour knot in his throat that tried to crawl up past his tongue. He considered stopping in Mayfield and getting drunk, but he never halted. He made the cow pony jog, and tried hard as he had since he left the —*C* to think of what he must tell her.

At her hitch rack, he almost lost it all. He didn't know to deal with the knife of sorrow stabbing his heart. He took off his hat and beat his leg stalking toward her front door.

"It happened like that banker said?" Kathren asked, coming out onto the porch.

"Yes."

She closed her eyes to cut off the flood coming from behind them, and he did the same as they held each other—for the last time.